The Best of Nancy Drew®

CLASSIC COLLECTION

Volume 1

The Secret of the Old Clock

The Bungalow Mystery

The Mystery of the 99 Steps

By Carolyn Keene

Grosset & Dunlap • New York

Acknowledgement is made to Mildred Wirt Benson, who under the pen name Carolyn Keene, wrote the original NANCY DREW books.

 THE BEST OF NANCY DREW CLASSIC COLLECTION Volume 1 published in 2004 by Grosset & Dunlap, a division of Penguin Young Readers Group, 345 Hudson Street, New York, New York 10014. NANCY DREW MYSTERY STORIES® is a registered trademark of Simon & Schuster, Inc. GROSSET & DUNLAP is a trademark of Penguin Group (USA) Inc. Printed in the U.S.A.

ISBN 0-448-44079-2 10 9 8 7 6 5

NANCY DREW MYSTERY STORIES®

The Secret of the Old Clock

BY CAROLYN KEENE

GROSSET & DUNLAP
Publishers • New York
A member of The Putnam & Grosset Group

Contents

CHAPTER I

The Rescue

NANCY DREW, an attractive girl of eighteen, was driving home along a country road in her new, dark-blue convertible. She had just delivered some legal papers for her father.

"It was sweet of Dad to give me this car for my birthday," she thought. "And it's fun to help him in his work."

Her father, Carson Drew, a well-known lawyer in their home town of River Heights, frequently discussed puzzling aspects of cases with his blond, blue-eyed daughter.

Smiling, Nancy said to herself, "Dad depends on my intuition."

An instant later she gasped in horror. From the lawn of a house just ahead of her a little girl about five years of age had darted into the roadway. A van, turning out of the driveway of the house, was barely fifty feet away from her. As the driver vigorously sounded the horn in warning, the child became confused and ran directly in front of the van. Miraculously, the little girl managed to cross the road safely and pull herself up onto a low wall, which formed one side of a bridge. But the next second, as the van sped away, the child lost her balance and toppled off the wall out of sight!

"Oh my goodness!" Nancy cried out, slamming on her brakes. She had visions of the child plunging into the water below, perhaps striking her head fatally on a rock!

Nancy leaped out of her car and dashed across the road. At the foot of the embankment, she could see the curly-haired little girl lying motionless, the right side of her body in the water.

"I hope—" Nancy dared not complete the harrowing thought as she climbed down the steep slope.

When she reached the child, she saw to her great relief that the little girl was breathing normally and no water had entered her nose or mouth. A quick examination showed that she had suffered no broken bones.

Gently Nancy lifted the little girl, and holding her firmly in both arms, struggled to the top of the embankment. Then she hurried across the road and up the driveway to the child's house.

At this moment the front door flew open and an elderly woman rushed out, crying, "Judy! Judy!"

The next second, the child lost her balance

"I'm sure she'll be all right," said Nancy quickly.

The woman, seeing Nancy's car, asked excitedly, "Did you run into her?"

"No, no. Judy fell off the bridge." Nancy quickly explained what had taken place.

By this time another woman, slightly younger, had hurried from the house. "Our baby! What has happened to her?"

As the woman reached out to take Judy, Nancy said soothingly, "Judy's going to be all right. I'll carry her into the house and lay her on a couch."

One of the women opened the screen door and the other directed, "This way."

Nancy carried her little burden through a hallway and into a small, old-fashioned living room. As soon as she laid the child on the couch, Judy began to murmur and turn her head from side to side.

"I believe she'll come to in a few minutes," said Nancy.

The two women watched Judy intently as they introduced themselves as Edna and Mary Turner, great-aunts of the little girl.

"Judy lives with us," explained Edna, the older sister. "We're bringing her up."

Nancy was somewhat surprised to hear that these elderly women were rearing such a small child. She gave her name and address, just as Judy opened her eyes and looked around. Seeing Nancy, she asked, "Who are you?"

"My name is Nancy. I'm glad to know you, Judy."

"Did you see me fall?"

Nancy nodded, as the child's Aunt Mary said, "She rescued you from the river after you fell in."

Judy began to cry. "I'll never, never run into the road again, really I won't!" she told her aunts.

Nancy said she was sure that Judy never would. She patted the child, who smiled up at her. Although Nancy felt that Judy would be all right, she decided to stay a few minutes longer to see if she could be of help. The child's wet clothes were removed and a robe put on her.

Mary Turner started for the kitchen door. "I'd better get some medication and wet compresses for Judy. She's getting a good-sized lump on her head. Nancy, will you come with me?"

She led the way to the kitchen and headed for a first-aid cabinet which hung on the wall.

"I want to apologize to you, Nancy, for thinking you hit Judy," the woman said. "I guess Edna and I lost our heads. You see, Judy is very precious to us. We brought up her mother, who had been an only child and was orphaned when she was a little girl. The same thing happened to Judy. Her parents were killed in a boat explosion three years ago. The poor little girl has no close relatives except Edna and me."

"Judy looks very healthy and happy," Nancy said quickly, "so I'm sure she must love it here."

Mary smiled. "We do the best we can on our small income. Sometimes it just doesn't suffice, though. We sold some old furniture to the two men in that van you saw. I don't know who they were, but I guess the price was all right."

Mary Turner's thoughts went back to little Judy. "She's so little now that Edna and I are able to manage with our small income. But we worry about the future. We're dressmakers but our fingers aren't so nimble with the needle as they used to be.

"To tell you the truth, Nancy, at the time Judy's parents were killed, Edna and I wondered whether we would be able to take care of Judy properly. But we decided to try it and now we wouldn't part with her for anything in the world. She's won our hearts completely."

Nancy was touched by the story. She knew what was in the minds of the Turner sisters—living costs would become higher, and with their advancing years, their own income would become lower.

"Unfortunately," Mary went on, "Judy's parents left very little money. But they were extremely bright people and Judy is going to be like them. She ought to study music and dancing, and have a college education. But I'm afraid we'll never be able to give her those things."

Nancy said reassuringly, "Judy may be able to win a scholarship, or get other financial aid."

Mary, finding Nancy a sympathetic listener, continued, "A cousin of our father's named Josiah Crowley used to help us. But he passed away a couple of months ago. For years he used to pay us long visits and was very generous with his money." Miss Turner sighed. "He always promised to remember us in his will—he loved little Judy—and I am afraid Edna and I came to depend on that in our plans for her. But he did not carry out his promise."

Nancy smiled understandingly and made no comment. But she did wonder why Mr. Crowley had changed his mind.

"Josiah went to live with some other cousins. After that, things changed. He rarely came to see us. But he was here just last February and said the same thing—that Edna and I were to inherit money from him. He had always helped us and it seemed strange that he should stop so suddenly."

Mary Turner looked at Nancy. "Maybe you know our well-to-do cousins that he went to stay with. They live in River Heights. They're the Richard Tophams."

"Do they have two daughters named Ada and Isabel?" Nancy asked. "If so, I know them."

"That's the family all right," replied Mary.

Nancy detected a hint of coolness in the woman's voice. "Do you like those two girls?" Miss Turner asked.

Nancy did not answer at once. She had been taught never to gossip. But finally she said tactfully, "Ada and Isabel were in high school with me. They were never my close friends. We—uh —didn't see eye to eye on various things."

By this time Mary Turner had selected a few items from the first-aid chest. Now she went to the refrigerator for some ice cubes. As she arranged the various articles on a tray, she said, "Well, when Cousin Josiah passed away, to our amazement Richard Topham produced a will which made him executor of the Crowley estate and left all the money to him, his wife, and the two girls."

"Yes. I did read that in the newspaper," Nancy recalled. "Is the estate a large one?"

"I understand there's considerable money in it," Mary Turner replied. "Some of Josiah's other cousins say he told them the same thing he told us, and they are planning to go to court about the matter." The woman shrugged. "But I guess a fight to break the will would be hopeless. Nevertheless, Edna and I cannot help feeling there *must* be a later will, although as yet no one has presented it."

Nancy followed Miss Turner into the living room. The cold compresses helped to reduce the swelling where Judy had hit her head on a rock. Convinced now that the little girl was all right, Nancy said she must leave.

"Come to see me again soon," Judy spoke up. "I like you, Nancy. "You're my saving girl."

"You bet I'll come," Nancy answered. "I like you too. You're a good sport!"

The child's great-aunts profusely thanked Nancy again for rescuing Judy. The visitor had barely reached the door when Edna suddenly said, "Mary, where's our silver teapot?"

"Why, right there on the tea table— Oh, it's gone!"

Edna ran into the dining room. "The silver candlesticks! They're gone too!"

Nancy had paused in the doorway, startled. "Do you mean the pieces have been stolen?" she asked.

"They must have been," replied Mary Turner, who was white with apprehension. "By those men who bought some furniture from us!"

Instantly Nancy thought of the men in the van. "Who were the men?" she asked.

"Oh, Mary, how could we have been so careless?" Edna Turner wailed. "We don't know who the men were. They just knocked on the door and asked if we had any old furniture that we wanted to sell. We'll never get the silver back!"

"Maybe you will!" said Nancy. "I'll call the police."

"Oh dear!" Mary said woefully. "Our phone is out of order."

"Then I'll try to catch up to the van!" Nancy declared. "What did the men look like?"

"They were short and heavy-set. One had dark hair, the other light. They had kind of large noses. That's about all I noticed."

"Me too," said Edna.

With a hasty good-by Nancy dashed from the house and ran to her car.

CHAPTER II

A Missing Will

THE BLUE convertible sped along the country road. Nancy smiled grimly.

"I'm afraid I'm exceeding the speed limit," she thought. "But I almost wish a trooper would stop me. Then I could tell him what happened to the poor Turner sisters."

Nancy watched the tire marks which the van driven by the thieves had evidently made in the dirt road. But a few miles farther on a feeling of dismay came over her. She had reached a V-shaped intersection of two highways. Both roads were paved, and since no tire impressions could be seen, Nancy did not know which highway the thieves had taken.

"Oh dear!" she sighed. "Now what shall I do?"

Nancy concluded that her wisest move would be to take the road which led to River Heights. There was a State Police barracks just a few miles ahead.

"I'll stop there and report the theft."

She kept looking for the van, which she recalled as charcoal gray. "I wish I'd seen the license number or the name of the firm that owns the van," Nancy said to herself ruefully.

When she reached State Police headquarters Nancy introduced herself to Captain Runcie and told about the robbery, giving what meager information she could about the suspects. The officer promised to send out an alarm immediately for the thieves and their charcoal-gray moving van.

Nancy continued her journey home, thinking of the Turners and their problems.

"I wonder why Mr. Josiah Crowley left all his money to the Tophams and none to his other relatives. Why did he change his mind? Those Tophams are well to do and don't need money as much as the Turners."

Nancy did not know Richard Topham, but she was acquainted with his wife, as well as his daughters. They were arrogant and unreasonable, and disliked by many of the shopkeepers in town. Ada and Isabel had been unpopular in high school. They had talked incessantly of money and social position, making themselves very obnoxious to the other students.

"I wonder," Nancy thought, "if a way can't be found so the Turners could get a share of the Crowley money. I'll ask Dad."

Five minutes later Nancy pulled into the double

garage and hurried across the lawn to the kitchen door of the Drews' large red-brick house. The building stood well back from the street, and was surrounded by tall, beautiful trees.

"Hello, Nancy," greeted the pleasant, slightly plump woman who opened the door. She was Hannah Gruen, housekeeper for the Drews, who had helped rear Nancy since the death of the girl's own mother many years before.

Nancy gave her a hug, then asked, "Dad home? I see his car is in the garage."

"Your father's in the living room and dinner will be ready in a few minutes."

Nancy went to say hello to her tall, handsome father, then hurried to wash her hands and comb her hair before the three who formed the Drew household sat down to dinner. During the meal Nancy related her adventure of the afternoon.

"What tricky thieves!" Hannah Gruen burst out. "Oh, I hope the police capture them!"

"They certainly took advantage of those Turner sisters," Mr. Drew commented.

"Mary and Edna are in financial difficulties," Nancy commented. "Isn't it a shame that Josiah Crowley didn't bequeath some of his estate to the Turners and other relatives who need the money?"

Carson Drew smiled affectionately at his only child, then said, "Yes, it is, Nancy. But unless a will written later turns up, that's the way it has to be."

"The Turners think there is another will," Nancy told him. "Wouldn't it be wonderful if it can be found?"

"I agree," spoke up Hannah. "It's well known in town that Mrs. Topham and her daughters were unkind to Josiah Crowley for some time before he died. Their excuse was that Josiah's eccentricities were extremely trying."

"The Tophams have never been noted for any charitable inclinations," Mr. Drew observed with a smile. "However, they did give Josiah a home."

"Only because they knew he was going to leave all his money to them," said Hannah. "If I'd been Josiah I wouldn't have stayed there." The housekeeper sighed. "But when people get old, they don't like change. And probably he put up with things rather than move."

She said the treatment the Tophams had accorded old Josiah Crowley had aroused a great deal of unfavorable comment throughout River Heights. Nancy had not known him personally, but she had often seen the elderly man on the street. Secretly she had regarded him as a rather nice, kindly person.

His wife had died during an influenza epidemic and after that he had made his home with various relatives. According to rumors, all these people had admitted that he had paid his board and done many favors for them. They in turn had been very kind to him, and though poor themselves, had tried to make Josiah Crowley comfortable and happy.

"Tell me everything you know about Mr. Crowley," Nancy urged her father.

The lawyer said that the old man had publicly declared he intended to provide in his will for several deserving relatives and friends. Then, three years before his death, the Topham family, who had never shown an interest in him, had experienced a sudden change of heart. They had begged Josiah Crowley to make his home with them, and at last he had consented. Shortly after he moved into the Topham house, Mr. Drew was told that the old man had decided to leave all his money to them.

Mr. Crowley, though failing in health, maintained a firm grip on life. But as time went on, he became more and more unhappy. He continued to live with the Tophams, but it was whispered about that he frequently slipped away to visit his other relatives and friends, and that he intended to change his will again.

"Then there must be a later will!" Nancy said hopefully.

Mr. Drew nodded, and went on, "One day Josiah Crowley became critically ill. Just before his death he attempted to communicate something to the doctor who attended him, but his words, other than 'will,' were unintelligible. After the funeral only one will came to light, giving the entire fortune to the Tophams."

"Dad, do you suppose Mr. Crowley was trying to tell the doctor something about another will which he had put some place where the Tophams couldn't find it?" Nancy asked.

"Very likely," the lawyer replied. "Probably he intended to leave his money to relatives who had been kind to him. But fate cheated him of the opportunity."

"Do you think anybody has looked for another will?" Nancy questioned.

"I don't know. But I'm sure of this. If another will shows up, Richard Topham will fight it. The estate is a considerable one, I understand, and they aren't the kind of people to share good fortune."

"Can't the present will be contested?" Nancy asked.

"I hear that other relatives have filed a claim, declaring they were told another will had been made in their favor. But unless it is located, I doubt that the matter will ever go further."

"But the Tophams don't deserve the fortune," Hannah Gruen remarked. "And besides, they don't need the money. It doesn't seem fair."

"It may not seem fair, but it is legal," Mr. Drew told her, "and I'm afraid nothing can be done about the situation."

"Poor Judy and her aunts!" said Nancy.

"There are others affected in the same way," her father remarked. "For instance, two young women who live on the River Road. I don't know their names. I understand they were not related to Mr. Crowley, but were great favorites of his. They are having a struggle and could use some extra money."

Nancy lapsed into silence. She felt strongly that a mystery lurked behind the Crowley case.

"Dad, don't *you* believe Josiah Crowley made a second will?" Nancy questioned suddenly.

"You sound like a trial lawyer, the way you cross-examine me," Mr. Drew protested, but with evident enjoyment. "To tell the truth, Nancy, I don't know what to think, but something did happen which might indicate that Mr. Crowley at least intended to make another will."

"Please go on!" Nancy begged impatiently.

"Well, one day nearly a year ago I was in the First National Bank when Crowley came in with Henry Rolsted."

"The attorney who specializes in wills and other estate matters?" Nancy inquired.

"Yes. I had no intention of listening to their conversation, but I couldn't help overhearing a few words that made me think they were discussing a will. Crowley made an appointment to call at Rolsted's office the following day."

"Oh!" cried Nancy excitedly. "That looks as though Mr. Crowley had made a new will, doesn't it? But why didn't Mr. Rolsted say something about it at the time of Mr. Crowley's death?"

"For one of many reasons," Mr. Drew replied. "In the first place, he may never have drawn a new will for Mr. Crowley. And even if he had, the old man might have changed his mind again and torn it up."

Before Nancy spoke again, she finished the delicious apple pudding which Hannah had made. Then she looked thoughtfully at her father. "Dad, Mr. Rolsted is an old friend of yours, isn't he?"

"Yes. An old friend and college classmate."

"Then won't you please ask him if he ever drew up a will for Mr. Crowley, or knows anything that might solve this mystery?"

"That's a rather delicate question, young lady. He may tell me it's none of my business!"

"You know he won't. You're such good friends he'll understand why you're taking a special interest in this case. Will you do it? Please!"

"I know you like to help people who are in trouble," her father said. "I suppose I could invite Mr. Rolsted to have lunch with me tomorrow—"

"Wonderful!" Nancy interrupted eagerly. "That would be a splendid opportunity to find out what he knows about a later will."

"All right. I'll try to arrange a date. How about joining us?"

Nancy's face lighted up as she said, "Oh, thank you, Dad. I'd love to. I hope it can be tomorrow, so we won't have to waste any time trying to find another will."

Mr. Drew smiled. "We?" he said. "You mean you might try to find a hidden will if Mr. Crowley wrote one?"

"I might." Nancy's eyes sparkled in anticipation.

CHAPTER III

An Unpleasant Meeting

"WHAT are your plans for this morning, Nancy?" her father asked at the breakfast table.

"I thought I'd do a little shopping," she replied. Her eyes twinkled. "There's a dance coming up at the country club and I'd like to get a new dress."

"Then will you phone me about lunch? Or better still, how about eating with me, whether Mr. Rolsted comes or not?"

"I'll be there!" Nancy declared gaily.

"All right. Drop in at my office about twelve-thirty. If Mr. Rolsted does accept my invitation, we'll try to find out something about Josiah Crowley's wills." Mr. Drew pushed back his chair. "I must hurry now or I'll be late getting downtown."

After her father had left, Nancy finished her breakfast, then went to the kitchen to help Hannah Gruen, who had already left the table.

"Any errands for me?" Nancy asked.

"Yes, dear. Here's a list," the housekeeper replied. "And good luck with your detective work."

Hannah Gruen gazed at the girl affectionately and several thoughts raced through her mind. In school Nancy had been very popular and had made many friends. But through no fault of her own, she had made two enemies, Ada and Isabel Topham. This worried Hannah. The sisters, intensely jealous of Nancy, had tried to discredit her in positions she had held in school. But loyal friends had always sprung to Nancy's defense. As a result, Ada and Isabel had become more unpleasant than ever to Nancy.

"Thanks for your encouragement," she said to Hannah a little later, giving her a hug.

"Whatever you do, Nancy, beware of those Topham sisters. They'd be only too happy to make things difficult for you."

"I promise to be on my guard."

Before leaving the house, Nancy phoned the Turners. She was glad to hear that Judy had suffered no ill effects from her fall. But she was disappointed that the police had found no clue to the thieves who had stolen the silverware.

"Please let me know if you learn anything," Nancy said, and Edna promised to do so.

Becomingly dressed in a tan cotton suit, Nancy set off in her convertible for the shopping district. She drove down the boulevard, and upon reaching the more congested streets, made her way skillfully through heavy traffic, then pulled into a parking lot.

"I think I'll try Taylor's Department Store first for a dress," she decided.

Taylor's was one of River Heights' finest stores. Nancy purchased several items for Hannah on the main floor, then went directly to the misses' wearing apparel section on the second floor.

Usually Nancy had no trouble finding a salesclerk. But this particular morning seemed to be an especially busy one in the department, and an extra rush of customers had temporarily overwhelmed the sales force.

Nancy sat down in a convenient chair to await her turn. Her thoughts wandered to the Turner sisters and little Judy. Would she be able to help them? She was suddenly brought out of her reverie by loud-voiced complaints.

"We've been standing here nearly ten minutes!" a shrill voice declared. "Send a saleswoman to us immediately!"

Nancy turned to see Ada and Isabel Topham speaking to the floor manager.

"I'm afraid I can't," the man replied regretfully. "There are a number of others ahead of you. All our salespeople are—"

"Perhaps you don't know who we are!" Ada interrupted rudely.

"Indeed I do," the floor manager told her wearily. "I will have a saleswoman here in a few moments. If you will only wait—"

"We're not accustomed to waiting," Isabel Topham told him icily.

"Such service!" Ada chimed in. "Do you realize that my father owns considerable stock in Taylor's? If we report your conduct to him, he could have you discharged."

"I'm sorry," the harassed man apologized. "But it is a rule of the store. You must await your turn."

Ada tossed her head and her eyes flashed angrily. This did nothing to improve her looks. In spite of the expensive clothes she wore, Ada was not attractive. She was very thin and sallow, with an expression of petulance. Now that her face was distorted with anger, she was almost ugly.

Isabel, the pride of the Topham family, was rather pretty, but her face lacked character. She had acquired an artificially elegant manner of speaking which, although irritating, was sometimes amusing. It was her mother's ambition that Isabel marry into a socially prominent family.

"I pity any future husband of hers!" Nancy thought with a chuckle.

Suddenly Ada and Isabel saw Nancy, who nodded a greeting. Isabel coldly returned the nod, but Ada gave no indication that she had even noticed Nancy.

At that moment a saleswoman hurried toward

the Topham sisters. At once they began to shower abuse upon the young woman for her failure to wait on them sooner.

"What is it you wish to look at, Miss Topham?" the clerk said, flushing.

"Evening dresses."

The saleswoman brought out several dresses. Nancy watched curiously as the Tophams, in an unpleasant frame of mind, tossed aside beautiful models with scarcely a second glance. They found fault with every garment.

"This is a very chic gown," the saleswoman told them hopefully, as she displayed a particularly attractive dress of lace and chiffon. "It arrived only this morning."

Ada picked it up, gave the dress one careless glance, then tossed it into a chair, as the distracted clerk went off to bring other frocks.

The fluffy gown slipped to the floor in a crumpled mass. To Nancy's horror Ada stepped on it as she turned to examine another dress. In disgust, Nancy went to pick it up.

"Leave that alone!" Ada cried out, her eyes blazing. "Nobody asked for your help."

"Are you buying this?" Nancy asked evenly.

"It's none of your business!"

As Nancy continued to hold the dress, Ada in a rage snatched it from her hands, causing a long tear in the chiffon skirt.

"Oh!" Isabel cried out. "Now you've done it! We'd better get out of here, Ada!"

"And why?" her haughty sister shrilled. "It was Nancy Drew's fault! She's always making trouble."

"It was *not* my fault," Nancy said.

"Come on, Ada," Isabel urged, "before that clerk gets back."

Reluctantly Ada followed Isabel out of the department. As they rushed toward a waiting elevator, Nancy gazed after them. At this moment the saleswoman reappeared with an armful of lovely frocks. She stared in bewilderment at the torn dress.

"Where did my customers go?" she asked Nancy worriedly.

Nancy pointed toward the elevator, but made no comment. Instead she said, "I'm looking for an evening dress myself. This torn one is very pretty. Do you think it could be mended?"

"Oh, I don't know," the woebegone clerk wailed. "I'll probably be held responsible and I can't afford to pay for the dress."

"I'm sure Taylor's wouldn't ask you to do that," Nancy said kindly. "If there's any trouble, I'll speak to the manager myself. What usually happens is that such a dress is greatly reduced."

"Thank you," the clerk replied. "I'll call Miss Reed, the fitter, and see what can be done."

"First, let me try on the dress," Nancy said, smiling.

They found a vacant fitting room and Nancy took off her suit and blouse. Then she slipped the lovely pale-blue dance creation over her head and the saleswoman zipped it up.

"It's darling on you," she said enthusiastically.

Nancy grinned. "I kind of like myself in it," she said. "Please call the fitter now."

Presently Miss Reed, a gray-haired woman, appeared. Within seconds she had made a change in an overlap of the chiffon skirt. The tear was no longer visible and the style of the dress was actually improved.

"I told our manager what happened," said the saleswoman. "If you want the dress, he will reduce the price fifty percent."

"How wonderful!" Nancy exclaimed. Laughing, she said, "That price will fit into my budget nicely. I'll take the dress. Please send it." She gave her name and address. To herself she added, "Ada Topham did me a favor. But if she ever finds out what happened, she'll certainly be burned up!" Nancy suppressed a giggle.

"It's been a real pleasure waiting on you, Miss Drew," the saleswoman said after Miss Reed left and Nancy was putting on her suit. "But how I dread to see those Topham sisters come in here! They're so unreasonable. And they'll be even worse when they get Josiah Crowley's money."

The woman lowered her voice. "The estate hasn't been settled, but the girls are counting on the fortune already. Last week I heard Ada say to her sister, 'Oh, I guess there's no question about our getting old Crowley's fortune. But I wish Father would stop worrying that somebody is going to show up with a later will which may do us out of it.' "

Nancy was too discreet to engage in gossip with the saleswoman. But she was interested and excited about the information. The fact that Mr. Topham was disturbed indicated to her that he too suspected Josiah Crowley had made a second will!

The conversation reminded Nancy of her date. She glanced at her wrist watch and saw that it was after twelve o'clock.

"I must hurry or I'll be late for an appointment with my dad," she told the saleswoman.

Nancy drove directly to her father's office. Although she was a few minutes ahead of the appointed time, she found that he was ready to leave.

"What luck, Dad?" Nancy asked eagerly. "Did Mr. Rolsted accept your luncheon invitation?"

"Yes. We are to meet him at the Royal Hotel in ten minutes. Do you still think I should quiz him about the Crowley will?"

"Oh, I'm more interested than ever in the case." She told her father about the saleswoman's gossipy remarks.

"Hm," said Mr. Drew. "It's not what you'd call evidence, but the old saying usually holds good, 'Where there's smoke, there's fire.' Come, let's go!"

The Royal Hotel was located less than a block away, and Nancy and her father quickly walked the distance. Mr. Rolsted was waiting in the lobby. Carson Drew introduced his daughter, then the three made their way to the dining room where a table had been reserved for them.

At first the conversation centered about a variety of subjects. As the luncheon progressed the two lawyers talked enthusiastically of their college days together and finally of their profession. Nancy began to fear that the subject of the Crowley estate might never be brought up.

Then, after the dessert course, Mr. Drew skillfully turned the conversation into a new channel and mentioned some strange cases which he had handled.

"By the way," he said, "I haven't heard the details of the Crowley case. How are the Tophams making out? I understand other relatives are trying to break the will."

For a moment Mr. Rolsted remained silent. Was he reluctant to enter into a discussion of the matter? Nancy wondered.

Finally the lawyer said quietly, "The settlement of the estate wasn't given to me, Carson. But I confess I've followed it rather closely because of something that happened a year ago. As the present will stands, I do not believe it can be broken."

"Then the Tophams fall heir to the entire estate," Mr. Drew commented.

"Yes, unless a more recent will is uncovered."

"Another will?" Carson Drew inquired innocently. "Then you believe Crowley made a second one?"

Mr. Rolsted hesitated as though uncertain whether or not he should divulge any further information. Then, with a quick glance about, he lowered his voice and said, "Of course this is strictly confidential—"

CHAPTER IV

Racing the Storm

"CONFIDENTIAL?" Mr. Drew repeated, looking at Mr. Rolsted. "You may rest assured that whatever you tell us will not be repeated to anyone."

"Well, I'll say this much," Mr. Rolsted went on, "about a year ago Josiah Crowley came to me and said he wanted to draw up a new will. He indicated that he intended to spread out his bequests among several people. He expressed a desire to write the will himself, and asked me a number of questions. I took him to my office and told him exactly how to proceed. When he left, he promised to have me look over the document after he had drawn it up."

"Then you actually saw the will?" Mr. Drew asked in surprise.

"No. Strange to say, Crowley never came back. I don't know whether he ever wrote the will or not."

"And if he did, there would be a chance that it would not be legal?" Nancy spoke up.

"Yes. He might have typed it and signed the paper without a witness. In this state at least two witnesses are required and three are advisable."

"What would happen," Nancy asked, "if a person were ill or dying and had no witness, and wanted to make a will?"

Mr. Rolsted smiled. "That sometimes happens. If the person writes the will himself by hand and signs it, so there's no doubt the same person did both, the surrogate's office will accept it for probate."

"Then if Mr. Crowley wrote out and signed a new will, it would be legal," Nancy commented.

"That's right. But there's another thing to remember. It's pretty risky for someone who is not a lawyer to draw up a will that cannot be broken."

Mr. Drew nodded. "If Josiah Crowley left any loophole in a will he wrote personally, the Tophams would drag the matter into court."

"Yes. It's a foregone conclusion that the Tophams will fight to keep the fortune whether they have a right to it or not. I believe some other relatives have filed a claim, but up to the moment they have no proof that a later will exists."

Although Nancy gave no indication of her feelings, the possibility that Mr. Crowley had made a new will thrilled her. As soon as Mr. Drew paid the luncheon check, the three arose and left the dining room. Mr. Rolsted took leave of Nancy and her father in the lobby.

"Well, Nancy, did you find out what you wanted to know?" Mr. Drew asked after the lawyer had left.

"Oh, Dad, it's just as I suspected. I'm sure Mr. Crowley did make a later will! He hid it some place! If only I could find out where!"

"It would be like looking for a needle in a haystack," Mr. Drew commented.

"I must figure out a way!" Nancy said with determination. "I want to help little Judy."

She awoke the next morning thinking about the mystery. But where should she start hunting for possible clues to a second will? She continued pondering about it while she showered and dressed.

As she entered the dining room, she was greeted with a cheery "Good morning" from her father and Hannah Gruen. During breakfast Mr. Drew said, "Nancy, would you do a little errand for me this morning?"

"Why, of course, Dad."

"I have a number of legal documents which must be delivered to Judge Hart at Masonville some time before noon. I'd take them myself, but I have several important appointments. I'd appreciate it if you would drive over there with them."

"I'll be glad to go," Nancy promised willingly.

"Besides, it's such a wonderful day. I'll enjoy the trip. Where are the papers?"

"At the office. You can drive me down and I'll get them for you."

Nancy, wearing a yellow sunback dress and jacket, hurried away to get her gloves and handbag. Before Mr. Drew had collected his own belongings, she had brought her car from the garage and was waiting for him at the front door.

"I put the top down so I can enjoy the sun," she explained as her father climbed in.

"Good idea. I haven't heard you mention the Crowley case yet today," Mr. Drew teased as they rode along. "Have you forgotten about it?"

Nancy's face clouded. "No, I haven't forgotten, but I must admit I *am* stumped as to where to search for clues."

"Maybe I can help you. I've learned that the two girls on River Road who expected to be remembered in the will are named Hoover. You might look them up on your return trip."

"That's great. I'll watch the mailboxes for their name."

When they reached the building where Mr. Drew had his office, Nancy parked the car and waited while her father went upstairs to get the legal documents to be delivered to Judge Hart. Returning a few minutes later, he placed a fat Manila envelope in his daughter's hand.

"Give this to the judge. You know where to find him?"

"Yes, Dad. In the old Merchants Trust Company Building."

"That's right."

Selecting a recently constructed highway, Nancy rode along, glancing occasionally at the neatly planted fields on either side. Beyond were rolling hills.

"Pretty," she commented to herself. "Oh, why can't all people be nice like this scenery and not make trouble?"

It was nearly eleven o'clock when she finally drove into Masonville. Nancy went at once to Judge Hart's office but was informed he had gone to the courthouse. Recalling that her father had mentioned the necessity of the papers being delivered before noon, she set off in search of the judge.

Nancy had considerable trouble trying to see him, and it was twelve o'clock when at last she delivered the Manila envelope into his hands.

"Thank you very much," he said. "I'll need these directly after lunch."

Nancy smiled. "Then I'm glad I found you."

When Judge Hart learned that Nancy was the daughter of Carson Drew, he at once insisted that she have luncheon with him and his wife at their home before returning to River Heights.

She accepted the invitation and spent a very

pleasant hour with the Harts. During the meal the judge laughingly asked if Nancy was still playing aide to her father.

"Oh, yes," she said, and at once told him about the Drews' interest in the Crowley case.

"Did you know Josiah Crowley or ever hear of him?" she asked.

Both the Harts nodded. "A maid who used to be with them, came to work for us after Mrs. Crowley's death," the judge explained. "Jane herself passed away a short time ago."

"We never met Josiah," Mrs. Hart added, "but Jane pointed him out to my husband and me one time down on Main Street."

"Did he have relatives or friends in town?" Nancy inquired.

"I think not," the judge replied.

Nancy wondered what old Josiah had been doing in Masonville if he had no relatives or friends there. The town was not known as a spot for sight-seeing. Her interest was further quickened when Mrs. Hart remarked that she had seen Mr. Crowley in town at another time also.

"How long ago was that?" the girl asked.

Mrs. Hart thought a minute, then replied, "Oh, less than a year, I'd say."

When luncheon was over, the judge said he must leave. Nancy told the Harts she too should go. She thanked them for their hospitality, then said good-by. Soon she was driving homeward.

"Why had Mr. Crowley gone to Masonville?" she asked herself. "Could it have had anything to do with a later will?"

Nancy had chosen a route which would take her to River Road. Half an hour later she turned into the beautiful country road which wound in and out along the Muskoka River, and began to look at the names on the mailboxes. "Hoover," she reminded herself.

About halfway to River Heights, while enjoying the pastoral scenes of cows standing knee-high in shallow sections of the stream, and sheep grazing on flower-dotted hillsides, Nancy suddenly realized the sun had been blotted out.

"A thunderstorm's on the way," she told herself, glancing at black clouds scudding across the sky. "Guess I'd better put the top of the car up."

She pressed the button on the dashboard to raise the top, but nothing happened. Puzzled, Nancy tried again. Still there was no response. By this time large drops of rain had started to fall.

"I'll get soaked," Nancy thought, as she looked around.

There was no shelter in sight. But ahead, past a steep rise, was a sharp bend in the road. Hopeful that there would be a house or barn beyond, Nancy started the car again.

Vivid forked lightning streaked across the sky. It was followed by an earth-shaking clap of thunder. The rain came down harder,

"Oh, why didn't I bring a raincoat?" Nancy wailed.

When Nancy swung around the bend, she was delighted to see a barn with lightning rods about a quarter mile ahead. Farther on stood a small white house.

"I wonder if that's the Hoover place," Nancy mused.

By now the storm was letting loose in all its fury. The sky was as dark as night and Nancy had to switch on her headlights to see the road. She was already thoroughly drenched and her thought of shelter at this point was one of safety rather than of keeping dry.

Nancy turned on the windshield wipers, but the rain was so blinding in its intensity, it was impossible to see more than a few feet ahead. Almost in an instant the road had dissolved into a sea of mud.

Nancy had been caught in a number of storms, but never one as violent as this. She feared a bad skid might land her in a ditch before she could reach the shelter of the barn.

"How much farther is it?" she worried. "It didn't seem this far away."

The next instant, to Nancy's right, a ball of fire rocketed down from the sky.

"Oh! That was close!" she thought fearfully. Her skin tingled from the electrical vibrations in the air.

A moment later a surge of relief swept over Nancy. "At last!" she breathed.

At the side of the road the barn loomed up. Its large double doors were wide open. Without hesitation, Nancy headed straight for the building and drove in.

The next moment she heard a piercing scream!

CHAPTER V

A Surprising Story

NANCY froze behind the wheel. Had she inadvertently hit someone? Her heart pounding in fright, she opened the car door to step out.

At the same instant a shadowy figure arose from a pile of hay near her. "I guess I must have scared you silly when I screamed," said a girl of Nancy's age, stepping forward.

"You— You're all right?" Nancy gasped.

"Yes. And I'm sorry I yelled. I came out here to check on our supply of feed for the chickens. I didn't think it was going to be a bad storm, so I didn't bother to go back to the house."

"It's pretty bad," said Nancy.

"Well, the storm terrified me," the girl continued. "I didn't hear your car coming, and when it rushed in here, I panicked."

Nancy began to breathe normally again, then

told the stranger her name and the fact that the mechanism for raising the top of the convertible was not working.

"That's a shame," said the girl. "And you must get your clothes dried. The storm is letting up. Let's dash over to the house. Grace will help you too. She's my sister. My name's Allison Hoover."

Hoover! Nancy was tempted to tell Allison that she had been planning to call, but she decided not to mention it at the moment. It might be better to do her sleuthing more subtly.

Nancy smiled at Allison. "Thanks a million. But first I'd like to wipe out the car. Are there any rags around the barn?"

Allison produced several and together the two girls mopped the water from the cushions and floor. By this time the rain had stopped. As Nancy and Allison sloshed through a series of puddles to the farmhouse, Nancy had a better chance to study her companion. She was tall, with reddish-blond hair and very fair skin. Her voice was musical and she had an attractive, lilting laugh.

The girls reached the run-down farmhouse and stamped the mud from their shoes on the back porch. Then Allison flung open the door, and they entered a cheerful kitchen.

As the door shut behind them, another girl who was just closing the oven of an old-fashioned range turned toward them in surprise.

"Grace, I've brought a visitor," Allison said

quickly. "Nancy, I want you to meet my sister. She's the mainstay of our family of two."

Grace Hoover cordially acknowledged the introduction and greeted Nancy with a warm smile. Nancy judged her to be at least four years older than Allison. Her face was rather serious, and it was evident from her manner that responsibility had fallen on her shoulders at an early age.

Nancy was attracted to both girls and responded to their friendly welcome. She put on a robe which Allison brought her and Grace hung her wet clothes near the range. Presently Grace pulled an ironing board from a closet with the intention of pressing Nancy's garments. But Nancy would not hear of this and began to iron them herself.

"This is fun," she said to the sisters. "I don't know what I would have done without you girls."

"It's great for us," Allison spoke up. "We don't have much company. To tell you the truth, we can't afford it."

Grace stepped to the stove, removed a golden-brown cake from the oven, and set it on the table to cool.

"But today we're not talking about money. It's Allison's birthday and this is a birthday cake. Nancy, if you're not in too much of a hurry, I wish you'd join us in a little celebration."

"Why, I'd love to," Nancy said.

"Grace's cakes are yummy," Allison declared.

"I'm not much of a cook myself. My department is taking care of the barn and the chickens."

Soon Nancy finished pressing her clothes and put them back on. Meanwhile, the cake had cooled and Grace started to spread the chocolate frosting.

"Suppose you two go into the living room and wait," she suggested. "I'll bring in the cake and tea."

Nancy followed Allison to the adjoining room. Although it was comfortable, the room did not contain much furniture. The floor had been painted and was scantily covered with handmade rag rugs. With the exception of an old-fashioned sofa, an inexpensive table, a few straight-backed chairs and an old oil stove which furnished heat in cold weather, there was little else in the room. However, dainty white curtains covered the windows, and Nancy realized that although the Hoovers were poor, they had tried hard to make their home attractive.

"Do you two girls live here alone all the time?" Nancy inquired.

Allison nodded. "Grace and I have been living here since Father died. That was two years ago. Mother passed away just before that," the girl added with a slight catch in her voice. "Their illnesses took every penny we had."

"I'm terribly sorry," Nancy remarked sympathetically. "It must be dreadfully hard for two girls to run the farm by themselves."

"Our farm isn't as large as it once was," Allison said quietly. "We have only a few acres left. I know you are too polite to ask how we manage, Nancy. Grace helps a dressmaker at Masonville whenever she can get work. She makes all her own clothes and mine too. And I raise chickens."

From just beyond the doorway suddenly came the strains of "Happy Birthday to you! Happy Birth—"

By this time Nancy had joined in. She and Grace finished "—day to you. Happy Birthday, dear Allison. Happy Birthday to you!"

Grace set the cake with eighteen lighted candles on the table. She and Nancy sang the second verse with the words "May you have many more!"

Tears stood in Allison's eyes. When the song ended, she grasped her sister in a tremendous hug. Then she gave Nancy one.

"This—this is the nicest birthday I've had in years," she quavered.

"And it's one of the most enjoyable I've ever attended," Nancy said sincerely.

Suddenly Allison began to sing a tuneful old English ballad about the birthday of a village lass. Nancy listened entranced to Allison's clear, bell-like tones. When she finished, Nancy applauded, then said:

"That was perfectly lovely. You have a beautiful voice, Allison!"

The singer laughed gaily. "Thank you, Nancy. I've always wanted to take lessons, but as you know, voice training is pretty expensive."

At that moment Grace brought in a tray of fragrant tea. As she poured three cups, Allison blew out the candles and served the cake.

"I've never tasted anything more delicious in all my life," Nancy said enthusiastically.

The three girls chatted like old friends. Finally the sun broke through the clouds. As Nancy rose to leave, she noticed an unusual picture on the wall opposite her and commented on its beauty.

"Uncle Josiah Crowley gave it to us," Allison told her. "If he were only alive now, things would be different."

At the mention of the name, Nancy sat down again. Was she going to pick up a clue to the possibility that Mr. Crowley had made a later will?

"He wasn't really our uncle," Grace explained. "But we loved him as much as though he were a relative." Her voice broke and for a moment she could not go on. Then, gaining control of herself, she continued, "He lived on the farm next to us—that was when Mother and Father were alive. All of Allison's and my misfortunes seemed to come at once."

"He was the dearest man you ever saw," Allison

added. "Some people thought him queer, but you never minded his peculiar ways after you knew him. Uncle Josiah was very good to us. He always told me that he'd back me in a singing career."

"Yes," Grace added. "Uncle Josiah used to say Allison sang as sweetly as a bird and he wanted to pay for lessons with a famous teacher. But after he went to live with the Tophams, he never said any more about it."

"He never liked it with the Tophams, though," Allison declared. "They weren't kind to him, and he used to slip away to visit us."

"Uncle Josiah often said that we seemed like his own children," Grace spoke up. "He brought us many nice gifts, but we loved him for himself and not his money. I remember, though, the very last day we saw him alive, he told us 'I have planned a big surprise to make you girls happy. But I can't tell you now what it is. You'll see it in my will.' Those were his very words."

"And then the Tophams got everything," Allison said. "He must have changed his mind for some reason."

"It's hard to believe he would forget his promise to us," Grace said sadly.

"Oh, wouldn't it be wonderful if a later will could be found!" Allison exclaimed.

"Yes," Nancy replied slowly. "I've heard that

Mr. Crowley told other people he was leaving money to them. The Turner sisters, for instance. Do you know them?"

"Slightly," Grace answered.

"My dad," Nancy went on, "is a lawyer and he and I are very much interested in this case. He even mentioned you girls, and to tell the truth I was on my way here to talk to you."

Allison impulsively grasped Nancy's arm. "You say your father is a lawyer? Grace and I are positive Uncle Josiah made a later will. Oh, if we could only engage your father to help us prove this!" Then a sad look came over her face. "But I'm forgetting—we wouldn't have any money to pay him if we should lose the case."

"Don't let that worry you," said Nancy kindly. "This is your birthday and you must be happy, Allison. My special wish for you is that before you're one year older, you'll inherit some of the Crowley money, so that you can take those singing lessons!"

CHAPTER VI

An Exciting Appointment

The Hoover girls walked out to the barn with Nancy. "Do come to see us again," Grace called, as the young detective climbed into her car.

"Yes, please do," Allison added.

Nancy promised that she would. "As soon as I have some news," she said.

Although the weather had cleared, the River Road remained muddy and slippery. Nancy found it necessary to drive with extreme care for the next two miles until she reached the main highway.

"No wonder this River Road isn't used much," she thought. "And how do Grace and Allison get to town?" Nancy wondered. She had not seen a car at the Hoover home and knew that no bus passed their door.

"I certainly wish," she thought, "that I or somebody else could locate a later will of Josiah Crowley's by which the Hoovers and the Turners would receive some much-needed money. I must tell Dad about this latest development."

She decided to see if her father was in his office and drove directly there. Nancy parked the car in a nearby lot. She surveyed the convertible ruefully as she climbed out.

"Poor thing! It certainly needs a bath!"

Nancy found Mr. Drew in. As she entered his private office, he arose from the desk chair to kiss her. "I'm glad you're here—and safe," the lawyer said. "I was worried about you when that violent storm came up. When Hannah phoned me that you weren't back, I began to regret I'd sent you on the errand."

His daughter grinned. "I'm back, all in one piece. I delivered the papers to Judge Hart and learned that he and his wife saw Mr. Crowley in Masonville a couple of times. Also, I talked to the Hoover girls."

She described her meeting with Allison and Grace Hoover and ended by asking her father if he could help them.

"From what you say, it does look as though Josiah Crowley might have made another will which included them as beneficiaries," Mr. Drew commented thoughtfully. "I'll be glad to do anything I can to help the Hoover girls."

He asked whether the sisters had given Nancy any specific information about Mr. Crowley's habits or other helpful clues. When Nancy shook her head, Mr. Drew suggested that she invite the girls to his office for a little conference. "Perhaps if I ask them some questions, it will recall helpful incidents." The lawyer studied his desk calendar for a moment, then looked up at his daughter. "How about tomorrow afternoon at two-forty-five? I can give them about half an hour."

For answer, Nancy gave her father a hug and then asked if she might use his telephone to call the Hoovers at once.

Grace and Allison eagerly accepted the Drews' invitation, and Nancy said she would drive out to bring them to the conference and take them home afterward.

"You're a doll!" cried Allison, who had answered the telephone. "Nancy, I just know you're going to solve this mystery!"

Suddenly an idea came to Nancy. She asked Allison how long the girls would be able to stay in River Heights.

"Oh, as long as you need us," Allison replied.

"Good. Then I'd like you both to stay and have supper with us," Nancy said.

"Sorry I can't join you," Mr. Drew told his daughter as she hung up. "I have a dinner engagement and conference in the evening."

Just then, the mayor of River Heights was shown into the lawyer's office, and Nancy arose to leave. She spoke to the mayor for a moment, then said, "See you later, Dad."

Before Nancy returned home, she stopped at an old-fashioned house on a side street. It was the home of Signor Mascagni, a famous voice teacher who had retired to the small city the year before, but took a few outstanding pupils. Nancy introduced herself to the white bushy-haired, florid-faced man, then said:

"Signor Mascagni, would you be willing to listen to the voice of a friend of mine and give your honest opinion as to whether or not she might become a great singer? If she might, and she can obtain the money for lessons, would you be able to take her as a pupil?"

Signor Mascagni studied Nancy for several minutes before replying. Finally he said, "You do not look like the kind of girl who would come here on a foolish errand. Ordinarily I do not accept beginners. But in this case I would be willing to hear your friend sing." He laughed. "Mind you, I will give you nothing but the truth, and if your friend does not measure up, I hope her feelings will not be hurt too deeply."

Nancy laughed too. "I like honesty," she said. "As a matter of fact, this girl knows nothing about what I am asking you. Coming here will be a complete surprise to her. I'm probably no judge of voices, but I think she's a natural. However, we will both appreciate having your opinion, and will certainly abide by it."

She arranged for a meeting the following afternoon at four o'clock and left Signor Mascagni's house in an excited mood. "Maybe I'm going way out on a limb," Nancy mused, "but this is another one of those hunches of mine that Dad talks about, and I must carry through."

When she picked up the Hoovers the following day, Nancy did not mention the appointment with the voice teacher. The three girls went directly to Mr. Drew's office and at once he began to quiz Grace and Allison about Mr. Crowley.

"I understand that he was a rather eccentric man," the lawyer began. "Suppose you tell me everything you can remember about what Josiah Crowley did and what he said which would help us figure out where he might have secreted a later will."

"Uncle Josiah was rather absent-minded," Grace spoke up. "I often saw him hunting for his spectacles, which he had pushed up on his head."

"Did he ever hide things?" Mr. Drew asked.

"Oh, yes." Allison laughed. "Uncle Josiah was always putting articles away in what he called a safe place. But the places were so safe he never could find the things again!"

"Then," Nancy spoke up excitedly, "Mr. Crowley could have hidden a will and then forgotten where?"

"I suppose so," Grace replied. "While living with the Tophams, I'm sure that's just what he would have done. One day when he was calling at our house he talked about the Tophams and the way they were trying to get all his money. 'I guess they think—just because I stay on—that they're going to get everything. But they'll be fooled when they find I've made another will,' he said with that odd little chuckle of his. 'This time I'm not going to trust it to any lawyer. I'll put it away in a place that I know will be safe.' "

Allison asked Mr. Drew, "Do you think Uncle Josiah hid another will somewhere in the Tophams' house?"

The lawyer looked down at his desk for several seconds before replying. "If he did, we would have a great fight on our hands, I'm afraid, trying to persuade the Tophams to let us make a search."

Another thought had come to Nancy and she shuddered at the idea. Perhaps the Tophams had been alerted by all the talk of a later will, had searched for it, discovered one, and by now destroyed it!

She flashed her father a questioning look and got the impression that he had the same thought. But there was no point in discouraging the Hoover girls by telling them this.

Mr. Drew continued to question the sisters until three-thirty, then said he had another appointment. He would do all he could to help the girls and would not charge them for his services.

"Unless they bring results," he added with a smile.

"You're very kind, just like your daughter," said Grace as she arose and shook hands with the lawyer. "You have no idea how much Allison and I appreciate what you're doing for us."

When the three girls reached Nancy's car, she told the sisters she wanted them to meet someone special in town, and drove directly to Signor Mascagni's home. As they went up to the front porch they could hear the sounds of a soprano voice singing an aria from *Tosca*.

"How beautiful!" Allison exclaimed softly.

The girls were admitted by a maid and asked to wait in a small room while Signor Mascagni's pupil finished her lesson. Puzzled, Allison waited for Nancy to explain.

"I have a surprise for you," Nancy said with a grin. "Signor Mascagni has promised to listen to your voice. If you pass the test, he'll consider taking you as a pupil—that is, after we find the money for voice lessons."

Allison was too dumfounded to speak, but Grace cried out, "Oh, Nancy, what are you going to do next? We've known you only twenty-four hours and you've already boosted our morale sky-high."

At this moment the door to the studio opened. The young soprano came out, followed by Signor Mascagni. He said good-by to his pupil, then invited the three callers into the studio. Nancy quickly introduced the Hoover sisters.

"And you are the singer," the man said almost

at once, addressing Allison. "I can tell from your speaking voice."

Apparently the teacher sensed that Allison had been taken by surprise and was a little nervous. Accordingly he began to talk on other subjects than music. He showed the girls several paintings in the room and pieces of statuary which had come from Italy.

"I prize them highly," he said.

"They are exquisite," Allison remarked.

Signor Mascagni walked to a rear window and pointed out a lovely garden in back of the house. Then, evidently satisfied that Allison was at ease, he led the way to the grand piano and sat down.

"Now what would you like to sing?" he asked Allison with a smile. "Please stand right here facing me."

"Something very simple," she replied. " 'America the Beautiful'?"

The teacher nodded, asked her what key she would like it played in, then began to accompany her. Allison sang as though inspired. Her voice sounded even more beautiful than it had at the farmhouse, Nancy thought. When Allison finished the song, Signor Mascagni made no comment. Instead he asked her to try a scale, then to sing single tones, jumping from octave to octave.

"You have a very fine range, Miss Hoover," was his only comment.

For half an hour he had Allison try short songs

in various keys and at one point joined with her in a duet. At last he turned around on the piano bench and faced Nancy and Grace.

"I believe," he said slowly, "I believe that some day we shall know Allison Hoover as an operatic star!"

Before the girls could say anything, he jumped up and turned to shake Allison's hand fervently. By this time the full import of his words had dawned on the young singer. Tears began to roll down her cheeks.

"Bravissimo! Bravissimo!" he exclaimed. "You sing, you cry, you smile! *Magnifico!* You will also be a dramatic actress *splendida."*

Nancy and Grace were nearly on the verge of tears also, they were so overwhelmed by the happy news. Then suddenly the three girls became serious, remembering that there was still the problem of money for lessons from this great man. They knew his fee per hour must be very high.

Allison suddenly began to talk and poured out her whole story to the white-haired teacher. "But I know," she declared with a brave smile, "that somehow I'm going to get the money for the lessons and I wouldn't want to take them from anybody but you, Signor Mascagni. I'll come back to you just as soon as I can. Thank you very, very much. Please, girls, I'd like to leave now."

As Allison rushed toward the front door, Signor Mascagni detained Nancy and Grace. "This Allison, she is wonderful!" he exclaimed. "I want to give her lessons to see that her training is correct." He threw up his hands and shook his head. "But I cannot afford to give the lessons free. Perhaps I could cut my price—"

"We'll find the money somehow, signor!" Nancy promised. Then she and Grace thanked the teacher and followed Allison outside.

At the Drew home that evening there were mixed emotions on everyone's part. Hannah Gruen had taken a great fancy to the Hoover sisters and the news of Allison's talent had thrilled her, as well as the girls. Conversation at supper was gay and animated. Nancy and Mrs. Gruen drove the sisters to their farm and on parting Nancy again promised to do all she could to help find a will from which the girls might possibly benefit.

But figuring out how to do this became a problem that seemed insurmountable to Nancy. At breakfast the following day, Mr. Drew suggested, "Nancy, perhaps if you'd give your mind a little rest from the Crowley matter, an inspiration about the case might come to you."

His daughter smiled. "Good idea, Dad. I think I'll take a walk in the fresh air and clear the cobwebs from my brain."

As soon as she finished eating, Nancy set out at a brisk pace. She headed for River Heights' attractive park to view the display of roses which was

Signor Muscugni shook Allison's hand fervently

always very beautiful. She had gone only a short distance along one of the paths when she caught sight of Isabel and Ada Topham seated on a bench not far ahead.

"They're the last people in the world I want to see right now," Nancy thought. "They'll probably say something mean to me and I'll lose my temper. When I think how Grace and Allison and the Turners could use just one-tenth of the Crowley money which the Tophams are going to inherit, I could just burst!"

Nancy had paused, wondering whether she should turn back. "No," she told herself, "I'll go on to see the roses. I'll take that path back of the Tophams and they won't notice me."

Nancy made her way along quietly, with no intention of eavesdropping on the two girls. But suddenly two words of their conversation came to her ears, bringing Nancy to an involuntary halt.

She had distinctly heard Isabel say—"the will."

In a flash Nancy's detective instincts were aroused and her heart pounded excitedly. "It must be Josiah Crowley's will they're talking about," she reasoned.

CHAPTER VII

The Angry Dog

WITH the instinct of a detective who dared not miss a clue, Nancy deliberately moved closer to the bench on which the Topham girls were seated.

"If there *should* be another will, I'm afraid we'd be out of luck." The words, in Ada's nasal voice, came clearly to Nancy.

Isabel's reply was in so low a tone that the young sleuth could just manage to catch the words, "Well, I, for one, don't believe Josiah Crowley ever made a later will." She gave a low laugh. "Mother watched him like a hawk."

"Or thought she did," Isabel retorted. "The old man got out of her clutches several times, don't forget."

"Yes, and what's worse, I'm sure Nancy Drew thinks he made a later will. That's why she's taking such an interest in those Hoover girls. I actually saw them go into Mr. Drew's office yesterday and it wasn't to deliver eggs! If Nancy gets her father interested, he might dig up another will. Oh, how I hate that interfering girl!"

At this Nancy could barely refrain from laughing. So the Tophams *were* concerned about the existence of a second will. With bated breath she listened further.

"You're such a worry wart, Ada. You can trust Dad and Mother to take care of things, no matter what happens," Isabel commented dryly. "They won't let that pile of money get away from us. It's ours by right, anyhow."

"You've got something there," Ada conceded. "We should have old Josiah's money after supporting and putting up with him for three years. That was pretty clever of Mother, never accepting any board money from Josiah Crowley!"

The conversation ended as Isabel and Ada arose from the bench and walked away. Nancy waited until they were out of sight, then emerged from her hiding place. Seating herself on the bench vacated by the Topham sisters, Nancy mulled over the remarks she had just overheard.

"There's no doubt in my mind now that if there is a later will, the Tophams haven't destroyed it. How thrilling! But where can it be?"

Nancy realized that to find it was a real challenge. "And I'd better hurry up before the Tophams stumble on it!"

For another ten minutes Nancy sat lost in

thought, sifting all the facts she had gleaned so far.

"There must be some clue I've overlooked," she told herself. Suddenly, with a cry of delight, she sprang to her feet. "Why didn't I think of that before! The Hoover girls and the Turners aren't the only ones who should have figured in this will. There are other relatives of Mr. Crowley who have filed a claim. I wonder who they are. If I could only talk with them, I might pick up a clue!"

Immediately Nancy set off for her father's office. He was engaged in an important conference when she arrived, and she had to wait ten minutes before being admitted to the inner office.

"Now what?" Mr. Drew asked, smiling, as she burst in upon him. "Have you solved the mystery or is your purse in need of a little change?"

Nancy's cheeks were flushed and her eyes danced with excitement. "Don't tease me," she protested. "I need some information!"

"At your service, Nancy."

The young sleuth poured out the story of the Topham sisters' conversation in the park, and told him of her own conclusions. Mr. Drew listened with interest until she had finished.

"Excellent deducting," he praised his daughter. "I'm afraid, though, I can't help you obtain the relatives' names. I don't know any of them."

Nancy looked disappointed. "Oh dear!" she sighed. "And I'm so anxious to find out right away. If I delay even a single day the Tophams may locate that other will—and destroy it."

The next instant her face brightened. "I know! I'll drive out and see the Turner sisters. They might be able to tell me who the other relatives are." Nancy arose and headed for the door.

"Just a minute," said the lawyer. "I wonder if you realize just what you are getting into, Nancy?"

"What do you mean?"

"Only this. Detective work isn't always the safest occupation in which to engage. I happen to know that Richard Topham is an unpleasant man when crossed. If you do find out anything which may frustrate him, the entire Topham family could make things extremely difficult for you."

"I'm not afraid of them, Dad."

"Good!" Mr. Drew exclaimed. "I was hoping you would say that. I'm glad you have the courage of your convictions, but I didn't want you to march off into battle without a knowledge of what you might be up against."

"Battle?"

"Yes. The Tophams won't give up the fortune without a bitter struggle. However, if they attempt to make serious trouble, I promise to deal with them myself."

"And if I do find the will?"

"I'll take the matter into court."

"Oh, thank you! There's no one like you in all the world."

After leaving her father's office, Nancy went directly home to get her car. When she told Hannah Gruen her plans, the housekeeper warned, "Don't become too deeply involved in this matter, dear. In your zeal to help other people, you may forget to be on your guard."

"I promise to be as careful as a pussycat walking up a slippery roof," Nancy assured the housekeeper with a grin, and left the house.

Quickly backing her car from the garage, she set off in the direction of the Turner home. The miles seemed to melt away as Nancy's thoughts raced from one idea to another. Before the young sleuth knew it she had reached the house.

"Hi, Judy!" she called to the little girl, who was playing in the yard with a midget badminton set.

The child looked very cunning in a pink play suit. The hand-embroidered Teddy bears on it were surely the work of her loving aunts.

"Hi, Nancy! I'm glad you came. Now I'll have somebody to play with," Judy said, running up to the visitor.

Obligingly Nancy took a racket and batted the feathered shuttlecock toward the child. "Hit the birdie," she called.

Judy missed but picked up the shuttlecock and whammed it nicely across the net. Nancy hit it back and this time the little girl caught the birdie on her racket and sent it over.

The game went on for several minutes, with

Judy crying out in delight. "You're the bestest batter I ever played with, Nancy," she declared.

After ten minutes of play, Nancy said, "Let's go into the house now, Judy. I want to talk to your aunties."

Judy skipped ahead and announced her new playmate's arrival.

"Hello, Nancy," the women said as she entered the living room.

"We were watching the game from the window," said Mary Turner. "This is a real thrill for Judy. Edna and I are very poor at hitting the birdie."

"It was lots of fun," Nancy replied. "I'm glad to see you all again."

She now asked whether the police had located the thieves who had taken the silver heirlooms from the house.

"Not yet," Mary answered. "And what's worse, we found that several other pieces had been taken too."

"What a shame!" Nancy exclaimed. "But I'm sure the stolen articles will be found." Then she added, "I came here on a particular mission."

"Yes?"

"Your story about Mr. Josiah Crowley intrigued me. Then, the other day, I met two girls, Grace and Allison Hoover, who told me of a similar promise from him regarding his will."

"How amazing!" Edna Turner exclaimed. "I

heard Josiah mention the Hoovers and Allison's beautiful voice."

"Dad and I have become very much interested in the case and are inclined to agree with you and the Hoovers that Mr. Crowley may have written another will shortly before his death and hidden it some place."

"Oh, wouldn't it be wonderful if such a will could be found!" Mary exclaimed. "It might mean all the difference in the world to Judy's future."

"What I want to do," Nancy went on, "is talk to as many of Mr. Crowley's relatives as I can find. Some place I may pick up a clue to where a more recent will is hidden. Tell me, do any of his other relatives live around here?"

"Yes. Three that I can think of," Edna answered.

She went on to say that two cousins, who had never married, lived on a farm just outside Titusville. "Their names are Fred and William Mathews."

Suddenly the Turner sisters blushed a deep pink. They glanced at each other, then back at Nancy. Finally Edna said:

"Many years ago Fred proposed to Mary, and William to me, and we came near accepting. But just at that time we had the great tragedy in the family and took Judy's mother to rear, so we decided not to marry."

An embarrassing pause was broken by Judy. "Some day my aunties are going to give me one of my mother's dollies, Nancy. Isn't that nice?"

"It certainly is," Nancy agreed. "And you must be sure to show it to me." Then she asked the sisters, "What relation are the Mathews to Mr. Crowley?"

"First cousins on his mother's side."

"Do you think they would mind my asking them some questions, even though I'm a stranger?"

"Not at all," Mary replied. "They're very fine gentlemen."

"And tell them Mary and I sent you," Edna added.

"How far is Titusville from here?" Nancy inquired.

"Oh, not more than five miles on Route 10A. You could drive there in a few minutes. It's on the way to Masonville. Nancy, won't you stay and have lunch with us?"

Eager to continue her work, the young sleuth was about to refuse, but Judy put in an invitation also. "Please, oh please, Nancy. And while my aunties are fixing it, you and I can play badminton."

"All right," Nancy agreed. "And thank you very much."

It was nearly two o'clock when she finally was ready to depart.

"Oh, Mary," said Edna suddenly, "we forgot to

tell Nancy about Josiah's wife's cousin, Mrs. Abby Rowen. She'd be apt to know more about the will than anyone else."

"That's right! You really should call on her, Nancy. She took care of Josiah one time when he was sick, and he thought the world of her. He often declared he intended to leave her something. She's a widow and has very little."

"Even a few thousand dollars would mean a lot to her," Edna added. "Abby must be over eighty years of age, and growing forgetful. She has no children and there's no one to look after her."

"Where shall I find Mrs. Rowen?" Nancy asked, hoping it was not far away.

"Abby lives on the West Lake Road," Edna responded. "It's a good many miles from here."

"Then I shan't have time to go there today," the young sleuth said. "But I'll surely see her as soon as I can. And now I must be going."

Nancy thanked the Turner sisters and said good-by. But before she could leave, Judy insisted upon showing how she could jump rope and do all kinds of dancing steps with a hoop on the lawn.

"Judy entertains us all the time," Mary remarked. "We believe she's very talented."

Nancy thought so too. As she drove off, she again hoped that money would become available for a very special education for Judy.

After Nancy had gone five miles along the designated route, she began to watch the mailboxes.

Soon she noticed one which bore the name *Mathews.* The farmhouse stood back a distance from the road and had a wide sweep of lawn in front of it. Near the house a man was riding a small tractor, mowing the grass.

Nancy drove down the narrow lane which led into the grounds, and stopped opposite the spot where the man was working. The man's back was toward her, and he apparently had not heard the car above the noise of the tractor, so she waited.

Looking toward the house, Nancy suddenly saw a sight that appalled her. Wedged between two stones of a broken wall was a police dog puppy whining pitifully. Nancy dashed forward and released the little animal. As it continued to whimper, she cuddled the pup in her arms and began to examine its paws.

"Why, you poor thing!" Nancy said, seeing a tear in the flesh of one hind leg. "This must be taken care of right away."

She decided to carry the puppy over to the man on the mower. As Nancy walked across the lane, she suddenly heard an angry growl near her. Looking back, she saw a huge police dog, evidently the pup's mother, bounding toward her.

"It's all right," Nancy called soothingly to the dog. "I'm not going to take your baby away."

She took two more strides, but got no farther. With a fierce snarl the dog leaped on Nancy, knocking her flat!

CHAPTER VIII

A Forgotten Secret

NANCY screamed for help, hoping to attract the farmer's attention. She expected momentarily to be bitten by the angry dog, but to her great relief the animal did not harm her.

The young sleuth's sudden fall had caused the puppy to fly from her arms. With a leap its mother was at the pup's side. She grabbed her baby by the back of its neck and trotted off toward the barn.

"O-o, that was a narrow escape." Nancy took a deep breath as she got to her feet, brushed herself off, and ruefully surveyed a tear in her sweater.

By this time the man on the tractor, having changed direction, saw the fracas and came running. He apologized for the dog's actions, but Nancy said quickly:

"It was my fault. I should have set the pup

down. Its mother probably thought I was trying to dognap her baby!"

"Possibly."

Nancy explained why she had picked up the little animal and the farmer said he would look at the cut later.

"I'm glad you weren't hurt," he added. "Thanks for being such a good scout about it. Did you come to see me or my brother?" he asked. "I'm Fred Mathews."

Nancy gave her name, and added that she was acquainted with the Turner sisters and others who had been told they would benefit under Josiah Crowley's will.

"My dad—the lawyer Carson Drew—and I are working on the case. We believe there might have been a later will than the one presented by Mr. Topham, and we'd like to find it."

"And you came to see if William and I could give you a clue?" Fred's bright blue eyes sparkled boyishly.

"That's right, Mr. Mathews. Also, did Mr. Crowley ever tell you he was going to leave you some money?"

"Indeed he did."

At this moment another man came from the house and Fred introduced him as his brother William. Both were tall, spare, and strong-muscled. Though their hair was gray, the men's faces were youthful and unwrinkled.

"Let's sit down under the tree here and discuss this," Fred suggested, leading the way to a group of rustic chairs. He told William of Nancy's request, then asked him, "Did Cousin Josiah ever give you any idea he'd made a will in which we were not beneficiaries?"

"No. I thought one would come to light when he died. To tell the truth, Miss Drew, Fred and I were thunderstruck at the will which left everything to the Tophams. That wasn't what Cousin Josiah led us to believe."

"It certainly wasn't," Fred spoke up. "But I guess William and I counted our chickens before they were hatched. We just about make ends meet here with our small fruit farm. Help and equipment cost such a lot. One thing we've always wanted to do, but couldn't afford, was to travel. We thought we'd use the money from Cousin Josiah to do that."

"But our dream bubble burst," said William. "No trips for us."

Nancy smiled. "Don't give up hope yet. Dad and I haven't."

She was disappointed that the brothers could offer her no clues about a place to look for another will. A little while later she left the farm and returned home.

"No new evidence," she told her father. "Let's hope Mrs. Abby Rowen has some!"

Early the next morning she set off for the elderly

woman's home, and reached her destination by asking directions of people living along West Lake Road.

"This must be Abby Rowen's house," Nancy told herself. "It fits the description."

She climbed out of her car and stood before the one-story frame building which was badly in need of paint and repair. The yard around it was overgrown with weeds, and the picket fence enclosing the cottage sagged dejectedly.

"The place looks deserted," Nancy mused. "But I'll see if Mrs. Rowen is at home."

Nancy made her way up the scraggly path to the house and rapped on the front door. There was no response. After a moment, she knocked again.

This time a muffled voice called, "Who's there? If you're a peddler, I don't want anything."

"I'm not selling anything," Nancy called out reassuringly. "Won't you let me in, please?"

There was a long silence, then the quavering voice replied, "I can't open the door. I've hurt myself and can't walk."

Nancy hesitated an instant before pushing open the door. As she stepped into the dreary living room, she saw a frail figure on the couch. Abby Rowen lay huddled under an old shawl, her withered face drawn with pain.

"I am Nancy Drew and I've come to help you, Mrs. Rowen."

The old lady turned her head and regarded Nancy with a stare of wonder.

"You've come to help me?" she repeated unbelievingly. "I didn't think anyone would ever bother about old Abby again."

"Here, let me arrange the pillows for you." Gently Nancy moved the old woman into a more comfortable position.

"Yesterday I fell down the cellar stairs," Mrs. Rowen explained. "I hurt my hip and sprained my ankle."

"Haven't you had a doctor?" Nancy asked in astonishment.

"No." Abby Rowen sighed. "Not a soul has been here and I couldn't get in touch with anybody. I have no telephone."

"Can you walk at all?" Nancy asked.

"A little."

"Then your hip isn't broken," Nancy said in relief. "Let me see your ankle. Oh my, it is swollen! I'll bandage it for you."

"There's a clean cloth in the closet in the kitchen," Abby told her. "I haven't any regular bandage."

"You really should have a doctor," Nancy remarked. "Let me drive you to one."

"I can't afford it," the old woman murmured. "My pension check hasn't come, and it's too small, anyway."

"Let me pay the doctor," Nancy offered.

Abby Rowen shook her head stubbornly. "I'll not take charity. I'd rather die first."

"Well, if you insist upon not having a doctor, I'm going to the nearest drugstore and get some bandaging and a few other things," Nancy told her. "But before I go, I'll make you a cup of tea."

"There's no tea in the house."

"Then I'll get a box. What else do you need?"

"I need 'most everything, but I can't afford anything right now. You might get me some tea and a loaf of bread. That's enough. You'll find the money in a jar in the cupboard. It's not very much, but it's all I have."

"I'll be back in a few minutes," Nancy promised.

She stopped in the kitchen long enough to examine the cupboards. With the exception of a little flour and sugar and a can of soup, there appeared to be nothing in the house to eat. Nancy found that the money jar contained less than five dollars.

"I'll not take any of it," she decided.

Quietly the young sleuth slipped out the back door. She drove quickly to the nearest store and ordered a stock of groceries. Then she stopped at a drugstore and purchased bandages and liniment.

Reaching the cottage, she carried the supplies inside and adeptly set about making Abby Rowen more comfortable. She bathed the swollen ankle and bound it neatly with the antiseptic bandage.

"It feels better already," Mrs. Rowen told her gratefully. "I don't know what would have happened to me if you hadn't come."

"Oh, someone would have dropped in," said Nancy cheerfully. She went to the kitchen and in a short while prepared tea and a light lunch for the elderly woman.

As Abby Rowen ate the nourishing meal, Nancy was gratified to observe that almost immediately her patient became more cheerful and seemed to gain strength. She sat up on the couch and appeared eager to talk with Nancy.

"There aren't many folks willing to come in and help an old lady. If Josiah Crowley had lived, things would have been different," she declared. "I could have paid someone to look after me."

"It's strange that he didn't provide for you in his will," Nancy replied quietly.

She did not wish to excite the woman by telling her real mission. Yet Nancy hoped that she might lead her tactfully into a discussion of Josiah Crowley's affairs without raising hopes which might never be realized.

"It's my opinion that Josiah did provide for me," Mrs. Rowen returned emphatically. "Many a time he said to me, 'Abby, you'll never need to worry. When I'm gone you'll be well taken care of by my will.' "

"And then everything was left to the Tophams," Nancy encouraged her to proceed.

"That was according to the first will," Abby Rowen stated.

"You mean there was another will?" Nancy inquired eagerly.

"Of course. Why, I saw that will with my own eyes!"

"You saw it!" Nancy gasped.

The old woman nodded gravely. "Mind, I didn't see what was in the will. One day Josiah came to call and give me some money. Right off I noticed he had a bunch of papers in his hand. 'Abby,' he said, 'I've made a new will. I didn't bother with a lawyer. I wrote it myself.' "

"How long ago was that?" Nancy asked quickly.

"Let me see." Abby Rowen frowned thoughtfully. "I can't remember the exact date. It was this past spring. Anyway, Josiah hinted that he'd done well by me. 'But, Josiah,' I said, 'are you sure it's legal to write it yourself?' 'Of course it is,' he said. 'A lawyer told me it was all right, just so long as I wrote it myself and signed it. But I did have it witnessed.' "

"Do you know who witnessed the will?" Nancy broke in.

"No. He didn't say."

"Haven't you any idea what became of the will?" Nancy asked hopefully.

"Well, I remember Josiah did say something about putting it where nobody could get it unless they had legal authority. But I really don't know what became of it."

"Are you certain that was all Mr. Crowley said?" Nancy inquired gently. She recalled the Turners saying that Abby had become forgetful.

The elderly woman shook her head and sighed. "Many a night I've lain awake trying to think what else he did say about where he would put the will. I just can't recollect."

"Try to think!" Nancy begged.

"I can't remember," Abby Rowen murmured hopelessly. "I've tried and tried." She leaned against the cushions and closed her eyes, as though the effort had exhausted her.

At that very moment the clock on the mantel chimed twelve. Abby's eyes fluttered open and an odd expression passed over her face.

For an instant she stared straight before her, then slowly turned her head and fastened her eyes on the clock.

CHAPTER IX

Helpful Disclosures

NANCY watched Abby Rowen intently as the mantel clock finished striking. The elderly woman's lips had begun to move.

"The clock!" she whispered. "That was it! The clock!"

Nancy gripped the arms of her chair in excitement. "Josiah Crowley hid the will in a clock?" she prompted.

"No—no, it wasn't that," Abby murmured, sighing again. "I know Josiah said something about a clock, but whatever it was has slipped my mind."

Silence descended over the room. Nancy was wondering what connection the timepiece could have with the missing will. Mrs. Rowen was staring at the clock, evidently still trying to probe her memory.

Suddenly she gave a low cry. "There! It came to me just like that!"

"What, Mrs. Rowen?" Nancy urged quietly, lest she startle the old woman into forgetfulness.

"A notebook!" Abby exclaimed triumphantly.

Nancy's heart gave a leap, but she forced herself to say calmly, "Please tell me more about this notebook."

"Well, one day not long before he passed away, Josiah said to me, 'Abby, after I'm dead, if my last will isn't found, you can learn about it in this little book of mine.' "

"Do you know what became of the notebook, Mrs. Rowen?"

"Oh dearie me! There goes my memory again. No, I don't."

Although baffled, Nancy felt a growing conviction that the whereabouts of the Crowley will was definitely tied up with a clock of some kind. But, she pondered, why did the striking of the mantel clock remind Abby Rowen of the notebook?

Impulsively Nancy got up and went over to the mantel. She looked inside the glass front and in the back. There were no papers inside.

Returning to her chair, Nancy asked the elderly woman, "What became of the furnishings of the Crowley home when he gave it up?"

"The Tophams got 'most everything."

"There must have been a family clock," Nancy mused, half to herself.

"A family clock?" Abby repeated. "Oh, yes, there was a clock."

"Can you describe it?"

"It was just an ordinary mantel type, something like mine—tall, with a square face," the woman told Nancy. "Only Josiah's was fancier. Had some kind of a moon on top."

"What became of the clock?" Nancy questioned.

"I suppose the Tophams got it, too."

At last Nancy, sure she had done all she could for Abby, and that she had learned as much as possible for the present, rose to depart. After saying good-by, she stopped at a neighboring house and asked the occupants to look in occasionally on the ailing woman.

"I think maybe one of the county's visiting nurses should see Mrs. Rowen," she suggested.

"I'll phone the agency," the neighbor offered. "Meanwhile, I'll go over myself. I'm so sorry I didn't know about Mrs. Rowen."

As Nancy drove toward River Heights, she jubilantly reviewed the new facts in the case. "Now, if I can only locate Mr. Crowley's notebook—or clock—or both!"

Nancy's brow knit in concentration. How would she go about tracking down the old timepiece?

"I guess," she concluded, "if the Tophams *do* have the clock, I'll have to pay them a visit!"

While she did not relish the idea of calling on

the unpleasant family, Nancy was determined to pursue every possible clue. "I can just see Ada's and Isabel's expressions when I appear at their front door," Nancy thought wryly. "Well, I'll think of some excuse to see them."

She was still mulling over the problem when she pulled into the driveway of her home and heard a familiar voice calling her name.

"Why, Helen Corning!" exclaimed Nancy, as a slim, attractive school friend of hers ran up. "I haven't seen you for days."

"I've been busy lately," Helen explained, "trying to sell six tickets for a charity ball. But I haven't had much luck. Would you like a couple?"

A sudden idea flashed into Nancy's mind at her friend's words. "Helen," she said excitedly, "I'll buy two of your tickets and sell the rest for you."

The other girl stared in astonishment. "Why, that's a wonderful offer, Nance. But—"

Nancy's eyes danced. "I know you think I've lost my mind. I really mean it, though. Please let me take the tickets! I can't tell you my reasons yet—except my cause is a worthy one."

Helen, looking relieved but bewildered, handed over the tickets. "This is really a break for me," she said. "Now I can leave for my aunt's Camp Avondale this evening as I'd hoped. It's at Moon Lake. I thought I'd never get off, with those tickets unsold!"

Nancy smiled "Have a grand time, Helen," she said.

"How about coming along? It's not expensive and there's room for lots more girls. We'd have loads of fun."

"I'd love to," Nancy replied, "but right now I can't get away."

"Maybe you can make it later," Helen suggested. "If so, just zip on up. I'll be there for two weeks before the regular summer camp opens."

The two friends chatted a little longer, then said good-by. Nancy put the car away, then walked slowly toward her house, looking meditatively at the charity tickets in her hand.

"These are to be my passport to the Tophams' stronghold!"

It was the following afternoon when Nancy approached the large pretentious house belonging to the Tophams.

Bracing herself for what she realized would be a trying interview, Nancy mounted the steps and rang the doorbell. "Here goes," she thought. "I must be subtle in this maneuver to keep from arousing the Tophams' suspicions!"

At that moment a maid opened the door, and with a condescending look, waited for Nancy to state her mission.

"Will you please tell Mrs. Topham that Nancy Drew is calling?" she requested. "I'm selling tickets for a charity dance. It's one of the most important functions of the year in River Heights," Nancy added impressively.

It seemed ages to the young sleuth before the maid returned and said that "Madame" would see her. Nancy was ushered into the living room, which was so bizarre in its decor she was startled.

"Such an expensive hodge-podge!" Nancy observed to herself, sitting down. She glanced at the pink carpet—which to her clashed with the red window draperies—and at an indiscriminate assortment of period furniture mixed with modern.

A haughty voice interrupted her thoughts. "Well, what do you want, Nancy?" Mrs. Topham had sailed grandly into the room and seated herself opposite Nancy.

"I'm selling—" Nancy began pleasantly.

"Oh, if you're selling things I'm not interested," the woman broke in rudely. "I can't be handing out money to every solicitor who comes along."

With difficulty Nancy suppressed an angry retort to the cutting remark. "Mrs. Topham," she said evenly, "perhaps your maid didn't make it clear. I am selling tickets to a charity ball which will be one of the loveliest affairs in River Heights this year."

"Oh!" A slight change came over Mrs. Topham's face. Nancy sensed that her words had struck a responsive chord. The woman was well known for her aspirations to be accepted by the best families in River Heights. "Well—"

To Nancy's dismay Mrs. Topham's response was cut off by the arrival of Ada and Isabel. The sisters entered the room, but did not at first notice Nancy's presence. They were intently carrying on a disgruntled conversation.

"Really!" Ada was complaining. "I'm positive that woman snubbed us deliberately."

Then she and Isabel caught sight of Nancy and stopped short. They stared coldly at the visitor.

"What are *you* doing here?" Isabel asked with a patronizing air.

Mrs. Topham answered her daughter's question. "Nancy is selling tickets to a charity dance, dear. It's to be a very important affair and I think it will be—er—beneficial—for us to be present."

Isabel tossed her head disdainfully. "Don't waste your money, Mother."

"Isabel's right," Ada chimed in. "We don't want to go to a ball just anybody can go to. We only attend the most exclusive affairs."

"Absolutely," Isabel declared in her haughtiest tone. "After all, Ada and I are very particular about the people we choose to meet."

Mrs. Topham hesitated, evidently influenced by her daughters' argument. Nancy's heart sank, and she feared her cause was lost. She fully realized that Ada and Isabel would stay away from the dance just to spite her.

As she debated what her next move should be, Richard Topham walked into the living room.

He was a thin man, with sparse graying hair. His manner was rather nervous. Mrs. Topham perfunctorily introduced Nancy to her husband.

"I gather you have some tickets to dispose of, Miss Drew," he said without ceremony. "How many?"

"Why, four," Nancy replied in some surprise.

"I'll take them all." Mr. Topham opened his wallet with a flourish and drew out a hundred-dollar bill. Here you are. Keep the change for your charity."

His daughters gasped and his wife exclaimed, "Richard! Have you lost your senses? All that money!"

"Listen," Mr. Topham retorted bluntly. "This donation will entitle us to have our names on the programs as patrons."

With this remark he slumped into a chair and buried himself in the financial section of the newspaper. His family stared at one another, but they knew that the matter was closed. They never dared disturb him when he was absorbed in the stock-market reports.

Nancy arose reluctantly. She still had not accomplished the real purpose of her visit, but she had no excuse for prolonging her stay. How could she find out about the Crowley clock? Was it the one on the mantelpiece?

"I must be going," she said. Then, looking at her wrist watch, she pretended that it had stopped and began to wind it. "What time is it, please?"

"There's a clock right in front of you—on the mantel," Ada said sharply.

Nancy looked at the timepiece. "So there is," she remarked casually. "Is it an heirloom, perhaps the old Crowley clock I've heard so much about?"

Mrs. Topham looked down her nose. "I should say not! This is a far more expensive one!"

Isabel also rose to Nancy's bait. "Cousin Josiah's old clock was a monstrosity. We wouldn't even have it cluttering up the attic!"

Nancy's hopes waned, but she asked quickly, "Oh, then you sold it?"

"No," Ada spoke up contemptuously. "Who'd give any money for that piece of junk? We sent it up to our bungalow at Moon Lake."

Moon Lake! The words hit Nancy like a thunderbolt. Not only had the Topham girl given Nancy the very information she sought, but Helen Corning's invitation to Camp Avondale provided a valid reason to visit the resort! Now if she could only figure out how to see the old clock!

As if Ada had read the visitor's thoughts, she said airily, "We have some really fine pieces up at the cottage, Nancy. If you ever get up that way, drop in to see them. The caretaker will show you around."

"Thank you. Thank you so much for everything," Nancy said, trying hard to conceal her excitement. As the door closed behind her, Nancy grinned in anticipation.

"What luck!" she told herself. "Moon Lake, here I come!"

CHAPTER X

Following a Clue

WITH soaring spirits, Nancy walked homeward. "I wonder," she thought, "how the Tophams will feel about Josiah Crowley's old clock if it costs them the inheritance they're counting on."

At dinner that night Nancy chatted with unusual animation, deciding not to tell of her exciting plans until after Hannah had served dessert.

Mr. Drew, however, sensed that big news was coming. "My dear," he said, laying a hand on his daughter's arm, "you look like the cat that swallowed the canary. What's the big scoop?"

Nancy giggled. "Oh, Dad. I can't keep any secrets from you." Then, as the table was cleared, the young sleuth told of her great stroke of luck. "And just think, Helen invited me to her aunt's camp!"

"Good," her father commented, smiling. "You

can combine business with pleasure, Nancy. Swimming and boating and fun with the girls will provide a much-needed vacation."

"May I start first thing in the morning?" his daughter asked.

"An excellent idea, Nancy. The change will do wonders for you. Go, by all means."

Hurriedly she packed a suitcase and the next morning was off to an early start.

Moon Lake was about a fifty-mile drive. One way to go was past the Hoover girls' farm and Nancy decided to stop there. As she approached the house, the young sleuth heard singing. It was coming from the barn.

"How beautiful!" Nancy thought, as the clear soprano voice went through a series of trills and flutelike scales.

In a moment the singer appeared and Nancy teasingly applauded. Allison's eyes danced. "Thanks. I was just trying to imitate some of the greats."

"You'll be great yourself one of these days," Nancy prophesied.

"Not unless I get some money to finance lessons," Allison said. "Any news, Nancy?"

"Sort of. I've had a little luck." At this moment Grace appeared and instantly invited Nancy to stay, but the young detective said she too had work to do. "I hope to have a good report for you soon," she added, and waved good-by.

Grace's face brightened and Allison declared cheerfully, "Then there's still hope? We are so lucky to have you as a friend, Nancy. Come see us again soon. Please."

Resuming her journey, Nancy soon branched off from the River Road and headed toward Moon Lake. As she drove along, her thoughts revolved constantly around the Crowley relatives and the Hoovers.

She sighed. "How different things would be for them now if Josiah Crowley hadn't been so secretive!"

Her reverie was ended by the sudden strange actions of her car. It kept veering to the left of the road in spite of her efforts to keep it in the middle. With foreboding, Nancy stopped and got out to make an inspection. As she had suspected, a rear tire was flat.

"Oh dear!" she murmured in disgust. "Such luck!"

Though Nancy was able to change a tire, she never relished the task. Quickly she took out the spare tire from the rear compartment, found the jack and lug wrench, and went to work. By the

time her job was completed, she was hot and a little breathless.

"Whew!" she exclaimed, as she started on her way again. "I'll be ready for a nice, cool swim in Moon Lake!"

It was after twelve o'clock when she came in sight of Camp Avondale, run by Helen's aunt. Through the tall trees Nancy caught a glimpse of cabins and tents. Beyond, the blue lake sparkled and glimmered in the sunlight.

As Nancy drove into the camp, a group of girls gathered about her car. Helen came running out of a cabin to greet her chum.

"Girls, it's Nancy Drew!" she exclaimed joyfully and made introductions. Nancy did not know any of the campers, but in no time they made her feel warmly welcome.

"Nancy," said Helen, "park your car back of the dining hall, then come have lunch."

"That sounds wonderful." Nancy laughed. "I'm nearly starved!"

First, she was escorted to the main building where she met Aunt Martha, the camp director, and registered.

"May she stay with me?" Helen asked.

"Certainly, dear. And I hope you have a splendid time, Nancy."

"I'm sure I shall, Aunt Martha."

As the two girls walked off Nancy told Helen

about selling the charity-dance tickets and gave her the money paid by Mr. Topham.

"He surely was generous!" Helen commented in surprise. Then she smiled wryly. "I have a feeling he did it more for social prestige than sympathy for the cause."

Nancy scarcely had time to deposit her suitcase under her cot and freshen up after the long ride when lunch was announced by the ringing of a bell. Campers hurried from all directions to the dining hall. The food was plain but appetizing and Nancy ate with zest.

The meal over, she was rushed from one activity to another. The girls insisted that she join them in a hike. Then came a cooling dip in the lake. Nancy enjoyed herself immensely, but the Crowley mystery was never far from her mind.

"I must find out where the Tophams' cottage is located," she reminded herself. "And next, manage to go there alone."

Nancy's opportunity to accomplish the first part of her quest came when Helen suggested about five o'clock, "How about going for a ride around the lake in the camp launch? There's just time before supper."

"Wonderful!" Nancy accepted readily. "By the way, can you see many of the summer cottages from the water?"

"Oh, yes. Lots of them."

Helen led her friend down to a small dock and with four other girls climbed into the launch, a medium-sized craft.

As one of the campers started the motor, Helen remarked, "It's always a relief to us when this engine starts. Once in a while it balks, but you never know when or where."

"Yes," spoke up a girl named Barby. "And when you're stuck this time of year, you're stuck. There are hardly any cottagers up here yet, so their boats are still in winter storage."

As the little launch turned out into the lake, Nancy was entranced with the beautiful sight before her. The delicate azure blue of the sky and the mellow gold of the late afternoon sun were reflected in the shimmering surface of the water.

"What a lovely scene for an oil painting!" she thought.

As they sped along, however, Nancy kept glancing at the cottages, intermingled with tall evergreen trees that bordered the shore line.

"The Tophams have a bungalow up here, haven't they?" she questioned casually.

"Yes, it's across the lake," Helen replied. "We'll come to it soon."

"Is anyone staying there now?"

"Oh, no, the cottage is closed. It's being looked after by Jeff Tucker, the caretaker. He's the tallest, skinniest man I've ever seen outside a circus."

"Is it hard to get to the place?"

"Not if you go by launch. But it's a long way if you take the road around the lake." Helen looked at her friend. "I didn't know you were particularly interested in the Tophams, Nancy."

"Oh, they're not friends of mine, as you know," Nancy returned hastily. "I was merely curious."

After a time, as the launch slowed down and chugged along close to shore, Helen pointed out a wide path through the woods. At the end of it stood a large, rambling white cottage.

"That's the Topham place," she said.

Trying not to appear too eager, Nancy looked intently at the bungalow. She made a quick mental note of its location.

"Tomorrow I'll visit that place and try to solve the mystery!" she told herself.

CHAPTER XI

An Unexpected Adventure

NANCY awoke the next morning to the fragrant odor of pines. Eager to start out for the Topham bungalow, she dressed quickly.

But in her plans she had reckoned without Helen Corning and her friends. From the moment breakfast was over, Nancy was swept into another whirlwind of activity by the campers of Avondale. The entire day passed without a chance for her to break away.

"Oh, Helen!" Nancy groaned as she tumbled into bed that night. "Tennis matches, canoe races, swimming, water skiing—it's been fun. But tomorrow I think I'll stay out of the activities."

Helen laughed gaily. "You'll change your mind after a sound sleep, Nancy. Wait and see."

For answer, Nancy murmured a sleepy good night. But even as she slipped into slumber, she vowed that in the morning she would not be deterred again from visiting the Tophams' summer place!

After breakfast the next day, Nancy stood firm in her resolve. When Helen urged her to accompany the girls on an all-day hike, Nancy shook her head.

"Thanks a lot, but please excuse me today, Helen."

Normally Nancy would have loved going on such a hike. But she had to achieve her plan of sleuthing. Helen, though disappointed, heeded her friend's plea and trudged off with the other campers into the woods.

As soon as they were out of sight, Nancy leaped into action. After obtaining Aunt Martha's permission to use the launch, she hurried down to the dock. Nancy had frequently handled motorboats and was confident she could manage this one.

"Now. Full speed ahead for the Tophams'!"

To her delight the motor started immediately, and Nancy steered out into the lake. As the launch cut through the water, a cool spray blew into her face. The young sleuth felt a thrill of excitement as she guided the craft toward her destination which might hold a solution to the mystery.

"If only the Tophams' caretaker will let me in when I get there!" she thought.

Nancy's heart beat somewhat faster as she neared her goal. But all of a sudden there was a sputter from the engine. The next instant, to Nancy's utter dismay, the motor gave one long wheeze and died.

"Oh!" she cried aloud.

Nancy knew that the tank held plenty of fuel, for she had checked this before departing. A moment later she recalled Helen's remark about the engine becoming balky at times.

With a sigh of impatience at the unexpected delay, Nancy examined the motor. For over an hour she worked on it, trying every adjustment she could think of. But her efforts were useless. There was not a sound of response from the motor.

"What miserable luck!" she said aloud. "Of all days for the motor to conk out! This means I won't get to the Topham cottage after all!"

For a moment Nancy was tempted to swim ashore. To be so close to the bungalow and not be able to reach it was tantalizing. But she resisted the impulse; she could not leave the boat stranded—it would drift off and she would be responsible.

"I'll just have to wait for a passing boat to rescue me," Nancy decided.

But fate was against her. The hours dragged by and not another craft appeared in sight. Nancy became increasingly uncomfortable as the hot sun beat down on her. Also, she was growing weak from hunger.

"And worst of all," Nancy thought gloomily,

"another whole day is being wasted. I want to get to the bottom of this mystery!"

To occupy her mind, Nancy concentrated once more on the motor. Determinedly she bent over the engine. It was not until the sun sank low in the sky that she sat up and drew a long breath.

"There!" she declared. "I've done everything. If it doesn't start now, it never will."

To her relief and astonishment, it responded with a steady roar as if nothing had ever gone wrong!

Nancy lost no time in heading back toward camp. She dared not attempt to visit the bungalow, since it would be dark very soon.

When finally she eased up to the dock, Nancy saw Helen and her friends awaiting her. They greeted her with delight.

"We were just going to send out a search party for you!" Helen exclaimed. She stopped abruptly and stared at her friend. "You're sunburned and covered with grease! What happened?"

Nancy laughed. "I had an extended sun bath." Then she gave a lighthearted account of her mishap as the campers trooped back to their cabins. When Helen learned that Nancy had had nothing to eat since breakfast, she went to the kitchen and brought back some food.

The following morning the young sleuth decided on her next move. Directly after breakfast she began packing.

When Helen entered the cabin she exclaimed in amazement, "Why, Nancy Drew! You're not leaving camp already!"

"I'm afraid I'll have to, Helen. Right after lunch. I may be back but I'm not sure, so I'd better take my bag with me."

"Don't you like it here?"

"Of course!" Nancy assured her. "I've had a wonderful time. It's just that there's something very important I must attend to at once."

Helen looked at her friend searchingly, then grinned. "Nancy Drew, you're working on some mystery with your father!"

"Well, sort of," Nancy admitted. "But I'll try to get back. Okay?"

"Oh, please do," Helen begged.

Nancy went to the office to pay Aunt Martha and explain her hasty departure. After lunch she set off in her car to a chorus of farewells from the campers, who sadly watched her depart.

She headed the car toward the end of the lake, then took the dirt road leading to the Topham cottage. Soon she came to a fork in the woods.

"Now, which way shall I turn for the bungalow?" she wondered. After a moment's hesitation, Nancy calculated that she should turn left toward the water and did so.

The going was rather rough due to ruts in the road. Two of them, deeper than the others, apparently had been made by a heavy truck.

"The tracks appear fresh," Nancy mused.

As she drove along, the young sleuth noticed a number of summer cottages. Most of them were still boarded up, since it was early in the season. As she gazed at one of them, the steering wheel was nearly wrenched from her hand by a crooked rut. As Nancy turned the steering wheel, to bring the car back to the center of the narrow road, one hand accidentally touched the horn. It blared loudly in the still woods.

"That must have scared all the birds and animals." Nancy chuckled.

Around a bend in the road, she caught sight of a white bungalow ahead on the right side of the road.

There was no sign at the entrance to the driveway to indicate who the owner was, but a wooded path leading down to the lake looked like the one she had seen from the water.

"I think I'll walk down to the shore and look at the cottage from there," Nancy determined. "Then I'll know for sure if this is the place Helen pointed out."

Nancy parked at the edge of the road and got out. To her surprise, she observed that the truck's tire marks turned into the driveway. A second set of tracks indicated that the vehicle had backed out and gone on down the road.

"Delivering supplies for the summer, no doubt," Nancy told herself.

She went down the path to the water, then turned around to look at the cottage.

"It's the Tophams' all right," Nancy decided.

Instead of coming back by way of the path, she decided to take a short cut through the woods. With mounting anticipation of solving the Crowley mystery, she reached the road and hurried up the driveway.

"I hope the caretaker is here," she thought.

Nancy suddenly stopped short with a gasp of astonishment. "Why, the Tophams must be moving out!"

The front and side doors of the cottage stood wide open. Some of the furniture on the porch was overturned and various small household items were strewn along the driveway.

Nancy bent to examine some marks in the soft earth. She noted that several were boot prints, while others were long lines probably caused by dragging cartons and furniture across the lawn.

"That must have been a moving van's tracks I saw," Nancy told herself. "But the Tophams didn't say anything about moving." She frowned in puzzlement.

Her feeling persisted and grew strong as she walked up the steps of the cottage porch. Nancy knocked loudly on the opened door. No response. Nancy rapped again. Silence.

Where was Jeff Tucker, the caretaker? Why wasn't he on hand to keep an eye on the moving activities? An air of complete desertion hung over the place.

"There's something very strange about this," she thought.

Curious and puzzled, Nancy entered the living room. Again her eyes met a scene of disorder. Except for a few small pieces, the room was bare of furniture. Even the draperies had been pulled from their rods and all floor coverings were gone.

"Hm! Most of the furnishings have been taken out," Nancy thought. "I suppose the movers will be back for the other odds and ends."

She made a careful tour of the first floor. All but one room had been virtually emptied. This was a small study. As Nancy entered it, she noticed that the rug lay rolled up and tied, and some of the furniture had evidently been shifted in readiness for moving.

"Funny I didn't hear anything about the Tophams deciding to give up their cottage," she murmured. "And I must say those moving men were awfully careless—"

A vague suspicion that had been forming in the back of Nancy's mind now came into startling focus. "Those men may not be movers!" she burst out. "They may be thieves!"

At once Nancy thought of the dark-gray van which had stopped at the Turners. "Those men may be the same ones who robbed them!"

That would explain, Nancy thought fearfully,

the evidences of the truck's hasty departure. "Probably the thieves were scared away when I sounded my horn!"

Nancy glanced about uneasily. What if the men were still nearby, watching for a chance to return and pick up the remaining valuables? The realization that she was alone, some distance from the nearest house, swept over her. A tingling sensation crept up Nancy's spine.

But resolutely she shook off her nervousness. "At least I must see if the Crowley clock is still here," Nancy reminded herself, and then went through the bungalow again.

She found no trace of the timepiece, however. "I guess the thieves took that too," Nancy concluded. "I'd better report this robbery to the police right now." She looked about for a phone but there was none. "I'll have to drive to the nearest State Police headquarters."

Nancy started toward the front door. Passing a window, she glanced out, then paused in sheer fright. A man, wearing a cap pulled low over his eyes, was stalking up the driveway toward the cottage. He was not tall and slender like the caretaker. This stranger was rather short and heavyset.

"This man fits the Turners' description! He must be one of the thieves who stole the silver heirlooms!" Nancy thought wildly.

CHAPTER XII

A Desperate Situation

For a moment Nancy stood frozen to the spot, positive that the man who was coming to the Topham cottage was one of the thieves.

But she hesitated only an instant. Then she turned and ran back into the study. Too late she realized that she had trapped herself, for this room had no other door.

Nancy started back toward the living room. But before she had taken half a dozen steps she knew that escape had been cut off from that direction. The man had reached the porch steps.

"It won't do a bit of good to talk to him," she reasoned. "I'll hide, and when he leaves, I'll follow him in my car and report him to the police!"

Frantically the young sleuth glanced about for a hiding place. A closet offered the only possible refuge. She scurried inside and closed the door.

Nancy was not a second too soon. She had scarcely shut the door when she heard the tread of the man's heavy shoes on the floor just outside. Peeping cautiously through a tiny crack in the door, she saw the heavy-set man come into the study. His face wore a cruel expression.

As he turned toward the closet where she huddled, Nancy hardly dared to breathe, lest her presence be detected. Apparently the man noticed nothing amiss, because his eyes rested only casually on the door.

Nancy's hiding place was anything but comfortable. It was dark and musty, and old clothing hung from nails on the walls. As dust assailed her nostrils, she held a handkerchief to her face.

"If I sneeze he'll surely find me," she told herself.

She felt around and once came close to ripping her hand on a sharp nail. Then she came upon something soft on a shelf and imagined it was a sleeping cat. She drew back, then touched it more cautiously.

"Only an old fur cap," she told herself in disgust. "O-oo, now I feel like sneezing more than ever!"

She held one hand over her mouth hard and waited in agony. But presently the desire to sneeze passed and Nancy breathed more freely.

When she dared to peep out through the crack a second time, she saw that two other rough-looking men had come into the room. One was short and stout, the other taller. Nancy was sure that neither of these two men was the caretaker, because Helen Corning had mentioned that the man was skinny.

The heavy-set man who had come in first seemed to be the leader, for he proceeded to issue orders. "Get a move on!" he growled. "We haven't got all day unless we want to be caught. That girl you saw, Jake, may be back any time from the shore. And she just might get snoopy."

The man addressed as Jake scowled. "What's the matter with you, Sid? Going chicken? If that girl comes around, we'll just give her a smooth story and send her on her way."

"Cut out the yaking," said Sid. "Parky, you and Jake take that desk out of here."

There was no doubt now in Nancy's mind. She was trapped by a clever gang of thieves! She could only continue to watch and listen helplessly from her hiding place.

The two men lifted the heavy piece of furniture and started with it to the door. But they did not move swiftly enough to satisfy the leader, and he berated them savagely.

Jake turned on him. "If you're in such a hurry, why don't you bring the van back to the driveway, instead of leaving it hidden on that road in the woods?"

"And have someone driving past here see us!" sneered the leader. "Now get going!"

Little by little the men stripped the room of

everything valuable. Nancy was given no opportunity to escape. Sid remained in the room while the others made several trips to the van.

"Well, I guess we have all the stuff that's worth anything now," Sid muttered at last.

He turned to follow his companions, who already had left the room, but in the doorway he paused for a final careful survey of the room.

At that same moment Nancy felt an uncontrollable urge to sneeze. She tried to muffle the sound, but to no avail.

The thief wheeled about. "Hey! What—"

Walking directly to the closet, he flung open the door. Instantly he spotted Nancy and angrily jerked her out.

"Spying on us, eh?" he snarled.

Nancy faced the man defiantly. "I wasn't spying on anyone."

"Then what were you doing in that closet?" the thief demanded, his eyes narrowing to slits.

"I came to see the caretaker."

"Looking for him in a funny place, ain't you?" the man sneered.

Nancy realized that she was in a desperate situation. But she steeled herself not to show any of her inward fears.

"I must keep calm," she told herself firmly. Aloud, she explained coolly, "I heard someone coming and I just felt a bit nervous."

"Well, you're going to be a lot more nervous,"

the man said threateningly. "This will be the last time you'll ever stick your nose in business that doesn't concern you!"

A fresh wave of fright swept over Nancy, but resolutely she held on to her courage. "You have no right to be here, helping yourself to the Tophams' furniture!" she retorted. "You should be turned over to the police!"

"Well, you'll never get the chance to do it." The ringleader laughed loudly. "You'll wish you'd never come snoopin' around here. I'll give you the same treatment the caretaker got."

"The caretaker!" Nancy gasped in horror. "What have you done to him?"

"You'll find out in good time."

Nancy gave a sudden agile twist, darted past the man, and raced for the door. The thief gave a cry of rage, and in one long leap overtook her. He caught Nancy roughly by the arm.

"Think you're smart, eh?" he snarled. "Well, I'm smarter!"

Nancy struggled to get away. She twisted and squirmed, kicked and clawed. But she was helpless in the viselike grip of the powerful man.

"Let me go!" Nancy cried, struggling harder. "Let me go!"

Sid, ignoring her pleas, half dragged her across the room. Opening the closet door, he flung her inside.

Nancy heard a key turn.

"Now you can spy all you want!" Sid sneered. "But to make sure nobody'll let you out, I'll just take this key along."

When Nancy could no longer hear the tramp of his heavy boots she was sure Sid had left the house. For a moment a feeling of great relief engulfed her.

But the next instant Nancy's heart gave a leap. As she heard the muffled roar of the van starting up in the distance, a horrifying realization gripped her.

"They've left me here to—to starve!" she thought frantically.

CHAPTER XIII

The Frustrating Wait

AT FIRST Nancy was too frightened to think logically. She beat upon the door with her fists, but the heavy oak panels would not give way.

"Help! Help!" she screamed.

At last, exhausted by her efforts to force the door open, she sank down on the floor. The house was as silent as a tomb. Bad as her predicament was, Nancy felt thankful that enough air seeped into the closet to permit normal breathing.

Although she had little hope that there was anyone within miles of the cottage, Nancy got to her feet, raised her voice, and again shouted for help. Her cries echoed through the empty house and seemed to mock her.

"Oh, why didn't I have enough sense to tell Helen where I was going?" she berated herself miserably. "The girls at camp will never dream that I came here."

Then Nancy remembered mournfully that her father thought she intended to remain at Camp Avondale for a week! He would not become alarmed over her absence until it was too late.

"Someone may find my car at the side of the road," Nancy reasoned, "but it isn't very likely. Few persons pass this way so early in the season."

She wondered, with a shudder, what had become of Jeff Tucker. The thief called Sid had hinted that the caretaker had received the same treatment as Nancy. If he was locked up somewhere, she could expect no aid from him.

"Those thieves will get so far away that even if I could get out of here, I'd be too late."

As the full significance of the situation dawned upon Nancy, panic again took possession of her. In a desperate attempt to break down the door, she threw her weight against it again and again. She pounded on the panels until her fingers were bruised and bleeding. At last she sank down again on the floor to rest and tried to force herself to reason calmly.

"I'm only wasting my strength this way. I *must* try to think logically."

Nancy recalled that it was sometimes possible to pick a lock with a wire. She removed a bobby pin from her hair, opened it, and began to work at the lock. But in the darkness she could not see and made no progress. After fifteen minutes she gave up the task in disgust.

"It's no use," she decided dejectedly. "I—I guess I'm in here for good."

She began to think of her father, of Hannah Gruen, of Helen Corning, and other dear friends. Would she ever see them again? As despondency claimed Nancy, she was dangerously near tears.

"This will never do," she reprimanded herself sternly. "I must keep my head and try to think of some way to escape."

The trapped girl began to rummage in the closet, hoping that by some lucky chance she might find a tool which would help her force the lock of the door. Nancy searched carefully through the pockets of every garment which hung from the hooks. She groped over every inch of the floor.

She found nothing useful, however, and the cloud of dust which she had stirred up made breathing more difficult than before. The closet had become uncomfortably warm by this time. Longingly she thought of the fresh air and cool lake water from which she was closed off.

Then, unexpectedly, Nancy's hand struck something hard. Quickly investigating with her fingers, she discovered a wooden rod suspended high overhead. It was fastened to either side wall and ran the length of the closet. Evidently it had once been used for dress and coat hangers.

"I might be able to use that rod to break out a panel of the door," Nancy thought hopefully. "It feels strong and it's about the right size."

She tugged at the rod with all her might. When it did not budge, she swung herself back and forth on it. At last, amid the cracking of plaster, one side gave way. Another hard jerk brought the rod down.

To Nancy's bitter disappointment, she found that unfortunately the rod was too long to use as a ram in the cramped space. But after further examination, she discovered that it had pointed ends.

"I might use this rod as a wedge in the crack," she thought hopefully.

The young sleuth inserted one end in the space between the hinges and the door, and threw all her weight against the rod. At first the door did not move in the slightest.

"That old Greek scientist, Archimedes, didn't know what he was talking about when he said the world could be moved with a lever," Nancy murmured. "I'd like to see him move this door!"

As she applied steady pressure to the rod a second time, she saw that the hinges were beginning to give. Encouraged, Nancy again pushed full force on the "lever."

"It's coming!" she cried.

Once more she threw her weight against the rod. A hinge tore from the casing and the door sagged. It was now easy to insert the wedge, and Nancy joyously realized that success would soon be hers. With renewed strength she continued her efforts.

Then, just as another hinge gave way, she was startled to hear footsteps. Someone came running into the study, and a heavy body hurled itself against the door of the closet.

For a moment Nancy was stunned. Could this be one of the thieves who had heard the noise she had made and had returned to make sure that she did not escape? She discarded the theory quickly. Surely the three men would want to get far away as quickly as possible. But who was this newcomer? One of the Tophams?

"So, one o' you ornery robbers got yourself locked up, did you?" came an indignant male voice. "That'll teach you to try puttin' one over on old Jeff Tucker. You won't be doin' any more pilferin'. I got you surrounded."

The caretaker! Nancy heaved a sigh of fervent relief. "Let me out!" she pleaded. "I'm not one of the thieves! If you'll only let me out of here, I'll explain everything!"

There was silence for a moment. Then the voice on the other side of the door said dubiously, "Say, you aimin' to throw me off, imitatin' a lady's voice? Well, it won't do you any good! No, sir. Old Jeff Tucker's not gettin' fooled again!"

Nancy decided to convince the man beyond doubt. She gave a long, loud feminine scream.

"All right, *all right,* ma'am. I believe you! No man could make that racket. This way out, lady!"

Expectantly Nancy waited. But the door did not open. Then she heard to her dismay:

"If that ain't the limit. The key's gone and I've left my ring o' extra keys somewhere. It's not in my pockets."

Nancy groaned. "Oh, Mr. Tucker, you must find it. Have you looked in every one of your pockets? Please hurry and get me out."

"Hold on, ma'am," the caretaker said soothingly. "I'll just check again."

Nancy was beginning to think she would still have to break down the door, when she heard Jeff Tucker exclaim, "Found it! You were right, ma'am. Key was in my back pocket all the time. It—"

"*Please* open the door!" Nancy broke in desperately.

A key turned in the lock and the bolt clicked. Joyfully Nancy pushed the door open and stepped out. For a moment the bright sunlight in the room almost blinded her. When her vision adjusted, she saw a very tall, thin, elderly man in blue shirt and overalls. He stared at her with concern and amazement.

"Mr. Tucker," she explained quickly, "I'm Nancy Drew. I was here looking for you when those awful thieves came and locked me in the closet." She paused and gazed at the caretaker. "I'm glad to see that you're all right. Their leader told me they'd locked you up too." She then asked the elderly man to tell his story.

Jeff Tucker seemed embarrassed as he began to speak. "I was plain hornswoggled by those critters, Miss Drew. They pulled up here in a movin' van, and told me I'd better get after some trespassers they'd seen nearby. So," the elderly man went on with a sigh, "I believed 'em. One of the men went with me down to the lake and locked me in a shed. I just got out." He shook his head sadly. "And all this time they was robbin' the place. Guess I'll be fired."

Secretly Nancy was inclined to agree, knowing the Tophams. But aloud she said reassuringly:

"Don't worry, Mr. Tucker. We'll report this robbery to the State Police immediately. Perhaps the troopers can catch the thieves before they get rid of the stolen furniture."

The caretaker looked somewhat relieved. "And I can sure give a good description o' those crooks. I'd never forget their ugly faces!"

"Fine," said Nancy. A sudden thought struck her. "Oh, before we go, Mr. Tucker, tell me, was there an old clock in this house? A tall, square-faced mantel clock?"

Jeff Tucker's bright blue eyes squinted. "Mantel clock? Hm. Why, sure enough!" He pointed to the mantel over the living-room fireplace. "Sat right up there. Got so used to seein' it, I couldn't remember for a minute. Don't know how come they took that too. Never thought it was worth much. The Tophams never bothered windin' the thing."

Nancy's pulse quickened. Knowing that the clock had been stolen, she was more eager than ever to have the thieves apprehended. She urged Jeff Tucker to hurry out to her car.

"Where's the nearest State Police headquarters?" she asked him as they climbed into the convertible.

"There's none till you get to Melborne, Miss Drew."

"We'll hurry."

Nancy headed as fast as possible for the highway. Would she succeed in heading off the thieves and recovering the old Crowley clock, so she could learn its secret?

CHAPTER XIV

A Tense Chase

"WHICH way is Melborne?" Nancy asked the caretaker when they reached the highway.

"Down there." He pointed.

"That's the direction the thieves took," Nancy told him, noting the dust and tire marks which revealed the van's exit onto the highway. "But," she added, glancing at the dashboard clock, "they're probably too far away by this time for us to catch them."

"Yes, ding it," Jeff muttered.

Nancy drove as rapidly as the law permitted toward Melborne. All the while, Jeff Tucker peered from one side of the road to the other.

"Those rascal thieves might just have nerve enough to stop an' count their loot," he said to Nancy. "So I'm keepin' a sharp eye peeled."

Nancy smiled in spite of the gravity of the situation. "Maybe," she replied. "Though I doubt that those men would be so reckless."

"Oh, I don't mean out in plain sight. They might have pulled off the road, back o' some o' these closed-up summer places."

"We'll watch for their tire marks on any dirt side road," the young sleuth said.

Jeff became so absorbed in looking for the van's tire marks that he never asked Nancy why she had come to see him at the Topham house.

"Those fake movers," he said, as they neared the outskirts of Melborne. "I wonder how far they went."

Nancy did not reply until they came to a crossroad, then she pointed. "They turned north here on this dirt road. How much farther is it to Melborne?"

"Only a mile."

As they came into the little town, Nancy asked her companion, "Which way to State Police headquarters?"

"Go right down Central Avenue to Maple Street. Turn left, and there it is."

Reaching headquarters, Nancy parked the car and hopped out. Jeff Tucker followed as she walked briskly into the office.

"I want to report a robbery," she told the desk sergeant after identifying herself.

For a moment the officer, taken aback, looked in astonishment at Nancy. "You've been robbed?" he asked. "In *our* town?"

"No, no!" Nancy cried out. She then gave a

Nancy reported what had taken place at the Tophams' cottage

quick but complete resume of what had taken place at the Tophams' cottage. Jeff Tucker added his account.

The police officer needed no further urging. Immediately he summoned four men and issued orders. "Now," he said, turning to Nancy, "have you any idea which road the thieves took?"

"Yes, Officer. When we passed the road crossing a mile outside of town, I saw their truck tracks on the dirt road leading north. I'll be glad to show you."

"Good. Lead the way. But first I'll send out a general alarm."

"Hurry!" Nancy begged as she started out. "Those thieves have at least an hour's head start!"

Jeff Tucker had been advised to return to his home. Accordingly he telephoned his son to come and pick him up in his car.

"Good luck!" he called, as the others pulled away. "I sure don't know how I'm goin' to break this to the Tophams."

Nancy was sorry for him, but she felt a thrill of excitement as she proceeded up the street, the police car following close behind.

Beyond the town, Nancy chose the road which she felt certain the thieves had used. The two cars sped along until Nancy unexpectedly came to a fork. Both branches were paved and no tire marks were visible. Nancy stopped. The police car pulled up alongside.

"What's the matter?" asked the officer in charge, whose name was Elton.

"I'm not sure which way to go now."

The policemen sprang from their automobile and began to examine the road. Officer Elton said that if a moving van had passed that way, its tire marks had been obliterated by other vehicles. It was impossible to tell which route the thieves had traveled.

"It'll be strictly guesswork from here," Officer Elton said to Nancy.

"In that case," replied Nancy, "it's my guess that the van went to the left." She pointed to a sign which read: *Garwin, 50 miles.* "Isn't Garwin a fairly large city?" she queried.

"Yes."

"Perhaps the thieves headed that way to dispose of the stolen furniture."

The officer nodded approvingly. "Sounds reasonable," he said. "Well, in any case, we can't go much farther, because we're near the state line."

Nancy had another thought. "I'll take the road to Garwin and swing around toward River Heights." She smiled. "If I see those thieves, I'll let you know."

"Well, you watch out, young lady. Those men may lock you up again!"

"I will. Anyhow, there'll be plenty of traffic as soon as I reach the main highway."

Without giving the policemen an opportunity

for further objection, Nancy started up and swung her car to the left. She noted in her rear-view mirror that the squad car had turned onto the right-hand road.

"The officers must have picked up a clue," Nancy said to herself. "But I certainly wish I could spot that van and maybe find a chance to look in the old clock!"

Nancy soon reached the main road. As mile after mile of highway spun behind her, Nancy's hopes grew dim. There were a number of side roads, any one of which the moving van might have taken to elude pursuers.

The young sleuth decided to adhere to her original theory—that Sid and his pals had headed for Garwin—and kept on the main highway.

"Those thieves think Jeff and I are still locked up and won't suspect they're being followed," she assured herself. Smiling, she thought hopefully, "In that case they won't be on their guard!"

About ten minutes later Nancy stopped at a service station to have her car refueled, and on impulse asked the attendant, "Did you by any chance see a moving van pass here recently?"

"Sure did, miss," was the prompt answer. "About half an hour ago. I noticed it because the driver was going at a terrific speed for a van."

Heartened, Nancy thanked him and resumed her pursuit, going past the turn for River Heights. "If only I can overtake the truck and somehow examine the Crowley clock before I have to report to the police!" she thought.

Again time elapsed and Nancy still saw no sign of a moving van on the highway. It was growing dusk and she decided that she would have to admit defeat.

"I never caught up to them." She sighed in disappointment, and turning into the opposite lane, headed back for the River Heights road.

Just then Nancy recalled that a little beyond the service station where she had stopped, she had noticed a rather run-down old inn. It was a slim hope, she knew, but the thieves might have put their van behind it while having a meal there.

"I'll go in and ask, anyhow," she decided.

Nancy increased her speed as much as she dared and within a few minutes came in sight of the inn. It stood back from the road a short distance and was half-hidden by tall trees. In front of the building a battered sign bearing the name *Black Horse Inn* creaked back and forth from a post. There was no sign of the van. Beyond the inn Nancy glimpsed a garage and a large barn. The doors to both were closed.

"I wonder," mused Nancy, "if the moving van is parked inside either one."

At the far side of the inn was a small woods with a narrow road leading into it. For safety's sake, Nancy thought it best to park her car on this little-used road.

She turned off the car lights, pocketed the key, and walked back to the curving driveway leading to the inn. As Nancy made her way forward, her heart pounded. There were tire marks which could belong to Sid's van! They led to the barn!

"Maybe those thieves are eating," she thought. "I'll look."

As Nancy stepped onto the porch, the sound of raucous laughter reached her ears. She tiptoed to a window and peered inside. What the young sleuth saw made her gasp, but she felt a glow of satisfaction.

In a dingy, dimly lighted room three men were seated about a table, eating voraciously. They were the thieves who had robbed the Topham bungalow!

CHAPTER XV

Nancy's Risky Undertaking

"I MUST notify the police at once!" Nancy told herself as she recognized the three thieves.

Turning away from the window, she crept noiselessly from the porch. She was about to make a dash for her car when a sudden thought occurred to her.

"If the gang have parked their van in the barn, now's my chance to look for the Crowley clock. I'm sure those men will be eating for a while, or they may even be staying overnight."

Acting on the impulse, Nancy sprinted to her car. Hastily she snatched a flashlight from the compartment, since it was now dark outside.

She made her way cautiously to the rear of the inn. Reaching the barn, she tried the closed doors, her heart pounding. They had not been locked!

As she slid back one of the doors, it squeaked in an alarming fashion. Anxiously Nancy glanced toward the inn, but so far as she could tell, her actions were unobserved. There was no one in sight.

Focusing her flashlight, she peered hopefully into the dark interior. A cry of satisfaction escaped her lips.

In front of her stood the moving van!

"What luck!" she exclaimed, snapping off her light.

With a last cautious glance in the direction of the inn, she hastily stepped inside and closed the barn door. With it shut, the interior of the barn was pitch dark.

Nancy switched on her flashlight again and played it over the moving van. She saw that its rear doors were closed.

Securing a firm grip on the handle, she gave it a quick turn. To her dismay the door did not open. The thieves had locked the van!

"Oh dear! Now what shall I do?" she wondered frantically. "I'll never be able to break the lock."

Desperately Nancy glanced about. She dared not remain many minutes in the barn, lest the thieves return and find her there. But she had to find out whether the Crowley clock was in the van.

"Perhaps the keys were left in the ignition," Nancy thought hopefully.

She rushed to the front of the van and clambered into the driver's seat. But there were no keys hanging from the ignition lock.

Nancy's mind worked frantically. She must find the keys! Perhaps the men had not taken them into the inn but had concealed them in the truck. Suddenly she remembered that people sometimes hide automobile keys under the floor mat. It was barely possible that the thieves had done this.

Hastily she pulled up a corner of the mat. Her flashlight revealed a small ring of keys!

"Luck was with me this time," she murmured, and quickly snatching up the ring, she ran back to the rear of the van.

After trying several of the keys, she at last found one which fitted the lock. Turning it, she jerked open the door. Nancy flashed her light about inside the truck. To her joy she recognized the van's contents as the furniture stolen from the Topham cottage!

"What will I do if the clock is on the bottom of the load?" Nancy wondered as she surveyed the pile of furniture. "I'll never find it."

Dexterously she swung herself up into the truck and flashed the light slowly about on chairs, tables, rugs, and boxes. There was no sign of the Crowley clock.

Then the beam rested for a moment on an object in a far corner. With a low cry of delight, Nancy saw that her search had been rewarded. Protected by a blanket, an old-fashioned mantel clock rested on top of a table in the very front of the van!

The young sleuth scrambled over the pieces of furniture as she tried to reach the clock. Her dress caught on something sharp and tore. Finally she arrived within arm's reach of the blanket. She grasped it and carefully pulled the clock toward her.

One glance at the timepiece assured her that it fitted the description Abby Rowen had given her. It had a square face and the top was ornamented with a crescent.

"The Crowley clock at last!" Nancy whispered almost unbelievingly.

But as she stood staring at it, her keen ears detected the sound of voices. The thieves!

"I'll be caught!" flashed through her mind. "And I won't be able to escape a second time!"

Clutching the blanket and the clock tightly in her arms, Nancy scrambled over the piled-up furniture as she struggled to get out of the truck before it was too late.

Reaching the door, she leaped lightly to the floor. She could now hear heavy footsteps coming closer and closer.

Nancy shut the truck doors as quickly as possible, and searched wildly for the keys.

"Oh, what did I do with them?" she thought frantically.

She saw that they had fallen to the floor and snatched them up. Hurriedly inserting the correct key in the lock, she secured the doors.

But as Nancy wheeled about she heard men's angry voices directly outside. Already someone was starting to slide back the barn door!

"Oh, what shall I do?" Nancy thought in despair. "I'm cornered!"

She realized instantly that she could not hope to run to the front of the car and place the keys under the mat where she had found them. "I'll just put them on the floor," she decided quickly. "Maybe the men will think they dropped them."

Then, glancing frantically about for a hiding place, Nancy saw an empty grain bin. Running to it, still holding the clock, she climbed inside and dropped the blanket over her head just as one of the barn doors slid open.

One of the men was speaking loudly. Nancy recognized the voice instantly. It belonged to Sid, the ringleader of the thieves.

"You had enough to eat," he growled. "We're goin' to get out of here before we have the cops down on our heads."

He climbed into the cab and turned on the headlights. Nancy held her breath. Would her hiding place be discovered? But the men apparently did not even look toward the bin.

In a moment Sid cried out, "What did you do with those keys? Thought you put 'em under the floor mat."

"I did."

"Well, they ain't here."

"Honest, boss, I—"

"Then come and find 'em, and don't be all night about it either!"

"All right. Get out of the way and give me a chance!"

As Jake went to the truck and began a careful search for the keys, Nancy listened fearfully from her hiding place.

"Say, if you've lost 'em—" the leader did not finish the threat, for at that moment the third man announced:

"Here they are on the floor! You must have thought you'd put 'em in your pocket, Jake, and dropped 'em instead."

"I didn't!" the other retorted.

The thieves were obviously in a quarrelsome mood. Just then the leader interposed:

"Cut out the yaking! We ain't got no time for a fight unless we want to land behind bars!"

"And if we do, it'll be your fault, Sid Sax. You left that girl to starve—"

"Shut up!" the leader snarled.

After a few more angry words, the three thieves climbed into the front seat and in a moment the engine started.

In relief Nancy heard the men go. The moment they were a safe distance from the barn, she climbed out of the bin.

Nancy watched long enough to make certain that the van had taken the road to Garwin. Then, snatching up her flashlight and clutching the precious clock in her arms, she turned and ran. "I'd better cut through the woods," she decided.

As Nancy darted among the trees, she cast an anxious glance over her shoulder, but to her intense relief she saw that she was not being followed. There seemed to be no one in the vicinity of the Black Horse Inn.

"I had a narrow escape that time," the young sleuth told herself as she ran. "I hate to think what might have happened if I had been discovered!" She clutched the mantel clock more tightly in her arms. "But it was worth the risk I took! I found the clock and maybe the secret of Josiah Crowley's will!"

Reaching the car, Nancy sprang inside. She took the key from her pocket and inserted it in the ignition lock.

"I'll notify the police as fast as I can," she decided. "Perhaps the state troopers can catch those men before they dispose of the furniture."

Then, just as Nancy was about to start the motor, her glance fell upon the Crowley clock which she had placed on the seat beside her. Did it contain old Josiah's mysterious notebook as she suspected?

"Oh, I must find out!" She got her flashlight.

Since the clock was too unwieldy to open inside the car, Nancy stepped out and laid it on the ground. She unfastened the glass door and ran her hand around the walls. There was nothing inside. She tried the back. Only the mechanism of the timepiece was there.

"Gone!" Nancy groaned. "Oh dear! Has my luck run out?"

Could it be, she wondered, that the Tophams had discovered the notebook only to destroy it? Nancy discarded this thought as quickly as it came to mind, for she recalled the conversation she had overheard between Ada and Isabel. No, the Tophams were as ignorant as herself concerning the location of a later will.

It was more likely that Abby Rowen had been confused in her story. After all, she had not declared that the notebook would be found inside the clock. Nancy herself had made the deduction.

"I was almost certain I'd find the notebook," she murmured in disappointment. But a moment later she took heart again. "It *must* be here somewhere," she told herself.

Turning the clock upside down, Nancy gave it a hard shake. Something inside moved. Hopefully she repeated the action.

"Unless I'm wrong," Nancy thought excitedly, "there's something inside this clock besides the works!" She examined it more closely. "An extra piece of cardboard back of the face! And something in between the two! The notebook maybe!"

After a vain attempt to remove the heavy cardboard face with her fingers, Nancy took a small screw driver from the glove compartment. With the tool it required but an instant to remove the two hands of the clock and jerk off the face.

As the cardboard fell to the floor, Nancy peered inside and gave a low cry of joy.

There, at one side of the clock, attached to a hook in the top, dangled a tiny dark-blue notebook!

CHAPTER XVI

The Capture

EAGERLY Nancy removed the little notebook from the hook. By holding the book directly under the beam of her flashlight, she could make out the words on the cover:

Property of Josiah Crowley.

"I've found it at last!" she thought excitedly.

Quickly turning the first few pages, she saw that they were yellowed with age. The writing was fine and cramped, and the ink had faded. The pages were crowded with business notations, and it was difficult to make out the words.

Nancy was thrilled, for she was positive that the notebook would disclose what Josiah Crowley had done with his last will. Yet, she realized that she could not hope to read through the book without a considerable loss of precious time. She must not delay another instant in reporting to the police.

"I'll read the notebook later," she decided, and

tucked it into her pocket. Then she put the clock together.

Hurriedly laying the timepiece back on the car seat, Nancy covered it with her coat and slid behind the wheel. Starting the engine, she swung the convertible onto the highway. Nancy cast an anxious glance in the direction the thieves had taken, and watched for side roads down which the men might turn to avoid the main highway.

"Perhaps I'd better phone the State Police from the first service station or store I come to."

Then suddenly she noticed a sign: *Alternate route to Garwin. Main road under repair.*

Reaching the intersection, she stopped to see if the familiar tire marks of the van indicated it had turned onto this dirt road. It had!

"Now what shall I do?"

As Nancy debated, she saw a car coming toward her. Her hopes soared. She could not be mistaken—it was a police prowl car with a red revolving roof light!

Instantly Nancy grabbed her own flashlight and jumped from the car. Standing at the side of the road, she waved her light and in a few minutes the police sedan stopped.

"I'm Nancy Drew," she said hurriedly to the two men inside. "Are you looking for the furniture thieves in the van?"

"Yes, we are. You're the girl who reported them?"

Nancy nodded, then pointed down the side road. "I think those are their tire marks. The men were at the Black Horse Inn, but left."

"You can identify them?" the driver asked.

"Oh, yes."

"Then please follow us. I'll radio for a car to approach the thieves' van from the other end of the road."

The police car sped down the bad road to Garwin, with Nancy following closely behind. They rode for several miles.

"Oh dear," thought Nancy, "I must have been wrong! We should have overtaken the van by this time."

Another ten minutes passed. Then, unexpectedly, she caught a glimpse of a red taillight on the road far ahead.

"It must be the van!" Nancy told herself hopefully. "The light doesn't appear to be moving fast enough for an automobile."

Evidently the police were of the same opinion, for at that moment their car slowed down. Nancy figured they would not stop the van until they saw the other police car arriving from the opposite direction. A few moments later she could see headlights in the distance.

The squad car in front of Nancy now sped ahead and pulled up alongside the van. "Pull over!" one of the officers shouted to the man in the cab.

Instead of doing so, the van put on a burst of

speed. But in order to avoid smashing into the oncoming squad car, the driver pulled too far to the right. The van swerved sharply. Its two right wheels went off into a deep ditch, and the vehicle toppled over.

In an instant the officers were out of the car and had the fugitives covered.

By this time Nancy, who had stopped her car at the side of the road, came running up. One of the officers turned to her and asked, "Can you identify these men?"

As a light was flashed upon each of the thieves in turn, Nancy nodded. "This one is Sid, who locked me in the closet," she declared, pointing to the leader. "The others are Jake and Parky."

The prisoners stared in complete disbelief. They were astounded to see Nancy Drew standing there. When it dawned on Sid that she evidently was responsible for their capture, he started to say something, then changed his mind and remained silent. The prisoners were quickly identified from licenses and other papers as wanted criminals.

One of the other officers opened the rear of the van and asked Nancy if she could identify the stolen furniture.

"Some of it," she replied. "That desk was taken from the room in which I was locked in the closet."

"Good enough," said the trooper. "These men will get long sentences for this. They'll be held on several charges. Are you willing to go with us and prefer charges against them?"

"Yes, if it's necessary," Nancy promised reluctantly. "But I don't live in this county and I'm eager to get home right away. Don't you have enough evidence against them? I think they're the same men who stole several silver heirlooms from the Turner sisters."

Sid and his companions winced, but did not speak.

"I see," said the trooper. "Well, I guess there's no need for you to go to headquarters now," the officer admitted. "I'll take your address, and if your testimony should be required, I'll get in touch with you."

When Nancy showed her driver's license as identification, the policeman glanced at her with new interest. Taking her aside, he said, "So you're the daughter of Carson Drew! I see you're following in his footsteps. Starting rather young, aren't you?"

Nancy laughed. "It was only by accident that I arrived at the Topham bungalow at the critical moment," she protested modestly.

"Not many girls would have used their wits the way you did," the officer observed. "Unless I'm mistaken, these fellows are old hands at this game. They're no doubt the men who have been stealing various things from around Moon Lake for a number of seasons. The residents will be mighty grateful for what you've done. And that Mrs. Topham you spoke of—she ought to give you a liberal reward for saving her household goods."

Nancy shook her head. "I don't want a reward, really I don't."

"Just the same you've earned one," insisted the officer, who said his name was Cowen. "If you'd like, I'll tell my chief the whole story and he'll take the matter up with this Mrs. Topham."

"You don't know her," Nancy remarked, "and I do. She'd never offer a reward. Even if she did, I wouldn't accept it." After a slight pause, she added, "In fact, I prefer that my name not be mentioned to her at all."

Officer Cowen shook his head in disbelief. "Well, all right, then. If you're sure you don't want any credit for capturing the thieves, I won't say anything. You're certain?"

"I am," Nancy replied firmly, "for a particular reason of my own."

The trooper smiled. "It must be a mighty good one."

"There *is* one favor you might do me," said Nancy. "Ask your chief to put in a good word for the caretaker, Jeff Tucker, to the Tophams. Perhaps then he won't lose his job."

"Be glad to," Officer Cowen promised. "And if you're really anxious not to figure in the case, I'll see if we can get along without your testimony."

Nancy thanked him, then suddenly thought of

the old clock. At the moment it was lying on the front seat of her car, less than a dozen yards away. Should she reveal this information? She decided against doing so in front of the thieves, who, though they could not hear what she had been saying, could see everything plainly. "I'll wait until a more opportune time," Nancy concluded.

It was agreed among the state policemen that one of them would stay to guard the van and keep a radio car standing by there. The other three troopers would take the captive thieves to headquarters.

The three prisoners, their faces sullen, were crowded into the car. One of the troopers took the wheel, while the one beside him kept the handcuffed trio closely covered.

Officer Cowen, a strapping, husky man, turned to Nancy. "I'll ride with you," he said. "You're going past headquarters on the main road?"

"I'm on my way to River Heights," she responded.

"Then the station is on your route. You can drop me off if you will."

"Why—why, of course," Nancy stammered. "I'll be glad to."

At once she had thought of the Crowley clock. What if Officer Cowen should not accept her explanation as to why she had helped herself to the heirloom and its strange contents? If this happened, her progress in solving the mystery might receive a serious setback! Even as these disturbing ideas raced through her mind, the trooper started toward the blue convertible.

Nancy braced herself. "I'll just have to 'fess up," she said to herself, "and take the consequences!"

CHAPTER XVII

Strange Instructions

For the next few seconds Nancy's mind worked like lightning as she rehearsed what she would say to Officer Cowen. One idea stood out clearly: the police were concerned in the theft of the furniture, so she would hand over the clock. But they were not involved in locating Mr. Crowley's missing will. For this reason the young sleuth felt justified in keeping the notebook. She would turn it over to her father, and let him decide what disposition should be made of it.

"After all," Nancy told herself, "Dad is handling the Crowley case for the Hoovers, and even the Turners and Mrs. Rowen, in a way."

By this time she and the trooper had reached her car. "Would you like me to drive?" he asked.

"Why—er—yes, if you wish," Nancy replied. "But first I want to show you something," she added, as he opened the door for her. "I have some stolen property here."

"What!"

Quickly Nancy explained that she had taken the responsibility of trying to learn whether or not the van held the stolen furniture. "I recognized a few of the pieces, and possibly this clock which the Tophams had told me about. I took that out to examine it. Then I never had a chance to get it back without being caught. I'm sure the Tophams will identify the old clock as their property."

Nancy's explanation seemed to satisfy the officer. "I'll take it to headquarters," he said. "Let's go!"

He laid the clock on the rear seat, then slid behind the wheel and drove off.

It was nearly midnight when Nancy, tired and worn from her long ride, reached the Drew home in River Heights. As she drove into the double garage, she noticed that her father's car was gone. A glance at the house disclosed that the windows were dark, with the exception of a light in the hall. Hannah Gruen must be in bed.

"Of course she's not expecting me," Nancy reasoned. "I wonder where Dad can be? Oh, I hope he'll get home soon. I want to tell him about my discovery right away."

After locking the garage door, she went to the kitchen entrance and let herself in.

Her eyes lighted on the refrigerator and suddenly Nancy realized she was very hungry. Many hours had passed since she had eaten. "Um, food!" she thought.

Just as Nancy opened the refrigerator door, she heard steps on the stairs and Hannah Gruen, wearing a sleepy look, appeared in robe and slippers.

"Nancy!" cried the housekeeper, instantly wide awake.

"Surprise, Hannah darling!" Nancy gave the housekeeper an affectionate hug and kiss. "I'm simply starved. Haven't had a bite since lunchtime."

"Why, you poor dear!" the housekeeper exclaimed in concern. "What happened? I'll fix you something right away."

As the two prepared a chicken sandwich, some cocoa, and Hannah cut a large slice of cinnamon cake over which she poured hot applesauce, Nancy told of her adventures.

The housekeeper's eyes widened. "Nancy, you might have been killed by those awful men. Well, I'm certainly glad they've been captured."

"So am I!" declared Nancy fervently as she finished the last crumb of cake. "And I hope the Turners get back their silver heirlooms."

"How about the Tophams?" Hannah Gruen questioned teasingly.

"Somehow," said Nancy with a wink, "that doesn't seem to worry me." Then she asked, "Where's Dad?"

"Working at his office," Hannah Gruen replied. "He phoned earlier that something unexpected had come up in connection with one of his cases."

"Then I'll wait for him," said Nancy. "You go back to bed. And thanks a million." The sleepy housekeeper did not demur.

Left alone, Nancy tidied the kitchen, then went to the living room.

"Now to find out what became of Josiah Crowley's last will," she thought excitedly, as she curled up in a comfortable chair near a reading lamp.

Carefully she thumbed the yellowed pages, for she was afraid they might tear. Evidently Josiah Crowley had used the same notebook for many years.

"He certainly knew how to save money," she mused.

Nancy read page after page, perusing various kinds of memoranda and many notations of property owned by Mr. Crowley. There were also figures on numerous business transactions in which he had been involved. Nancy was surprised at the long list of stocks, bonds, and notes which apparently belonged to the estate.

"I had no idea Josiah Crowley was worth so much," she murmured.

After a time Nancy grew impatient at the seemingly endless list of figures. She skipped several pages of the little notebook, and turned toward the end where Mr. Crowley had listed his possessions.

"Why, what's this?" she asked herself. Fastened to one page was a very thin, flat key with a tag marked 148.

Suddenly a phrase on the opposite page, "My last will and testament," caught and held Nancy's attention. Eagerly she began to read the whole section.

"I've found it!" she exclaimed excitedly. "I'm glad I didn't give up the search!"

The notation concerning the will was brief. Nancy assumed the cramped writing was Josiah Crowley's. It read:

To whom it may concern: My last will and testament will be found in safe-deposit box number 148 in the Merchants Trust Company. The box is under the name of Josiah Johnston.

"And this is the key to the box!" Nancy told herself.

For several moments the young sleuth sat staring ahead of her. It seemed unbelievable that she had solved the mystery. But surely there could no mistake. The date of the entry in the notebook was recent and the ink had not faded as it had on the earlier pages.

"There *is* a later will!" Nancy exclaimed aloud. "Oh, if only it leaves something to the Turners, and the Mathews, and Abby Rowen, and the Hoover girls! Then Allison could take voice lessons and little Judy would be taken care of, and—"

Nancy hurriedly read on, hoping to learn something definite. But although she carefully examined every page in the book, there was no other mention of the will, nor any clue to its contents.

"No wonder the document didn't come to light," Nancy mused. "Who would have thought of looking for it in a safe-deposit box under the name of Josiah Johnston? In his desire for safekeeping, Josiah Crowley nearly defeated his own purpose."

Her thoughts were interrupted as she heard a car turn into the driveway. Rushing to the window, Nancy saw her father pull into the garage. She ran to meet him at the kitchen door.

"Why, hello, Nancy," he greeted her in surprise. "If I had known you were here, I'd have come home sooner. I was doing some special work on a case. Back from Moon Lake ahead of schedule, aren't you?"

"Yes," Nancy admitted, trying to hide her excitement. "But for a good reason."

Before her father could hang up his hat in the hall closet, she plunged into the story of her adventures and ended by showing him the notebook which she had found inside the mantel clock. When she had finished, Carson Drew stared at his daughter with mingled pride and amazement.

"You're a good detective, Nancy. You've picked up an excellent clue," he said.

"Dad, I thought it best not tell the police about

the notebook. We don't want to reveal the secret of another will to the executor mentioned in the old one."

"You mean Mr. Topham. I agree," the lawyer replied. "The new will may name someone else as executor." He smiled. "I think you and I should try to see this will. But," he added, "which Merchants Trust Company is it in? There must be dozens of banks by that name."

Nancy suddenly snapped her fingers. "Dad, I believe I know. You recall that Judge Hart and his wife told me they had seen Josiah Crowley in Masonville a couple of times. And there's a Merchants Trust Company there."

Mr. Drew looked at his daughter admiringly. "I believe you have the answer, Nancy. And Judge Hart is just the man to help us. I'll phone him in the morning. Well, I guess we both need some sleep."

As the lawyer kissed his daughter good night, he added, "My dear, you were in serious danger when you encountered those thieves. I don't like to have you take such risks. I am very grateful indeed that you are back home safe."

"The Tophams aren't going to thank me when they find out what I have done," Nancy said, as she went up the stairs ahead of her father. "In fact, we may have a battle on our hands, Dad."

"That's right, Nancy. And it will be just as well that they don't learn the details of how the will was found until the matter is settled beyond a doubt."

"I'm certainly curious to find out if the new will left anything to the Tophams," said Nancy.

"If not," her father put in, "your discovery will strike them at an especially awkward time."

Nancy paused on the stairs and turned to face her father. "What do you mean?"

"Well, there's talk about town that Richard Topham has been losing heavily in the stock market this past month. He has been getting credit at a number of places on the strength of the inheritance, and I suspect he is depending on Crowley's money to pull him through a tight spot. He's making every effort to speed up the settlement of the estate."

"Then we'd better hurry," said Nancy, resuming the climb.

"Don't build your hopes too high," Mr. Drew advised her wisely. "There may be a slip, you know."

"How?"

"We may fail to find the will in the safe-deposit box."

"Oh, I can't believe it, Dad. The notebook says it's there!"

"Then," the lawyer continued, "there is a chance that Josiah Crowley didn't dispose of the fortune as the Turners and the Hoovers and others expected he would."

"But he promised all those people—"

"I know, Nancy. But there's just the possibility that the notation in the notebook was wishful thinking and Mr. Crowley never got around to making the new will."

"You can discourage me all you want to, Dad, but I'm not going to stop hoping!" Nancy said. "Oh, I can scarcely wait for morning to come!"

Her father laughed. "You're an incurable optimist! Now put Josiah Crowley out of your mind and get a good night's sleep."

At the door of her bedroom Nancy hesitated, then turned back toward the stairs.

"What's up?" Mr. Drew asked.

Without answering Nancy ran down to the living room, picked up the notebook which lay on the table, and hurried back up the carpeted steps.

"After all I've gone through to get my hands on this," she told her father, "I'm not going to take any chances!" Nancy laughed. "Tonight I'll sleep with it under my pillow!"

CHAPTER XVIII

A Suspenseful Search

WHEN Nancy awoke the following morning, bright sunlight was streaming through her open bedroom window. As her eyes turned toward the clock on her dresser, she was alarmed to see that it was a little after nine o'clock.

"How could I have overslept on a morning like this?" she chided herself.

Quickly running her hand under the pillow, she brought out the Crowley notebook and surveyed it with satisfaction.

"What a surprise the Tophams are going to get!" she murmured softly.

After hastily bathing and dressing, Nancy hurried downstairs looking very attractive in a blue summer sweater suit. She kissed Hannah Gruen, who said a cheery good morning and told Nancy that Mr. Drew had already left for his office.

"Oh dear," Nancy said, "I wonder if he forgot our date?"

"No indeed," the housekeeper replied. "He phoned Judge Hart and expects word from him by ten o'clock. He'll let you know the result. My goodness, Nancy, you've really made a big discovery. I do hope everything turns out for the best."

She went into the kitchen but returned in a moment with a plate of crisp, golden waffles.

"Better eat your breakfast," she advised. "Your dad may call any minute."

Nancy ate a dish of strawberries, then started on the waffles. "These are yummy," she stated, pouring maple syrup over a second one.

She had just finished eating when the phone rang. Mr. Drew was calling to say Judge Hart had made arrangements at the bank. "Come to my office with the notebook and key, Nancy. We'll start from here."

"I'll be right down, Dad."

Nancy went upstairs for her purse, then drove to her father's office.

"I have the notebook with me," she told the lawyer. "Do you want it?"

"We'll take the book along. I want to show it to the head of the trust department at the bank," Mr. Drew said. "It's our proof we have good reason for taking a look in Mr. Crowley's box."

After leaving a number of instructions with his private secretary, Carson Drew followed his daughter from the office. He took his place beside her in the convertible.

"I'll never get over it if we don't find a newer will," Nancy declared, as they drove along. A flush of excitement had tinted her cheeks and her eyes were bright.

"You must remember one thing, Nancy," returned her father calmly. "Crowley was an odd person and did things in an odd way. A will may be there, and again it may not. Perhaps he only left further directions to finding it.

"I remember one case in Canada years ago. An eccentric Frenchman died and left directions to look in a trunk of old clothes for a will. In the pocket of a coat were found further instructions to look in a closet of his home. There his family found a note telling them to look in a copper boiler.

"The boiler had disappeared but was finally located in a curiosity shop. Inside, pasted on the bottom, was what proved to be a word puzzle in Chinese. The old Frenchman's heirs were about to give up in despair when a Chinese solved the puzzle and the old man's fortune was found—a bag of gold under a board in his bedroom floor!"

"At least they found it," said Nancy.

The trip to Masonville was quickly accomplished, and Nancy parked the car in front of the Merchants Trust Company.

Father and daughter alighted and entered the

bank. Mr. Drew gave his name and asked to see the president. After a few minutes' wait they were ushered into a private conference room. An elderly man, Mr. Jensen, arose to greet them.

The introductions over, Mr. Drew hastened to state his mission. Before he could finish the story, the bank president broke in.

"Judge Hart has told me the story. I'll call Mr. Warren, our trust officer."

He picked up his desk phone and in a few minutes Mr. Warren appeared and was introduced. Nancy now brought out the notebook, opened it to the important page, and handed it to the men to read.

When they finished, Mr. Jensen said, "What a mystery!"

Mr. Warren pulled from his pocket the file card which the owner of Box 148 had filled out in the name of Josiah Johnston. The two samples of cramped handwritings were compared.

"I would say," Mr. Drew spoke up, "that there is no doubt but that Crowley and Johnston were the same person."

"I agree," asserted Mr. Jensen, and his trust officer nodded.

"Then there's no reason why we shouldn't open the box?" Mr. Drew asked.

"None," Mr. Warren replied. "Of course nothing may be removed, you understand."

"All I want to see," Nancy spoke up, "is whether

there is a will in the box, the date on it, who the executor is, and who the heirs are."

The bankers smiled and Mr. Jensen said, "You're hoping to solve four mysteries all at once! Well, let's get started."

With Mr. Warren in the lead, the four walked toward the rear of the bank to the vault of the trust department. A guard opened the door and they went through. Mr. Jensen took the key from Mr. Crowley's notebook, while Mr. Warren opened the first part of the double safety lock with the bank key. Then he inserted the key from the notebook. It fitted!

In a moment he lifted out Deposit Box Number 148. It was a small one and not heavy, he said.

"We'll take this into a private room," Mr. Jensen stated. He, Nancy, and Mr. Drew followed the trust officer down a corridor of cubbyhole rooms until they reached one not in use.

"Now," said Mr. Jensen, when the door was closed behind them, "we shall see how many—if any—of the mysteries are solved."

Nancy held her breath as he raised the lid of the box. All peered inside. The box was empty, except for one bulky document in the bottom.

"Oh, it must be the will!" Nancy exclaimed.

"It is a will," Mr. Jensen announced, after a hasty glance at the first page. "Josiah Crowley's last will and testament."

"When was it written?" Nancy asked quickly.

"In March of this year," Mr. Jensen told her.

"Oh, Dad," Nancy cried, "this was later than the will the Tophams submitted for probate!"

"That's right."

"Let's read it right away," Nancy begged.

Mr. Jensen handed the sheets to Mr. Drew. "Maybe you can decipher this. The handwriting is too much for me."

The lawyer took the will. Then, as Nancy looked over his shoulder, he haltingly read aloud, giving an interpretation rather than a word by word account.

"Mr. Jensen—Mr. Warren, your bank has been named as executor," he said.

"Very good." The president smiled. "But I expect Mr. Topham won't be happy to hear this."

Mr. Drew had turned to the last page. "The signature of Josiah is in order," he remarked, "and there are two witnesses—Dr. Nesbitt and Thomas Wackley. No wonder this will didn't come to light. Both those men died in April."

As Nancy tried to decipher the handwriting, she noticed to her delight that the Hoover girls and Abby Rowen were mentioned.

At this moment the president said, "Mr. Drew, the bank's regular lawyer had just left for Europe on an extended vacation. Since you and your daughter have solved the mystery and are so vitally interested in it, would you handle this case for us?"

Nancy held her breath as Mr. Jensen opened the safe-deposit box

Nancy's eyes sparkled and Mr. Drew smiled. "I'd certainly be very glad to," he said.

"What instructions have you for us?" Mr. Warren asked.

Mr. Drew thought a moment, then said, "Because of the unusual aspects of this case, I believe that first of all I'd like you to have photostats of the will made, so I can study the contents carefully."

"We'll be happy to do that," Mr. Jensen replied. "And then?"

"After I'm sure everything is legal," Mr. Drew went on, "I'll deliver the original will for probate and notify the people who will benefit from Mr. Crowley's estate."

"Fine," said Mr. Jensen. "We have photostating equipment right here. I'll have a couple of copies made while you wait. Or shall I send them to your office?"

Mr. Drew glanced at his daughter. "We'll wait," he said, smiling.

While the photostats were being made, Nancy's mind was racing. "Oh, I hope Allison receives enough money to pay for singing lessons, and the other deserving people get nice amounts," she whispered to her father, who nodded.

The wait seemed interminable to Nancy, who could not sit still. She walked back and forth until finally her father remarked teasingly, "You're like a caged lion."

Nancy pretended to pout. "At least I'm not growling," she said, and Mr. Drew grinned.

Soon a messenger brought back the will, together with two photostats of the document.

"Thank you," said Mr. Jensen, who handed the photostatic copies to Mr. Drew.

"I'll work on this at once," the lawyer promised as he put the papers in his brief case. Then he and his daughter left the bank.

Mr. Drew insisted that he and Nancy stop for lunch and refused to let her look at the will while they were waiting to be served. "Relax, young lady," he warned. "There's no point in letting any prying eyes know our secret."

As he saw his daughter's animation fading, Mr. Drew said, "Suppose you come to my office with me and we'll work on the problem together. I'll have the will typed. In this way its full meaning can be understood more easily."

"Oh, thanks, Dad," said Nancy.

In the lawyer's office the young sleuth sat down beside his typist, Miss Lamby. As each page came from the machine, Nancy read it avidly.

"Mr. Crowley certainly seemed to know the correct phraseology for drawing up a will," she remarked.

Finally, when the typing had been completed, Nancy said to the secretary, "I have a lot of questions to ask Dad."

Miss Lamby smiled. "If they're legal ones, he'll

know all the answers," she said. "There's no better lawyer in River Heights than your father."

Nancy smiled as she dashed into her father's office. The two Drews sat down to study Josiah Crowley's last will and testament.

"If this does prove to be legal," said Nancy, "it will certainly be a blow to the Tophams."

"I'm afraid so."

"Dad, when you call a meeting of all the relatives and read the will aloud," Nancy said, "please may I be there?"

Mr. Drew laughed. "I'll humor you this time, Nancy. You may be present when the Tophams get the surprise of their lives!"

CHAPTER XIX

Startling Revelations

"DAD, it's nearly two o'clock now. Mr. Crowley's relatives should be here in a few minutes! I'm so excited!"

Carson Drew, who stood in the living room of the Drew home with Mr. Warren from the bank, smiled at his daughter as she fluttered about, arranging chairs.

"I believe you're more thrilled than if you were inheriting the fortune yourself," he remarked.

"I am thrilled," Nancy admitted. "I can scarcely wait until the will is read aloud. Won't everyone be surprised? Especially the Tophams. Do you think they will come?"

"Oh, yes, the Tophams will be here. And, unless I am mistaken, they will bring a lawyer with them. Just as soon as they learned that another will had come to light, they began to worry. They will certainly want to hear what is in this one."

"Are you certain the will we found can't be broken?" Nancy inquired anxiously.

"Of course I can't be certain, Nancy. But I have gone over it carefully, and so far as I can tell, it is technically perfect. I also asked a couple of lawyer friends and they agree. Josiah Crowley was peculiar in some ways, but he was a very smart man. I'll promise you the Tophams will have a difficult time if they try to contest this will."

"The bank will help you fight," Mr. Warren put in.

With the exception of Abby Rowen, who was still confined to bed, all the old gentleman's relatives had promised to be present. Grace and Allison Hoover, although not relatives, had also been invited.

"It's too bad Mrs. Rowen can't come," said Nancy. "But I'll take the news to her this very afternoon."

"The size of the fortune will probably be a great surprise to everyone but the Tophams," said her father with a smile. "Nancy, you did a remarkable piece of detective work."

"It was fun," she said modestly. "And I can hardly wait to have it all cleared up."

"We may have some trying minutes with the Tophams, Nancy," her father warned.

"Yes, I suppose so. I expect anybody would be sorry to see a fortune slip away. . . . Dad, I see

Grace and Allison coming up the walk now," Nancy announced, glancing out the window.

She greeted them with kisses and escorted the sisters into the living room, where she introduced them to Mr. Warren. As Allison sat down, she whispered to Nancy:

"Is it true a later will has been found?"

"You and Grace have no cause to worry," Nancy assured her with a mysterious smile.

The doorbell rang. This time Nancy admitted Edna and Mary Turner, who were dressed as if for a party. With them was little Judy, who threw herself into Nancy's arms. A few minutes later the Mathews brothers, William and Fred, arrived.

"I guess everyone is here except the Tophams," Mr. Drew commented. "We had better wait for them a few minutes."

There was no need to wait, for at that moment the bell rang sharply. Nancy opened the door and the four members of the Topham family walked in haughtily, merely nodding to the others in the room. As Mr. Drew had predicted, they were accompanied by a lawyer.

"Why have we been called here?" Mrs. Topham demanded, addressing Mr. Drew. "Have you the audacity to claim that another will has been found?"

"I have a will written only this past March, Mrs. Topham," Carson Drew replied evenly. "And I'd like to introduce to all of you Mr. John Warren, trust officer of the Merchants Trust Company, of Masonville, which has been named as executor."

"It's preposterous!" Mrs. Topham stormed. "Josiah Crowley made only one will and in that he left everything to us with my husband as executor."

"It looks like a conspiracy to me," Ada added tartly, as she gazed coldly upon the relatives and friends who were seated about the room.

Isabel did not speak, but tossed her head contemptuously. Richard Topham likewise did not offer a comment, but uneasily seated himself beside his own attorney.

"If you will please be seated, Mrs. Topham, I will read the will," Mr. Drew suggested.

Reluctantly Mrs. Topham sat down.

"As I have said," Mr. Drew began, "a recent will of the late Josiah Crowley was found in a safe-deposit box in the Masonville bank. The will is unusually long, and with your permission I will read from a typed copy only the portions which have to do with the disposal of the property. But first I want to ask Mr. Topham what value he puts on the estate."

"A hundred thousand after taxes," the man replied.

"Oh!" the Turners exclaimed, and Mary said, "I had no idea Josiah had that much money."

"Nor I," Edna agreed.

Mr. Drew picked up several typewritten sheets from the table, and began to read in a clear voice:

" 'I, Josiah Crowley, do make this my last will and testament, hereby revoking all former wills by me at any time made. I give and bequeath all my property, real and personal, as follows:

" 'To my beloved friends and neighbors, Grace and Allison Hoover, a sum equal to twenty per cent of my estate, share and share alike.' "

"I must be dreaming!" Grace gasped.

"You mean I'm going to get ten thousand dollars?" Allison cried out. She burst into tears. "Oh, Nancy, you did this for me! Now I can have my voice lessons."

Isabel Topham eyed her disdainfully. "It would take more than ten thousand dollars to make a singer out of you!" she said maliciously.

"Quiet!" commanded her father. "Let's hear what else this will says."

His daughter subsided, but his wife exclaimed spitefully, "The will is a fraud. The Hoovers aren't even relatives."

"It is no fraud," Mr. Drew told her quietly. Again he picked up the will and began to read:

" 'To Abby Rowen, my late wife's cousin, in consideration of her kindness to me, a sum equal to ten per cent of my estate.' "

"Oh, I'm so glad," Grace murmured. "Now she'll be able to get the medical and other attention she needs."

"And have someone live at her house to take care of her," said Nancy.

"That old lady gets ten thousand dollars?" Ada Topham said harshly. "What did she ever do for Cousin Josiah?" Angrily she turned to her mother. "We took care of him for years—she didn't!"

"I'll say not," Isabel echoed, her voice tart.

" 'To my cousins, Fred and William Mathews, a sum equal to twenty per cent of my estate, share and share alike,' " Mr. Drew read.

"We didn't expect that much," Fred Mathews declared in genuine surprise. "Josiah was very kind." Fred smiled. "Now we can take a trip like we've always wanted to do, William."

"That's right. I just can't believe it. A long trip on an ocean liner or a plane."

" 'To my cousins, Edna and Mary Turner, twenty per cent of my estate, share and share alike.' "

"Oh, how generous!" Edna murmured. "Now little Judy can have the things we've always wanted to give her."

"Yes," said Mary Turner. "Oh, I feel so relieved."

"Aren't we mentioned at all?" Mrs. Topham broke in sharply.

Mr. Drew smiled. "Yes, you are mentioned. I'm coming to that now. 'To Richard Topham, five thousand dollars. To Grace and Allison Hoover—' "

"Hold on!" cried Mrs. Topham. "What about me and the girls?"

"No money was left to you," the lawyer stated simply.

Isabel gave a shriek. "Oh, no! Oh, no! Oh, Mother, all those bills! What'll we do?"

Ada too had cried out. "I'll have to go to work! Oh, I can't bear the thought of it!"

When the furor died down, Mr. Drew read on, " 'To Grace and Allison Hoover my household furniture now in the possession of Mrs. Richard Topham.' "

There was a gasp of surprise from everyone in the room, and Mrs. Topham half arose from her chair. It was generally known in River Heights that she had practically confiscated Josiah Crowley's furniture at the time he had been induced to make his home with the Tophams.

"How insulting!" the woman cried. "Does Josiah Crowley dare hint that I took his furniture?"

"I'm sure I don't know what was in his mind at the time he wrote the will," Mr. Drew told her with a smile.

Grace Hoover interposed quickly, "We have enough furniture without Josiah Crowley's."

Allison nodded. "We'll not take any of it from you, Mrs. Topham."

Mr. Drew carefully folded the document he had been reading, and after placing it in his pocket, he said to the people in the room:

"That is all, except that there is a proviso for the executor to pay all Mr. Crowley's just debts, including his funeral expenses, and that what balance is left in the estate goes to the Manningham Old Men's Home. I understand Josiah Crowley kept his assets in a liquid state. It will not be difficult to convert the estate into cash. For that reason I should think it would be possible to draw on your inheritances at once."

Ada wheeled upon Nancy, her face convulsed with anger. "You engineered this whole thing, Nancy Drew!" she accused bitterly.

"Any good I've done I'm happy about," Nancy answered.

"We'll break the will!" Mrs. Topham announced firmly.

CHAPTER XX

A Happy Finale

"OF COURSE you may take the matter into court if you like," Mr. Drew responded to Mrs. Topham's threat. "But I warn you it will be a waste of your time and money. If you don't wish to accept my judgment, ask your own lawyer."

"Mr. Drew is right," the other lawyer said, after arising and looking carefully at the legal document which Mr. Drew took from his pocket.

"Oh, he is, is he?" Mrs. Topham retorted. "If that's all you know about law, you're discharged! We'll get another lawyer and we'll fight to the last ditch!"

With that she arose and stalked from the room. Isabel and Ada followed, after bestowing a withering glance upon Nancy. Mr. Topham brought up the rear. As soon as the door had closed behind them, their lawyer arose and picked up his brief case.

"Well, I can't say I'm sorry to be taken off the case," he remarked as he, too, took his leave. "But I advise you to be on your guard. That woman is certainly belligerent."

At once the atmosphere in the Drew living room became less strained, though each person was fearful Mrs. Topham would make trouble. Everyone began to talk at once.

"Oh, Nancy, I can hardly believe it yet!" Allison declared happily. "The money means so much to Grace and me! And we owe it all to you, Nancy Drew! You haven't told us how you came to find the will, but I know you were responsible."

When the Hoover girls and Mr. Crowley's relatives begged her for the details, Nancy told of her adventure with the thieves at Moon Lake. After she had finished the story, they praised her highly for what she had done.

"We'll never be able to thank you enough," Grace said quietly. "But after the estate has been settled, we'll try to show our appreciation."

It was on the tip of Nancy's tongue to say that she did not want a reward, when Mr. Drew turned the conversation into a different channel.

"Mrs. Topham will not give up the money without a fight," he warned. "My advice would be to go along as you have until the court has decided to accept this will as the final one. However, if Mrs. Topham and her daughters bring the matter into court, I'll give them a battle they'll never forget!"

After thanking Mr. Drew and Nancy for everything they had done, the relatives and friends departed. Allison and Grace were the last to leave. On the porch, Allison paused to hug Nancy and say, "Please let us know what develops. I'm so eager to start taking voice lessons."

Nancy wanted to set off at once to see Abby Rowen and tell her the good news. But upon second thought she decided to wait. Suppose the Tophams succeeded in upsetting the whole case!

For a week Nancy waited impatiently to hear the result of the battle over the will. As she and her father had anticipated, Mrs. Topham was fighting bitterly for the Crowley estate. She had put forth the claim that the will Nancy had unearthed was a forged document.

"This suspense is just awful," Nancy told her father one morning. "When are we going to get final word?"

"I can't answer that, Nancy. But apparently Mr. Topham thinks it's a losing battle. I suppose you've heard about the family."

"Why, no, what about them?"

"They're practically bankrupt. Richard Topham has been losing steadily on the stock market of late. After his failure to recover the Crowley fortune, the banks reduced his credit. He's been forced to give up his beautiful home."

"No, really? How that must hurt Mrs. Topham and the two girls!"

"Yes, it's undoubtedly a bitter pill to swallow. They are moving into a small house this week, and from now on they'll have to give up their extravagant way of living. Both girls are working. Personally, I think it will be good for them."

Word came that the three furniture thieves had finally confessed to many robberies and their unsold loot was recovered. Among the pieces were all the heirlooms they had stolen from the Turners.

One evening Mr. Drew came home wearing a broad smile. Facing Nancy and laying both hands on her shoulders, he said:

"We've won, my dear. The will you located has been accepted as the last one Mr. Crowley wrote."

"Oh, Dad, how wonderful!" she cried, whirling her father about in a little dance. "First thing tomorrow morning, may I go and tell Allison and Grace and the others?"

"I think that would be a fine idea. Of course the bank and I will formally notify them later."

The following morning Nancy was the first one downstairs and started breakfast before Hannah Gruen appeared.

"My goodness, you're an early bird, Nancy," the housekeeper said with a smile. "Big day, eh?"

"*Very* big," Nancy replied.

As soon as the family had eaten, Hannah said,

"Never mind helping me today. You run along and make those people happy as soon as possible."

"Oh, thank you, Hannah. I'll leave right away."

Nancy, dressed in a simple green linen sports dress with a matching sweater, kissed her little family good-by and drove off. Her first stop was at the Mathews brothers. They greeted her affably, then waited for Nancy to speak.

"I have good news," she said, her eyes dancing. "Mrs. Topham lost her case. The will Dad and I found has been accepted for probate. You will receive the inheritance Mr. Crowley left you!"

"Praise be!" Fred cried. "And we never would have received it if it hadn't been for you." His brother nodded in agreement.

To cover her embarrassment at their praise, Nancy reached into a pocket and pulled out a handful of travel folders and airline schedules. "I thought you might like to look at these. Now I must hurry off and tell the other heirs."

As she drove away, the two men smiled, waved, then immediately began to look at the folders. "I hope they have a grand trip," Nancy thought.

Half an hour later she pulled into the driveway of the Turner home. Before the car stopped, Judy came racing from the front door. As Nancy stepped out, the little girl threw herself into the young sleuth's arms. "Nancy, guess what! My aunties found an old, old doll that belonged to my mommy and they gave it to me. Come and see her. She's pretty as can be."

Judy pulled Nancy by the hand up the steps and into the house. "There she is," the child said proudly, pointing to a blond, curly-haired doll seated in a tiny rocking chair.

"Why, she's darling," Nancy commented. "And, Judy, she looks like you, dimples and all."

Judy nodded. "And Aunt Mary says she looks like my mommy did when she was a little girl, so I'm always going to take very good care of my dolly."

At this moment her great-aunts came from the rear of the house to greet their caller.

"I see," said Nancy, "that you have made Judy very happy. Now it's my turn to pass along good news to you," and she told about their inheritance.

The women smiled happily and tears came to their eyes. Then suddenly Edna Turner gave Nancy an impulsive hug. "You dear, dear girl!" she half sobbed with joy. "Now Judy will always be well taken care of and receive the kind of schooling we think she should have!"

Mary kissed Nancy and thanked the young sleuth for her untiring efforts to see justice done. Judy, meanwhile, looked on in puzzlement at the scene. But sensing that it called for her participation, she grabbed up her new doll and began to dance around with it.

"Now you can go to school too, Carol," she told her doll.

It was hard for Nancy to break away from the Turners, but she reminded them that she still had two calls to make.

"But come back soon," Judy said.

When Nancy arrived at Abby Rowen's she was delighted to find her seated by the window in a chair. Her kind neighbor, Mrs. Jones, was there preparing food for the invalid. To this Nancy added a jar of homemade beef broth and a casserole of rice and chicken which Hannah Gruen had insisted upon sending.

"Can you stay a little while?" Mrs. Jones asked. "I ought to run home for half an hour, then I'll come back."

"She's been so kind," Abby Rowen spoke up. "Today she took my laundry home to wash and iron." After the woman had left, Abby went on, "The folks around here have been very thoughtful of me, but I just can't impose on them any longer. Yet I haven't any money—"

Nancy took the invalid's hand in hers and smiled. "I came to tell you that now you have lots of money, left to you by Josiah Crowley."

"What! You mean I won't have to depend on just my little pension any longer? Bless Josiah! Nancy, I never could believe that my cousin would go back on his word."

Nancy ate some broth and crackers with Abby

Rowen and told the whole story. The old woman's eyes began to sparkle and color came into her cheeks. "Oh, this is so wonderful!" she said. Then she chuckled. "It does my heart good to know you outwitted those uppity Topham women!"

Nancy grinned, then said soberly, "If I hadn't become involved in this mystery, I might never have met several wonderful people—and their names aren't Topham!"

Abby Rowen laughed aloud—the first time Nancy had heard her do this. She laughed again just as the neighbor returned. Mrs. Jones, amazed, had no chance to exclaim over the elderly woman's high spirits. Abby launched into an account of her inheritance.

As soon as Mrs. Rowen finished the story, Nancy said good-by and left. She now headed straight for the Hoover farm. The two sisters were working in a flower bed.

"Hi!" Nancy called.

"Hi, yourself. How's everything?" Allison asked, as she brushed some dirt off her hands and came forward with Grace.

"Hurry and change your clothes," Nancy said. "I have a surprise for you."

"You mean we're going somewhere?" Grace inquired.

"That's right. To Signor Mascagni's so Allison can sign up for lessons."

"Oh, Nancy, you mean—?"

"Yes. The inheritance is yours!"

"I can't believe it! I can't believe it!" Allison cried out ecstatically. She grabbed the other two girls and whirled them around.

"It's simply marvelous," said Grace. "Marvelous. Oh, Nancy, you and Mr. Crowley are just the dearest friends we've ever had." Then, seeing Nancy's deep blush, she added, "Come on, Allison. Let's get dressed."

Nancy waited in the garden. Fifteen minutes later the sisters were ready to leave for River Heights. "But before we go," said Grace, "Allison and I want to give you something—it's sort of a reward."

"Something very special," her sister broke in.

"Oh, I don't want any reward," Nancy objected quickly.

"Please take this one," Allison spoke up.

She led the way to the living-room mantel. There stood the Crowley clock. "We received it this morning from the Tophams," Grace explained.

Allison added, "We think you earned this heirloom, Nancy, and somehow Grace and I feel Mr. Crowley would want you to have it."

"Why, thank you," said Nancy.

She was thrilled, and gazed meditatively at the old clock. Though quaint, it was not handsome, she thought. But for her it certainly held a special significance. She was too modest to explain to Allison and Grace why she would prize the heirloom, and besides, her feeling was something she could not put into words. Actually she had become attached to the clock because of its association with her recent adventure.

"This is the first mystery I've solved alone," she thought. "I wonder if I'll ever have another one half so thrilling."

As Nancy stood looking wistfully at the old clock she little dreamed that in the near future she would be involved in *The Hidden Staircase* mystery, a far more baffling case than the one she had just solved. But somehow, as Nancy gazed at the timepiece, she sensed that exciting days were soon to come.

Nancy ceased daydreaming as the clock was handed to her and looked at the Hoover girls. "I'll always prize this clock as a trophy of my first venture as a detective," she said with a broad smile.

NANCY DREW MYSTERY STORIES®

The Bungalow Mystery

BY CAROLYN KEENE

GROSSET & DUNLAP
Publishers • New York
A member of The Putnam & Grosset Group

Contents

CHAPTER I

A Blinding Storm

"LOOK at those black storm clouds!" Nancy Drew pointed out to her friend, Helen Corning, who was seated beside her in the bow of the small red motorboat.

Nancy, blue-eyed, and with reddish-gold glints in her blond hair, was at the wheel. She gazed anxiously across a long expanse of water to the distant shores of Twin Lakes. The Pinecrest Motel, where the eighteen-year-old girl and her older friend were staying, was almost two miles away on the smaller of the two lakes.

Helen Corning, dark-haired and petite, looked at Nancy with concern. "I think we're in for a cloudburst," she said, "and Twin Lakes becomes as rough as the ocean in a storm."

A few minutes later angry waves began to beat against the sides of the boat.

"Are there life preservers aboard, Helen?" Nancy asked.

"No," Helen answered fearfully.

Nancy set her chin grimly. Although it was only four o'clock in the afternoon, the sky was becoming increasingly dark. The pleasant summer breeze, which had been blowing earlier, was turning into a stiff wind.

"It's getting harder to keep on course," Nancy remarked, gripping the wheel more tightly.

As she increased the boat's speed to the maximum, the craft fairly leaped through the water, dashing spray into the girls' faces.

"I wonder if there are any raincoats in the lockers," said Helen.

"Please look," Nancy requested. "We'll be drenched by the time we reach the motel dock."

Luckily Helen found two plastic coats. She slipped into one, then helped Nancy into the other.

A streak of forked lightning cut across the sky, momentarily disclosing a thick mass of ugly clouds. The lightning was followed by an ominous crack of thunder, which caused the girls to jump.

"This is terrible!" Helen wailed.

A moment later the wind began to howl. It struck the boat with a force which made Helen grasp the railing next to her for support. Another dazzling flash of lightning illuminated the sky, and simultaneously a deluge of rain began to descend.

Nancy peered ahead into the dimness. The shore line had vanished and the blinding rain made it impossible for her to see more than a few feet beyond the bow of the boat.

"At least we have half a tank of fuel," Nancy announced, trying to sound optimistic. "We'll reach shore soon, I'm sure."

"I wouldn't bet on that," Helen said nervously.

A worried expression furrowed the young pilot's brow. The boat was making little progress against the wind. If anything happened to the motor they would be at the mercy of the waves.

A few minutes later the rain came down even harder. The wind continued to blow a raging gale and the waves seemed higher.

The girls leaned forward, trying to get their bearings. As a jagged ribbon of lightning illuminated the path ahead, Helen screamed, "About!"

Nancy froze with horror. A tremendous log was floating directly into the path of the motorboat!

Her heart pounding, the young skipper gave the wheel a vicious turn, but not quickly enough. With a splintering crash, the bow of the boat struck the log!

The impact sent Helen sprawling to the deck. Nancy clung to the steering wheel, but was thrown forward violently.

"Helen, are you hurt?" she asked.

"I— I'm all right. Are you?" she stammered, as Nancy helped Helen to her feet. Both girls were breathing heavily.

By now the small boat was listing sharply to starboard. Nancy saw instantly that the log had torn a jagged hole in the side of the craft. Water was pouring in rapidly.

"Quick, Helen!" Nancy ordered tersely. "You bail and I'll try to stop the leak!"

She sprang forward, tore off her raincoat, and stuffed it into the hole. Helen, meanwhile, found a rusty can and began to bail. Despite their efforts, water continued to pour through the opening.

"Let's shout for help!" Nancy cried above the wind, but she doubted that there was any other craft on the lake.

The girls cupped their hands to their lips and shouted frantically. Their only answer was the howl of the gale and the steady beat of rain

"Louder!" Helen urged, and they screamed until they were hoarse.

"It's no use," Nancy said at last. "We'll have to think of something else."

Just then Nancy saw a giant wave bearing down on them. She met it head on, hoping to ride the crest, but a deluge of water almost inundated the girls. They were flung overboard and the motor-boat sank to the bottom of the lake!

An excellent swimmer, Nancy managed to get her head above water almost immediately. Her first thought was for Helen. What had become of her?

Treading water, Nancy glanced about. Helen was not in sight.

"I must find her!" Nancy thought desperately. "She may have been injured!"

Then, several yards away, Nancy saw a white hand flash above the water. With powerful crawl strokes she plowed through the waves to the spot. The hand had vanished!

Nancy made a neat surface dive. Opening her eyes, she tried to see through the clouded water but to no avail. At last, she surfaced and drew in a deep breath.

Clearing her eyes, Nancy was relieved to spot her friend several feet ahead. Helen was floating on her back. Strong strokes brought Nancy directly behind her friend.

"My arms feel numb," Helen said weakly. "Guess I hit them on the boat."

"Don't worry," said Nancy. "Just lie still and I'll tow you to shore."

Nancy, however, had grave misgivings regarding her ability to accomplish this in the turbulent water. She needed every ounce of strength to swim the distance alone. *Could* she manage to save Helen? The storm had made the water very cold. Nancy prayed that she would not get a cramp and both girls go down.

"Hold your breath when you see a wave coming," she instructed Helen. as they started off.

At frequent intervals Nancy shouted for help, although she felt it was wasted energy. On and on they went.

Helen noticed finally that Nancy's breathing showed the great strain on her. "Save yourself," she begged. "Go on to shore without me."

"Never!" said Nancy, as a huge wave bore down upon the two girls, smothering them in its impact.

Feebly, Nancy struggled back to the surface with her burden. "One more like that and I'll be through," she said to herself.

Just then Nancy thought she detected a voice above the roar of the wind. Was it her imagination or had she really heard someone call?

"Help!" she screamed.

This time there could be no mistake, for she distinguished the words:

"Hold on! I'm coming!"

Through the blinding rain Nancy caught a glimpse of a dark object. A rowboat! If only she could hold out until it reached her!

"Over here!" Nancy cried loudly, waving.

As the boat approached, she fully expected to see it swamped. The boat swept safely toward the two girls, barely avoiding a crash, however. To Nancy's surprise, there was only one occupant in the boat—a slender, auburn-haired girl of about sixteen.

Twice she tried to bring the boat alongside the swimmers, but failed. The third time, as the craft swept past, Nancy lunged forward and caught the side of it. She dragged Helen along, supporting her with one hand until she, too, secured a hold.

"Can you climb aboard?" their rescuer asked. "I'll balance the boat while you get in."

Nancy explained about the submerged motorboat and Helen's useless arms.

With the strange girl and Nancy working together, they managed to get Helen into the craft. Then Nancy pulled herself over the side.

"Safe!" Helen said in relief. "I don't know how to thank you," she told their rescuer.

"Are you both all right?" asked the strange girl. "We're not far from the beach—otherwise, I couldn't have heard your cries for help in this wind."

"You were very brave to come for us," said Nancy. "I'm Nancy Drew and this is Helen Corning."

The girl at the oars stared at Nancy with keen interest. "I'm Laura Pendleton," she said. "I read in a newspaper about one of the mysteries you solved. I may need your help some day soon, Nancy."

Without another word Laura bent over her oars again.

"I'll help you row," Nancy offered, snatching up an extra oar from the bottom of the rowboat, and wondering what Laura Pendleton's mystery was.

Using the oar like a paddle, Nancy attempted to keep the boat on course. As she and Laura made some progress against the wind and waves, Helen took new hope.

"I think we're going to make it!" she said in relief. "Oh!"

A vivid flash of lightning illuminated the water. Directly ahead, through the rain, she and Nancy caught a glimpse of the rocky shore line.

"The rocks, Laura! Be careful or we'll be dashed against them!" Helen cried out, as the rowboat was tossed and slapped by the crashing waves.

Another zigzag streak of lightning disclosed the shore line more distinctly. A short distance out from the land and directly in front of their boat stood the ugly protruding nose of a jagged boulder!

CHAPTER II

Uninvited Guests

For an instant Nancy panicked. Would the girls be able to steer clear of the menacing rocks? A collision seemed unavoidable!

"We'll be killed!" gasped Helen.

"Row to the left, Laura!" Nancy commanded. "It's our only chance."

With a burst of energy the rowers turned the boat and deftly avoided the jagged boulder. An oncoming wave pushed them farther out of danger.

"There's a cove ahead!" Laura shouted above the wind. "We'll try to make it."

In another five minutes they reached the cove. Here the water was comparatively quiet.

"Thank goodness!" Helen murmured. "Oh, you girls are wonderful!"

As Nancy's oar struck a sand bar, she dropped it and quickly stepped out into water up to her knees. Laura followed and the two girls pulled the boat up onto the beach. Then they helped Helen Corning step onto firm sand.

"How do your arms feel now?" Nancy asked her.

"Better," Helen replied. "But I'm freezing." Her teeth were chattering.

Nancy herself was cold. She squinted through the darkness and rain, trying to see where they were. It seemed to be a desolate spot.

"Where are we?" she asked Laura. "Is there some place nearby where we can sit out the storm and get warm?"

"The only place I know," Laura replied, "is a bungalow I passed a while ago as I was walking along the beach. It's to our right, secluded among the trees."

"Sounds fine," Nancy said. "Let's hurry!"

The three bedraggled girls stumbled along the beach. Water oozed from Laura's sandals. Nancy and Helen had kicked theirs off in the lake and now slipped and slid in their soggy socks.

Presently the girls reached a small, concealed building, a one-and-a-half-storied weather-beaten bungalow which stood a short distance from the water's edge. The upper level nestled into the steep, wooded hillside. Since there was no light inside, Nancy assumed no one was there. She knocked. No answer. Nancy tried to open the door. It was locked.

"Looks as if we're out of luck," said Helen.

But Nancy was not easily discouraged, and she knew it was imperative for the girls to get warm. Her father, a well-known lawyer, had trained her to be self-reliant. He frequently handled mystery cases, and Nancy had often helped him in unearthing valuable clues.

In addition, Nancy had solved some mystery cases on her own—one involving an old clock and another a haunted house. There, Nancy had aided its owners to discover a hidden staircase which led to the capture of the mansion's "ghost."

"I'm sure that the owner of this bungalow will forgive us for going in," Nancy said.

There was a small window to the right of the door. She tried it and found to her relief that it was unlocked.

"That's a lucky break," said Helen, as Nancy opened the window.

Fortunately, it was low enough to the ground for the girls to hoist themselves through easily.

"Whew!" Laura exclaimed, as the wind almost blew them inside. She helped Nancy close the window.

It was pitch dark inside the building. Nancy groped around for a light switch, finally found one, and flicked it on. A small bulb in the ceiling disclosed nothing except two canoes and a wooden bench which stood against one wall.

"Maybe it's only a boathouse," said Helen, flopping wearily onto the bench.

The girls noticed a narrow flight of stairs leading to the second floor.

"I wonder," Nancy mused, "if we might find something up there to wrap around us. Or maybe even some towels to dry ourselves off with. Let's see."

Laura followed Nancy to the rear of the building. Seeing a light switch for the upper story, Nancy turned it and the two girls climbed the steps. To their surprise, the second floor of the bungalow was furnished with two cots and blankets, a table and chairs, tiny refrigerator, a sink, and a two-burner electric stove.

"We're in luck!" Nancy exclaimed happily. "Come on up, Helen," she called.

Laura spotted an open closet in a corner of the room. It was well stocked with food. She held up a can of prepared cocoa.

"Under the circumstances," she said, "I doubt that the owner of this place would object if we made something warm to drink."

Helen and Nancy agreed. Within a short time the three girls had taken off their wet clothing and were wrapped in blankets. Laura had turned on one burner of the stove and made hot chocolate.

"Umm, this is good," Nancy said contentedly.

Both she and Helen again thanked Laura profusely for coming to their rescue, and said they had been trying to get back to the Pinecrest Motel.

"Are you staying there?" Laura questioned.

"For a week," Helen replied. "My Aunt June is coming tomorrow. She was supposed to ride up with us Thursday from River Heights where we live, but was detained. She's going to help design my dress for my marriage to Jim Archer. He's in Europe now on business for an oil company. When he returns to the States, we'll be married."

Nancy Drew asked Laura if she, too, was a summer visitor at the resort. When her question met with silence, Nancy was surprised to see tears gathering in Laura's eyes.

"I'm sorry, Laura," Nancy said instantly. "You've been through a terrible ordeal. You should be resting instead of talking."

"Of course," Helen agreed.

Laura blinked her eyes, then said soberly, "You don't understand. You see, my mother passed away a month ago and—" She could not continue.

Nancy impulsively put an arm around Laura's shoulders. "I do understand," she said, and told of losing her own mother at the age of three.

Helen added, "Nancy lives with her father, a lawyer, and Hannah Gruen, their housekeeper."

"I'm an orphan," Laura stated simply. "My father was in a boat accident nearly six years ago." She explained that Mr. Pendleton's sailboat had capsized during a storm. He had been alone and no one had been near enough to save him.

"That's why," Laura added, "I knew I had to save whoever was crying for help on the lake today. I love to walk in a storm."

Nancy and Helen felt their hearts go out to the parentless girl. Not only was Laura brave, but also she showed great strength of character.

"With whom are you staying now?" Nancy asked Laura.

The girl looked troubled. "I'm alone at the moment. I checked in at the Montewago Hotel just this morning. But my guardian Jacob Aborn and his wife Marian are to arrive some time this evening. They're taking me to their summer home at Melrose Lake. I believe it's near here."

"Yes, it is," Nancy said.

"Do you know the Aborns?" Helen asked.

Laura said that she did not remember the couple. Her mother had frequently spoken of them, however.

"Mr. Aborn is distantly related to my mother, and it was her request that he become my legal guardian in case of her death."

Laura gave a slight sob, then went on, "But no answer came from our lawyer's letter to Mr. Aborn, who was traveling."

"How strange!" Nancy remarked.

"Finally I wrote to Mr. and Mrs. Aborn myself at the Melrose Lake address," Laura said. "The truth was I needed some money as a down payment on tuition at the boarding school I attend."

"And they replied?" Nancy asked.

"Yes. Mr. Aborn told me to come here and he and his wife would meet me."

Helen interrupted. "Then everything's settled, so you should be happy."

The girl shook her head. "I feel I'm not wanted. The letter wasn't cordial. Oh dear, what shall I do?"

Nancy gave Laura a hug. "You'll be at school and during vacations you can visit friends. And you have a new friend named Nancy Drew!"

"Oh, Nancy, you're sweet." Laura smiled for the first time, but in a moment her mood became sad again. "Living that way isn't like having your own home. Mother and I had such wonderful times together." She brushed away a few tears.

Nancy wanted to learn more but saw by her waterproof watch that it was six o'clock. Laura would have to hurry off to meet her guardian. The sky was getting lighter and the rain had almost stopped.

"We'd better leave," she suggested to Helen and Laura.

The girls washed the cups and saucepan, dressed, and put the blankets where they had found them. Before leaving the bungalow, Nancy wrote a note of thanks to the owner, signing it "Three grateful girls."

As they were parting, Laura said, "If my guardians don't arrive I'll call you and arrange a date for tomorrow."

"Please do!" Nancy and Helen urged, and waved good-by.

When they reached the Pinecrest Motel, the two girls went at once to talk to Mr. Franklin, the manager. They told him about the sunken motorboat, expressing extreme regret, and assured him that their parents would pay for the craft.

"Don't worry about that," the manager said. "We have insurance which takes care of such accidents. I'm just glad you girls are all right."

At that moment a short, thin woman swaggered into the office. Her print dress was mud-splattered and she had lost the heel to one shoe. Her wet, bleached hair clung to her head in an unbecoming fashion.

Ignoring Nancy and Helen, who were still conversing with Mr. Franklin, the woman said bluntly, "Is there anyone here who can change a tire for me? I just had a flat half a mile away."

"I'm afraid not," Mr. Franklin apologized. "I'm busy in the office and most of the help are off this evening."

"That's great!" the woman said angrily. "What am I supposed to do—walk to the Montewago Hotel? I'm late already!"

Although Nancy thought the stranded motorist was being extremely rude, she, nevertheless, suggested that the woman telephone a nearby service station. "I'm sure they'll send someone out to help you."

This idea was received with a snort as sparks of annoyance flashed in the woman's pale-blue eyes. "I'll think about that!" she said sarcastically, and, turning, limped toward the telephone booth. She banged the door shut behind her.

The three spectators looked after her with disgust and Helen said, "Some people don't deserve a helping hand."

The irate stranger was still in the booth when Nancy and Helen went off to their room on the ground floor. After a bath and change of clothes the girls felt better. A tasty dinner in the restaurant restored their energy and they played shuffleboard under the floodlights.

The next morning, as the two friends dressed, Helen asked, "Do you think Laura Pendleton will call us?" Helen was putting on Bermuda shorts and a candy-striped blouse.

"I imagine so," said Nancy, "unless her guardian and his wife took her to Melrose Lake last night."

"How far is that from here?" Helen inquired.

Nancy consulted a road map. "About twenty-five miles," she replied. Then, as she was putting on loafers, someone knocked on the door. Nancy went to see who it was.

Laura Pendleton stood in the doorway. She looked very pretty in a becoming pink cotton dress. But the girl's eyes were shadowed and she seemed highly distressed.

"Oh, Nancy—Helen!" Laura exclaimed. "I just had to come see you as soon as I could!"

"We're glad you did," Nancy said. "Come in." Before she could continue, Laura flung herself on Helen's bed and started to sob.

"What's wrong, Laura?" Nancy asked in concern, going over to her.

Slowly the girl sat up and wiped away her tears with a handkerchief. She apologized for her behavior, then said, "I don't think I'm going to be happy living with the Aborns—at least not with Mrs. Aborn!"

Troubled, Nancy asked Laura whether the guardian and his wife had arrived the evening before.

"Only Mrs. Aborn," Laura replied. "She came to my room about an hour after I left you girls.

She was wet and in a very nasty mood. Apparently she'd had a flat tire on the road and was delayed in getting help from some gasoline station."

Nancy and Helen exchanged significant glances. Mrs. Aborn sounded like the woman they had met in Mr. Franklin's office!

"What does your guardian's wife look like, Laura?" Helen asked with interest.

"She's blond, small, and thin. And I guess she was terribly upset about all the trouble she'd had. I understood this and tried to make her comfortable in the extra bedroom, but—"

Laura went on to say that Mrs. Aborn, instead of calming down, had become even more unpleasant, blaming the girl for making it necessary for her to drive to Twin Lakes in the bad storm.

"She said that Mary, my mother, had spoiled me and that I was going to have to toe the mark in her home— Oh, what will I do?" Laura asked.

Nancy did not know, but said Mrs. Aborn's behavior was inexcusable. Then she asked whether Laura's mother had known the guardian's wife well.

Instead of replying to the question, Laura said absently, "Mrs. Aborn called my mother 'Mary.' But, Nancy, Mother's name was Marie!"

CHAPTER III

Strange Guardians

NANCY was almost certain now that she and Helen had met the unpleasant Mrs. Aborn the night before. The woman's quarrelsome mood had extended to Laura.

Aloud Helen said, "But don't forget it's no fun to have car trouble on a bad night. That is apt to make anyone cross."

"I suppose so," Laura conceded.

"How was Mrs. Aborn this morning?" Nancy asked.

Laura's face brightened somewhat as she admitted that the woman had been pleasant and charming. "Mrs. Aborn apologized for her actions last night and said both she and her husband could hardly wait for me to come and live with them."

"I see," said Nancy, but with inward reservations.

"I guess I'm being foolish to worry." Laura smiled. "Mrs. Aborn did say she had met Mother only once, so that could explain the name mix-up."

"Where is Mr. Aborn?" Helen asked.

"He's arriving after lunch today. He was detained on business."

Nancy was puzzled. The Aborns' behavior was unusual and thoughtless, she felt.

"Mrs. Aborn is having her hair set at the beauty parlor in the hotel," Laura explained. "She suggested that I take a taxi here this morning if I felt I had to see you two—which I insisted I did," Laura said, grinning cheerfully.

Suddenly Nancy smiled. "I'm starved." She asked Laura to have a second breakfast with her and Helen in the motel restaurant.

"And afterward," Helen went on, "let's ask Marty Malone—the girl we met yesterday, Nancy—to make a foursome in tennis."

"Great!" said Laura to both suggestions.

When the three girls stepped outside, Nancy took a deep breath of air. She loved the earthy smell of the forests surrounding the lake resort, particularly the scent of the tall pines.

"What a day!" she exclaimed. Only a few fleecy white clouds broke the clear blue sky.

"The weatherman must be on our side." Helen chuckled.

A little later Nancy lent Laura tennis clothes, and the girls went to meet Marty Malone. Soon the four were playing a lively set on the courts located behind the motel. Laura and Nancy, who were partners, won. Helen and Marty took the second set.

"You're a terrific player, Nancy!" Laura exclaimed, as she scored a point during set three.

"Thanks," Nancy said, as they changed courts for service. "Where did you learn to play so well?"

"Private lessons." Laura grimaced. "At boarding school. Mother insisted. Before her illness she was a great sportswoman."

When Nancy and Laura had won the third set, Laura called for time out. "I must go back to the hotel now," she said. "It's almost noon."

After Laura had changed her clothes, Nancy offered to drive her to the hotel. The three girls piled into Nancy's blue convertible. Ten minutes later they drew up in front of the spacious Montewago Hotel. It was several stories high and stood a long distance back from the main road. In front stretched a green lawn bordered by beds of multicolored gladioli, dahlias, and giant asters.

"It's beautiful!" Nancy commented, as Laura stepped from the car.

Helen pointed to an attractive outdoor swimming pool to the right of the hotel. It was filled with bathers. Laura said that there was also a riding stable behind the Montewago.

"There are a lot of families here," Laura said wistfully. "I wish I could stay." Then hastily she thanked Nancy for driving her over.

"I loved doing it," Nancy replied. "I hope we see each other again, Laura."

"So do I," Helen added.

Laura snapped her fingers. "I have a wonderful idea! Why don't you girls come back around three o'clock? You can meet my guardians. And if there's time, we can join the other young people at a tea dance scheduled for four."

"Fine!" Nancy said at once.

"Come directly to my room." Laura waved good-by.

Nancy detected a worried expression on Laura's face, and knew she hated the thought of meeting her strange new guardian.

The young sleuth was so quiet on the return trip that Helen said, "Penny for your thoughts, Nancy."

Her friend smiled. "I've concluded that the Pendletons must have been wealthy."

"What gives you that idea?"

"It's very expensive to live year round in New York hotels where Laura lived and she also mentioned boarding school. In addition," Nancy enumerated, "Laura's clothes have that simple but expensive look—you know what I mean."

"Yes," said Helen. "Well, if you're right, Mr. Aborn will control a great deal of money while he's managing Laura's affairs."

"In the case of a minor," said Nancy, "an inheritance is held in trust until she is twenty-one, Dad says. That's five years for Mr. Aborn. I hope he'll be a wise guardian."

She turned onto Lakeview Lane, a long, straight road bordered by woods. There were no homes along the way but a sign ahead advertised Sterling's real-estate office. Suddenly Nancy stopped.

"I think I'll run in here for a minute," she said, "and ask who owns that bungalow we helped ourselves to."

She walked into the office, introduced herself to Mr. Sterling, an elderly man, and told him the purpose of her call. The realtor grinned. "Any port in a storm is all right, I'm sure."

He said that the bungalow was owned by one of his clients. He had rented it a week before to a Mrs. Frank Marshall from Pittsburgh.

"I guess she fixed up the second floor," Mr. Sterling added. "She and her husband plan to use the place week ends. I'll pass the word along to Mrs. Marshall that you were there."

"I left a note but didn't sign it," Nancy said.

"Perhaps some time I'll stop in person and thank the Marshalls."

Returning to the car, she told Helen what she had learned. "Just for fun let's go out to the bungalow now."

A quarter of a mile farther on Nancy made a right-hand turn which brought them out on the lake drive. Below them, the girls could see the bungalow they had visited.

Suddenly a black foreign car pulled out of the lane that led down to the bungalow. Gaining speed, the automobile came toward Nancy's convertible.

"Watch out!" Helen yelled, jerking to attention as the vehicle passed and nearly sideswiped them.

Nancy slowed down and stopped. She looked back at the car which was almost out of sight. "Some drivers don't deserve a license," she said. "Do you suppose that was Mr. Marshall?"

Helen shrugged. "He wore a straw hat pulled low over his forehead. All I could see was the sleeve of his tan-and-white jacket."

"That's quite a bit," Nancy teased, "in so short a time."

Helen laughed. "Close association with you is making me more observant," she said.

When the girls reached the Pinecrest Motel, Helen exclaimed, "There's Aunt June!" While

Nancy parked, the dark-haired girl slipped from the convertible and hurried to the porch outside the room they occupied.

"Hello, Helen dear." The slim, stylishly dressed woman, with softly waved black hair, smiled at her niece.

Helen returned the greeting and gave her father's younger sister a kiss. "When did you arrive?" she asked. "Have you been waiting long?"

"No. I got here half an hour ago."

The attractive-looking woman was a buyer for a River Heights department store. She told Helen of a retailing problem which had prevented her departure with the girls, then turned to greet Nancy with enthusiasm.

"Isn't this a lovely spot?" Nancy remarked, and Aunt June Corning agreed that the view of the lake was superb.

After learning that Aunt June had not had lunch, the three went into the tearoom. When they had given their order, Miss Corning said, "I have some slightly bad news for you, Nancy."

"What's happened?"

"Well, just before I left River Heights, I phoned your housekeeper to see if she had any messages for you. To my surprise Dr. Darby answered. He said that Mrs. Gruen had sprained her ankle early this morning, and she must not walk for a couple of days."

"I'll call Dad right away and talk to him," said Nancy with concern.

"Wait!" Aunt June said. "Dr. Darby mentioned that your father left on a business trip today before the accident occurred."

"That means Hannah is all alone," Nancy said, rising. "I'll have to go home at once. Will you both excuse me for a minute, please?"

She went to a telephone booth and dialed the Drews' next-door neighbor, Mrs. Gleason. Nancy was relieved to hear that the woman's sister was taking care of Hannah for the afternoon. The housekeeper was in no pain and resting comfortably.

The young sleuth did some rapid thinking. If she left for River Heights late that afternoon she could still fulfill her promise to Laura to meet her guardian and arrive home in time to cook Hannah's supper.

"Will you please tell Mrs. Gruen I'll see her at six o'clock," Nancy requested, and Mrs. Gleason agreed to do this.

When Nancy returned to the others, Helen was telling her aunt of the adventure on the lake and Laura Pendleton's story.

"How dreadful for the girl!" exlaimed Miss Corning. "I feel very sorry for her."

Nancy now told of her plans to return home, and although Helen and her aunt were disappointed, they agreed that it was the right thing to do.

"But before I leave," said Nancy, "I want to meet Mr. and Mrs. Aborn."

After lunch Nancy packed her suitcase, put it in the car, and paid her motel bill. Soon it was time for her and Helen to leave for the Montewago Hotel.

"Are you sure you won't accompany us, Aunt June?" asked Helen.

Miss Corning shook her head. "I'm a little tired," she said, "and besides, I must unpack."

A short while later the two girls entered the Montewago lobby. Nancy made her way directly to the desk and after a brief wait was informed that Miss Pendleton would receive the girls in her suite. An elevator took them to the third floor.

Scarcely had they knocked on the door when Laura opened it. "Oh, I'm so glad you came," she cried out, smiling with relief.

Laura led the girls into a well-appointed living room with a bedroom on either side. As Nancy stepped inside, she saw a man and a woman seated in chairs near a picture window. In a glance Nancy realized that she and Helen had been right about Mrs. Aborn being the woman they had met the night before. Right now she looked more friendly.

Jacob Aborn arose and smiled graciously. He

was a well-built, somewhat stocky man in his early fifties. His face was square, and his small brown eyes were shifty.

When Laura introduced the girls, Mrs. Aborn rushed toward them. "Darlings!" she said, giving Helen and Nancy a butterfly peck on their cheeks. "You've been so good to poor Laura."

"Perfect bricks!" Mr. Aborn said gruffly. He extended a hand first to Nancy, then to Helen. "The reason I'm late in getting Laura is that I want everything to be perfect for her arrival at our Melrose Lake house."

Nancy was sure Mrs. Aborn recognized the callers and was embarrassed to admit it. They said nothing. There was an awkward silence until Laura said, "Well, let's all sit down."

For a few minutes everyone chatted generally, then Helen asked, "When are you leaving, Mr. Aborn?"

"In half an hour," was the reply. "Laura is tired and I want to get her settled before suppertime."

Mrs. Aborn broke in, "Yes, the poor child needs a lot of rest and good care."

Laura Pendleton seemed annoyed to be treated as a child and an invalid. "I'm fine," she stated defiantly. Turning to Nancy, she said quietly, "I'm afraid that we can't attend the hotel tea dance."

"That's all right," Nancy replied. She told of Hannah's accident and the fact that she must soon head for home.

"Are you all packed, Laura?" Mr. Aborn asked.

"Yes, except to get Mother's jewelry from the hotel safe."

"I'll do that for you, dear," Mrs. Aborn volunteered, rising. She smoothed her skirt restlessly.

Laura said, "Thank you, but I must present the receipt in person." She excused herself, saying she would be right back.

As Laura left the suite, Mr. Aborn turned to the two guests. "I wish Marie Pendleton had been a little more cautious with her inheritance from her husband," he confided.

"What do you mean?" Nancy asked.

"Laura is practically penniless," her guardian explained. "Mrs. Pendleton's illness and the way she lived took almost all her funds."

Nancy and Helen were surprised and dismayed to hear this.

"It doesn't matter, though," Mrs. Aborn said. "We have ample means to provide for Laura. She'll have everything she needs."

Nancy was confused by the woman's seemingly dual personality. She could be crude as on the evening before, or sweet as she appeared now. Perhaps, at heart, she meant well. Nancy hoped so for Laura's sake, but a strange feeling of distrust persisted.

When Laura returned, Helen and Nancy said they must be on their way. The friends shook hands.

"We never can thank you enough, Laura, for coming to our rescue yesterday," Helen said gratefully.

"That's right," Nancy agreed. "If you hadn't come along at that moment we'd probably be at the bottom of the lake!"

Laura shuddered. "Oh, I'm sure you would have reached shore some way! But I am glad I could help and it's been such fun knowing you. I hope you'll come to see me while I'm at Melrose Lake."

"We will," Nancy promised. "What is your address there?"

"Anyone can direct you to my house," Mr. Aborn said heartily. "It's well known in that section."

His wife tapped her foot on the floor. "Jacob, it's getting late," she hinted.

Nancy and Helen hastily bade the Aborns good-by and walked toward the door of the suite with Laura. Suddenly Helen turned around.

"It's lucky you brought two cars!" she called back. "Laura has a lot of luggage."

Without another word, Helen gave Laura a quick kiss and walked into the corridor. Nancy followed a moment later.

"Why did you say that?" Nancy questioned Helen as they rode down in the elevator.

The dark-haired girl signaled for silence. There were several other people in the car. When they stepped out into the lobby Nancy repeated her question.

Helen grabbed her chum's arm excitedly. "I couldn't resist it!" she exclaimed. "Jacob Aborn was the driver in the tan-and-white sports jacket I saw coming out of the road by the bungalow this morning! The driver of the black foreign car!"

CHAPTER IV

The Tree Crash

IF HELEN was right about Mr. Aborn's being the driver of the foreign car, then it should be in the hotel parking lot, Nancy thought.

"Let's take a look," she suggested.

The girls walked to the rear of the hotel where Nancy had left her own convertible. They scouted the lot. There was no sign of a black foreign car. Helen asked the attendant if one had been driven in that day. The man said no.

Helen was puzzled. "I was so sure I was right."

"You still could be," said Nancy. "The car may be parked somewhere else. Mrs. Aborn may have picked up her husband at some other point."

Puzzled, she and Helen climbed into the convertible and Nancy started the engine. As she drove back to the Pinecrest Motel, Helen remarked:

"I don't care for either Mr. or Mrs. Aborn. Their friendliness seems forced, and their promises don't ring true."

"I agree." Nancy nodded. "By the way, did you notice how Laura's guardian went out of his way to tell us she was penniless? And we were total strangers."

"I certainly did," Helen replied. "It was in very bad taste, I'd say."

"As soon as Hannah's ankle is better," Nancy declared, "I'm coming back here. Let's pay Laura a visit together at Melrose Lake. I feel very uneasy about her."

"A wonderful idea!" Helen exclaimed.

When they reached the motel, she got out. "I hope Hannah's foot improves quickly," she said, and waved Nancy out of sight.

A minute later Nancy was on the main highway which paralleled Twin Lakes for some distance. Presently, as she left the lake area, Nancy cast a speculative glance toward the sky. Did she imagine it or was it beginning to cloud over?

Nancy glanced at the speedometer. She was nearly halfway to River Heights. "Maybe I can get home before the storm breaks," she told herself.

A quarter of a mile farther on Nancy saw an obstruction in the road and brought the convertible to a halt. A huge sign read:

DETOUR. BRIDGE OUT. TAKE MELROSE LAKE ROAD. An arrow pointed to the left.

"Just when I'm in a hurry!" Nancy fumed, knowing she would have to go miles out of her way before reaching the River Heights road.

Another anxious glance at the sky told her there was no time to be lost. Already huge storm clouds were appearing.

"I'll be caught in another cloudburst like the one on the lake," she thought.

Hastily she headed the car down the Melrose Lake detour, a narrow, rutty road bordered with tall pines and thick shrubbery. Nancy was forced to reduce her speed to ten miles an hour, and even then it seemed as though the car would shake to pieces.

Within a few minutes it grew so dark that Nancy snapped on the headlights. Giant raindrops began to strike the windshield. In a short time they were followed by a blinding downpour, and the deep ruts in the road filled up like miniature streams.

"I'm in for it now," Nancy groaned, as the car crept up a hill.

Before she could reach a level stretch on the other side of the hill, the storm broke in all its fury. Trees along the roadside twisted and bent before the onslaughts of the rushing wind.

It was difficult for Nancy to see the road ahead.

She crawled along, endeavoring to keep the convertible's wheels out of deep ruts. As she swerved to avoid a particularly large puddle, a blinding tongue of lightning streaked directly in front of the car.

There was a flash of fire and simultaneously a deafening roar. For an instant, Nancy thought the car had been struck.

Almost blinded, the girl jammed on the brakes in time to hear a splintering, ripping noise. Before her horrified eyes a pine tree fell earthward. The convertible seemed to be directly in its line of fall!

"Oh!" Nancy gasped, as the tree missed her car by inches, landing directly in front of it.

Nancy felt as though she were frozen in her seat. How closely she had escaped possible death! When she was breathing normally again, Nancy ruefully surveyed the tree which blocked the road. What was she to do?

"I can't go back because the bridge is out," she told herself. "And there probably isn't anyone within miles of this place." She suddenly realized she had not seen another car going in either direction.

As Nancy continued to gaze at the fallen tree, she decided it could be moved by two people.

"Too bad I'm not twins," she thought. "I wonder how long it will be before someone comes past here."

Finally Nancy decided to try pulling the tree aside. She reached in the back seat for plastic boots and a raincoat with a hood. After putting these on, she stepped outside.

Gingerly picking her way through the mud and heavy rain, she walked to the fallen pine. She grasped the branches and tugged with all her might. The tree did not budge. Nancy next tried rolling it. This, too, she found was impossible.

"Oh, this is maddening," she thought, feeling completely frustrated.

As another low roll of thunder broke the quietness of the woods, Nancy was delighted to see headlights approaching. A moment later a small jeep pulled up behind her car.

The driver's door opened and a young man's voice said, "Hello there! Having trouble?"

"I sure am," said Nancy, as he walked toward her and stood outlined in the convertible's headlights. He appeared to be about seventeen, had dark hair, and twinkling eyes. Quickly Nancy explained about the fallen tree.

"Wow! You were lucky that it missed you!" the boy cried, then added, "It will be easy for the three of us to move the tree."

"Three?" Nancy questioned.

He laughed. "My sister's in the jeep," he explained, then called out, "Come on out, Cath!"

They were joined by a pretty girl, whom Nancy guessed to be fourteen years old. Introductions were exchanged. The brother and sister were Jim and Cathy Donnell. They lived off the next main highway and were returning home from visiting friends.

"I'm glad we came by," Cathy said. "There's only one house on this road and the people haven't moved in yet for the summer."

After Jim had pulled some tangled pine branches away from the convertible, he and the two girls were able to lift the trunk. Little by little they moved the tree far enough aside so that the cars could drive ahead.

"I'll report this to the highway patrol when we get home," said Jim.

"Thanks so much for your help," Nancy told the brother and sister. "By the way, do you know a Mr. and Mrs. Aborn who live at Melrose Lake?"

"We certainly do," said Cathy. "They're the ones whose house is on this route. It's a lovely place, with a lane leading to the house. You passed it about a mile back. The Aborns just bought the place."

"It's a small world," Nancy observed. She told the Donnells, however, that they were wrong

Nancy tried to pull the fallen tree aside

about the Aborns not being at their home, and explained about meeting the couple and Laura Pendleton at Twin Lakes.

"That's funny," said Jim. He explained that his parents had known the Aborns for years. "They used to have a place on the other side of the larger lake, and bought this new house only a month ago. They mentioned that Laura Pendleton was coming to visit them, but said they were taking an extensive trip first."

"I see," said Nancy, thinking, "Another strange angle to this thing!" Aloud she asked, "Is Mrs. Aborn a blond-haired woman, rather small and slight, Cathy?"

"Yes."

Jim said that he and Cathy must say good-by. Their parents would be worried if they did not arrive home soon.

"We'll tell Mother and Dad about the Aborns and Laura," said Jim. "We're all keen to meet Laura. The Aborns think she must be tops!"

"And we want to introduce Laura to our friends here at the lake," Cathy added.

"Grand!" Nancy said enthusiastically. "Laura has had a pretty sad time recently. She needs friends."

The three said good-by and got into their own cars. As Nancy drove on, she kept mulling over the Aborn-Pendleton enigma. She inferred from the Donnells' remarks that the man and his wife were very acceptable people. But Nancy certainly had not received this impression of them.

"I can't wait to meet them again," she thought, "and see how they're treating Laura."

By the time Nancy reached the end of the detour, the storm was over. A little later she turned into the Drews' driveway and parked near the front porch of the large red-brick house. She climbed from the car and made a dash for the porch with her suitcase.

As she inserted her key in the lock and pushed the front door open, a voice called out from the living room, "Nancy? Is that you?"

"Yes, Hannah. Be right in."

Nancy took off her raincoat and boots and put them in the vestibule closet. Then she hurried into the living room and hugged the motherly-looking woman, who was reclining on the sofa.

"Hannah! I'm so sorry about your ankle. How are you feeling?"

A worried expression faded from the housekeeper's face as she said, "I'm fine, now that you're home. This storm has been dreadful and I was concerned about you being on the road. Helen phoned that you were on your way."

Nancy told of the fallen tree at Melrose Lake, and how it had taken her longer than she had planned to make the trip.

"Goodness!" the housekeeper exclaimed. Then she smiled. "Nancy, you're like a cat with nine lives, the way you so often just miss being injured."

Nancy laughed. Then, becoming serious, she asked, "Where did Dad go?"

"To the state capital," Hannah replied, "and that reminds me, dear—you're to call Mr. Drew at eight tonight—" She gave Nancy a slip of paper with a telephone number on it.

"Did he say what he wanted?" Nancy inquired.

A look of concern appeared on Hannah's face as she said, "Mr. Drew wishes you to help him with an embezzlement case he's investigating!"

CHAPTER V

The Unexpected Prowler

AN EMBEZZLEMENT case! Nancy was excited. What, she wondered, did her father want her to do? The young detective longed to place a call to him immediately, but knew she must wait until eight o'clock.

"Where is Mrs. Gleason's sister?" she asked.

Hannah said that the woman had left a short while before, after hearing that Nancy would be home by suppertime.

"But first she fixed a chicken casserole dish for us," Hannah added. "It's all ready to pop in the oven. My dear, I hate to bother you—"

Nancy grinned mischievously and teased, "You mean you hate to have anyone else but you reign in your kitchen. Don't worry, Hannah, I'll be neat."

"Oh posh!" said Hannah. She blushed and gave Nancy a loving glance.

Humming softly, Nancy went to the modern pink-and-white kitchen. The casserole, which looked tempting, stood on one of the gleaming counter tops. After lighting the oven, Nancy placed the dish inside to heat.

She set two wooden trays with doilies, napkins, and silver. Then, after placing bread and butter on each, Nancy poured two glasses of milk. Lastly, she made a crisp salad of lettuce and tomatoes and marinated it with a tangy French dressing.

While waiting for the casserole, Nancy went back to the living room. Hannah was reading the evening paper.

"You're a wonderful help, dear," the housekeeper said gratefully, looking up. "Tell me, did you enjoy your vacation?"

"It was lovely," said Nancy, and described the resort. She then told Hannah of the adventure on Twin Lakes and of Laura Pendleton and the Aborns.

"Hannah, wouldn't it be nice if Laura could visit us sometime soon?"

"It certainly would."

By now their supper was ready and Nancy brought it in on the trays. After they had eaten, she put the dishes in the washer, then helped Hannah, who was using crutches, upstairs to bed.

Nancy then went out to put her car in the garage, and returned to the house just as the clock was striking eight. She went to place the call to Carson Drew.

Nancy looked at the series of numbers on the slip of paper Hannah had given her:

942 HA 5-4727

She dialed the long-distance number, and after one brief ring the phone on the other end was picked up.

"Hotel Williamston," the switchboard operator answered.

"May I speak with Mr. Carson Drew?" his daughter requested.

"One moment, please."

There was a pause, then the operator's voice said, "I'm sorry but Mr. Drew checked out this evening."

"Did he say where he was going?" Nancy inquired in amazement.

The desk clerk said no. Nancy thanked him and hung up, feeling oddly upset. It was unlike her father to change his plans without calling home to tell where he would be. Could anything have happened to him? she wondered.

Since Hannah was asleep, Nancy did not awaken her to discuss the matter. Leaving on a light in the lower hall, she went to her own room and unpacked, deep in thought. As she hung up her dresses in the closet the young sleuth wondered if her father might be following a new clue in another city.

Deciding that this probably was what had happened and that she would hear from her father the next morning, Nancy felt reassured, took a bath, and went to bed. She fell asleep almost immediately.

Several hours later Nancy was awakened by the sound of a dull thud. She sat up and groped for the bedside light. Turning it on, she got out of bed and slipped into her robe and slippers.

"I hope Hannah hasn't fallen out of bed," Nancy thought worriedly, and hurried down the carpeted hall to the housekeeper's room.

Peering in the bedroom door, Nancy saw that Hannah was sound asleep. Puzzled, Nancy went back to her own room. The girl detective had almost decided she had been dreaming, then she heard an even louder noise.

The creaky window in the ground-floor library was being opened! Someone was entering the house!

Alarmed, Nancy decided to call the police and tiptoed to the bedside telephone in Mr. Drew's room. When the sergeant answered, she told him she would unlock the front door.

Nancy tiptoed quietly down the stairs. Upon reaching the ground floor, she eyed the closed door of the library, located at the far end of the living room. Not a sound came from the library which Mr. Drew used as a study.

With bated breath Nancy moved toward the front door and opened it. At that instant the library door was flung open. A man's dark figure was outlined in the doorway. Nancy's heart skipped three beats.

As Nancy debated whether to run outdoors or upstairs, she heard a loud chuckle. At the same time, a table lamp was turned on.

"Dad!" cried Nancy in disbelief, as color flooded back into her face. "Is it really you?"

"Of course!" said Carson Drew, a tall, distinguished-looking man who right now seemed a little sheepish.

He placed the brief case he was carrying on a table, then walked toward Nancy with outstretched arms. His daughter rushed into them and gave Mr. Drew a loving kiss.

"You're the best-looking burglar I've ever seen!" Nancy declared, and told her father of fearing the house was being entered. Then she clapped a hand to her face. "The police! I notified the police when I heard the window creaking open."

At that very moment father and daughter heard a car stop outside. Two policemen rushed in.

"Where's the burglar?"

"Right here," Mr. Drew confessed. "I forgot my house key. Sorry to put you to this trouble."

The policemen grinned and one said, "I wish all our burglary cases were solved this easy!" A few minutes later the officers left.

Mr. Drew explained to Nancy that he had hesitated about ringing the doorbell and disturbing Mrs. Gruen and Nancy. Recalling that one of the windows in the library did not close completely and needed repair, he removed the screen and opened the window.

"I'm sorry I scared you. I flew home tonight rather unexpectedly and didn't have a chance to let you know, Nancy."

"Has there been a new development in your embezzlement case, Dad?" she inquired.

Mr. Drew nodded. "Yes, but since it's late I suggest we both go to bed. We can talk about it in the morning."

Nancy stifled a yawn. "Good idea," she agreed.

Father and daughter turned off the lights and went upstairs. Both slept soundly until eight o'clock the following morning when Nancy was awakened by Hannah.

"Get up, sleepyhead!" said the housekeeper. Teasingly she prodded Nancy's foot with the tip of a wooden crutch while leaning on another one. "It's a beautiful day!"

Nancy jerked awake, rubbing her eyes. "Hannah!" she gasped. "What are you doing up?"

The housekeeper smiled. "One day of staying off my feet will keep me well for a year," she declared. "Besides, I feel fine this morning."

"But Dr. Darby said—" Nancy began.

"Stuff and nonsense!" Hannah replied tartly. "He left me these crutches to use and that's what I intend to do with them. Nancy, is your father home? I noticed his door is closed."

"Yes, Hannah." Nancy related the burglar scare.

The housekeeper smiled in amusement. Then, with a swish of her skirt, she turned and clumped out of the room. She paused at the door, winked at Nancy, and said:

"Pancakes and sausage at eight-thirty—and you tell your dad that I'm going to squeeze some extra-juicy oranges."

Mr. Drew was awake also. Nancy could hear the buzz of his electric razor! It was good, she thought, for the little family to be home again.

In half an hour they were seated in the cheerful breakfast room. As they began to eat, Mr. Drew caught up on the latest news and listened with concern to the story of Nancy's two storm adventures.

"I'm grateful that you're here safely beside me," he said gravely.

When the lawyer heard about Laura Pendleton and the Aborns, he frowned. "I agree with you, Nancy, it does sound strange," he said. "But you should not interfere with Laura and her guardians unless she asks you to. They may turn out to be very nice people."

"I agree," said Hannah, then added pointedly, "But if things should prove otherwise, Mr. Drew?"

"Then I'd be happy to help Laura have another guardian appointed by the court," the lawyer replied. "In the meantime, Nancy, let's invite Laura to spend a few days with us very soon."

Nancy beamed. "Thanks, Dad. That's just what I wanted to do."

When the meal was finished and the dishes had been put in the washer, Mr. Drew and Nancy went to his study, a comfortable room with book-lined shelves, deep-seated leather chairs, and a wide, highly polished mahogany desk.

Nancy sat down in a yellow club chair, then said eagerly, "Come on, Dad, don't hold out on me any longer about this case of yours."

Mr. Drew smiled, and absently fingered a glass paperweight. Sitting down, he began to talk.

Mr. Drew's client, a Mr. Seward, was the president of the Monroe National Bank in Monroe. It had branches throughout the country, including one in River Heights. During a recent audit, many valuable securities had been discovered missing from the main bank's vault. Most of the securities were bonds which read "Payable to Bearer."

"How dreadful!" said Nancy. "It means that whoever has the bonds can cash them."

"That's right." Mr. Drew said that the bonds belonged to various bank clients throughout the country. In all cases the clients had inherited money and had asked the bank as custodian to invest it for them. A Mr. Hamilton was put in charge. This was a very common bank procedure: the bank made the investments and paid the dividends to the individual, thus relieving the person of handling his own transactions.

"I was called in on the case," Carson Drew said, "by Mr. Sill, manager of our River Heights branch, when Mr. Seward advised him that a number of the missing securities belong to residents in our community. Mr. Seward felt this was an odd coincidence."

"It is," Nancy agreed. "Have you any idea who might have taken the property?"

Mr. Drew said no. So far the evidence pointed to Mr. Hamilton, although the man was a highly trusted officer.

"What about the people who work in the vault?" Nancy asked, wrinkling her forehead.

"They're being checked on now. Most of these

employees have worked for the bank a long time, however. At present two of them are on vacation, so the investigation may take some time."

"Couldn't you find out where they went?" Nancy asked.

"We've tried that," her father replied, "but they're not at their homes and the neighbors don't know where they're vacationing. We'll just have to wait until the men get home."

"I see," Nancy agreed.

"The main thing is," said Mr. Drew, "that Mr. Seward doesn't want any publicity about the theft. The bank will continue to pay dividends to the security holders, of course. My assignment is to find the missing property and the guilty person."

"A big order," said Nancy. "How are you going to do this?"

Carson Drew said he was presently checking on employees other than Hamilton who worked in the custodian department. Also, he was trying to find out if there might be a tie-in between the thief and one or more of the persons whose property was missing.

"There must be several people behind this theft," the lawyer explained. "It's pretty difficult in these times to rob a bank, with all the security measures they employ. Nothing is impossible, however, if a plan is well worked out."

"Sounds like an exciting case, Dad," said Nancy. "What can I do to help?"

In reply Mr. Drew gave Nancy a slip of paper with four names on it and their corresponding River Heights addresses. They were: Mrs. William Farley, Mr. Herbert Brown, Mrs. John Stewart, Mr. Stephen Dowd. None of the names was familiar to the young detective.

"These are the local people whose securities are missing," Mr. Drew said. "Think of some reason to meet these people," he directed. "See what kind of homes they have, and try to get an insight into their characters. This is a very vague assignment, but I feel you may find out something incriminating about one of them—you see, we have to be very careful not to arouse suspicion in a case of this type."

"I'll do my best," Nancy assured him.

"The out-of-town names I'll check myself," her father explained. "They live in various large cities around the country, so I'll have to be away a good bit during the next few weeks."

"I'll get busy on these names right away," Nancy said. She gave her father a quick hug. "You're an old dear to let me help you!"

"Promise me you'll be careful," the lawyer warned. "An embezzler can be a dangerous person. And in this case whoever is behind the thefts is playing for big stakes."

The young sleuth said she would take every precaution. As Nancy stood up, the telephone rang.

"I'll get it, Dad," she offered, and hurried to pick up the receiver of the hall phone.

A low-pitched feminine voice said tersely, "Nancy? Nancy Drew?"

"Yes. This is Nancy speaking."

As she held on, waiting for the caller's identification, she heard sounds of a scuffle on the other end of the receiver. This was followed by a cry of pain and a loud *crash!*

CHAPTER VI

An Invitation to Sleuth

"WHO is this?" Nancy asked.

But the caller had cut off the connection. What had happened to her? Nancy wondered. Certainly she had sounded very distressed. Nancy hung up and waited for a second call, but the phone did not ring.

"Who was it?" Mr. Drew asked, coming into the hall.

Nancy told what had occurred.

"You didn't recognize the voice?" he remarked.

"No, so I can't call back. Oh dear, someone is in trouble, I just know it. And here I stand helpless to do a thing! It's maddening!"

"It certainly is," her father said. "Well, dear, I must run down to the office." Presently he left the house.

After seeing that Hannah was comfortable, Nancy went to her bedroom and thoughtfully opened the closet door.

"This is as good a day as any to start Dad's investigation," she thought.

Nancy took out a two-piece navy-blue dress which made her look older than her eighteen years. Next, she found a pair of comfortable low-heeled pumps.

For several minutes Nancy experimented with various hair styles. She finally chose a simple off-the-face arrangement. Nancy put on tiny pearl earrings, dusted her nose lightly with powder, and finally added a dash of lipstick.

After she had changed her clothes and given herself a final appraisal, Nancy went to Hannah's room to tell her she was going out for a while.

"Gracious, Nancy," said the housekeeper, giving the girl a sharp glance, "you look awfully businesslike today. Where are you going?"

"Dad asked me to look up something for him," she said. "I'll be back in time for lunch."

"Don't worry about that," said Hannah. "I can get around. Have a good time, dear."

When Nancy left the house she consulted the list Mr. Drew had given her. Mrs. William Farley, the first name on the paper, lived on Acorn Street, seven blocks from the Drew residence.

Nancy set out at a brisk pace, rehearsing in her

mind the approach on which she had decided. One of the girl's favorite community projects was a recreational youth center located in downtown River Heights. The center always needed volunteer helpers as well as entertainers for the children.

"A good way to find out something about Dad's suspects," Nancy decided, "is to see how they will respond to a needy cause. And I'll be telling the truth when I say that I'm working for the organization."

This resolved, Nancy soon reached a modest white house which was set back from the street a short distance. The front walk was outlined with pink and white petunias and the grass was well tended.

Nancy rang the bell. The door was opened almost immediately by an elderly woman with wavy white hair and the greenest, most alert, eyes Nancy had ever seen.

"Yes?" she inquired pleasantly.

Nancy introduced herself, then explained the purpose of her call. She was invited inside.

"Please be seated," said the woman, sitting down herself. Nancy chose a Duncan Phyfe rocking chair covered with a black floral print.

The hostess smiled. "I'd be glad to help you with your project, my dear," she said, "although I have no talent. Also, I don't leave this house very much. I'm a recent widow, you see, and I haven't been too well lately."

Nancy expressed sympathy and said she understood completely. She liked this friendly little woman on first sight.

"Would a small check help your cause?" the widow asked. "Perhaps you could buy some equipment for the children."

"That would be wonderful," Nancy said. "But I'm not soliciting funds."

Mrs. Farley smiled shyly. "I realize this," she said. "But there's so little I can do to help others. Mr. Farley left most of his estate, which was modest, in trust. And I have only a tiny income to live on."

The woman arose, and despite Nancy's protests, went to the desk where she wrote out a check.

Nancy thanked her profusely, for she realized that this was a sacrifice on the widow's part.

"I'm glad I can help," said Mrs. Farley. "Please come see me again and tell me how the youth center is coming along."

Nancy promised to do this. After a few more minutes of conversation, she bade Mrs. Farley good-by and left the house.

"If I'm a judge of human nature," thought Nancy, "that woman never did a mean thing in her life!"

When she reached the sidewalk, Nancy took out Mr. Drew's list from her handbag. Thoughtfully she crossed out Mrs. Farley's name.

Herbert Brown, the next suspect, lived in River Heights Estates, a rather exclusive housing area located on the outskirts of the city.

"It's kind of a long walk," Nancy told herself. "But it will do me good."

As Nancy strolled along, she was so engrossed with her thoughts that she failed to notice a tan sedan whose driver cruised by, honked the horn, then pulled over to the curb.

As the door opened, a good-looking young man about eighteen called, "Hi, Nancy!"

To her surprise, she saw Don Cameron, who had been a fellow student in River Heights High School. Nancy had, in fact, gone to the Spring Prom with the tall, black-haired boy.

"Hello, Don," she said. "What are you doing home? I thought you were working on your uncle's farm this summer before going to college."

Don grinned engagingly. "I've been picking string beans and berries and hoeing potatoes for nearly a month," he replied. "But I have a leave of absence to attend my sister's wedding this Friday."

Nancy had read of Janet Cameron's wedding plans in the *River Heights Gazette* two weeks before. "Jan must be excited!" she exclaimed.

"Everyone at home is going 'round in circles," Don stated, laughing. "Bill Bent, my brother-in-law-to-be, is no better.

"By the way, Nancy," Don continued, "I intended calling you later today. If you're free Thursday afternoon and evening I'd like to have you go to a barbecue party with me. It's being given in honor of Jan and Bill."

"I'd love to," said Nancy. "Where will it be?"

"At the Herbert Browns' home in River Heights Estates," Don said. "Their daughter, Lynn, is Jan's maid of honor."

Herbert Brown! One of the possible suspects in the bank security theft! Nancy could scarcely conceal her excitement. Although she did not like the idea of spying on a host, here was an excellent chance for her to find out what Mr. Brown was like.

"What time does the barbecue begin?" Nancy asked.

"I'll call for you at four," said Don.

He offered to drive Nancy home, and she hopped in beside him. When the young sleuth entered the house, she found Hannah in the living room.

"My goodness," the housekeeper exclaimed, "you haven't solved the mystery already!"

"I gave up," Nancy teased.

"What!"

With a grin Nancy told why she had postponed her trip. "I'll get some lunch for us," Nancy offered, "and then drive to the other two places on the list."

Hannah chuckled. "Since you said you'd be home," she said, "I prepared a fresh fruit salad—it's in the refrigerator. And rolls ready to pop into the oven."

"You're a fine patient!" Nancy scolded.

"I feel better keeping busy," Hannah countered.

Nancy asked whether there had been any telephone calls in her absence.

"No. But you did get a post card in the mail."

Nancy went to the mail tray in the hall and recognized Helen Corning's writing. The message read:

Dear Nancy:

Aunt June and I have decided to take a week's automobile trip up North. Will return directly to River Heights. Plan to stop and see Laura Pendleton on our way. Hope Hannah is better.

Love,
Helen

Nancy read the card aloud and commented, "I hope Helen lets me know how everything is at the Aborns' home. Anyway, I'm going to call

Laura myself in a few days to find out how she is and make a date with her to come here."

"Do you think her guardian will let her leave his care so soon?" the housekeeper asked, as she reached for her crutches.

When there was no reply, Hannah looked out toward the hall. Nancy's normally rosy complexion was deadly white. She looked as if she were about to faint!

CHAPTER VII

A Startling Assignment

"NANCY! Nancy! What's wrong with you?" Hannah cried out, as she tried to hurry to the girl's side.

As the housekeeper limped toward her, Nancy snapped to attention. "I'm all right, Hannah," she said. "But Helen's post card—it brought back the phone call I had this morning—"

Nancy told Mrs. Gruen about the call which had ended so abruptly with a cry of pain. "The caller's voice sounded vaguely familiar, but I couldn't place it," she explained. "Now I think I know who it was."

"Who?" said Hannah.

"Laura Pendleton! I believe someone was trying to stop her from talking to me!"

"Mercy!" Hannah exclaimed, sinking weakly into a soft chair. "Do you think it was one of the

Aborns, Nancy? And why would they do such a thing?"

Nancy shrugged. "I'm going to call the Aborn home right now."

While Hannah listened nervously, Nancy picked up the phone and dialed Information. When the operator replied, Nancy asked for Jacob Aborn's number.

The operator cut off for a minute, then reported, "I'm sorry, miss, but that number has been temporarily disconnected!"

"Can you tell me when this was done?" Nancy requested tersely.

"I'm sorry. I have no further information."

Nancy thanked the operator and hung up.

"It sounds suspicious," Hannah remarked, "but, Nancy, the Aborns may have changed their plans and gone away with Laura for a vacation somewhere else."

"I know one way to find out," said Nancy with determination. She reminded Hannah of the young couple, Cathy and Jim Donnell, who had helped move the fallen tree at Melrose Lake.

"I'll ask them if they've seen Laura or the Aborns," Nancy explained.

Hannah sighed. "You're just like your father," she said, "and he certainly is astute. But I'm worried that you're becoming involved in another complicated mystery."

Nancy tweaked Hannah's cheek. "The more there are, the better I like them!"

The housekeeper smiled. She said that while Nancy was calling Cathy and Jim she would put lunch on the table.

"Fine. I'll help you in a moment."

As Hannah hobbled to the kitchen, Nancy got the Donnells' number and dialed it. After two rings a girl's voice said, "Hello!"

"Cathy?" Nancy inquired.

"Yes."

Nancy gave her name. "Do you remember me?" she asked.

"Of course," said Cathy. "My family and I were talking about you just a short while ago. Jim and I told them about the Aborns' being home and we all went over this morning to say hello and meet Laura. But the house was closed. Nobody's staying there."

"Oh!" said Nancy, disappointed. She explained that this was her reason for calling, and told of the Aborns' telephone having been disconnected.

Cathy already knew this, and added, "Dad found a note on the back porch telling the milkman to discontinue deliveries until further notice."

"Cathy, does Mr. Aborn own a foreign make of car?" Nancy queried.

"Why, no," Cathy replied. She added that her

parents thought the Aborns might have planned suddenly to take a short trip somewhere. "I'm sure that we'll hear from them in a few days. If we do, I'll call you, Nancy."

"Fine," said the young detective. "Remember me to Jim. Good-by."

Deeply troubled, Nancy went to the kitchen and told Hannah what Cathy had said.

"Chances are," said the housekeeper, "the call you received this morning was not from Laura at all. You know a lot of people, dear."

Nancy replied that usually when someone had to break a telephone conversation in an abrupt manner the person called back as soon as possible to explain what had happened.

"That's true," Hannah admitted. "It's very strange."

After lunch Hannah said she was going next door to visit with Mrs. Gleason. Nancy helped her to the neighbor's front porch. Then Nancy backed her convertible from the garage and headed for Mr. Drew's downtown office.

"I'll report my progress so far regarding his suspects."

Nancy parked the car in a lot adjoining a large building where lawyers, doctors, and other professional people had offices. Mr. Drew's suite was on the fifth floor. A few minutes later Nancy greeted her father's secretary, Miss Hanson.

"My, how pretty you look, Nancy!" said the efficient young woman, who had been with Carson Drew for the past five years.

"Thank you." Nancy blushed a trifle. "You look lovely yourself."

When the lawyer learned that his daughter had arrived, Carson Drew at once asked Nancy to come into his office.

"I can see by the gleam in your eyes, Nancy, that you have some information for me."

Nancy told him of her interview with Mrs. Farley. "In my opinion, she's a woman of very fine character." Then Nancy mentioned the invitation to the barbecue party at Mr. Herbert Brown's home.

Mr. Drew raised his eyes and chuckled. "Better than I expected."

"My main reason for coming was to tell you something else," Nancy said.

She quickly reviewed the latest developments in the Laura Pendleton case. Mr. Drew listened quietly. Finally he said:

"There's something odd about all this. Nancy, I must leave River Heights on the three-o'clock plane this afternoon for Cincinnati, but I'll be home by Sunday. Why don't we plan to drive to the Aborns' home later that afternoon and see for ourselves what the story is? They may have returned by then."

"That's a grand idea!" Nancy exclaimed. Then, knowing that he was busy, she kissed her father good-by and wished him a successful trip.

"I'll call you every night at eight!" Mr. Drew promised, and Nancy left the office.

On the way down in the elevator, Nancy asked Hank, the operator, if he knew where Hilo Street was located. Mrs. John Stewart, the third suspect, lived in an apartment at this address.

"I know the general area," Nancy added. "It's about three miles from here on the eastern side of the city."

"That's right," Hank said. "It's a classy neighborhood! All high-priced apartment buildings. I believe Hilo Street runs off East Main."

Nancy thanked him, then went to her convertible. She drove carefully through the city traffic and finally reached Hilo Street. Mrs. Stewart's apartment house was Number 76.

Nancy scanned the buildings and found that this one was the largest on the street. It was ultramodern in design and about twenty stories high. After parking her car, she smoothed her hair and got out.

A red-coated doorman nodded pleasantly to the young detective as she entered the building a minute later. Nancy checked the directory and saw that Mrs. Stewart was in Apartment Three on the fourth floor. She rang the elevator button.

Almost instantly, aluminum doors slid open noiselessly, and Nancy stepped inside the carpeted elevator. It was self-operated, and Nancy pushed the fourth-floor control.

Her heart was pounding with excitement. Would Mrs. Stewart prove to be a link in the embezzlement case? Nancy hoped to find a clue this time!

When the elevator stopped at the fourth floor, Nancy got out and easily located Apartment Three. She pressed the doorbell.

A trim-looking maid, a rather harassed expression on her pretty face, opened the door immediately. "Oh, hello!" she said. "You must be the walker."

"Why, no—" Nancy began, but before she could explain, the maid went into the living room, leaving the door ajar.

As Nancy, speechless, glanced hastily into the apartment beyond, the maid reappeared. She was leading a pair of frisky black-and-white French poodles by a gold-linked leash.

"Here!" she said abruptly, thrusting the leash into Nancy's hand. "Their names are Irene and Frederika. Mrs. Stewart says to take them for a nice, long walk!"

Before Nancy could utter a word, the door was closed with an emphatic bang!

CHAPTER VIII

The Frightened Runaway

NANCY DREW, dog tender! This was a new title, the young detective thought. As she burst into laughter, the two poodles began to yap excitedly and dance around in little circles.

"Hello, girls," Nancy said to them, and bent down to pat the friendly animals. She then rang the doorbell with determination.

This time the door was opened by a tremendously stout woman whose chubby face was framed by a mass of fuzzy brown curls.

"Yes?" she inquired coyly. "Have you had some trouble with the babies? I told Collette to give you explicit instructions."

Nancy smothered a giggle. "Are you Mrs. Stewart?" she asked briskly.

"Of course," the woman said impatiently.

Nancy introduced herself and said that a mistake had been made. She was not the dog walker, but had come to solicit Mrs. Stewart's aid for the River Heights Youth Center.

"Oh dear!" Mrs. Stewart blushed, obviously flustered. "Collette's made a mistake. I'm sorry." She jerked the leash from Nancy and gave the poodles a loving glance. "Mama will give you both cookies while we wait for your real walker."

Nancy cleared her throat and Mrs. Stewart's glance returned to the caller. "Oh, yes—your project. I'm afraid that we'll have to discuss it another time. I'm having an afternoon musicale featuring the most divine violinist—Professor Le Bojo. He is expected any moment—"

"I understand," Nancy nodded. "Perhaps I can return later when Mr. Stewart is home?"

"He left today for a fishing trip in Maine," Mrs. Stewart replied. She added somewhat angrily, "I simply don't understand Gerald—he doesn't appreciate our home life here with the children!" Her glance swept toward the poodles.

Nancy managed to keep a straight face, said good-by to Mrs. Stewart, and left. When she returned to her car Nancy reached the conclusion that Mrs. Stewart was hardly the type to plan a bank swindle!

"Her poor husband," Nancy thought with a laugh.

There was only one more name for Nancy to check today—Mr. Stephen Dowd. She drove out Hilo Street and headed across the city. The man's address was in a business zone which was partly residential, although most of the homes were two-family dwellings.

After a little difficulty, Nancy found the house she sought—a brown duplex situated between a gasoline station and a tailor shop. She parked and went up the walk. Mr. Dowd's half of the house was on the right-hand side.

The young sleuth rang the bell and waited. No answer. She pushed the button again. Still no one came to the door.

"Maybe I can find out something from his next-door neighbor," Nancy thought hopefully.

As she was about to ring the bell on the left, the door was opened by a young woman, a shopping bag in her hand. She appeared startled to see Nancy.

The young sleuth smiled pleasantly. "I came to call on Mr. Dowd," she explained. "He's probably at work?"

"No. Mr. and Mrs. Dowd are both away now—on tour with a show, they said. They board here. I'm Mrs. Wyman."

"Are they entertainers?" Nancy inquired with interest, and explained about the youth center.

Mrs. Wyman said the couple were actors, but

she did not know what parts they played. "Since moving here two months ago, they've been away a great deal of the time."

Nancy thanked Mrs. Wyman and said she would call again. "They sound like the type of people I'm looking for to help amuse the children," she explained.

Nancy drove away, but told herself they would bear further investigation. It seemed unnatural that they would not have told what parts they were playing.

Nancy felt a little discouraged about her findings so far. She realized that she could do nothing else until she met Herbert Brown the next afternoon.

"I think I'll go home, get my bathing suit, and head for the club," she decided. The day was becoming very warm.

Fifteen minutes later Nancy parked in her driveway. As she was about to insert her key in the front lock, the door was opened from inside.

Laura Pendleton, wan and disheveled, stared at the young detective!

"Laura!" Nancy gasped. She could hardly believe her eyes.

"Hello, Nancy," her friend said, as Hannah Gruen came into view, walking slowly on her crutches.

"Come in, Nancy," the housekeeper invited

urgently. "Laura's been waiting for you over an hour. She's terribly upset—"

The three went into the living room and Nancy sat down on the couch beside the visitor. Before Nancy could ask why she was in River Heights, Laura burst into tears.

"Oh, I'm so unhappy!" she sobbed. "That's why I ran away!"

Nancy gently stroked Laura's hair and waited for the hysterical girl to calm down. Then she said quietly, "Tell me everything that has happened since I saw you last."

Slowly Laura started to speak. After Nancy and Helen had left the hotel suite, Mr. Aborn said he had to attend to some business for a short while. He had left the hotel. Meanwhile, Laura and Mrs. Aborn had checked out and waited for the guardian in his blue sedan, which was parked in the hotel lot.

"Where did Mr. Aborn go?" asked Nancy.

"I don't know, but when he met us a short while later he was carrying a brief case. As we started toward Melrose Lake, Mrs. Aborn asked what I had done with Mother's jewelry. When I said it was in my handbag she asked me to give it to her for safekeeping. I said I would when we got home."

"Then you *did* go directly to Melrose Lake?" Nancy questioned.

"Yes," Laura replied. She hesitated, then went on with her story. "The Aborns showed me to my room and I started to unpack.

"I found I needed more hangers," the girl went on, "but when I went to the door to ask Mrs. Aborn for them, I discovered it was locked on the outside."

"Locked!" Hannah gasped and Nancy was shocked.

Laura nodded. "I was so frightened," she said, "that at first I didn't know what to do. Then I heard voices coming from the Aborns' room. I lay down on the floor so I could hear them better and listened.

"Marian Aborn said, 'What did you lock her in for—she doesn't know anything!' and my guardian replied, 'Not yet, but she's a smart kid. See if you can gain her confidence and get hold of the jewels.' "

As Laura paused, a terrible thought came to Nancy. Were the Aborns *thieves?* But they could not be, she argued, if Marie Pendleton had trusted the couple to take care of her daughter. "And besides, I gather the Donnells think they are nice people." Aloud she asked, "What happened next?"

"I thought I must have heard them wrong," the auburn-haired girl said slowly, "but I suddenly remembered Mother telling me always to take good care of her jewelry. So I took it from my handbag and hid it underneath the mattress of the bed.

"Just as I finished doing this, the door to my room opened. Mrs. Aborn stood there, looking very friendly. She offered to help unpack my bags, and admired several dresses as I hung them in the closet—"

"And then—" Nancy pressed.

Laura said that she and Mrs. Aborn had prepared a tasty dinner, then she and the couple had watched television for a while.

"Just before we went upstairs to bed, Mrs. Aborn said it would be a good idea for me to put my mother's jewels in the wall safe in the living room. I agreed and said that I would give them to her in the morning."

"What was Mrs. Aborn's reaction to this?" Hannah asked.

"Oh, both she and her husband became very angry. They said that apparently I didn't trust them to take care of a few insignificant gems, while they in turn had the responsibility of caring for a penniless orphan! Oh, Nancy, I thought Mother had a lot of money! Mrs. Aborn yelled at me and said I was ungrateful and a big burden to them. They were sorry they had ever agreed to take me!

"I can't explain how I felt," Laura went on, her

hands shaking with nervousness. "I was just numb. Then I burst into tears and rushed to my room."

Laura said that finally she had fallen asleep and awakened this morning to find she was again locked in.

"At eight o'clock Mrs. Aborn opened the door, acting very friendly, and said breakfast was ready in the kitchen."

"Was anything said about last night?" Nancy asked.

Laura said no, that the Aborns had acted as though nothing had happened. "But a strange thing occurred after breakfast," Laura stated. "Mr. Aborn took a small package from the refrigerator and left the house, saying he would be back later. Before he went he said I would be sorry if I didn't co-operate with them!"

"I presume he meant to hand over the jewels," Hannah guessed, and Laura nodded.

"I knew then that I had to leave their house and also get word to Nancy. While Mrs. Aborn was emptying the rubbish I tried to use the phone, but she caught me and twisted my arm, then hung up the receiver!"

"You see, I was right, Hannah!" Nancy exclaimed, and told Laura her theory about the call.

"Were you locked up again?" Hannah asked.

Laura explained that before Mrs. Aborn could do this she had run past her and barricaded herself inside the bedroom, not wanting the jewels to be unguarded. At that moment the doorbell had rung. Apparently Mrs. Aborn had not answered it, for the woman had kept quiet for a long while on the first floor.

"So I quickly took my handbag and the jewels, and climbed down a trellis outside my window," Laura said. "Once I was on the detour I was lucky enough to get a ride to the highway and there I caught a bus to River Heights. I took a taxi to your house."

As Laura sat back with an exhausted sigh, Hannah stood up. "You're worn out, dear," the housekeeper said. "I'm going to get you a cup of hot tea and you're not to say another word until you've drunk it!"

With that, she bustled out of the room and returned shortly with a small tray on which was a cup of hot tea and a piece of toast. By the time Laura had finished the snack, color had returned to her cheeks and she looked more relaxed.

"I wonder if we should report your experience to the police," Nancy mused.

"What could we tell them?" Laura quavered.

"That's the point," Nancy continued. "We could tell them that the Aborns tried to get your jewels, but of course they would deny it all. It would be their word against yours."

"And I don't have definite proof!" Laura said dejectedly.

Nancy patted the girl's hand. "We'll do everything we can to help you, Laura. You've really had a terrible experience, you poor girl."

"Nancy, you're a real friend," Laura said. Tears came into her eyes. "Mr. Aborn is my legal guardian—I saw the papers—but what am I going to do?"

"You'll stay with us," Hannah said quickly, "and when Mr. Drew comes home he'll know how to handle the situation."

Nancy was quiet, but she was doing a lot of figuring. Something mysterious was going on at Melrose Lake. She intended to find out for herself what it was.

CHAPTER IX

A Valuable Inheritance

IF IT had been possible Nancy would have started out for Melrose Lake at once, but she felt that Laura needed her. Besides, there was a job to do for her father at the Browns' barbecue next day.

"Helping Dad comes first," Nancy decided.

Laura spoke again of her mother's affairs. "She used to say I'd always be financially independent if anything happened to her."

"We'll find out," Nancy said, and then took Laura upstairs so she might shower and rest.

In the meantime, Nancy selected some of her own clothes for the visitor. When she appeared at the dinner table, Hannah declared that Laura looked pretty as a picture and much more relaxed.

"I am—thanks to both of you," their guest said gratefully.

When the meal was finished the two girls sat out on the Drews' porch. To cheer up her guest, Nancy told Laura of her funny experience with the French poodles, while trying to get volunteers for the youth center. The young detective did not mention her real reason for calling at the apartment.

Laura giggled. "I wish I could have been with you," she said. "Tell me, Nancy, have you any souvenirs of the mysteries you've solved?"

"Two trophies." Nancy displayed a mantel clock and a valuable silver urn. Laughingly she told Laura that her father often said she would have the house cluttered before she finished her career!

Just then the telephone rang and Hannah called from upstairs that Mr. Drew was on the line. Nancy hurried to talk with him.

"Nancy, I've come across some evidence that indicates Mr. Hamilton, or some person working for him in the trust department, was behind the security thefts. A detective is tailing Hamilton, and if he tries to leave town, the Monroe police will be notified."

"How about the others in his department?" Nancy asked.

"They're being watched, too, but not so steadily. Of course we don't want to arrest an innocent man."

Nancy said she hoped the guilty person would make a misstep soon so the case might be solved, and told her father what she had learned of the River Heights suspects since she had seen him.

He suggested that she keep trying to contact the Dowds. "And that reminds me," the lawyer said. "You can forget about Mr. Herbert Brown being suspicious." He explained that Brown was a personal friend of the bank president's and had been cleared.

Nancy was relieved to hear this. "I'll keep trying to get in touch with the Dowds," she promised.

Next, she told her father about Laura Pendleton's flight from the Aborns' home. "Do you think we should report her experience with them to the police?" she asked.

Mr. Drew said no, that so far the two girls had only their suspicions of the couple's dishonesty, even though Laura had overheard them talking about her jewels. "You need some concrete evidence before calling in the authorities," he stated.

"I thought I'd run up to Melrose Lake and do some sleuthing," she said.

"All right, but keep out of danger," he warned. "I'll be eager to hear what you find out. We'll have a conference when I get home and decide what we can do for Laura."

"Thanks, Dad." A moment later they bade each other good night and hung up.

As the teen-aged detective started for the porch, she had an inspiration. It was not essential now for her to meet Herbert Brown. If Don Cameron would agree to take Laura as a substitute to the barbecue party, it would leave Nancy free to go to Melrose Lake the next day!

"I'll ask Don if he'd mind. If he does—well, that's that."

Hopefully Nancy dialed the Cameron house. Don answered and the girl detective told him the problem.

"Wow! A real mystery!" he remarked. "If I didn't know what sleuthing means to you, Nancy, I'd say you were just trying to brush me off. But you have me feeling sorry for this Laura Pendleton, too. Okay. If she's willing to go with me, I'll be glad to take her. But I'm sure sorry you can't make it. See you another time."

"Thanks, Don. I shan't forget this. Of course if Laura won't go, I'll keep the date. 'By now."

As Nancy walked toward the porch, she smilingly crossed her fingers, hoping that Laura would agree to the plan. Stepping outside, Nancy asked, "How would you like to go to a barbecue tomorrow, Laura?"

The girl's face glowed with anticipation. "It would be fun!" she exclaimed. "Where, Nancy?"

When the plan was explained, Laura said, "Oh, but I don't want to take your date away from you."

"Don and I have already arranged everything," Nancy assured her. Then she told of her desire to do some sleuthing at Melrose Lake.

At once Laura said she was afraid to have Nancy go to the Aborns' home. "There's no telling what my guardian might do to you," she said fearfully. "He has a terrible temper, and if he learns you're helping me—"

"He won't learn that," Nancy said determinedly.

Reluctantly Laura agreed to Nancy's whole scheme. "But if anything should happen to you, I— I'd just want to die!" she declared.

Before the girls went to bed, Hannah suggested that Laura's jewelry be put into the wall safe in Mr. Drew's study.

"Dad, Hannah, and I are the only persons who know the combination," Nancy told Laura.

"It would be a good idea," the brown-eyed girl replied. "First, I'd like to show you some of Mother's treasures. She gave them to me before her last illness."

"Do you have this in writing?" Hannah asked.

"Yes, I do. Why?"

"Then the jewelry wouldn't be part of your

mother's estate," Mrs. Gruen answered, "and there'd be no tax on it."

Laura took a package from her handbag and opened it. She displayed a string of priceless matched pearls, a gorgeous diamond clip and earrings, several jeweled pins set with rubies, pearls, and emeralds, and six rings, including one with a brilliant star sapphire.

Nancy and Hannah were astounded. "Why, this is the most beautiful collection I've ever seen!" Nancy exclaimed. She pointed to a ring set with a perfect aquamarine. "I love this!"

Laura smiled. "That was Mother's favorite," she said. "My father gave it to her on their first wedding anniversary."

"Thank goodness your guardian didn't find these things!" Hannah declared.

Finally the jewels were put into the safe and everyone went to bed.

Nancy awoke at seven o'clock the next morning. After taking a shower, she decided to wear a forest-green cotton dress and flat-heeled brown play shoes.

Laura was still sleeping when Nancy joined Mrs. Gruen at breakfast. The housekeeper was using a cane.

"My ankle feels almost as good as new," Hannah announced. "I've discarded the crutches."

Nancy was delighted to hear this. As they ate, she and the housekeeper talked about the young sleuth's trip.

"I'll worry about you every second until you return home," Mrs. Gruen declared. "If you're not here by ten thirty, I'll notify the police."

Nancy grinned. "I'll try to be here by supper-time. If not, I'll call you."

A short while later Nancy battled the early-morning traffic through the city. Reaching the outskirts, she took the road to Melrose Lake.

"Poor Laura," she thought, wondering what the day would disclose about the girl's strange guardian and his wife.

If Laura were really penniless, maybe the man thought he had a legitimate right to take and sell the jewelry for the girl's support. But his wife had bragged about having plenty of money to take care of their ward.

After a time Nancy came to the Melrose Lake detour. Laura had told her there was a sign marked "Eagle Rock" in front of the lane leading to her guardian's property.

Presently Nancy approached the spot where the pine tree had fallen. Fortunately, it had been removed.

She drove more slowly, afraid of inadvertently missing the Eagle Rock sign. Then, sighting the turnoff, Nancy left the detour.

"This ring was Mother's favorite," Laura said

She had gone but a few hundred feet along the Aborns' road when she decided it might be safer to walk. After parking along the side of the roadway, she started off. In a few minutes Nancy suddenly caught sight of a man walking rapidly through the woods. He carried a small bundle under his arm.

"Jacob Aborn!" she thought, recognizing his profile and the peculiar stoop of his shoulders.

Nancy recalled Laura's story of her guardian taking a small package from the refrigerator and leaving the house with it. What was in the bundle and where was he taking it?

"I'm going to find out!" Nancy declared. Without hesitation, she quietly plunged into the thicket. Following at a safe distance she managed to keep the man in sight.

"He doesn't seem to be worried about being followed," Nancy thought. "He must not have heard my car when I turned into the lane." She continued her musing. "I'm glad I wore this green dress. It's good camouflage!"

Just then a twig crackled under her foot, breaking the stillness of the woods. Jacob Aborn turned and looked back, frowning. He stood a minute, listening intently. Only by ducking quickly behind a large bush had Nancy avoided detection.

"I'd better be more careful if I don't want to get caught," she warned herself.

As the man continued through the forest Nancy followed, painstakingly avoiding twigs or loose stones. She kept well behind him.

"Wouldn't it be a joke on me if he's just a bird watcher!" She giggled at the thought. "And maybe that package has his lunch in it!"

Laughing to herself, Nancy picked her way through the woods as she trailed Laura Pendleton's guardian. Suddenly he disappeared behind a clump of high blueberry bushes. Nancy hurried forward. When she reached the spot the girl detective looked about in all directions.

"Which way did he go?" she asked herself.

Jacob Aborn seemed to have vanished into thin air!

CHAPTER X

The Danger Sign

ALERT for possible danger, Nancy moved forward with the utmost caution. It occurred to her that possibly Aborn had become aware he was being followed and had hidden in the bushes to watch the pursuer.

"I'll walk into a trap!" Nancy thought with alarm. "Mr. Aborn will learn I'm spying on him and everything will be ruined!"

With great caution she moved from one bush and tree to another. Laura's guardian was not hiding behind any of them.

"That's funny," Nancy said to herself.

She examined the ground, almost expecting there would be a cave or secret tunnel in the vicinity. But the earth was firm and in many places very rocky.

Finally Nancy came to a tiny clearing. On the far side attached to a large oak was a crudely printed wooden sign which read:

PRIVATE PROPERTY. KEEP OUT. DANGER!

"I wonder if that's where Mr. Aborn went and why?" the young detective asked herself.

She waited several minutes, then decided to cross the clearing. She was not stopped. Entering the woods again, she saw a dilapidated shack. The windows had been boarded up, and the roof sagged.

"One good gust of wind would blow the place over," Nancy said to herself.

She stepped from among the bushes and stood in the shadow of the trees, curiously surveying the building. Was it possible that Jacob Aborn had entered it?

Nancy's eyes searched the ground for footprints. Directly ahead, in the soft earth, she saw the fresh mark of a man's shoe. Instantly her suspicions were confirmed.

Jacob Aborn had come this way!

"I'll just have a look at this shack," the young sleuth decided.

After quickly glancing about to make certain she was not being watched, Nancy hurried forward. Tiptoeing across the front porch, she quietly tried the door. It was locked. Nancy walked around to the rear door and found that it likewise was securely fastened.

Although disappointed, Nancy was unwilling to give up. Making a complete circuit of the shack, she saw a window from which several boards had fallen. It was too high for her to peer through. Nancy returned to the rear of the building to get an old box that she had seen. She set it beneath the window and mounted it.

Pressing her face against the glass, she gazed inside. The room, apparently a kitchen, was bare of furniture and covered with dust and cobwebs.

"I wish I could get inside," Nancy thought.

She was about to climb down from the box when a strange feeling came over her. Though she had heard no sound, Nancy sensed that unfriendly eyes were watching her every move.

Before she could turn around and look over her shoulder, a coarse, angry voice barked into her ear:

"What are you doing here, young lady?"

Nancy wheeled and faced Jacob Aborn!

With as much dignity as she could muster, the girl detective stepped to the ground and regarded the man with composure. His eyes burned with rage.

"I was merely curious," Nancy replied. "And may I ask why *you* are here?"

"Yes, I'll tell you. I'm looking for my ward."

"You mean Laura Pendleton?"

"Yes. Who else? I thought maybe she was hiding here. But nobody's in the shack."

"Why in the world would Laura hide in this ramshackle place?" Nancy asked, trying to show as much surprise as possible.

"Search me," Mr. Aborn said, then added angrily, his eyes boring Nancy's, "Laura has run away!"

"Run away?" Nancy repeated.

"Yes. Yesterday. I'll tell you something about that ward of mine—" A crafty light came into Jacob Aborn's eyes as he went on, "At times she acts unbalanced—thinks folks don't treat her right."

"Indeed?" said Nancy, pretending to be shocked.

By now Laura's guardian had calmed down. When he spoke again he was once more the pleasant man Nancy had met at the Montewago Hotel.

"It's for Laura's own good that she ought to return home," he said. "Mrs. Aborn is dreadfully upset. She loves Laura just like a mother. Miss Drew, have you heard from Laura by any chance?"

Nancy was on her guard. "Why should I hear from her?" she countered. "We never met until that accident on the lake and she came to rescue my friend Helen and me."

Mr. Aborn did not pursue the subject. Instead, he said, "Laura's a nervous, high-strung girl. Why, do you know she locked herself in her room the entire time she was with us—wouldn't eat, or even let us try to help her?"

"Terrible!" Nancy said, pretending to be shocked. "Laura does need help."

Secretly Nancy felt that Jacob Aborn was telling this version of the locked-door story to cover his own actions, in case they came to light.

"Have you notified the police, Mr. Aborn?" she asked, probing for further information.

"We have a private detective working on the matter," the man stated. "We don't want any bad publicity because of dear Marie Pendleton's memory. She entrusted Laura to my care because she knew how much my wife and I would love the girl."

Nancy suddenly was finding it hard to concentrate on what Mr. Aborn was saying. Was she wrong or had she heard a sound inside the shack?

"This is very strange," she told herself. "But I don't dare pursue the subject or Mr. Aborn will really become suspicious." Aloud she said, "I certainly hope Laura is all right. Well, I must go now. I have some friends here at Melrose Lake I plan to call on." She paused, then added lightly, "In fact, I believe you know them, Mr. Aborn—the Donnell family."

The man looked startled, then recovered himself. "Oh, yes. Fine family. Say hello to them for me, please."

Nancy promised that she would. Since Mr. Aborn made no move to accompany her, she said good-by and walked rapidly back to the spot where her convertible was parked.

As Nancy climbed into it, she cast a glance over her shoulder. There was no sign of Mr. Aborn. Had he gone into the shack? Was someone there? Had he been delivering packages to the person?

Nancy started the car's motor and backed out to the main road. As she drove along, her thoughts were entirely on Mr. Aborn. She had no doubt but that the man had been lying about Laura's behavior.

"I must find out more about that man," Nancy decided.

Reaching the highway, she stopped at a service station, had the gas tank of her car filled, and asked directions to the Donnell home. The attendant told her how to reach the place, and a short while later Nancy drew up before a lovely redwood house located well off the road.

She got out and rang the front doorbell. There was no answer. Nancy walked around to the back of the house. A gardener was there, trimming the flower beds.

"Howdy, miss!" the elderly man hailed her. "Looking for the Donnells?"

"Yes. Are they away?" Nancy inquired.

"Yep. They're visiting relatives in Crescent Gardens 'til tonight. Any message?"

Nancy said no, that she would call again, and thanked the man. As she drove away Nancy was disappointed that she had been unable to pick up any information regarding Mr. Aborn.

"I don't want to leave Melrose Lake until I have learned *something* to help Laura," she thought. "Mr. Aborn may trace her whereabouts to our home and force Laura to return with him before Dad gets back to town. I suppose he has a legal right to do it."

At last an idea came to Nancy. "I'll go to one of the hotels on the lake and engage a room. Then, after it gets dark, I'll do a little more investigating."

Fortunately, Nancy always carried an overnight case in her car trunk. It contained pajamas and robe, two changes of clothing, toilet articles, and, this time of year, a bathing suit.

Presently she saw a large white building ahead of her. Its green lawn sloped down to the sandy beach. On the stone pillar at the side of the driveway was the sign: *Beach Cliff Hotel.*

"I think I'll stop here," Nancy decided. She parked her car and entered the pleasant lobby. In a few minutes she had registered and been taken to a comfortable room overlooking the lake.

"I'll telephone home," Nancy said to herself, "and tell Hannah where I am."

As Nancy placed the call, a chilling thought suddenly popped into her mind. Perhaps the detective whom Aborn had engaged had already traced the runaway girl, and knew Nancy had not told all she knew about Laura. If so, Nancy might find that her guest had already been whisked away from the Drew home!

CHAPTER XI

Trapped!

WHEN Hannah Gruen answered the telephone at the Drew residence, Nancy at once asked, "Is Laura all right?"

"Why, of course," Hannah answered in surprise. "She's upstairs setting her hair for the party this afternoon."

"Well, tell her to be very careful," Nancy urged. "Mr. Aborn has a detective looking for her!"

"Oh dear!" exclaimed Mrs. Gruen. "And when will you be home, Nancy?"

The young detective explained where she was and that she planned to stay at Melrose Lake and do more sleuthing.

"I think I may be on the trail of something big."

"I don't like the idea of you prowling around the Aborns' home in the dead of night," the housekeeper objected.

"I'll be careful," Nancy promised. "I may even get home tonight."

"Well, all right," Hannah consented reluctantly. "By the way, Nancy, I had a repairman fix the window in Mr. Drew's study this morning, and also requested the police to keep a lookout for anything suspicious going on in this neighborhood."

"Wonderful!" Nancy said, feeling relieved. "Any more news?"

"Everything's quiet here," Hannah reported. "And Laura seems happy."

Laura came to speak to Nancy and was alarmed when she heard that a detective was looking for her. "But I won't go back to those awful Aborns! They can't make me! If they try it, I'll—I'll run right to the police!"

"That's a good idea," said Nancy. "By the way, I'd like to do some sleuthing at the Aborn house. I may want to get inside without ringing the bell." The young sleuth chuckled. "Since it's now your house too, may I have permission to go in and look around?"

"You certainly may," said Laura with a giggle. "If no doors are unlocked, try my bedroom window. I left it open a crack and there's a sturdy rose trellis right alongside it."

"Terrific!" said Nancy elatedly.

After she completed the call, Nancy went to

the hotel coffee shop for a hearty lunch. Since it was now almost one thirty, the room was empty.

After eating, Nancy put on her bathing suit and wandered down to the beach. A boy in attendance gave her a towel and Nancy stretched out on the sand, unaware of the steadfast glance of a couple hidden behind a large green-and-white striped umbrella not far away. They nodded to each other, then when Nancy was not looking, they quickly left the beach.

"Guess we're safe," the woman muttered. "She's here to stay and have a good time."

As the strong rays of the sun beat down on the unsuspecting girl, she rehearsed her plan for the evening. When it was dark she would visit both Jacob Aborn's home and also the shack in the woods, if time permitted.

"I'll miss Dad's call tonight," Nancy reflected.

Standing up half an hour later, Nancy put on her bathing cap and walked to the water. She stuck her toe in. The lake water felt icy cold, and Nancy noticed that there were more people on the beach than in swimming. Nevertheless, she waded out to where it was deep enough to make a surface dive and plunged in. Once she was wet, the water was invigorating.

After swimming for a while, Nancy came back to her beach towel and dried off. Then she returned to her room, showered, and slept for two hours, realizing that the rest would give her more endurance for the evening ahead.

Awakening at six o'clock, Nancy put on the simple black cotton dress from her suitcase and pumps. After brushing her hair until it snapped with electricity, she was ready for supper.

"What will it be this evening, miss?" asked the friendly waitress.

Nancy selected steak, a baked potato, and tossed salad, then sat back to enjoy the soft dinner music playing in the background. The orchestra was in an adjoining lounge.

Nearby diners regarded the lone girl with interest, for the prospect of the daring adventure had brought a becoming flush to her cheeks.

"If I'm wrong in suspecting Jacob Aborn of being dishonest," thought Nancy, "then I guess I'd better give up sleuthing!"

Upon leaving the dining room an hour later, she lingered on the porch for a few minutes, watching couples dance. As a red-haired young man began to walk toward Nancy with an invitation in his eyes for her to dance, she hastily went to her room.

Chuckling to herself, Nancy said aloud, "Romance and detective work won't mix tonight!" Then she changed to walking shoes, sweater, and skirt.

The moment it became dark enough for her

purpose, Nancy left the hotel in her car. As she drew near the Aborns' lane a short while later, she turned the convertible off the road and ran it into a clump of bushes where it would not be seen.

Switching off the engine and locking the doors, Nancy started down the lane leading to the house, holding her flashlight securely. She found the windows of the house dark.

"The Aborns are out, I guess," she told herself. "Well, that means I can do some looking around."

Circling the structure cautiously, Nancy noted that the second-floor wing, where the bedrooms apparently were located, was in the back. She found the trellis easily.

"I'll try the doors first," Nancy decided, and darted to the front. Gently turning the handle, she found the door locked.

An investigation of two other doors revealed that they, too, were securely fastened.

"I guess I'll have to climb after all," Nancy said to herself.

As quietly as possible, she climbed the trellis. It wobbled and creaked a little but did not give way. When Nancy reached the window ledge of Laura's bedroom, she found to her delight that the window raised easily. She crawled through and switched on her flashlight.

As Nancy tiptoed across the room, which was in

disorder, she heard a noise. Halting, she listened. A car was approaching the house. Looking out the window she could barely make out the figures of a man and a woman who alighted. Who were they and what should Nancy do?

"I'll stay right here," she determined.

As Nancy waited tensely she realized someone was walking up the stairs. Quickly Nancy closed the window without a sound. As she looked around for a hiding place she saw a closet, and darted inside it, switching off her flashlight. Crouched in a far corner behind some of Laura's dresses, Nancy scarcely dared to breathe.

The door to the room was opened a moment later and the boudoir lamps switched on. Cautiously Nancy peered out through the keyhole in the closet door. She saw Jacob Aborn!

The man went directly to Laura's dressing table. Apparently he had not heard Nancy, for he did not glance toward the closet.

Ruthlessly he jerked out drawers from the dressing table and emptied their contents upon the bed. As he surveyed the assortment of tiny bottles, boxes, and other paraphernalia, Laura's guardian gave a disgusted grunt.

"Last place to look!" he said, as if addressing someone out in the hall, probably his wife. "Guess Laura really took the jewels with her. Well, I'll soon have them back!"

Nancy's heart leaped. There was no longer any doubt in her mind as to the character of this man. She was now certain that his sole interest in Laura was to get possession of her property! Only the girl's opportune escape from the house had prevented him from seizing the valuable jewelry collection!

"Laura's mother couldn't have known his true character, or she wouldn't have entrusted her daughter to Aborn's care," Nancy pondered.

Her thoughts came to an abrupt end as the man moved toward the closet. Fearfully, Nancy ducked down behind Laura's dresses again and fervently hoped that she would not be discovered.

Suddenly, as Nancy's legs began to grow cramped, the closet door was jerked violently open. Jacob Aborn looked in!

CHAPTER XII

A Black Abyss

As JACOB ABORN stared into the closet where Nancy was hiding, the girl detective wished wildly that she were invisible. There was no telling what harm the man might inflict if he saw her!

"He has such a violent temper," Nancy realized.

But Aborn's glance did not stray to the dress section. Instead, he reached up for two large suitcases which were on a shelf above the clothes. He set them on the floor outside and shut the closet door.

Beads of perspiration trickled down Nancy's neck as she relaxed. Presently she heard the man leave the room and shut the hall door with a loud bang.

Nancy waited a moment, then left her hiding

place. "I suppose I'd better leave while I can," she advised herself.

But running away from a chance to pick up a clue was not in Nancy's nature. As she heard Laura's guardian descending the stairs to the first floor, she became aware of a woman's voice somewhere below. Nancy decided, "I'll stay and see what's going on."

Before leaving Laura's bedroom she gave it a final searching look and shook her head, puzzled. The room was one which Nancy would be happy to call her own. The feminine furnishings and good colonial pieces showed evidence of discerning taste. They did not fit the Aborns' character. Perhaps an interior decorator had planned it!

"One could believe from this room that the Aborns really wanted Laura," Nancy pondered.

It just did not make sense. Many criminals, Nancy knew, laid the groundwork to lull any suspicion on the part of their victim, then cornered him. But Laura had not even been settled in her new home when the Aborns had begun to persecute her.

Soundlessly Nancy opened the bedroom door, and keeping her flashlight low to the floor, tiptoed along the carpeted hall. Step by step, she edged down the stairway to the floor below. Here there was no sign of activity but Nancy saw a light shining through louvered doors to her left.

"That's probably the kitchen. The Aborns are in there," she thought.

A moment later the woman said, "Here's the combination. I'll pack this stuff while you open the safe."

Quickly Nancy stole into the living room and hastily ducked out of sight behind a large sofa. She was just in time. One of the louvered doors opened and Laura's guardian came into the living room carrying a suitcase. He flicked on a table lamp.

Near it hung the small oil painting of a ship. Aborn lifted it from the wall and set the picture against a chair.

Nancy's eyes widened as she saw that the painting had concealed a wall safe. Aborn deftly twirled the dial to the left, then several notches to the right, and back to the left again. He swung the safe door open.

With a grunt of satisfaction, the man removed several packages of bank notes and some papers which looked like stock certificates. Mr. Aborn chortled and called to his wife:

"When we get the rest of these cashed, you and I will be set for life—thanks to Laura and a few others."

Nancy, startled, almost gave herself away. So Laura did have a sizable inheritance other than the jewelry! But how had the securities reached the safe? Had Aborn brought them here or was he stealing them from someone else? Nancy felt more confused by the moment.

As her thoughts raced, Aborn replaced the loose papers in the safe and closed it. Then he put the money and securities into the suitcase. Giving a tired yawn, he switched off the lamp and left the room.

"Guess I'll turn in," he called to his wife. "Got to be up early tomorrow and get Fred. You ready?"

"Yes."

Marian Aborn came from the kitchen carrying the other bag. Together the couple ascended the stairs. Nancy heard a bedroom door above close.

"Now I must get the police," the girl detective thought.

She paused for several seconds, after coming from behind the couch, to stretch her cramped limbs. "I'd better go out the front door," she decided. "The bedrooms don't overlook that."

Noiselessly Nancy slipped outside and started for her hidden car. Then a temptation came to her. "Why don't I investigate that shack in the woods first? I may have an even bigger story to tell the police! I'll do it!"

Taking a deep breath of air, Nancy hurried toward the path leading to the dilapidated building. Had she been right about having heard someone inside? Was he a friend or an enemy of Aborn's? Were the packages being carried there and what did they contain? Loot?

"Maybe just food," Nancy concluded. "But being taken to whom?"

Beaming her flashlight on the ground, the young detective soon picked up the trail she had taken earlier in the day. It was quiet and eerie as she stumbled along the uneven ground. Nancy became apprehensive once or twice as she heard scuffling noises of forest creatures in the underbrush, but went on.

"I wish Dad were here now," she thought fervently.

Nancy reached the shack without mishap and paused in front of it. A sixth sense seemed to tell her there was someone inside who needed help. No person would stay in such a place unless forced to.

"This is no time for me to hesitate," she told herself.

As Nancy moved toward the rear of the tumble-down building, she glanced at her flashlight and was alarmed to see that it was beginning to grow dim.

"Just my luck when I need it the most!"

In an attempt to save the battery, Nancy switched off the light. As her eyes became accustomed to the darkness, she moved toward the window she had looked through earlier that day. Appraising it, the young sleuth realized that the window ledge was too high from the ground for her to climb through unassisted, even when standing on the box.

Undaunted, she began to examine the other windows. On the south side of the shack she found one which opened from the rickety porch. It was boarded up.

"This is my entry," Nancy determined.

She began searching the yard for something with which to pry off the boards, and finally found a stout stick. Nancy began wedging it between the boards with all her might.

The first board offered stubborn resistance. Then, with a groan and a squeak, it gave way. The remaining boards were removed with less difficulty.

To Nancy's joy, the window was unlocked! Pushing it up, she beamed her flashlight inside. The room beyond was bare and quiet as a tomb.

"Well, here comes Nancy Drew, housebreaker and spy!" Nancy thought with amused determination. "It's certain now no one lives here."

When she was halfway through the window the young sleuth hesitated without knowing just why. She glanced back over her shoulder. A queer sensation made Nancy quiver as she turned searching eyes toward the woods.

"How silly!" she scolded herself. "No one's there. It's just nerves."

Bravely Nancy swung herself through the window. Hastily she moved toward an adjoining room, noting that her flashlight was growing dimmer. Soon she would be left in total darkness! She must hurry!

Her light revealed a small room, also empty, its walls and floor dusty from long lack of any occupant's care. Nancy was disappointed to find nothing of interest.

"I'd better leave and drive to police headquarters," she thought.

Just then Nancy's flashlight revealed a trap door in the floor. Quickly she moved over toward it. But she had taken only a few steps when an unusual sound arrested her attention. Had she heard a board creak behind her, or was it a night sound from the woods?

After hesitating a second, Nancy again started for the trap door. As she reached down to grasp the ring in it, her body became tense.

This time there was no mistake. She had heard a peculiar sound which seemed to come from beneath the floor.

"It sounded like a groan!" Nancy decided. She felt cold all over.

Someone was imprisoned in the cellar! Who? And why?

As Nancy tugged at the ring, another idea came to her. This might be a trap laid for her!

"Oh, what should I do?" she thought, hesitating. There was still time to run away from danger.

But the fear that some person was in distress gave her the courage to open the trap door. As it swung upward, Nancy saw before her a flight of stone steps, leading down into complete darkness. A gust of damp, musty air struck her in the face and momentarily repulsed her.

Nancy glanced nervously at her flashlight. The battery could not last much longer. Already the light was so weak that she could barely see the steps in front of her. Did she dare investigate the cellar?

"It won't take long," she thought.

She descended the steps and came to a landing. The rest of the stairway went toward the left. Nancy peered anxiously into the black abyss below.

To her horror, she saw a man stretched out full length on a bench. His face was turned upward and Nancy caught a full glimpse of the countenance.

He was Jacob Aborn!

CHAPTER XIII

An Actor's Ruse

SPELLBOUND, Nancy stood like a stone image, gazing down into the face of Jacob Aborn. How had the man reached the bungalow ahead of her? What was he doing sleeping in the musty cellar of the old shack?

As these thoughts flashed through Nancy's mind, the beam of her flashlight flickered again. Then it went out, leaving her in total darkness.

Sheer panic took possession of the girl detective. Something very strange was going on! She must not be caught in a trap!

Turning, she gave a low cry and stumbled up the stairway and toward the window through which she had entered. Her flight was abruptly checked as she banged one foot on something metallic that moved ahead of her. In a second she smelled kerosene.

"A lantern!" she decided.

The thought of a light gave her hope. She felt around and discovered an old-time oil lantern.

Collecting her wits, she stopped and listened for any sounds of pursuit. There were none. The shack appeared as deserted and silent as before.

"I'm sure that was Jacob Aborn down in the cellar," Nancy thought in perplexity. "I didn't imagine it. But how did he get here so fast? After I left his house I didn't waste much time."

Suddenly an amazing thought came to Nancy. Was the man she had seen by chance a brother, even a twin, of Jacob Aborn? He might be honest and Jacob had found him in the way!

"I'm going to find out!" Nancy declared excitedly.

Eagerly she reached into the pocket of her dress, recalling that at dinner she had taken a pack of matches from the hotel dining table for her souvenir collection. Good! The pack was still there!

Striking a match she was pleased to discover that the lantern was half full of oil. Someone had used it recently, for the glass was clean. Nancy lighted the wick and a flame spurted up. Carrying the lantern, she returned to the trap door.

Suddenly, from below, Nancy heard a moan of pain. This was followed by a pitiful cry of "Help!"

"That settles it," the worried girl thought.

As she descended the steps, the lantern's flick-

From below came a pitiful cry of "Help!"

ering glow revealed that the cellar was dungeon-like, with solid stone walls and no windows.

She held the light high above the figure on the bench. A man, deathly pale, was lying where she had first seen him.

But he was not Laura's guardian!

"There's certainly a startling resemblance, though," Nancy thought, her heart filled with pity for this unfortunate stranger.

Dropping to her knees, she felt his pulse. It was faint but regular.

"He's just unconscious," she told herself in relief.

At the same time, Nancy saw with horror a large chain around the man's waist. It was attached to the prisoner in such a way that it allowed him some freedom of motion and yet held him captive. Was Jacob Aborn responsible for this atrocity? Nancy wondered angrily.

"I must do something to revive this man," she decided, "and get him away from here."

Picking up the lantern, Nancy mounted the cellar steps two at a time. She headed for a small sink in one corner of the room above, where she had seen a pump.

After a search through the cupboard she at last found a battered tin cup. Quickly pumping water into it, she returned to the cellar.

Nancy wet her handkerchief and applied it

gently to the prisoner's forehead. Then she sprinkled a little of the water on his face and chafed his wrists. The man stirred slightly and moaned.

As she gazed anxiously into his face, Nancy wondered how she could have mistaken him for Jacob Aborn. Although the two men were of the same age, and had similar facial characteristics, the prisoner was gaunt and thin. His features, contrary to Mr. Aborn's, were gentle and relaxed.

Now Nancy saw that the man was slowly regaining consciousness. As his eyes fluttered open he cried "Help!" feebly, then stared into Nancy's face, amazed.

"Help has come," Nancy said quietly.

The man attempted to raise himself to a sitting position with Nancy's aid. "Didn't—think—help—would—ever come," he murmured. Then he saw the cup in Nancy's hand and asked for water.

Nancy steadied the cup while he drank. Finally the man leaned against the wall. "First water I've had in twenty-four hours," he said more clearly.

The young sleuth was horrified. She introduced herself, then asked, "Who are you—and who did this terrible thing to you?"

A bitter expression passed over the prisoner's face. "I'm Jacob Aborn," he said. "A crook by the name of Stumpy Dowd took over my house, imprisoned me here, and somehow or other arranged for my new ward, Laura Pendleton, to come to my home earlier than she was expected. Yesterday he told me that he had the girl's inheritance in his possession—and showed bonds to prove it."

"You're Jacob Aborn!" Nancy repeated, as the prisoner, exhausted by these words, leaned against the wall.

Quickly Nancy's mind flashed back to everything that had happened since she had met Laura. The puzzling questions that had bothered her about the girl's guardian now became clear. Most of all, it was a relief to know that the person to whom Marie Pendleton had entrusted her daughter's care was not a criminal.

Equally important, Nancy realized that Stephen Dowd—alias Stumpy—used his talent as an actor and skill with make-up to fool other people, and then probably swindled them. The young sleuth wondered if there was a tie-in between Laura's inheritance and the Monroe National Bank thefts of stocks and bonds. She must find out from Jacob Aborn, but the police should be notified immediately, as well as her father.

Aloud Nancy said, "I want to hear the whole story of what has happened to you, Mr. Aborn, but first—"

Briefly, she told of having met the man who had impersonated him and of seeing Laura at Twin Lakes. Nancy was about to add that Laura was now at her home when Mr. Aborn said:

"If Stumpy caught you here once today we'd better get out right now!" He told Nancy that Dowd kept the key to the padlock on his chains on a hook near the stairway.

"This is a lucky break," said Nancy. She snatched the lantern from the floor and started toward the stairs.

"Please hurry," Mr. Aborn said faintly. "Stumpy Dowd is a dangerous criminal! He boasted to me that he and his accomplices have victimized several people besides Laura!"

Nancy anxiously moved the lantern up and down, illuminating the dingy walls. Just above her head to the left she finally saw the hook, with a key dangling from it.

"I have it!" she exclaimed triumphantly.

As Nancy hurried back to Mr. Aborn's side she speculated on how the Dowds had found out about Mr. Aborn, his wife, and Laura.

"I'll have you free in a minute, Mr. Aborn," Nancy said, as she stooped over the bench.

While she worked on the rusty lock, Nancy asked if he had known the Dowds previously.

"Yes," he replied. "Mrs. Dowd was hired by my wife as a maid to come when we arrived. Soon after I reached the house her husband came. He grew quite loud and abusive and when I objected he knocked me unconscious. When I came to, I was chained in this cellar."

"How dreadful!" Nancy exclaimed. "But where is your wife?" she asked.

"She had to go to Florida unexpectedly. Her mother, who lives there, had an emergency operation. Marian went down to be with her and I moved into our new home." Mr. Aborn sighed. "Of course I haven't heard a word from her since I've been tied up here!"

"You'll be able to find out about her now," Nancy assured him. "Do you know how many people are working with Stumpy Dowd?"

"One or two others besides his wife, I believe. Stumpy Dowd is secretive about some things, although he boasted a lot. I did hear him mention the name Fred, but I don't know who he is."

When the padlock finally snapped open Nancy's spirits soared. Now the suitcase of securities that Stumpy Dowd had packed could be retrieved. The criminals could be apprehended and her father's case perhaps solved!

Meanwhile, neither Nancy nor Mr. Aborn had noticed a dark figure creeping slowly down the steps. Near and nearer the man came, a stout cane gripped tightly in his right hand.

"That's wonderful, Nancy!" Mr. Aborn exclaimed. "Now if I just knew where Laura is." As he spoke Mr. Aborn glanced up. A look of horror froze his face.

"Look out, Nancy!" he shouted.

CHAPTER XIV

A Desperate Situation

THE WARNING came too late. Before Nancy could turn, the end of the cane crashed down on her head. With a low moan of pain, she sagged to the floor and lay still.

How long she remained unconscious, the young sleuth did not know. When at last she opened her eyes Nancy found herself stretched out on the cold floor of the cellar. Bewildered, it was a full minute before she could account for the splitting pain in her head.

Then, with a shudder, the young sleuth remembered what had happened. She had been struck down from behind. Who was her assailant?

Nancy became aware that someone was standing over her, but objects whirled before her eyes and she could not distinguish the face. Then, gradually, her vision cleared. She saw Stumpy Dowd gazing down upon her, a satisfied leer on his face.

"Well, Miss Drew," he said mockingly, "we meet again. You've gotten in my way once too often!"

As Nancy started to speak, Dowd reached down. Catching Nancy by an arm, he jerked her roughly to her feet. Nancy was so weak that she nearly fell over.

Nevertheless, with a show of spirit, she said, "You'll regret this, I promise you!"

"Let the girl go," Jacob Aborn pleaded from the other side of the room. "Do anything you like to me, but set her free." Nancy saw that he was again padlocked.

Stumpy Dowd glared at his other prisoner. "It's quite impossible for me to release either of you," he said calmly. "You see, you both know too much."

Nancy was aware that resistance would be useless. Right now she did not have the strength to make a break for the stairs. But as the criminal began to unwind a long rope, Nancy realized that unless she thought of something the situation would be desperate. There would be no way to escape!

As Stumpy began to bind Nancy's feet together he said sarcastically, "Mr. Aborn will enjoy having company. And you two have so much to talk about."

An idea suddenly came to Nancy. She remembered that a detective who had called on her father a few months before had told her how it was possible to hold one's hands while being bound so as to slip the bonds later. He had given a demonstration.

"If I can only remember the correct position," Nancy prayed fervently.

When Dowd began to bind Nancy's wrists she tried to follow the detective's instructions. As the ropes cut into her flesh it seemed to Nancy that she must have made a mistake. Certainly there was little space between her wrists and the bonds.

"And now, just to make sure you won't get away—" Stumpy muttered with a sneer.

He took the end of the rope and ran it through a ring in the wall, knotting the rope fast.

"I guess that will hold you for a while and teach you not to meddle in affairs that are none of your business!" the man added.

Nancy Drew had never been so angry in her life, but she realized that any argument she might give would only provoke the man to further torture. So she set her jaw grimly and kept still.

"You'll pay for this, Dowd!" Jacob Aborn spoke up in a quavering voice. "When I get free—"

"When you get free!" Stumpy Dowd taunted.

"That's a laugh. Why, you fool, how do you propose to get help? If it hadn't been for this meddlesome Drew girl only the rats would have known you were here!"

Nancy could not help but remark quietly, "The police will catch you in the end."

"I doubt it," Dowd said with confidence. "I've covered my trail thoroughly. I've made plans to leave the country and I'd like to see the police or anyone else catch me!" He turned to Laura's guardian. "First, of course, we'll have to get the jewels away from Laura."

"How do you propose to do that," Nancy asked quickly, "when you don't know where she is?"

Stumpy Dowd laughed. "That's what you think. Laura is at your home in River Heights, Nancy Drew!"

As Nancy blinked, a look of horror came into Mr. Aborn's eyes. Nancy knew he was wondering why she had not mentioned Laura's being at her home. Also, he realized that his last hope of keeping Laura's whereabouts unknown was gone.

Nancy, too, was worried. What did Stumpy plan to do? Right now, he looked pleased at his prisoners' reactions.

"My wife overheard Laura placing a call to Nancy Drew in River Heights yesterday morning. When Laura ran away, we had a hunch she would go there. I asked my detective to find out."

Dowd said the sleuth had seen Laura leaving the house that afternoon with a young man. "I presume she left her jewels behind," he added. "But we'll get them before we leave this area!"

"Don't try anything foolish," Nancy warned.

"All my plans are well made," Dowd said coolly. "Too bad you aren't more cautious, Miss Drew."

He said that his wife had felt a draft in the house and gone downstairs to find the front door part way open. Then she had seen a girl heading into the woods and had awakened him. Dowd had figured out that it might be Nancy.

"That's the end of my story," he said, "except to tell you, Aborn, I sold your blue sedan this morning. The money helped pay for my new foreign car."

Jacob Aborn was so furious he almost choked. "You robber! You kidnaper!" he cried out.

"Tut, tut, none of that!" Dowd said. "You'll get your blood pressure up."

"Laura's not in your clutches, and she won't get there!" Aborn stormed. "And I can support her without any inheritance!"

Dowd shrugged. "It won't do any good to threaten me. You're my prisoner and don't forget it! After the jewels are mine—"

Nancy felt as if she would choke with rage. Mr. Aborn closed his eyes and seemed to have fainted.

Meanwhile, Stumpy Dowd had replaced the key on the wall—the hook supporting it, Nancy saw, was far out of the two prisoners' reach.

"You can think of this in the days ahead," the crook taunted. "And now—good-by!"

Turning, he ambled up the steps. Nancy heard mocking laughter as the trap door was slammed shut. Soon a deathlike quiet fell on the shack.

"Mr. Aborn!" Nancy called.

There was no answer. Nancy's heart beat wildly. Was the man only in a faint or had something worse happened to him?

Holding her breath, she strained her ears to see if she could detect any sign of life. A few seconds later Nancy caught faint sounds of inhaling and exhaling.

"Thank goodness," she thought.

Presently the man stirred, and regaining consciousness, looked about. Seeing Nancy, he exclaimed, "Now I remember! We were so near freedom."

"Yes, we were, Mr. Aborn. And we may get out of here yet. I'm trying to slip this rope off my wrists. In the meantime, I want to tell you why I didn't mention that Laura is at my home. I was about to do so when you urged that we leave the shack as fast as possible."

"I see and I forgive you," said Mr. Aborn. "Never having met you, Dowd's announcement gave me a momentary feeling of distrust in you. But that's gone now."

"Then would you mind telling me about Laura's mother and the estate she left?" Nancy requested, as she worked to free her hands.

"I'll be glad to. Mrs. Pendleton appointed the Monroe National Bank executor of her estate and me as Laura's guardian. During Mrs. Pendleton's long illness she had all her securities taken from her private safe-deposit box and put in care of the bank. They were turned over to the custodian department and kept in the bank's personal vault."

"Then how could Stumpy Dowd get them?" Nancy asked.

"That's the mystery. He didn't say."

Nancy was convinced now that a good portion of Laura's inheritance must be among the securities stolen from the bank. She asked whether Mrs. Pendleton had left a large estate.

Mr. Aborn nodded. "Laura is a very wealthy young woman," he said, then went on to explain that at the time of Mrs. Pendleton's death, the Aborns were abroad. Upon their arrival in New York, Mrs. Aborn had received word of her mother's illness. It was then that Laura had been asked to postpone coming to Melrose Lake until his wife's return.

"Laura was staying on at her boarding school

with the headmistress until our trip to Melrose."

"She never received your letter," Nancy told him. "The Dowds must have intercepted it. Soon they told her to come."

Just then Nancy thought she had found the trick to freeing her hands, but a moment later she sighed in discouragement. The rope still bound her wrists.

"At least we have a light," she said. Fortunately, Stumpy Dowd had forgotten the lantern.

"Yes, but the oil is burning low," Mr. Aborn remarked quietly. "When it's gone we'll be in the dark—as I have been for the past two weeks."

Nancy shuddered. "Did Stumpy bring you food in little packages?"

"Yes, when he thought of it. He kept me alive just to pump me for information, and threatened to harm Laura if I didn't tell him what he wanted to know."

Suddenly Nancy felt the rope which chafed her wrists slacken. At the same time the light went out. The cellar was plunged into darkness.

CHAPTER XV

Plans for Rescue

BACK in River Heights, meanwhile, Hannah Gruen had spent a restless and worried evening, expecting to hear Nancy's convertible pull into the driveway at any moment. Moreover, Mr. Drew had failed to call at the appointed hour and Hannah had no knowledge of how to contact the lawyer.

At ten thirty, when the front doorbell rang, the housekeeper limped hurriedly to answer it. Instantly she felt a sense of keen disappointment.

"Oh, hello, Laura," she said, and turned to greet Don Cameron. "Did you have a good time at the barbecue?"

"It was wonderful!" Laura exclaimed happily, as she and Don entered the house.

"Certainly was fun," Don agreed. "Too bad Nancy wasn't with us. Where is she, Mrs. Gruen?"

At these words tears welled up in Hannah's eyes. She told of not hearing from either Nancy or Mr. Drew that evening. "I'm so upset," she said. "What will we do? Call the police?"

"Probably Nancy decided to stay overnight at the Beach Cliff Hotel," Laura said at once. "Have you called there to find out?"

"No, because Nancy always calls when she changes her plans."

Don, greatly concerned, went at once to the telephone. Impatiently the young man waited for a response to his ring.

The hotel telephone operator answered. When Don asked for Nancy Drew, the girl said, "Just a moment." It was nearly five minutes before she told him:

"We are unable to reach your party. Miss Drew is not in the hotel."

"Then she didn't check out earlier this evening?" Don inquired.

"No. Miss Drew is still registered."

Don Cameron hung up, a drawn expression on his face. He told the others what he had learned.

"Oh, I just know something has happened to Nancy!" Laura cried, her lower lip quivering with nervousness. "And it's all my fault."

Hannah took the girl into her arms. "You must not feel this way," she said gently. "Nancy is trying to help you because she wants to."

Don spoke up, "I don't know whether we should notify the police or drive to Melrose Lake ourselves."

As the three hesitated, they heard an automobile stop in front of the house. Then a door slammed. Don looked out the window.

"It's a man," he said. "He's coming to the door."

Don opened the door to Carson Drew, who came inside immediately. He greeted Hannah and Don. Then, after being introduced to Laura Pendleton and bidding her welcome to his home, the lawyer asked:

"Where's Nancy? Upstairs?"

When told that his daughter had not returned from her investigation at Melrose Lake, the lawyer was gravely concerned.

"I don't like the sound of this at all," he said. "I had no idea that Nancy was planning to sleuth in Mr. Aborn's home at night."

"She mentioned something about wanting to pay another visit to a mysterious shack in the woods, Mr. Drew," Hannah volunteered. "But I don't know where it's located."

Carson Drew's anxiety deepened. "It would be just like Nancy to follow up a good clue," he said, "particularly if she thinks there is something odd about the shack. She never gives up until she figures out the solution to whatever the problem is."

Despite his worry, Nancy's father uttered these words proudly. He had often admired the initiative his daughter displayed when she was trying to unravel a mystery.

"I think you're on the right track, Mr. Drew," Don Cameron said thoughtfully. "Since Nancy hasn't returned to the hotel, there are three possibilities—she's had car trouble, something has happened to her in the woods—"

"Or the Aborns have discovered Nancy prowling about their house," Laura put in fearfully. "And if that is the case, there's no telling what they may do to her!"

The girl quickly mentioned a few of the things which had happened in her brief stay at the Aborns.

"I'll leave for Melrose Lake immediately," Mr. Drew announced. "If I don't find Nancy in a very short time, I'm going to notify the police that she's missing!"

The others begged Mr. Drew to let them accompany him. The lawyer thought it best for Hannah to remain at home in case Nancy should call.

"But I'll be glad to have you accompany me, Laura and Don," he added.

Don hurried to the telephone to notify his parents of the plan, while Laura went for a coat.

Then they went outside and got into Mr. Drew's car.

"Be sure to call me as soon as you've found out something!" Hannah called.

"Don't worry, we will!"

Nancy's father was a skillful driver and right now he was intent upon reaching the lake as soon as possible. He could barely restrain himself from breaking the speed limits.

"This is one time I wish I had a helicopter," he told the two young people.

"It wouldn't do you much good at Melrose Lake, Mr. Drew," said Laura. "It's a pretty thickly wooded area. I doubt that you'd find a landing strip."

Don realized that this remark, although unintentional, heightened Carson Drew's worry about Nancy being lost in the woods. He changed the subject quickly.

"I thought you weren't due home until Sunday, sir," Don said.

"That's right," the lawyer replied, his eyes intent on the highway ahead. "In Cincinnati late this afternoon I had a call from Chief McGinnis of the River Heights police. He thought it was imperative for me to return home immediately."

Mr. Drew proceeded to tell Don and Laura the complete story of the embezzlement case.

Laura looked worried. "The Monroe National Bank had my mother's securities!" she exclaimed. "You don't suppose—"

"Maybe," Don put in, "Nancy learned something in connection with this at the Aborn house and is staying to get more information."

"Oh, she shouldn't have done it!" Laura cried out fearfully.

"Now there may not be anything to your theory," Mr. Drew remarked. "Don't borrow trouble."

Don patted Laura's shoulder. "Sure. We have enough worries as it is. Mr. Drew, you were telling us why you came back early."

"Yes. Although I'm making a private investigation for Mr. Seward, the bank president, Chief McGinnis has been helping me on an unofficial basis. We're old friends, you see.

"When Nancy told me that two of the suspects—the Dowds—were in the acting profession and had been out of town recently, I had a hunch they might tie in with the case. I asked the chief to check on any past records the couple might have, and call me in Cincinnati."

At this point Carson Drew explained that Chief McGinnis had learned that the Dowds both had records for theft and embezzlement. Each had served prison terms. Using various aliases, they had either acted or worked in theaters in several states and among other crimes had robbed the ticket offices.

"When the chief told me this," said Carson Drew, "I asked him to take the list of missing securities to various brokerage offices in the River Heights area. He did this and found that during the past few days all of them had been sold by a woman."

"The same woman?" Don asked.

"Apparently not," Mr. Drew replied. "At least when Chief McGinnis asked for the woman's description it was different every time."

"How odd!" Laura exclaimed. "Could it have been Mrs. Dowd? Since she's an actress she must be good at disguise."

"You may be right," Mr. Drew acknowledged. "Anyway, the chief sent two officers to their house to pick up the Dowds for questioning."

"Did they find them?" Don asked eagerly.

The lawyer shook his head. "When the police got to the house they learned that the actor and actress had had a man caller earlier in the day and that the three had left together. Mr. Dowd said they would not be back."

"How discouraging for you"—Laura sighed in sympathy—"but I'm sure you'll find them."

"There's a state alarm out for the couple," Mr. Drew said. "They shouldn't be able to get very far."

"What do the Dowds look like?" Laura asked.

In reply, the lawyer took two photographs from his breast pocket and handed them to her.

Laura held the pictures toward the light on the dashboard. She shook her head in disbelief. "These are the Dowds?" she repeated.

"Yes, why? Have you seen them before?"

Laura said in a tense voice, "I know them as Mr. and Mrs. Aborn. Oh, Mr. Drew, if they've caught Nancy, she's in real danger!"

CHAPTER XVI

A Speedy Getaway

UNAWARE that help was coming, Nancy worked feverishly to slip her hands out of the ropes in the dark cellar of the shack.

"How are you doing?" Jacob Aborn asked her.

"The bonds are becoming looser," Nancy replied.

Suddenly she recalled Hannah's promise to send the police to the Aborns' home if she had not returned at a reasonable hour. When she told the imprisoned man about this, it seemed to give him courage.

However, to herself Nancy said, "By that time those criminals will have escaped. They may even prevent Hannah from carrying out her plan! And both Laura and Hannah may be harmed!"

As if to offset this alarming possibility, the ropes around Nancy's hands suddenly pulled free.

"I did it!" she exclaimed, and Mr. Aborn sprang from his bench, crying, "We'll be able to escape!"

Nancy did not respond, for she was working grimly at the ropes which bound her feet. "If I could only see!" she muttered.

Then she remembered the packet of matches in her skirt pocket. She took it out and lighted a match, which she stuck in a crack in the wall. As the light burned she worked to untie the knots that bound her ankles. Several more matches were used before she was free.

"Miss Drew, you're the most ingenious girl I've ever met!" Mr. Aborn said admiringly. "I wish I could think that fast. It just occurred to me that there's a can of kerosene under the stairs. You might fill the lantern."

Nancy found the can and in a few seconds the place was aglow with light.

"Now I'll open the padlock again," Nancy told Mr. Aborn.

After getting the key she hurried to the side of Laura's guardian. A minute later the chains fell to the floor with a loud thud.

"At last!" Jacob Aborn cried in relief.

"Our next step," said Nancy, "is to get out of here as fast as we can and then try to alert the police."

"It's my bet," her companion said, "that Dowd has already skipped town."

Nancy was inclined to agree, but since the swindler had not expected his two prisoners to escape, he might still be at the Aborn house with his wife.

"We'll head for my car," Nancy said, "and decide what we'll do when we reach it."

Jacob Aborn moved forward several steps, then his knees began to tremble. "My legs will be all right after I've used them for a few minutes," he apologized.

But try as he would, the man was unable to climb the stairway unassisted. Nancy reached out a strong arm to help him. At last they reached the top of the stairway.

The young sleuth led the way to the door, unbolted it, and the two stepped outside.

"What a relief!" Jacob Aborn gasped, filling his lungs with pure air.

In the east, the moon had risen over the woods and the sky was peppered with stars. The route among the trees would be easy to find in the clear night. Yet Nancy glanced uneasily at her companion, wondering if he would be able to walk to the car.

As if reading her thoughts, Aborn said, "I'm fine now. Let's go!"

Nancy offered her arm again, and at a slow pace they walked across the clearing and entered the woods. They had gone but a short way when Mr. Aborn sank down on a log, breathing heavily.

"You go on without me, Nancy," he said in a voice shaky with fatigue. "I can't do it."

"Just rest here for a moment," Nancy said encouragingly, unwilling to leave the man.

Shortly, Mr. Aborn felt he could continue. Leaning heavily on Nancy, he moved forward, refusing to pause again even for a brief rest.

"You're a very kind girl to help me," he said hoarsely.

Nancy replied modestly, "I'm *so* glad I found you. Think of what it means to Laura to have her real guardian found! I know she will be happy living with you and your wife."

At the mention of his wife's name Mr. Aborn said he was grateful that she had gone away before the Dowds invaded their home. "She might have been made a prisoner too!" he declared.

Presently, with a feeling of relief, Nancy caught sight of her convertible standing among the bushes where she had left it. After she had helped Mr. Aborn into the front seat, Nancy took her place behind the steering wheel.

"Now we'll drive to the nearest police station," she announced. "You direct me."

She inserted the key and tried the starter. To Nancy's surprise, the motor did not turn over.

"That's funny," she said, and tried again. Nothing happened. Next, Nancy glanced at the fuel gauge. It registered half full.

"I wonder if your battery's dead," Mr. Aborn said in a faint voice.

"I think not," Nancy replied, as she reached into the glove compartment and took out an extra flashlight she kept there for emergencies.

She got out of the car, lifted the hood, and flashed her light inside. She had taken a course in automobile mechanics and knew the possible sources of trouble.

"I see what the trouble is," Nancy called. "The distributor has been uncapped and the rotor's missing! This is sabotage!" Without this necessary part the car could not start. "I'm sure that Mr. Dowd is the saboteur," she added angrily.

Mr. Aborn sighed resignedly. "Stumpy Dowd leaves no stones unturned," he said in a tired voice. "Just in case we might escape he wanted to make certain we'd have no transportation. I'm afraid, Nancy, that we'll have to go to the main highway for help."

As Mr. Aborn spoke, Nancy heard a car motor not far away. Eagerly she looked to right and left but saw no approaching headlights.

"Quick! Duck down!" Mr. Aborn whispered, and Nancy crouched in the bushes alongside her car.

A dark foreign sports car emerged from the Eagle Rock lane, then made a left-hand turn in the direction of Twin Lakes!

"It's the Dowds making a getaway!" Mr. Aborn said. "We're too late!"

Nancy was alarmed by this turn of events. She wondered why Stumpy Dowd was not heading toward River Heights. Had he given up the idea of going to the Drews' residence and forcing Laura Pendleton to give him the jewels? Or was he taking an alternative route there?

"Oh dear! I wish there were a telephone nearby!" Nancy moaned. She told Mr. Aborn that his had been disconnected.

Jacob Aborn spoke up. "Nancy, I'm sure that Dowd and his wife have left my house for good. I think the best plan is for us to go there."

"Yes," Nancy agreed. "After you're safely inside I'll go for help."

"I can't let you do that," Jacob Aborn protested. "Few cars come along this road at night. You'll have an extremely long walk before you reach the main highway."

Silently Nancy agreed, but she also noted that the man's strength was almost spent. She helped him from the car, and the two slowly approached the lane that led to Mr. Aborn's house.

"Oh, if I could only get my hands on that scoundrel!" the man muttered.

The thought gave him new strength, and he moved forward again. Cautiously the two crept toward the house, approaching it from the rear.

"We'd better make certain that no one's here," Nancy whispered.

As they drew near the back door she saw that it stood ajar, as though someone had left hurriedly without taking time to shut it.

With Jacob Aborn close behind her, Nancy stepped cautiously into the kitchen. There was profound silence. The place appeared deserted.

Crossing the room on tiptoe, Nancy and Mr. Aborn walked toward the living room. He clicked on a light. Everything was in disorder. A chair had been overturned and papers were scattered about.

"The Dowds certainly made a thorough search," Nancy remarked.

Just then Mr. Aborn's eyes fell upon the wall safe which stood open. With a cry of alarm he tottered across the room to look inside. Everything had been taken out.

Mr. Aborn groaned. He told Nancy that a sizable sum of his own money had been in the safe, along with shares of negotiable stock. Stumpy Dowd had forced him to tell the safe's combination on threat of harming Laura.

Mr. Aborn, white as starch, sank into a nearby chair and buried his head in his hands. "Nearly all my securities were in there," he said. One quick glance at him told Nancy that the man was on the verge of a complete collapse. She could not leave him alone, yet how could she get help without doing so?

A second later she and Mr. Aborn were startled to hear a car driving up the lane. Were the Dowds returning? Had the couple merely gone out for a while, or had they forgotten something in their hasty flight?

Nancy's next thought was far worse than either of these. Had Stumpy Dowd somehow learned that his two prisoners had escaped?

CHAPTER XVII

Two-way Detecting

As THE automobile pulled to a halt, Mr. Aborn slumped to the floor in a faint. Evidently he had shared Nancy's thought that the Dowds were returning, and would force their way in. The terrifying thought that he might become a prisoner again had been too much for the exhausted man.

"Oh!" Nancy cried out.

From the window Nancy saw four people hurriedly alighting from the car. A moment later the bell rang and a woman's voice cried, "Mr. Aborn —Mr. Aborn—please let us in. It's the Donnells!"

Nancy hurried to the front door and flung it open. "Cathy! Jim!" she cried out. "Oh, you don't know how glad I am to see you!"

The two young people introduced Nancy to their parents, a good-looking couple in their forties. Then they stepped inside.

"What are you doing here, Nancy?" Jim Donnell asked, puzzled at the girl's disheveled appearance. "What's going on?"

Nancy replied by saying Mr. Aborn was ill, and there was no time for further explanation right now. She hastily led the family into the living room. When they saw their unconscious friend on the floor, Mrs. Donnell rushed forward with an excited cry.

"How dreadful!" she exclaimed.

As she knelt down, the kindly woman said she was a registered nurse. After a brief examination of the patient she reported that Mr. Aborn appeared to be suffering from malnutrition and shock.

While Jim and his father lifted him onto the couch, Nancy told what had happened to him. The Donnells were stunned.

Before they could discuss it, however, Nancy turned to Jim. "Two phone calls must be made right away," she said. "Would you be able to take care of them for me?"

"Glad to," the boy said. "I suppose you want me to notify the police to pick up Stumpy Dowd—"

"Yes," Nancy said tersely, and described the black foreign car.

She next asked Jim to call Chief McGinnis at River Heights and tell him to have extra men patrol the Drew home. "Find out if Mrs. Gruen and

Laura are all right," she requested, "and see if our housekeeper knows where to get in touch with Dad."

Jim said he would do all of these things. As soon as he returned, he would try to fix Nancy's car.

After Jim left, Nancy turned to the others. Mr. Aborn had regained consciousness and said he felt better and able to talk.

"Lillian," he said, giving Mrs. Donnell a wan smile, "the angels must have sent you. How did you know we were in trouble here?"

"We didn't for sure," Mr. Donnell replied gravely, "until tonight—it's a long story."

The gray-haired man said that he and his wife had been amazed to hear on Tuesday from their children that Marian Aborn had returned from Florida and that she and Jacob had met Laura Pendleton at Twin Lakes.

"We were sure you would have told us of your change of plans, if this were true, Jacob," he said to his old friend. "Anyway, we came over here yesterday morning to say hello and meet Laura. No one answered the bell."

"We concluded," said Mrs. Donnell, "that Nancy Drew had been mistaken in thinking that you were coming back here—anyway, we remembered you saying that due to the illness of Marian's mother you would not be able to come here with Laura until after your wife's return."

"That's right," said Mr. Aborn. He explained to Nancy that first there had been legal technicalities regarding his appointment as the orphan's guardian, since he had been living in another state. That was why his ward had remained at her boarding school.

Mrs. Donnell went on to say that this evening they had received a telephone call from Mrs. Aborn who was still in Florida. "Marian had tried several times to get you and was upset to learn that the phone here was disconnected. She called us to see why."

"My wife hadn't heard from me in over two weeks," Mr. Aborn stated.

Mrs. Donnell said, "But Marian thought she had. Mrs. Aborn sent telegrams here and replies came to her in Florida."

Mr. Donnell said that when the family heard that Marian Aborn was indeed in Florida, they were fearful something was terribly wrong.

"We told Marian what we knew, suggested she come home immediately, and said we would come over here right away to see what we could uncover."

"Thank goodness you did," Nancy sighed, and Mr. Aborn gave his friends a grateful smile. Then he asked, "How is Marian's mother?"

"Getting along very well."

"When will my wife arrive?" Mr. Aborn asked anxiously.

"She's taking a night plane from Miami to the Hamilton airport," Mrs. Donnell replied. "My husband will meet her."

Cathy's mother then went to the kitchen to prepare a light meal for Mr. Aborn. Nancy excused herself and went to wash her face, legs, and grimy hands. Refreshed, she returned to the living room, wondering what was keeping Jim so long.

"He'll be here soon, Nancy," said Cathy.

"I'll feel much better when I know everything's all right at home," Nancy replied.

While Mr. Aborn ate, the pretty detective told the others of Stumpy Dowd's connection with Mr. Drew's case.

"What a story!" Mr. Donnell exclaimed.

Nancy excused herself for a moment and went to the front door to listen for Jim's car. As she stood on the steps her heart suddenly leaped. A tall figure stood up from behind a bush near the front steps.

"Nancy?" a man's voice called softly.

Nancy knew who it was. "Dad!" she cried out.

Carson Drew leaped the steps and gave his daughter a resounding kiss. "Are you all right?" he whispered.

When Nancy said yes, and that it was safe to

talk aloud, Don Cameron and Laura emerged from some shrubbery.

"We saw lights and heard voices," Laura explained. "We thought it was the Aborns. What's going on here, Nancy?"

"Yes, tell us!" Don urged.

Once again Nancy explained what had happened. Carson Drew listened to his daughter's story of her encounter with the thief, a stern expression on his face.

"You were lucky to come out of this so well," he remarked.

"Yes," Laura agreed. "And it's so wonderful to have a guardian whom you say is nice!"

"Mr. Aborn is a fine person, Laura," Nancy said. "I'll take you in to meet him in a minute."

Carson Drew now brought Nancy up to date on his news, and ended by saying, "We were so worried we drove here immediately, not even taking time to call the police."

Don added that they had left Mr. Drew's car at the end of the lane and were scouting the house to see if Nancy were inside when she had appeared on the front steps.

"How many times I wished you were here!" said Nancy. She now suggested that everyone come into the house to meet the others. "Jim Donnell," she added, "should return any minute."

"I'll wait for the young man out here and act

as guard in case the Dowds show up," Carson Drew said, sitting down on a step. "The rest of you run along—"

As Nancy walked inside with Don and Laura she saw that Mr. and Mrs. Donnell were helping Mr. Aborn up the stairs to his bedroom. Hearing voices, the guardian turned, looked at his ward, and exclaimed:

"Laura dear—at last—I'd know you anywhere! You look just like your mother!"

"Mr. Aborn!" Laura cried out. She raced up the steps and gave her guardian a big kiss.

Introductions were quickly made, and when Mr. Aborn was settled in his bed, he had a visit with Laura and Nancy. But after they had chatted for a few minutes the girls could see that the man needed sleep badly.

"We'll say good night now," said Nancy. "Sweet dreams." She turned off the light, and they went downstairs.

When Nancy and Laura reached the first floor, they found Mr. Drew and Jim Donnell talking in the hall with a state trooper. While Cathy took Laura aside, Nancy walked toward the group.

She was introduced to Sergeant Murphy, then Carson Drew explained to her that the state police were putting all available cars on the chase and hoped to round up the Dowds and their accomplice shortly.

"Good!" Nancy exclaimed. "But what about Mrs. Gruen?"

Sergeant Murphy said that he had talked with Chief McGinnis. The River Heights official had immediately sent a patrol car and four men to the Drews' home.

"Your housekeeper was relieved to hear that you, Miss Drew, had been found," he reported. "Nothing unusual has happened at your home tonight. But it will be closely guarded until the Dowds and their accomplice are caught."

"Oh, I'm glad," said Nancy. Sergeant Murphy left, after saying he would check back later.

Nancy and Mr. Drew walked into the living room, and she introduced her father to Mr. and Mrs. Donnell and Cathy. After a few minutes of excited conversation, the young sleuth said:

"Dad, I have a hunch that the man 'Fred' whom Stumpy Dowd mentioned is someone employed at the Monroe National Bank. Tell me, was Mrs. Pendleton's name ever mentioned in connection with the missing securities?"

Mr. Drew shook his head. "No, Nancy, it wasn't."

"Then," said Nancy, "I think we're going to find that Laura's bonds were never deposited in the bank's vault. Whoever took them and passed them on to Stumpy Dowd must be someone who works in the custodian department of the bank."

"That's good reasoning, Nancy," her father agreed, "but we have checked almost all the employees and they've been given a clean bill of health. One man, Mr. Hamilton's assistant, has been on vacation and we won't be able to interview him for another week or so."

"What's the man's name?" Nancy asked.

Mr. Drew consulted a list of names which he took from his pocket. "William Frednich."

Nancy snapped her fingers. "Frednich! Maybe *he's* the 'Fred' the Dowds were talking about. And if he is," she continued excitedly, "I think they're together and I believe I know where the Dowds are hiding out with this man!"

Carson Drew looked at his daughter in amazement. "Where?" he asked.

"Not far from here," Nancy said mysteriously. Then she jumped up from her chair. "Let's find out, Dad!"

CHAPTER XVIII

Night Trail

CARSON DREW, startled, looked at his daughter. "Where do you think the Dowds and Fred are hiding, Nancy?"

"In a bungalow on Twin Lakes—the one I told you we stayed in after Laura rescued us," she explained. "My main reasons for thinking so are these: I saw a black foreign car come from there, and the place was well-stocked with food. Fred may have been living there."

"Go on. This is interesting," the lawyer said.

Nancy's hunch was that the thieves had first planned the bank theft, then the Dowds had rented the bungalow under an assumed name.

"Makes sense." Carson Drew nodded.

"Fred," Nancy continued, "knew of Laura's large estate and jewelry, and got the idea of having Stumpy Dowd impersonate Mr. Aborn. In order to get the jewelry they had to have Laura with them, so they decided to take her to the Melrose Lake house."

"Good logic," said Mr. Drew. "Then, when the real Mr. Aborn appeared, they had to kidnap him temporarily. Well, we'll follow your hunch. Shall we go?"

The others offered to go, but Mr. Drew thought that the Donnells should stay with Mr. Aborn and Laura.

"Please do," Nancy added. "After all, my hunch could be wrong. The Dowds may return here."

"We'll nab 'em if they do!" Jim said determinedly.

A few minutes later Mr. Drew's car was on the detour again, heading for the Twin Lakes road. When they reached it, there were no other cars in evidence.

"That's odd," said Nancy, knowing that this was the only road which connected the two resorts.

"Oh, oh!" said Don. "Look!"

Mr. Drew had also seen a small red light a few hundred feet distant. He slowed up. Ahead was a gate obstruction across the highway. On it was nailed a sign which read:

ROAD UNDER CONSTRUCTION
Travel at your own risk

"This is great!" Mr. Drew remarked unhappily.

"Maybe it won't be too bad," Nancy said. "I came this way the other day and I think I know all the turns."

"Why don't we try it, sir?" Don spoke up.

"All right."

Don got out of the car and moved the barrier enough so Mr. Drew could drive through. They went slowly, because of the steam shovels, bulldozers, and equipment parked along the road.

To make matters worse, the pavement was gone in places where repairs were being made. The car tires wallowed in soft dirt.

Soon, however, they reached the end of the construction section and Carson Drew stepped on the accelerator. The car responded with a burst of speed.

"We're not far from Twin Lakes now," Nancy said as she spotted a few familiar landmarks.

Don wanted to know what the plan would be when they reached the bungalow. Mr. Drew said they would first check to see if the foreign car were in the vicinity. "Of course it will be hidden."

"Next," Nancy added, "we'll have to make sure Fred and the Dowds are there, and not some innocent people. But if Stumpy's there, we'll notify the police. Right, Dad?"

"Unless Dowd sees us first," he said grimly.

Nancy said she hoped this would not happen.

"But I suppose they probably will have someone acting as a lookout."

"As I understand it, Nancy," said her father, "the bungalow is in an isolated spot."

"Yes, and there are a lot of trees around it."

"Could anyone inside the house make a getaway by boat?" Don asked.

"Not easily," Nancy answered. "The bungalow is not built over the water. It's some distance from the lake and there's no dock where a boat could be tied." Presently she said, "We're about a mile from the bungalow."

Carson Drew's face tensed. He drove to a point about a tenth of a mile from the lane leading down to the bungalow, then stopped the car in a clearing off the road.

"We'll cover the rest of the distance on foot," he announced.

As Nancy got out the right-hand side of the car after Don she glanced at the luminous dial on the clock. It was three o'clock in the morning!

Walking three abreast, the sleuths saw the bungalow below. It was in darkness.

"I don't see any sign of a car," Don whispered to Nancy, as he guided her by the arm.

Carson Drew was silent, but suddenly he jerked to attention. A twig had snapped. Now they saw a man walking toward the trio through the woods!

As Don, Nancy, and Mr. Drew ducked behind

some shrubbery, they noticed that the man approaching them was carrying a fishing pole and a box of the type ordinarily used for bait.

Passing by the watchers, he walked unhurriedly toward the beach. At this moment the moon chose to show itself brilliantly, and Nancy observed that the man was tall and heavy.

"Hello, Sam," he said, and now the watchers could see a rowboat and passenger gliding out of the shadows.

"I hope the fish are biting well this morning." His voice carried clearly in the stillness.

The fisherman deposited his gear in the boat, and the two companions shoved off. They were barely out of sight when Don whispered hoarsely, "A light in the bungalow."

From the second-story window had come a flash of light. It did not reappear.

"Someone's up there!" Nancy whispered. "Maybe the fisherman alerted him."

"Let's circle the house," said Carson Drew, and suggested that he take the left half of the circle while Nancy and Don took the right. They would meet back at this same spot in a few minutes.

"Be careful now," he warned the young people.

"You too, Dad," Nancy said.

The route Nancy and Don took led past the door into the first floor of the boathouse bungalow. Cautiously they listened at the exit. There was no sound from within. They went on to the beach side.

The two tiptoed among the shadows as far as the center of the rear of the building without incident, then quietly returned to the meeting place. When they arrived, Mr. Drew was not there.

"That's funny," said Nancy, a little alarmed. "Where *is* Dad?"

Just then she and Don heard a low groan. It seemed to come from behind a tree about twenty feet away. Forgetting caution, the couple rushed to the spot. Behind its broad trunk a man lay sprawled on the ground. Mr. Drew!

"Dad!" Nancy exclaimed, kneeling down. She felt the lawyer's pulse. It was steady.

"I think he was knocked out," said Don angrily. "Nancy, you're right about this being a hide-out. We must get the police!"

"And right away!" Nancy agreed, as Carson Drew sat up groggily. In a moment he could talk.

The lawyer said that after leaving Nancy and Don he had started around the bungalow. Someone had come from behind and struck him. "I suppose he dragged me here."

"Stumpy Dowd, I'll bet!" Nancy exclaimed. "And this may mean that he and his wife made a getaway while Don and I were on the other side of the bungalow! Dad, do you feel well enough to try to follow them?"

"Yes, but where did they go?" he asked. "And how? By boat, car, or on foot?"

As if in answer to his question, the three suddenly saw in the clear moonlight the figures of two men and a woman running up the bungalow lane toward the road. Each man carried a big suitcase. Laura's inheritance and Mr. Aborn's little fortune!

"After them!" Don cried.

But Mr. Drew could not make it. He tottered unsteadily and leaned against the pine. "Go on!" he said.

"No!" Nancy replied quickly. "Don, bring Dad's car here, will you?"

As the boy started off, the trio heard the muffled backfire of an automobile coming from the direction of the woods across the main road.

"Hurry, Don!" Nancy urged. "They had a car hidden there."

By the time Don returned, Carson Drew felt better. He suggested that Nancy drive, since she was more familiar with the road. When everyone was in the car, with the lawyer in the rear seat, they took off.

Upon reaching the road, the young sleuth turned right. "I think this is the direction the other car took," she said. "Anyway, it leads to Stamford, where I know there's a state police headquarters."

Carson Drew sat up groggily

The road became rough and was full of sharp turns. Nancy drove fast but carefully, slowing at each curve. There was no sign of another car until Don suddenly cried out:

"I think we're approaching a car!"

Nancy peered forward intently. She saw nothing but the road ahead.

"It's hidden now by that hill in front of us," Don told her.

There was a long moment of suspense, then Nancy exclaimed, "I see it!"

"Do you think it's the Dowds?" Don asked.

"It could be," Mr. Drew replied.

As the car reached a smooth, straight piece of road, Nancy put it to a faster and faster pace.

"We're gaining on them!" Don said exuberantly.

Little by little the Drew sedan crept up on the car ahead. Soon its headlights spotlighted the rear of the other vehicle—a black foreign car! Three figures were silhouetted inside it!

At the same moment Nancy caught sight of a huge black-and-white checkerboard sign at the side of the road. A bad curve ahead! With well-timed precision, Nancy eased up on her speed and gradually used her brake, knowing that abrupt pressure might cause a bad skid.

"That other driver isn't paying any attention to the warning!" Don exclaimed.

The snakelike curve was only a few hundred feet ahead on a steep downgrade. The occupants of the Drew sedan held their breath. Would the others make the turn? There came a violent screech of brakes.

"Oh no!" Nancy cried out in horror.

As she and her companions watched, the foreign car shot off the edge of the road and plunged down a steep cliff!

CHAPTER XIX

Missing Property

STUNNED by the accident to the speeding car, Nancy brought the sedan to a halt at the curve. Everyone inside was reluctant to look down into the ravine below, from which there was not a sound.

But only for an instant. Then Carson Drew urged, "Out, everyone, quickly! We must do what we can for those people!"

Nancy and Don sprang from the car and rushed to the edge of the road. The lawyer was close behind them.

As the three gazed down into the ravine, the first light of dawn revealed that the foreign car had rolled nearly to the bottom of it and overturned against a boulder. A wheel had been torn loose from its axle and the body had been smashed in. There was no sign of any of the three occupants.

A silence held the trio above. It was inconceivable that anyone in the wreck could be alive!

At last Carson Drew found his voice. "I guess we'd better notify the police and emergency squad," he said.

Don agreed, but Nancy thought they should first see if by chance any of the accident victims were alive.

Mr. Drew and Don nodded, and followed Nancy as she scrambled down the incline. Nancy, in the lead, gasped as she saw the body of a strange man, apparently not the driver, which had been flung out of the car into a clump of bushes near the wreck. She also noticed gasoline spilling from a hole in the tank. Vaguely she thought of fire and an explosion.

"Hurry!" she urged.

As the three drew closer they saw a man's leg and a woman's high-heeled shoe protruding from beneath the left-hand side of the car.

With frantic haste Don and Mr. Drew dragged the man out, while Nancy tugged at the woman's body. Stumpy Dowd and his wife! Both were breathing, but unconscious. The victims, cut and badly bruised, were carried to a safe place on the grass.

"Now let's see about the other man, Mr. Drew," urged Don.

As they headed for the bushes where he lay,

Nancy stared at the car. "The suitcases!" she thought. "Laura's inheritance and Mr. Aborn's little fortune! I must get them out before they may be burned up!"

Crawling under the wreck, she began to grope about frantically. Her hand struck a suitcase and she dragged it out.

At that instant Nancy realized how hot the metal was. There might be spontaneous combustion at any second. She must work fast to save the second suitcase!

"It's the only way I can ever repay Laura for saving my life on Twin Lakes!" Nancy thought.

By feeling around she found the bag and triumphantly brought it out, only to be jerked from the scene by Carson Drew and Don.

"Nancy!" Carson Drew cried, white-faced and horror-stricken. "Are you mad? Those suitcases aren't worth your life!"

There was a sudden explosion. Then flames enveloped the car and the dry grass in the immediate vicinity began to burn.

Don Cameron shuddered, but looked at Nancy, admiration showing in his eyes. "You're the most courageous girl I've ever met," he said slowly. "Nancy, you might have been killed!"

As she herself realized what a narrow escape she had had, Nancy breathed a prayer of thanksgiving.

She was shaken and silent as the men threw dirt on the flames to keep them from spreading. When they finished, Don told Nancy that he and Mr. Drew thought the third man would be all right, although the stranger as well as the Dowds were injured, perhaps seriously.

"Now I suppose we must get the three of them to a hospital as fast as we can," he said.

At that moment they all heard the low whine of an ambulance alarm. This was followed by a police siren.

Nancy, Mr. Drew, and Don looked at one another hopefully. "Do you suppose—" Nancy began.

She was right. Help had come! A moment later police and emergency squad cars stopped at the top of the ravine. Four officers, two stretcher-bearers, and an intern, clad in white, hurried down to the group.

"Thank goodness," said Mr. Drew. Introductions were quickly made, then he asked, "How did you know about the accident?"

An officer, Lieutenant Gill, told him that a farmer living not far away had seen the speeding car go off the road and notified headquarters.

"When we heard it was a black foreign car, we were suspicious immediately," he said. "Can you identify these people as the Dowds?"

"From pictures, yes," said Mr. Drew, and briefly told the whole story of the Dowd affair up to the present moment.

"And I can testify that they were impersonating the Aborns," Nancy added.

"Anybody know who the other man is?" Lieutenant Gill inquired.

"I believe," Mr. Drew replied, "that he's William Frednich, assistant to the president of the River Heights branch of the Monroe National Bank. He's suspected of removing certain securities from the bank."

During this conversation the intern had been examining the accident victims and the attendants had laid them on stretchers. The doctor reported that the victims had been given first aid and had revived. They would be in good shape after a short stay in the hospital.

"They'll get a nice long rest after that," said Lieutenant Gill, "in the state pen. I shan't try to question them now."

As the prisoners were carried up to the ambulance, with the others following, Lieutenant Gill explained to the Dowds how Nancy had saved them from being burned in the wreckage.

"I don't believe it," said Stumpy ungratefully.

His wife was more gracious. "Thanks, Miss Drew. And I want to tell you I'm tired of this whole business. You're only a kid but you've really taught me a lesson."

Nancy did not answer. She found herself choking up, and tears came into her eyes.

As the ambulance moved away, Nancy, quickly brushing her moist eyes dry with the backs of her hands, turned toward the east. She observed that a beautiful sunrise was beginning to flood the sky with brilliant color.

Don yawned. "What do you say we head for home?" he suggested. "Otherwise, I'll never be able to make my sister's wedding this evening."

"Oh dear!" Nancy exclaimed. "I forgot all about it. Please forgive us for keeping you up all night."

Don grinned. "I wouldn't have missed this excitement for anything!"

"I suggest," said Mr. Drew, "that we go back to Nancy's hotel and the Drews will get some sleep. Don, you take my car and return to River Heights. Later, Nancy and I will take a taxi and pick up her convertible at the Aborns'."

"Thank you, sir. I'll do that."

While the three had been talking, Lieutenant Gill had been wedging open one of the two locked suitcases which Nancy had taken from the wrecked car. Mr. Drew and the others walked over as he lifted the lid.

The bag was jammed with feminine clothing. There were several dresses, a large make-up kit, pieces of lingerie, shoes, and several wigs—a gray one, a black hairpiece, and one which was decidedly auburn.

"That clinches it, Dad!" Nancy exclaimed. "Mrs. Dowd must have gone around in disguise to cash the bonds."

"But where's the money she got?" Don asked.

"It must be in the other bag," Nancy suggested, "together with securities and money belonging to Laura Pendleton, Mr. Aborn, and River Heights bank clients."

Lieutenant Gill opened the second suitcase. It contained men's clothing and toilet articles.

"Nancy, you risked your life for this!" Don exclaimed.

Nancy Drew could not believe her eyes. Had she been mistaken in believing that Stumpy Dowd had put the contents of Mr. Aborn's safe in the bags? Quickly she glanced down at the foreign car. Had Laura's inheritance and other people's money burned in it?

The thought stunned the young sleuth. But in a moment an idea came to her.

"There's just a possibility the papers *are* here," she said.

All eyes turned on the girl detective, as the group awaited a further explanation.

CHAPTER XX

A Surprise Gift

"I'M SURE," said Nancy, "that Mr. Dowd not only put the money and securities in one of these suitcases, but never removed them!"

"Then *where* are they?" Don asked.

Nancy smiled. "These bags may have false bottoms!"

Lieutenant Gill said, "Why, of course. I should have thought of that."

Kneeling down, he soon found that Nancy was right. The bottom of each bag opened up, disclosing packages of thousand-dollar bills and securities.

"Good thinking, Nancy," said Don admiringly. "You're a whiz of a detective, all right."

It took Mr. Drew and the officers several minutes to count the large sum of money and make a rough estimate of the value of the stocks and bonds. When they finished, the officer gave Carson Drew a receipt to turn over to the president of the Monroe National Bank. Meanwhile, he would take the stolen property to police headquarters and send on a detailed report.

A few minutes later Nancy's group said good-by to the officers, and returned to Mr. Drew's car. When they reached the Beach Cliff Hotel, Nancy and Mr. Drew got out. They thanked Don for all he had done.

"Don't mention it." The young man grinned. Turning to Nancy, he added, "I kept my date with you yesterday after all!"

As he got into the driver's seat Don said that when he returned the car to the Drews' home he would tell Hannah Gruen what had happened.

It was now very light. Nancy and her father, exhausted, could hardly wait to get a few hours sleep. They tumbled into their beds and slept until noon, then met in the hotel dining room for a hearty brunch.

"How's your head, Dad?" Nancy asked.

"Sound as ever!" Carson Drew said, grinning. "I don't even have a bump."

"Then we have a date," Nancy told him, waving a note. "This was at the desk. I picked it up. The clerk said Jim Donnell left it a little while ago."

"The date's with him?" Mr. Drew asked.

"No. Laura Pendleton. She says she and the

Aborns are thrilled by the news which the police relayed and would like us to come to their house as soon as possible. What do you say, Dad?"

"We'll go."

As Nancy finished her pancakes and sausages she remarked that she could hardly wait to start for the Aborns' home. "I wonder if the Dowds have confessed everything and what Mr. Frednich had to say."

"In my opinion it's an open and shut case," the lawyer replied.

While Mr. Drew paid the hotel bill, Nancy called a taxi and soon the Drews were heading for Eagle Rock Lane. Reaching it, they got out of the cab and the lawyer paid the driver.

Nancy slid in behind the steering wheel of her convertible, as Mr. Drew got in on the other side. The motor started at once. "Good old Jim," Nancy said with a smile, and drove up the lane to the Aborn home.

As she parked, the front door was opened by a woman of about forty-five. Her pretty face showed humor, kindness, and intelligence.

After the Drews had introduced themselves, the woman said she was Marian Aborn and had reached home "in the wee small hours" because her plane was late. "I've been most eager to meet you two," she added, smiling. "How can I ever thank you for all you've done?"

As the callers went inside, Laura Pendleton hurried down from the second floor. After greeting Mr. Drew she gave Nancy a kiss and exclaimed, "Everything is so wonderful—you've captured the thieves and recovered all the money—and I have the nicest guardians anyone could ever hope for!"

"And Jacob and I have a daughter to love!" said Marian Aborn, smiling fondly at Laura.

Nancy asked how Mr. Aborn felt. His wife said, "Come see for yourselves," and led the way to a small study at the rear of the house.

She knocked, then opened the door, and Nancy heard the steady drum of typewriter keys. Jacob Aborn was seated behind the machine.

The erstwhile cellar prisoner already looked like a new man. His face was flooded with color, and his eyes were alert and happy. Now he stood up, greeted the Drews, and expressed his great appreciation for all they had done in recovering his and Laura's property.

He grinned at Nancy. "First time a girl ever risked her life for me!" he said. "To show my appreciation I'm writing my adventure. You know, writing is my business. If I sell this one to a magazine, I'm going to give the proceeds to Nancy's favorite charity—the River Heights Youth Center!"

"Why, that's terrific!" Nancy exclaimed.

Mrs. Aborn's face sobered. She said that she

had not yet heard the entire story of what had happened. Before anyone had a chance to tell her, the doorbell rang. Lieutenant Gill walked in with Chief McGinnis of River Heights and another man. While Nancy greeted the officers, her father hurried to shake hands with the stranger.

"This is Mr. Seward, president of the Monroe National Bank," he announced a moment later, and introduced the dignified white-haired man.

The president's glance included the policemen as he said, "I want to thank all of you in person for the splendid job you did in capturing the Dowds and the two bank employees involved in the thefts."

"There is a fourth man?" Nancy asked in amazement.

Mr. Seward explained that Alma Dowd's brother, Joe Jackson, had been employed by the Monroe National Bank in their vault department for some time. He and Frednich had cooked up the scheme of taking the securities. They had done this between audits of the bank's holdings. Frednich, in his job as assistant custodian, had known exactly how to place his hands on the valuable stocks and bonds.

"Frednich overheard Mrs. Pendleton's discussion with me about Laura and the large estate she would inherit some day," Mr. Seward said, "and also that Mr. Aborn would be her guardian.

When Frednich learned that Laura Pendleton had a valuable jewelry collection, he instantly thought of a swindle scheme. Frednich had chanced to meet Mr. Aborn one time while vacationing at Melrose Lake. He had been amazed by the strong resemblance between Aborn and Stumpy Dowd, whom Alma's brother had introduced to Frednich. He asked Dowd to impersonate Mr. Aborn and to move up the date when Laura would come to the guardian's home. He even deposited some securities with the bank in Stumpy's name, so there would be no question of Dowd's having anything to do with the thefts."

"Where is Joe Jackson now?" Nancy asked.

Chief McGinnis said he would answer this question. "We caught him cruising by the Drews' home. When we stopped the car, he tried to escape. After the whole story broke, we got a confession from him. He was going to burglarize your home, Nancy, to find the jewels."

"There's one thing I don't understand," said Mrs. Aborn. "Why did the Dowds rent the bungalow when they had helped themselves to this house?"

Nancy grinned. "I'm sure I know," she said. "Dowd was smart enough not to want either Frednich or Jackson to stay here—just in case anyone from the bank traced the thefts to them before Dowd could make a getaway. So he had Alma

Dowd rent the bungalow and convinced Frednich that it was a good hide-out."

After Mr. Aborn and Laura had signed statements for the police, the officers and Mr. Seward left. Nancy suddenly felt a sense of loneliness and realized it was because her work on the case was at an end. Would another mystery come her way to solve? she wondered. And it did. In less than a week, Nancy was facing up to the challenge of *The Mystery at Lilac Inn.*

Nancy and her father now said good-by to the family at Eagle Rock. As Nancy gave Laura a farewell hug, she asked, "When will you come to get your jewelry?"

Laura consulted her guardian, who said the next day would be convenient for them to drive to River Heights. "Will three o'clock be all right?"

"Yes indeed."

The following afternoon Laura Pendleton and the Aborns arrived promptly. After iced tea and some of Hannah's delicious open-faced sandwiches, Laura whispered to Mr. Drew that she would love to get her jewelry from the safe. Excusing himself, Nancy's father left the room and returned in a few minutes with the package, which he handed to Laura.

Nancy, meanwhile, was listening to Jacob Aborn's surprising news that he had finished his story and was sending it to a leading magazine.

"Wonderful!" said Nancy. As she said this, she looked up to see Laura standing before her. In the girl's hand was the beautiful aquamarine ring Nancy had admired earlier in the week.

"I'd like you to wear this," Laura said shyly, "as a reminder that our friendship began on the water." Quickly she slipped the ring on the third finger of Nancy's right hand.

The pretty detective gave an exclamation of delight and admired the gift for a long moment. Then she showed it to the others. At last she turned to Laura and said with genuine sincerity:

"The ring is priceless and I'll always treasure it as a reminder of you—although no one can place a value on a true friendship like ours."

Seeing tears in Laura's eyes, Nancy added quickly with a grin, "Even if we had to be shipwrecked to get an introduction!"

NANCY DREW MYSTERY STORIES®

The Mystery of the 99 Steps

BY CAROLYN KEENE

GROSSET & DUNLAP
Publishers • New York
A member of The Putnam & Grosset Group

Contents

CHAPTER I

The Strange Dream

"How exciting, Nancy! Your dad really wants Bess and me to go to France with you?" Nancy's tomboy friend exclaimed over the telephone.

"Yes, George, to help us solve a couple of mysteries. How about you girls having dinner with me tonight and I'll tell you the details."

"Give me a hint," George begged. "I can hardly wait!"

Nancy Drew laughed. "My case involves a weird dream."

"A dream!" George exclaimed. "Hypers! And what's your dad's case about?"

"Too confidential for the phone," Nancy replied. "Be here at five so we can talk it over before dinner. I'll call Bess."

Bess Marvin and George Fayne were cousins. Like Nancy, they were eighteen, and had been friends of the attractive, titian-haired girl detective for a long time. They arrived promptly. Blond Bess's warm smile revealed two dimples. George, with close-cropped dark hair, was slim and athletic—the exact opposite of her slightly plump cousin.

"We both have permission to go to France, Nancy," said Bess, "but please, *please* don't get me into any scary situations the way you have in your other mysteries."

Nancy grinned and put an arm affectionately around Bess. "I can't promise, but—"

"Of course you can't," George interrupted. "Besides, that's what makes solving mysteries so exciting. Now tell us all about everything."

The three girls went into the living room, where a cheerful blaze crackled in the fireplace. This was an unseasonably cool June day. Bess and George seated themselves in comfortable chairs, but Nancy remained standing, her back to the fire. Her blue eyes glistened excitedly.

"Begin!" George urged. "From your expression I'd say we shouldn't waste a minute getting these mysteries solved."

"How'd you guess?" said Nancy. "Dad has already gone to Paris on his case. We're to meet him at a hotel there and after a couple of days in Paris we girls will go for a visit to a large chateau in the country."

Bess's face glowed. "A real chateau! Divine!"

"Not only that," Nancy went on, smiling,

"we're having dinner guests tonight—they live in the chateau."

"We'll be staying with them?" Bess asked.

"No, they're visiting in the States for a few weeks and staying right in this house. You girls and I will be exchange guests."

George chuckled. "Will I be in exchange for a boy?"

Laughingly Nancy replied, "They're girls—Marie and Monique Bardot." She explained that arrangements had been made between her father and an aunt of the Bardot sisters. Carson Drew was a prominent attorney, who often was called upon to handle difficult cases. Frequently his daughter helped him.

"The girls' aunt, who is a few years older than their mother," Nancy continued, "lives here in River Heights. Marie and Monique are with her right now. But her apartment is too small to accommodate overnight guests. Mrs. Blair is the person with one of the mysteries—mine. She asked me to solve it."

Nancy went to stand by the fire. "You both know Mrs. Josette Blair, don't you?"

"Of course!" said Bess. "She's that lovely woman who lives in the apartment house near us. Don't tell me she's having more trouble and so soon after her husband and son were killed in that car accident. Now she has a sprained ankle! Poor Mrs. Blair," Bess added sympathetically.

"This is another kind of trouble," Nancy told the cousins. "It's weird. Every night Mrs. Blair has a horrible nightmare and wakes up with her heart pounding. In her dream she's blindfolded and is about to fall down a long flight of stairs, with someone whispering, '99 steps.'"

"How horrible!" Bess murmured.

"But," put in practical George, "at least it's only a dream. What's the mystery?"

"The mystery of the 99 steps," Nancy answered. "You see, Mrs. Blair lived in various places in France as a small child, and actually had this frightening experience, but she can't remember where or anything else about it. For years she did not think of what happened but recently had the dream again. Then something occurred that has really frightened her."

"What was it?" George asked.

Nancy said that Mrs. Blair had received a letter from Paris, written in French. "Unfortunately, in a moment of panic she destroyed the message. There was only one sentence in it. 'Tell no one about the 99 steps. Monsieur Neuf'!"

"Mr. Nine, eh?" Bess murmured, and Nancy nodded.

"It's our job," she continued, "to find Monsieur Neuf and where the 99 steps are, and—well, solve the mystery so poor Mrs. Blair can sleep peacefully again."

As Nancy stooped to poke the fire and put on

another log, Bess groaned. "I can see danger ahead with this mysterious Mr. Nine."

Suddenly the three girls were startled by a loud whirring noise. "A helicopter!" George cried out. "It's awfully close!"

The girls listened tensely, knowing it was against a River Heights ordinance for any aircraft to fly so low over the residential area. Was the pilot in trouble?

An instant later a strong downdraft of air burst from the chimney. It sent sparks, soot, and ashes over Nancy and into the room.

"Oh, Nancy!" Bess screamed.

She rushed forward with George to help Nancy. They patted out the sparks in her hair and on her sweater. Then George trampled some burning fragments on the carpet.

The scream had brought Mrs. Hannah Gruen, the Drews' housekeeper, running from the kitchen. She was a kind, pleasant-faced woman who had helped to rear Nancy since the sudden death of Mrs. Drew when the girl was three years old.

Hannah exclaimed, "What happened? Oh, my goodness!" she added, seeing Nancy covered with soot and ashes.

"That helicopter!" George exclaimed. "I'll bet it caused this mess!"

While Bess told Mrs. Gruen about the chimney episode and Nancy went upstairs to bathe, George dashed outdoors. She could see the helicopter in the distance, apparently getting ready to land at the River Heights airport.

"That pilot ought to be reported!" George thought angrily.

When Nancy came downstairs, George mentioned this and Nancy agreed. "I'll drive out to the airport tomorrow morning to see about it."

"In the meantime, Detective Drew," put in Bess, "tell us more about your mystery. For instance, how did Mr. Nine find out where Mrs. Blair is?"

"I suppose from her relatives in France. We'll ask Marie and Monique when they come. Maybe they can give us some other clues, too."

At that moment a taxi drove up and two attractive, dark-haired girls alighted. Each carried a large and a small suitcase. Nancy went to the door to meet them.

"You are Nancy Drew?" asked the taller of the pair, smiling. She had a musical voice with a delightful accent.

Nancy smiled. "*Oui*. And you are Marie, *n'est-ce pas?*" She turned to the shorter girl. "Hello, Monique. Please come in, and welcome!"

As soon as the Bardots were in the hall, Nancy introduced Bess, George, and Mrs. Gruen. Then the visitors' bags were carried upstairs.

"What a charming house!" exclaimed Monique when all the girls were seated in the living room. "You are very kind to invite us, Nancy.

George and Bess rushed forward to help Nancy

We do not want to be any trouble. Mrs. Gruen must give us something to do."

Conversation turned to Mrs. Josette Blair's mystery. The sisters felt sure none of the family in France had given their aunt's address to anyone. Marie and Monique were worried about the mysterious message she had received.

"Perhaps Tante Josette should go away," said Marie.

"I'm sure Mrs. Gruen would be glad to have her stay here," Nancy offered. "Perhaps she wouldn't be so frightened if she weren't alone."

"Merci bien," Monique said gratefully.

Presently Hannah announced dinner. At the table the group continued to discuss the mystery of the 99 steps, but the French visitors could shed no light on the subject. Nancy did not refer to her father's case. Bess and George, though disappointed, realized that it was a confidential matter and Nancy would tell them about it later.

Nancy herself was thinking, "I'll drive Bess and George home and tell them Dad's mystery then."

A luscious-looking lemon meringue pie had just been served by Hannah Gruen when the front doorbell rang.

"I'll get it," said Nancy. "Excuse me."

At the door Nancy was startled to see a man wearing a half mask! "This is the home of the Drews?" he asked in a strong French accent.

"Y-yes," Nancy replied. Fearful he would force his way inside, she held the door firmly.

The masked man did not try to enter, and Nancy made quick mental notes of his appearance. He was tall, with exceptionally long arms and feet.

The stranger, who wore heavy leather gloves, handed Nancy a sealed envelope, turned on his heel, and left. She noted that he walked with a slight limp and wondered if this was genuine. He disappeared down the winding driveway and Nancy closed the door. The typewritten address on the envelope was to Mr. and Miss Drew.

"Why was the man wearing heavy leather gloves—in June? This could be a dangerous trick," Nancy thought, her detective instinct for caution aroused.

She carried the envelope upstairs. To be rid of any possible contamination from it, Nancy washed her hands thoroughly, then put on leather gloves.

Using a letter opener, she carefully slit the envelope. A single sheet fell out with a typed message:

STAY OUT OF FRANCE!
MONSIEUR NEUF

"Monsieur Neuf!" Nancy thought in dismay. "Was he the man who brought this?"

CHAPTER II

The Frightened Financier

AT ONCE Nancy rushed to the telephone in her father's bedroom and called Mrs. Blair. She told her of the warning note and asked if the first message from Monsieur Neuf had been typed also.

"Yes, on a French typewriter. You know many of the keys have different characters."

"Then the warning I just received was typed on another machine—an American one," Nancy said. "Monsieur Neuf probably has a confederate in this country. By the way, Mrs. Blair, we were going to suggest that you stay here with our housekeeper and your nieces while Dad and I are away."

"That's sweet of you," said Mrs. Blair. "Let me think it over. It's you I'm worried about—not myself. I don't want you to take any undue risks for me."

Nancy replied in as lighthearted a tone as she could muster, "Oh, don't worry, Mrs. Blair, I must take risks when solving a mystery."

Some traps and scary situations in which she had found herself flashed through the young detective's mind, from her very first mystery involving *The Secret of the Old Clock* to her recent adventure—capturing *The Phantom of Pine Hill.*

"I'm sure you do take risks," Mrs. Blair said. "But I beg of you, be careful."

When Nancy returned to the dining room, she told the others about the masked man who had left the warning note. Everyone looked worried.

"Oh dear! You are in danger, Nancy, because of Monique and me," Marie burst out. "We will leave."

"No indeed you won't," Nancy replied firmly. "Monsieur Neuf is trying to keep me from going to France. But I'll go just the same. Dad wants me there. Besides, I have a job to do. I must solve your aunt's mystery. After I leave, I hope you people won't be bothered again."

Marie and Monique glanced at each other, as if unconvinced, but finally they smiled. Monique said, "Nancy, you are brave as well as kind. We will remain."

All the girls thanked Mrs. Gruen for the delicious meal, then insisted that she watch television while they cleared the table and tidied the kitchen. Shortly afterward, when Marie and

Monique excused themselves to unpack, Bess and George declared they must leave. Nancy offered to drive them home.

As soon as the three girls were on their way, George said, "Now tell us about your father's case."

Nancy chuckled. "He calls it 'The Case of the Frightened Financier.' "

Bess giggled. "Who is this money man?" she asked. "And what's he frightened about? The stock market?"

"His name is Monsieur Charles Leblanc. We don't know why he's frightened."

Bess murmured dreamily, "Frenchman. Mmm!"

Nancy went on, "He lives in a chateau in the Loire River valley, and his office and a factory he manages are in Paris. He's wealthy and influential in business circles but inherited most of his financial empire. Lately he has become very secretive—is drawing large sums of cash from banks and threatens to close up his factory."

"And put all those people out of work?" George broke in.

"Right. He has sold large holdings of stocks and bonds, too, which isn't good for the country's economy."

"Nancy, how does your dad fit into this picture?" Bess asked.

"Monsieur Leblanc's business associates have

engaged Dad to find out what has scared him into doing this. An American lawyer on vacation in France wouldn't be suspected by the 'frightened financier' of trying to learn what's going on."

As Nancy finished speaking, she pulled up in front of the Marvins' home. The girls said good night and Nancy went on to the Faynes'.

"By the way," said George, "when are we taking off?"

"Day after tomorrow. Meet you at the airport eight-thirty A.M. sharp. Good night."

During the drive home Nancy's thoughts dwelt on the mystery. On a deserted street she was suddenly startled when a man stepped off the curb directly into her path! He limped forward, then fell. Nancy jerked the steering wheel hard and jammed on her brakes to avoid hitting him. Shaken, she stared out at the prone figure.

"Help!" he cried, with a French accent. "I am sick!"

Nancy's first instinct was to assist him, but instead she reached for the door locks and snapped them. *The man on the pavement was the masked messenger who had come to her house earlier.* This must be a trick! He had followed her and knew the route she probably would take home!

Quickly Nancy pulled the car near the opposite curb and drove off. In the rear-view mirror she could see the man picking himself up and limping to the sidewalk. On a chance she had been wrong, Nancy stopped a patrol car and told her story.

"We'll investigate at once, miss," said the driver.

A little while after arriving home Nancy telephoned police headquarters and learned that the suspect had vanished. The young sleuth, convinced the man had been feigning illness, told her French friends and Hannah of the incident.

Mrs. Gruen sighed. "Thank goodness you're home safe."

Marie and Monique looked concerned, but made no comment. Nancy felt sure they were wondering if all American households were as full of excitement as this one!

The trying events were forgotten temporarily, when the visitors offered to sing duets in French. Nancy and Hannah were delighted.

"These are old madrigals from the Loire valley where we live," Monique explained. "You will hear them often while you are there."

"The songs are beautiful," Nancy said, clapping.

Mrs. Gruen applauded loudly. "This is just like having a free ticket to a lovely concert," she said, smiling.

Before the group went to bed, Nancy invited the visitors to accompany her to the airport the next day. She told them about the helicopter that had buzzed the Drew home.

The three girls arrived there in the middle of the morning. Nancy spoke to the man at the regular service counter and was directed to the office of a private helicopter company.

A young man at a desk had to be prompted twice before replying to Nancy's question. He kept staring with a smile at the two French girls.

"Oh, yes," he finally said to Nancy, "a man was up with me yesterday—the one who's going to build the helipad on your roof."

Nancy stared at the young pilot, speechless. Then she said, "You're kidding!"

"Kidding, the girl says!" He rolled his eyes around and shrugged his shoulders. "No, this is for real."

Suddenly Nancy realized the pilot had been the victim of a hoax that perhaps tied in with Monsieur Neuf. She decided to be cagey in her questioning.

"Who told *you?*" she asked.

"Why, the man I took up. Guess you know him—James Chase."

"Was he from the—er—company that's going to build the helipad on our roof?" Nancy asked.

"Yes. He showed me a letter from the A B Heliport Construction Company signed by the president. I don't remember his name. It said what they were going to do and asked if I'd fly him low over your house. I got permission to do it."

"Next time you fly low you'd better be more careful," Nancy warned. "We had a fire going and you caused a downdraft that could have set our house on fire."

"Gosh, I'm sorry about that."

"I don't know this James Chase," Nancy said. "What does he look like?"

The pilot grinned. "Queer-looking duck about fifty-five years old. Real long face and arms and feet. Limped a little."

"Anything else?" Nancy asked, her pulses quickening.

"Well, he spoke with a French accent."

Nancy thanked the pilot for his information and left with her guests. When the three were out of earshot of his office, Nancy said excitedly, "James Chase is the masked man who came to my house!"

Marie and her sister exchanged quick glances. "Nancy," Marie burst out, "we think we know who this man is. His name is not James Chase!"

CHAPTER III

The Green Lion

"You know who the masked man is?" Nancy cried out unbelievingly.

"We are not acquainted with him," Marie answered. "But I'm sure he was a gardener at the chateau of friends of ours. He was discharged for not being honest. In fact he was later suspected of stealing large sums of money from several shops."

Monique spoke up. "We remember him because he was so odd looking, although I don't recall he limped. His first name was Claude. We don't know the rest."

"And," Nancy said, "he could be Monsieur Neuf! But if Neuf is trying to keep people away from the 99 steps, why would he leave France? Girls, you've given me a very valuable clue, anyway. Since you say Claude was not honest, and he's using an assumed name and sent that warning note to Dad and me, I think our police should be alerted."

When they reached headquarters, Nancy took the Bardot sisters inside to have them meet Chief McGinnis. The middle-aged, rugged-looking officer, a good friend of the Drews, greeted them all with a warm smile.

"I'm glad to meet your French visitors, Nancy," he said.

"You'll be doubly glad," said Nancy, "when they tell you about the man who is trying to keep me from going to Paris."

After Chief McGinnis had listened to the story, he nodded gravely and turned to the Bardots. "Will you young ladies compose a cable to your friends and ask for Claude's last name and his address in France. I'll send it, but the reply will come to your house, Nancy."

The officer winked, adding, "I wouldn't want the Bardots' friends to think Marie and Monique are having trouble with the River Heights' police!"

"Oh, no, no," said Marie, and the sisters laughed.

Everyone was pleased at the quick response that came from France. The three girls, after a sightseeing trip on the Muskoka River, arrived home at five o'clock. Hannah Gruen had just taken the message over the telephone. It said: *Name Claude Aubert. Whereabouts unknown.*

"Good and bad news at the same time," Nancy remarked. "Apparently Claude the gardener has disappeared from his home town. But won't *he* be surprised when our River Heights police pick him up!"

She dialed headquarters at once. Chief McGinnis was still there. Upon hearing Nancy's report, he said, "I'll get in touch with immigration authorities in Washington at once to check if Aubert entered this country legally. Most offices will be closing, but I'll call anyhow." He paused. "My men are out looking for this Frenchman. When do you leave, Nancy?"

"At eight tomorrow morning."

"Well, if I have any news before then I'll let you know. Good-by now."

"Good-by, and thanks!"

Monique turned to Nancy. "Oh, I hope the police catch Claude! He may try to harm you again before you leave."

The telephone rang. Nancy answered. "Hi, Bess! What's up?"

"You must help us out—tonight."

"How?"

"By performing anything you like. Play the piano, do tricks, tell a mystery story."

"Bess, what *are* you talking about? Is this some kind of gag?"

"No, indeed, Nancy. This is the night the Teeners Club entertains the Towners Club, remember? You had to decline because of your trip."

"Sorry, Bess," said Nancy. "I'm afraid I must decline again for the same reason. I haven't finished packing yet, and I told Mrs. Blair I'd drop in to see her. She was trying to find some clues for me from old diaries of her mother's."

"But, Nancy, we need one more number. We Teeners can't disappoint the older folks. Couldn't you just—?"

"Bess," Nancy said suddenly, "I just had a brainstorm. Maybe Marie and Monique will sing some madrigals."

"Marvelous!" Bess exclaimed. "Oh, Nancy, you're a whiz. Hurry up and ask them."

At first the French girls demurred, feeling that they did not sing well enough to perform in public. When Nancy, backed by Mrs. Gruen, assured the sisters they sang beautifully, the girls consented.

Monique said happily, "Marie and I brought old-time costumes used by singers in the Loire valley. We thought Tante Josette would like to see them."

"That's great," said Nancy, hugging the girls.

When she told Bess the good news, there was a squeal of delight from the other end of the wire. "I'll pick up Marie and Monique at seven-thirty," said Bess.

Nancy requested that the sisters come last on the program. "I'll try to finish my visit with Mrs. Blair in time to hear them."

A little later when Marie and Monique came downstairs in their costumes, Nancy and Mrs. Gruen clapped in admiration. The long-skirted bouffant dresses with tight bodices were made of fine flowered silk. Marie's was blue and trimmed with narrow strips of matching velvet. Her sister's was rose color with festoons of shirred white lace. The girls' hair was piled high on their heads and they had powdered it to look like the wigs worn by the elegant ladies of the eighteenth century. On one cheek of each singer was a tiny black patch, another custom of the day.

"You will make a great hit," Mrs. Gruen prophesied.

"Merci beaucoup," said Marie, her cheeks flushed with excitement. "Mrs. Gruen, are you not going?"

"I hadn't planned to, since Nancy was not performing," the housekeeper replied.

At once the three girls urged her to attend. Hannah beamed. "All right. It won't take me long to change."

She hurried to her room and soon returned in a becoming navy-blue dress. A few moments later Bess arrived for her passengers and they left. Nancy set off in her car for Mrs. Blair's apartment.

The attractive woman, about forty years old, opened the door and said eagerly, "I found some notes in Mother's diary that may help us."

She sat down beside Nancy on a low couch in the living room and opened a small red-velvet-covered book. The writing was precise and quite faded in places.

"I've had a hard time deciphering this," said Mrs. Blair. "It tells mostly of my parents' travels, and mentions that I went along sometimes. But I was always with my governess."

"Then the experience you dream about," Nancy guessed, "could have included your governess. Is she still living in France?"

"I really don't know. To me she was just 'Mademoiselle' and that is what she's called in the diary. She was very kind, I remember. I was only three years old at the time."

Mrs. Blair gave the names of several famous chateaux they had visited. Another was where Marie and Monique lived.

Nancy's eyes sparkled. "Now we have something to work on! We'll go to each chateau and look for the 99 steps!"

"Another place mentioned in the diary, Chateau Loire, was mostly in ruins," Mrs. Blair went on. "It says the place was haunted by a ghostly alchemist who carried on his work there. You know, Nancy, in olden times people were superstitious about chemists and their experiments, and they were forbidden by law to work their 'miracles.'"

"But they did it in secret?" Nancy asked.

"Oh, yes. They had all kinds of signs, and symbols and special words to indicate to other people in their group what they had accomplished."

"How clever—and daring!" said Nancy.

Mrs. Blair arose and took a book from a shelf. It too was in French. She showed it to Nancy. "One of the interesting sets of symbols includes a Red King, White Queen, Gray Wolf, Black Crow, and Green Lion. The Red King stood for gold; the White Queen, for silver. I don't understand the meaning of the crow, but the Green Lion—he's a bad one. He devours the sun—or in other words, he's acid making the silver or gold look green."

"That's fascinating!" Nancy exclaimed.

"Yes, it is," the woman agreed. "And it's hard to realize that the forbidden art of alchemy finally became the basis for our modern chemistry. In the sixteenth century alchemists believed that minerals grew, so certain mines were closed to give the metals a chance to rest and grow."

Nancy listened intently as Mrs. Blair went on, "For a long time people laughed at this idea. But today chemists have discovered that metals do literally grow and change, though very slowly. My goodness!" the woman exclaimed. "We have wandered off the subject of our mystery, Nancy. But actually I didn't find any other clues to my dream or the 99 steps' incident of my childhood."

Nancy glanced at her wrist watch. She was reluctant to leave, but would still have time to hear Marie and Monique perform. She invited Mrs. Blair to accompany her, but the woman declined because of her sprained ankle.

Nancy arose, saying she must go. "You have given me a lot to work on, Mrs. Blair. I'll certainly be busy in France! *Au revoir,* and I hope I'll soon have good news for you."

Nancy hurried to the school auditorium where the Teeners were giving their show. She quietly slid into a rear seat in the dim light.

The Bardot sisters had just been announced and came out before the footlights. Standing with their heads close together, they began to sing. At the end of the number the applause was terrific.

As it died down, and the sisters started the second madrigal, Nancy's eyes wandered over the audience. Suddenly she caught her breath. Directly across the aisle in the center of a row sat Claude Aubert!

"I must get the police before he leaves!" Nancy thought. Quickly and unobtrusively she made her way outside.

CHAPTER IV

Backstage Scare

WHEN Nancy reached the street she looked back to see if Claude Aubert were following, but evidently he had been unaware of her presence in the auditorium. She ran to a nearby street telephone and called police headquarters.

The officer on duty promised to send two plain-clothes detectives to the school at once. Nancy said she would meet them in the lobby, and hurried back to the school. As she entered the lobby she heard enthusiastic clapping and assumed Marie and Monique had finished their act.

"Oh, I hope Claude doesn't come out here before those detectives arrive," Nancy thought worriedly. She peered inside the auditorium. He was still in his seat.

Fortunately the audience insisted upon encores. Just before the show ended, Detective Panzer and Detective Keely walked into the lobby.

Nancy quickly led them inside and pointed out their quarry. Suddenly Claude Aubert arose, pushed into the side aisle, and, without limping, hurried toward the stage.

"Come on!" Nancy urged the detectives. "He may be planning to harm the Bardots!"

The three hurried after the French ex-gardener. He went through the door that led up a short flight of stairs to the stage. To the left of the steps was an exit to the parking lot. When the pursuers reached the spot, the suspect was not in sight.

"Where did he go?" Nancy asked in dismay.

Detective Panzer yanked open the exit door and reported, "I don't see him." He and Keely dashed outside.

The next instant a scream came from somewhere backstage. Electrified, Nancy raced up the steps where a throng milled about on stage. Many persons were asking, "What happened?"

A sob could be heard above the noise. Nancy went to investigate and found Monique in hysterics. Marie was trying to comfort her.

Seeing Nancy, they cried out together, "He threatened us!"

"Claude Aubert?"

"Yes," said Monique. "He grasped my arm so hard I screamed. Then Claude said in French,

" 'If you sisters let Nancy Drew go to France, you will suffer and she will too!' "

"He *must* be Monsieur Neuf!" Marie added fearfully.

"Where did he go?" Nancy asked.

Marie pointed to the opposite side of the stage from where Nancy had entered. When Nancy reached it, she found an exit to a walk that ran behind the building to the parking lot.

Nancy was elated. Mr. Nine was trapped! The walk ran between the school and a high concrete wall. There was no way out except through the parking lot. By this time the detectives must have nabbed the suspect!

Nancy dashed along the walk to the lot and stared ahead. A large crowd was making its way to the cars and some of the automobiles had already started to move out. The detectives were not in sight. Neither was Claude Aubert.

"Oh great!" Nancy groaned in disgust. Then she took heart. "Maybe he's already been captured and is on his way to jail!"

Nevertheless, Nancy searched thoroughly among the cars, but saw neither Claude Aubert nor the detectives. She returned to the stage. By this time Monique had calmed down and was receiving congratulations with her sister from many persons for their excellent performance.

"You certainly made a hit," said Bess, coming up with George. "Just as Hannah said."

"Oh, thank you." The Bardots smiled.

George added, "Someone told us a fresh guy came up and bothered you. Who was he?"

"A Frenchman who threatened Marie and me if we let Nancy make the trip."

"Such nerve!" George exclaimed. "What's his name?"

Nancy whispered it, then brought Bess and George up to date, telling of her suspicion that Aubert was Monsieur Neuf.

"Wow!" said George. "Mr. Nine must be worried you'll solve the mystery."

In a low tone Nancy said, "We'd better go home, and I'll call headquarters to see what happened to the detectives."

They found Mrs. Gruen waiting in Nancy's convertible. After bidding good night to Bess and George, Nancy drove off. The housekeeper was astounded at the story of the threat.

"Starting tonight, I'm going to keep the burglar alarm on all the time!" she declared. "I'm glad we had it put in."

Nancy grinned. "Marie and Monique, be careful not to come home unexpectedly. You may scare Hannah."

"Just the same," said Mrs. Gruen, "I don't like this whole thing. Nancy, perhaps you ought to postpone your trip for at least a few days."

"I can't," Nancy replied. "Dad and Mrs. Blair are counting on me. Let's not worry until we find out if Claude Aubert has been captured."

As soon as she reached home Nancy telephoned the police. The suspect, she learned, had not been brought in. Furthermore, Detective Panzer and Detective Keely had neither returned nor phoned a report.

"We assume they're still tailing their man," the desk sergeant added.

Nancy hung up, her mind in a turmoil. How had Claude Aubert escaped? Where would he show up next?

"I'll bet," she thought, "that it will be right here. I'm glad the burglar alarm is on."

After a pre-bedtime snack, Mrs. Gruen and the girls went upstairs. Nancy, who had some final packing to do, was the last one to retire. Some time later she was awakened abruptly by a loud ringing.

The burglar alarm had gone off!

Instantly the young detective was out of bed and pulling on her robe and slippers. She dashed to a window and leaned out, hoping to spot the intruder. Seeing no one, Nancy sped to her father's room in the front of the house and peered below.

"Oh, they've caught him!" she exulted.

In the rays of a flashlight, the two plainclothesmen were holding a tall, long-faced man. Aubert? Just then Mrs. Gruen, Marie, and Monique rushed in.

Nancy cried out, "The detectives got the burglar! Hurry! Let's go down!"

She quickly led the way, turning on lights as she went, and flung open the front door. The detectives marched their prisoner, now limping, into the hall. Claude Aubert!

"Hello, Miss Drew," said Detective Keely. "We saw your lights go on and thought you'd like to know we got this fellow."

"Bud here and I had a wild chase," Panzer told Nancy. "We got clues to Aubert from people all over town who saw him, but we missed him every time. We figured he might come here, so Bud and I hid near your house and waited. We let him try to jimmy the window, then nabbed him red-handed."

Nancy expressed the theory that the fugitive had eluded them at the school by running in front of the stage curtains, jumping from the platform, and mingling with the crowd leaving the auditorium. The policemen agreed. "That's why we all missed him," said Detective Keely.

The prisoner was prodded into the living room. His black eyes glared malevolently at the three girls. The man's lips moved but no intelligible sounds came through them. A quick search of his pockets by Keely revealed no passport or other identification.

As soon as Mrs. Gruen and the girls were

seated, Detective Panzer ordered, "Okay, Aubert. Talk! Tell everything from the beginning. Why and how did you sneak into this country and under what name?"

Silence.

Nancy spoke to the detectives. "I haven't introduced my friends from France—Marie and Monique Bardot. Perhaps they can act as interpreters."

"Good idea," Detective Keely agreed.

Marie was spokesman. She relayed questions from Nancy and the police to the prisoner about the threatening letters to Mrs. Blair and the Drews; the helicopter ride; the faked illness in front of Nancy's car, and his inconsistent limping. No answers from Aubert.

Finally Detective Panzer said, "We'll go now. A night in jail may loosen this man's tongue. He'll learn he can't run around threatening people."

After the men had left, Mrs. Gruen said, "We should all be thankful that awful man is in custody. Nancy—you, Bess, and George can go to France with nothing to worry about."

Nancy merely smiled. She was not so sure! The group exchanged good nights again and retired. Soon Nancy began to dream. She kept chasing after a man who carried a large sign reading:

BEWARE M. NEUF

Then a great crowd of people in old-fashioned costumes came swarming from the ruins of a chateau. They carried large bells which they were ringing lustily.

Suddenly the dream ended. Nancy was wide awake. Bells, bells! Then she realized what was happening. The burglar alarm had gone off again!

CHAPTER V

Prowler Without Footprints

When Nancy reached the top of the stairway Mrs. Gruen was there. Marie and Monique appeared a few seconds later. The group hurried down and flooded the first floor with light and turned off the alarm. No sign of a prowler.

"Let's divide up and search," Nancy suggested. "Marie and Monique, will you examine the windows? Hannah, please try the doors. I'll search for anyone hiding."

The four separated. There was tense silence as the hunt went on. Nancy looked in closets, behind draperies and furniture. She found no one.

"I guess the intruder was scared away," she thought. "At least we know he wasn't Claude Aubert!"

At that moment Marie called from the dining room, "Please come here, everybody!"

The others rushed to her side. She was pointing

to a side window which had been jimmied between the sashes and the lock broken. The intruder probably had been frightened by the burglar alarm before he had a chance to climb in.

"There will be footprints outside," Mrs. Gruen spoke up.

"We'll look," Nancy said, and went for a flashlight.

The quartet trooped outdoors to the dining-room window. A few feet away from it they stopped and Nancy beamed her light over the area.

"No footprints!" Hannah exclaimed. "If somebody tried to get in the house from here, he must have been a ghost!"

Nancy had been studying the ground. Now she pointed to a series of evenly spaced holes. "I think they were made by stilts."

"Stilts!" Monique exclaimed. "You mean the person who tried to get into your house was walking on stilts?"

"That's my guess," Nancy replied.

Mrs. Gruen gave a sigh. "It seems to me that every time we have a chance to pick up a clue, somebody outwits us."

Nancy smiled. "Stilts might be a better give-away than footprints," she said cheerfully. "I'm sure there aren't many thieves who use them."

Monique asked, "Then you think the intruder meant to steal something?"

Hannah Gruen answered. "He was either a thief or intended to harm us."

Nancy's own feeling was that the stilt walker might be linked with her mystery. She returned to the house and called the police. The sergeant at the desk was amazed to hear of the second attempted break-in.

"Two alarms in one night!" he exclaimed. "But this one sounds like some boy's prank," he commented. "Probably a town hood. I'll make an investigation and see if anybody on our list of troublemakers owns a pair of stilts. Miss Drew, perhaps you have some ideas yourself about who the person was and why he wanted to break in."

"No, I haven't," she answered, "unless there's a connection between him and Claude Aubert."

The officer whistled. "In any case, I'll speak to the chief about having a detective watch your house every night until this prowler mystery is solved."

"Thank you and I'll hunt around our place for more clues," she offered.

Again Nancy organized a search party. Marie and Monique were assigned to the house. The sisters frankly admitted they did not know what to look for.

"Oh, anything that seems odd to you," Nancy replied. "For instance, table silver missing or disturbed." Even though she felt that the intruder had not entered the house, Nancy did not want to miss an opportunity to track down the slightest piece of evidence.

She and Mrs. Gruen began searching the grounds. A single set of stilt marks came from the street, ran along the curved driveway, then turned toward the window.

"There should be two sets of marks," Nancy said. "One coming and one going."

She asked Hannah to go into the house and put on the back porch and garage lights. As soon as this was done, Nancy extinguished her flashlight and stared intently at the ground.

She noticed that the top branches of a bush near the forced window were broken. Nancy looked beyond the shrub and saw that the stilt marks went across the rear lawn toward the garage.

"I guess the man stepped over the bush," she thought.

As Nancy hastened forward to follow the marks, the housekeeper joined her. Side by side the two hurried to the double garage. The door behind Nancy's convertible had been left open. As she and Hannah approached it, they stared in astonishment. Propped against the inside of the rear window of the car was a large cardboard sign. On it, printed in green crayon, were the words:

BEWARE THE GREEN LION

"How strange!" Mrs. Gruen murmured.

"How strange!" Hannah murmured

At that moment a patrol car came up the driveway and an officer stepped out. He introduced himself as Detective Braun. "Are you Miss Nancy Drew?"

"Yes. And this is Mrs. Gruen who lives with us."

The headlights of the police car had shown up the warning sign vividly. "For Pete's sake, what's that all about?" the detective asked.

"We just found it," Nancy told him. "I think the person who tried to get into our house intended to leave the warning in some room. When he was scared away, he put it here."

"Do you know what it means?" Detective Braun asked.

"I'm not sure, but the message may have something to do with a mystery I'm trying to solve." Nancy told about the old alchemists' codes, some of which Mrs. Blair had shown her.

"One man used the Green Lion as a symbol that he had figured out how to make gold look green."

Detective Braun shook his head. "This wasn't the stunt of a kid on stilts," he said. "It's a real warning."

Mrs. Gruen nodded. "I'm afraid you're right and this means trouble for Nancy in France after all. She's leaving early tomorrow morning."

Nancy, seeing how worried the housekeeper was, tried to sound lighthearted. "Not *tomorrow* morning, Hannah dear," she said teasingly. "It's already morning! Do you realize I'll be leaving home in about four hours?"

Hannah gasped. "You're right. What a terrible night you've had—just when you need a good rest!"

Braun said he would take the sign back to headquarters and have it examined for fingerprints.

"Good night," Nancy said. "And thank you."

At eight o'clock the young sleuth was ready to leave. She and Hannah Gruen and the Bardots drove to the airport in the convertible. The housekeeper would bring the car back. Marie and Monique were sad when it came time to say good-by at the loading gate.

Marie said, "I want to see Tante Josette's mystery solved, but please don't let yourself be harmed, Nancy dear."

Monique added, "Do not spend all your time on your detective work. France is so lovely to see, and please have some fun."

"I will," Nancy promised.

She had begun to worry about Bess and George, who had not yet arrived.

But a minute later the two girls came dashing up with their parents. The cousins said quick hellos and good-bys. Then the three travelers waved adieus and walked to a four-engine craft that would take them to New York. There they would change planes.

Nancy motioned Bess to a window seat while she took one next to her on the aisle. George sat across from her. Seat belts were fastened and in a few minutes the craft taxied down the runway and took off.

As soon as the lighted "Fasten Your Seat Belt" sign was turned off and the girls unbuckled their straps, Nancy said to George, "Sit on the arm of my chair. I have something exciting to tell you and Bess."

When she finished her recital of the night's adventures, both her friends gaped unbelievingly. Then Bess said worriedly, "More trouble—now with a green lion!"

George snorted. "Sounds ridiculous to me. The alchemist who worked out that code lived hundreds of years ago. Somebody came across it just by chance and is using those words to try to scare you, Nancy."

The girl detective frowned. "What puzzles me is, where does everything fit? I have a feeling it'll be some time before I put this jigsaw together."

As she spoke, Nancy could hardly hold back a yawn and slept during most of the flight to New York. Here the girls boarded a larger plane and jetted off to Paris. After they had been cleared through customs the next morning, Mr. Drew met his daughter and her friends. The tall handsome man beamed in delight at seeing the girls.

"I've been mighty lonesome without you,

Nancy," he said. "I'll enjoy showing this beautiful city to you. Now tell me, how is your mystery coming?"

Nancy chuckled. "I have one villain in jail already." She was amused at her father's upraised eyebrows and quickly reported all that had happened.

"I can hardly believe it," the lawyer said. "Well done, Nancy. You're way ahead of me."

In lowered tones, Mr. Drew continued, "I haven't learned yet why Monsieur Leblanc is acting so strangely. Whenever I meet the man I find him very pleasant but not a hard worker, though he goes to his office regularly. He hasn't given a hint as to why he is selling his investments at such an alarming rate."

Mr. Drew remarked that he was very much interested in the warning *Beware the Green Lion.*

"Dad, I've been assuming the warning was linked with my mystery," she said, "but now I wonder if it was meant for you, too. After all, the first one from Monsieur Neuf was addressed to both of us."

"You could be right."

When the travelers reached the heart of Paris, they were intrigued by the wide boulevards with their beautiful buildings and the spectacular Eiffel Tower.

"What would you girls like to visit first?" Mr. Drew asked.

George responded at once, "Notre Dame. I want to see those ugly gargoyles."

The lawyer laughed and nodded. "Notre Dame it shall be, as soon as we have checked into our hotel on the Rue de la Paix and you girls have unpacked. I have reserved a large room for you with three beds."

In an hour the group was ready for the sightseeing trip. Mr. Drew called a taxi and they drove directly to the street called Double D'Arcole in front of the famous old cathedral.

As they stepped from the cab, Bess exclaimed, "Oh, it's gorgeous! Goodness, look at all the carvings and statues! There must be hundreds!"

"There are," Mr. Drew agreed. "Would you girls like to climb to the top of one of the two towers? You can get a better look at some of the gargoyles and also a magnificent view of the city."

"Yes, let's," George urged.

Mr. Drew led the girls around the corner into a side street with several sidewalk cafes opposite the north wall of the cathedral. A narrow doorway opened upon an even narrower circular stone staircase. The steps were precipitous and on one side barely had toe room.

"I hope we don't meet anyone coming down," Bess remarked, frowning.

Nancy went first, with Bess directly behind her. George came next and Mr. Drew brought up the rear. The stairway was rather dark in spots where light could not filter through the tiny square openings in the outer wall.

Nancy was silently counting the steps. "I may as well begin my sleuthing and see if there are any clues on the 99th step," she thought.

Slowly she and the others spiraled their way upward. Nancy had just passed the 99th step, without having seen anything significant, when she started around a sharp turn. Coming down toward her was an enormously fat woman, who blocked the entire width of the staircase.

Without regard for those below her, she descended swiftly and thoughtlessly, not moving sideways to give Nancy any room. Dismayed, Nancy stood on her toes and tried to hug the wall which was too flat to give any handhold.

"S'il vous plait—" Nancy began.

The fat woman paid no attention. She pushed against Nancy so hard that the girl lost her balance! She fell against Bess, who in turn dropped backward onto George. Unable to keep her balance, George desperately clawed the air!

Would they all go tumbling to the bottom?

CHAPTER VI

Double Take

As the three girls tumbled down the circular stairway, Mr. Drew braced himself to try stopping them. He held one hand firmly against the inner wall and leaned forward. As the impact came he teetered, but only momentarily. The girls, too, had pressed against the stone side and this had helped to break the fall.

"Oh, thank you!" Bess cried out. "I was never so scared in my life!"

She, George, and Nancy regained their balance. The fat woman who had caused the accident had paused for only an instant. With a curt *pardon* she went on down the stairway.

The Americans laughed off the incident, but all of them sincerely hoped they would not meet any more overweight persons on the steps!

"How much farther to the top?" Bess asked, puffing a little.

Mr. Drew said that the Notre Dame tower was 226 feet high. "You should be glad you're not going to the tip of the spire," he said with a chuckle. "That's 296 feet from the ground."

"It's a tremendous building, isn't it?" Nancy remarked.

Mr. Drew nodded. "And some outstanding historical events have taken place here, including two coronations of enormous pomp and ceremony—for Henry V of England and Napoleon I."

By this time Nancy had reached the top step and walked out onto the platform of the tower with its shoulder-high stone railing. A few feet ahead of her a massive stone gargoyle protruded from the roof. It looked like some strange prehistoric bird overlooking the swift-flowing River Seine below.

As Bess reached Nancy's side, she commented, "This gargoyle and the others I can see around this tower are so ugly they're almost handsome!"

George turned to Mr. Drew. "Who ever thought up gargoyles and what does the name mean?"

"I understand," Mr. Drew replied, "that these figures are really rainspouts. Gargoyle is derived from a medieval French word meaning gurgle or gargle. As to why they were made to look so grotesque, it's thought this was a whim of the designer and the architects."

Mr. Drew and the girls walked from one end

of the platform to the other viewing as much of Paris as they could. The thing they noticed particularly was that practically all the buildings except churches had flat roofs.

"They were also in vogue in our country around the turn of the century," said Mr. Drew, "but we went back to the gabled variety. Now the flat ones are becoming popular again for large buildings. Give you one guess why."

"So helicopters can land on them," Nancy replied. Smiling, she said, "Dad, will we have to change our roof for the helipad?"

George chuckled. "Paris is ready for the future. A helipad on every roof! And the Drews won't be far behind!"

Nancy glanced down at the street from which they had entered the tower. Suddenly she grabbed her father's arm.

"Dad! That man down there! He looks like Claude Aubert!"

Mr. Drew was surprised and Bess and George dashed to Nancy's side. The man on the street was gazing upward directly at the group.

"But you said Claude Aubert was in the River Heights' jail!" Mr. Drew exclaimed.

At that moment the man apparently sensed that they were looking at him. He turned on his heel and walked away quickly.

"He's not limping!" Bess exclaimed.

As George gazed after him, she said, "Hard to

believe he escaped from jail and got over here so fast!"

Nancy remained silent, but her father spoke up. "It's possible Aubert had someone put up bail money for him, then he jumped bail and managed to catch an overseas plane somewhere."

When Nancy still did not put forth an opinion, Mr. Drew asked, "What's your theory?"

"Rather startling," she replied, "but I have a hunch this man is Claude Aubert's brother, perhaps an identical twin."

"Then which one," said George, "is the real Monsieur Neuf?"

Nancy frowned. "I don't know, but I believe they're working together—Claude in the United States, this man over here. It's my guess we've been followed ever since we arrived."

A frightened look came over Bess's face. "Then we didn't leave the danger behind. Nancy, supposing the men are brothers, do you think one calls himself the Green Lion?"

"Possibly. In any case, we should find out at once if Claude Aubert did escape, or jump bail. I'll phone Chief McGinnis as soon as we leave here."

Mr. Drew liked the idea and the four left the tower immediately. When they reached the street, Nancy suggested that Bess and George go inside the cathedral while she and her father looked for a telephone.

"There's a delightful little garden in back of Notre Dame," said Mr. Drew. "Suppose we all meet there in half an hour."

The group separated. Nancy and her father found a restaurant which had a telephone booth and Nancy put in a call to River Heights. She was told there would be a delay of fifteen minutes.

"I'll wait," she said in French. "Will you please ring me at this number?"

The operator promised to do so. Nancy and her father sat down at a nearby table and ordered some French pastry and hot chocolate. When the food arrived, Mr. Drew chuckled and said, "Wouldn't Bess be goggle-eyed over this pastry?" Nancy grinned.

Ten minutes later the telephone rang and she jumped to answer it. "Chief McGinnis?"

"Yes. You're calling from Paris, Nancy?" he said. "It must be important."

"It is. Tell me, is Claude Aubert still in jail?"

"Sure. Why?"

Quickly Nancy told him about the man she had seen. "Could you find out from Aubert if he has a brother who looks like him, perhaps a twin?"

"Hold on!" The chief was gone for several minutes.

Finally McGinnis came back and said that Aubert had refused to answer. "That makes me think you may have guessed correctly," the officer told Nancy. "By the way, we've observed that his limp is phony. Anyhow, I will report your suspicions to the Paris police."

Nancy told the chief where she was staying and thanked him for his help. She asked about the stilt walker. The man had not been found yet.

As Nancy emerged from the booth and rejoined her father, she was beaming.

"Don't tell me," said Mr. Drew. "I know from your expression you're on the right track."

Nancy laughed. "I shouldn't wear my secrets on my face." Then she remarked softly, "If this other man is Claude Aubert's brother and is following us, we should turn the tables and follow him."

"A neat trick if you can do it," the lawyer said. "But we'll keep our eyes open."

The Drews made a tour of the breathtaking interior of Notre Dame. Nancy was awed by its vastness and the beauty of the stained-glass windows and the many statues. She paused before one of the Virgin Mary, whose lovely face looked down at arms which had once cradled an infant.

"The baby's statue was mysteriously taken away," her father explained. "Stolen apparently."

"How dreadful!" Nancy exclaimed. "And how sad!"

She and her father left the cathedral and walked down the side street to the open garden at the rear. Bess and George were waiting for them and admiring the colorful beds of zinnias and petunias. The four sat down on chairs and Nancy told the cousins of her talk with Chief McGinnis. She urged that wherever they all went, each one try to spot the man she thought was Claude's brother. A few minutes later Mr. Drew suggested that they go back to the hotel and have lunch.

"That's a grand idea," Bess spoke up. "I'm starved!"

She arose, and before heading toward the street, turned slowly in a complete circle, hoping she might see the suspect. Suddenly her eyes became riveted on a black lamppost which stood near high bushes and trees at the back of the garden. She had spied a figure crouching behind the post.

"Nancy," Bess whispered quickly, "I think I see Mr. Nine!"

CHAPTER VII

Exciting Steps

As Bess pointed toward the lamppost, the man crouching behind it seemed to realize he had been discovered. He sprang up and plunged into a mass of bushes and trees behind him.

"Let's chase him!" Nancy urged, and the whole group took off in pursuit.

George reached the other side of the shrubbery first. She cried out, "I see him! He's heading for the back street!"

When they came to the Rue du Cloître, they could see their quarry running to the south.

"We mustn't let him escape!" called Mr. Drew. "You girls go on. I can't run as fast as I used to."

Nancy soon caught up to George. But at the corner of the Quai de l'Archêveché, they were stopped by a policeman wearing a tight-fitting, dark-blue tunic suit, white gauntlets, and a high-crowned, peaked cap.

"Why are you in such a hurry?" he called out in French.

Nancy pointed down the street toward the fugitive. "He is a suspect trying to get away from us!"

The officer's eyebrows lifted. "Suspected of what?" he asked.

For a moment Nancy was stumped. What did she suspect the man of? Only of being Claude Aubert's brother. Finally she said, "He has been watching and following us. We want to find out why."

By this time Mr. Drew and Bess had reached the group. The lawyer introduced himself and the girls and showed his identification.

"I beg the pardon of the Americans," the policeman said, and waved them on.

But Nancy shook her head. "Too late. Look!"

At that moment the long-armed man was jumping into a taxi. Disappointedly his pursuers watched it drive out of sight.

The policeman said cheerfully, "If the man is following you, he will be seen again. What is his name?"

"We do not know," Nancy replied. "We think it may be Aubert. By any chance, have you ever heard of a Claude Aubert?"

The officer stared at her. "*Mais oui,* mademoiselle! Claude Aubert is a well-known forger. Some time ago he faked the signature on a large check and was nearly caught by our captain, but he got away. You mean, that man you were chasing is Claude?"

"No, he's in jail in the States," Nancy replied, then added that Captain McGinnis was going to get in touch with the Paris police. On a hunch she asked whose signature Claude Aubert had forged. The group was astounded to learn it was that of Charles Leblanc! The "frightened financier"!

Nancy and her father were elated over this clue, which might prove a strong link between his case and Nancy's.

As calmly as she could, Nancy asked the officer where Claude Aubert had lived at the time he vanished. The policeman gave her the address of an apartment house in the section of Paris known as the Left Bank.

The Drews thanked him for the information and walked back toward Notre Dame. Mr. Drew suggested they have lunch at one of the sidewalk cafes instead of returning to the hotel, then go to Aubert's apartment house.

"That would be fun," Bess said eagerly. "Some fine French food will step up my brainpower. You'd like that, wouldn't you, Nancy?"

Her friend laughed. "This mystery is becoming so complicated, I can use all the help you can give me."

Mr. Drew selected a pleasant cafe and the group seated themselves at a small table. After their luncheon orders of cheese soufflé had been given, the lawyer said in a low tone, "Monsieur Leblanc's office building is not far from Aubert's apartment."

George asked, "Do you think that fact has a bearing on your case, Mr. Drew?"

The lawyer shrugged. "At least it's a strange coincidence."

When they finished eating, Mr. Drew suggested that on their way to the Left Bank, they stop at the famous Louvre to view some of the paintings and statuary. A taxi took them to the massive museum which had once been a palace.

Bess sighed. "It would take us a week to see everything in this place," she commented.

Mr. Drew smiled. "You're right, Bess, but there are certain priceless art objects you must not miss —for instance, the Winged Victory."

George grinned. "She's the lady with the wings but no head, isn't she?"

"That's the one," Mr. Drew answered.

"The Venus de Milo statue is here too," Nancy said.

"That's right."

George chuckled. "She's the beautiful lady without any arms. Where did she lose them?"

"I haven't heard," the lawyer said with a grin, "or I might look for them."

Bess announced, "One thing *I* want to see is Leonardo da Vinci's portrait of Mona Lisa."

Mr. Drew said that apparently this was considered the most valuable art treasure in the Louvre, since it was more heavily protected than any of the other pieces.

When the group reached the famous painting, they found it guarded by an iron rail and two uniformed men, who carefully watched each visitor.

"Mona Lisa's face is lovely," Nancy remarked. "Just looking at her portrait gives me a peaceful feeling."

The River Heights visitors stayed for an hour in the famous old building. Then, weary, they decided to stop walking and drive across the Seine to Claude Aubert's former home. The concierge in charge of the apartment house was a rather gruff man of about fifty. At first he seemed unwilling to answer any of their questions about the forger.

"It was bad enough having the police come here disturbing me!" he complained, growing red in the face. "Who are you?"

Nancy smiled disarmingly. She decided to shoot a direct question at him. Could she get him to answer?

"What's Claude Aubert's twin's name?" she asked.

Without hesitation, the concierge replied, "Louis."

Nancy could hardly keep from shouting her

delight. Mr. Drew, Bess, and George also found it difficult to maintain calm expressions.

"Oh, yes," Nancy said nonchalantly. "Let me see, where does Louis live?"

The man did not answer at once, but finally he said, "It is out in the country. I do not know the name of the place." Suddenly he went on, "You know, Louis is the bright one. Claude is a bit slow. He just does what his brother tells him to."

Mr. Drew put in casually, "Louis keeps busy, no doubt. We saw him today from a distance. What's he doing now?"

"Oh, he is some sort of scientist. That business with formulas and flasks and such is beyond me."

Nancy's intuition told her they were getting nearer and nearer to an excellent clue. Again she smiled at the concierge. "Would it be possible for us to see where Claude used to live?"

Actually Nancy did not expect to find any clue in the apartment. What she did want to do was count the number of steps to Aubert's living quarters. It was just possible there might be 99 and there would be some significance to this!

"I can show you which apartment it is," the concierge replied. "But I cannot admit you because a young man and his wife occupy it now."

As he led the way up the stairs, Nancy moved backward to the front door. Then, as she walked forward again, she began to count. It took her ten steps to the stairway. She added each tread as the group climbed. On the second floor there were ten steps to the next stairway. The concierge went on up, and Nancy continued to count. When they reached the top, she found there were 69 steps in the two stairways.

"Maybe—just maybe—" Nancy told herself.

Would there be ten steps to the Aubert apartment? There were. The total was 99!

"But now that I have the information, how can I use it?" Nancy thought. "The number may have been a signal between Louis and Claude or between Claude and some pals of his to meet here in connection with his forgeries. But where does it fit in with Mrs. Blair's dream?"

Meanwhile, the Drews and their companions had pretended to gaze with interest at the apartment door, then returned to the front entrance. Mr. Drew thanked the concierge, hailed a taxi, and the callers went back to their hotel.

"I have a surprise for you girls this evening," said Mr. Drew. "We're invited to a soirée. It's being held by friends of mine especially for you girls to meet Monsieur Charles Leblanc and see what you can learn."

"It sounds wonderful!" Bess remarked.

The lawyer turned to his daughter and smiled. "If you can get as much information from Monsieur Leblanc as you did from the policeman and the concierge, I'll buy you a special gift from Paris!"

Nancy laughed. "I'll do my best to win it!"

After tea and a short rest, Mr. Drew and the girls dressed in evening clothes and taxied to a beautiful mansion near the Bois de Boulogne Park. The large stone building had several steps leading up to a massive carved doorway. The house was brilliantly lighted, and strains of music from inside floated to the ears of the arriving guests.

"How divine!" Bess murmured.

Mr. Drew alighted first. He was just helping Nancy out when a car came up behind their taxi, and without braking, smashed into it. Despite her father's efforts to save Nancy, she was knocked off-balance and thrown full force to the pavement!

CHAPTER VIII

Dancing Sleuths

THE impact snapped Bess and George against the rear seat of the taxi, then bounced them onto the floor. The driver was also jolted, although less severely.

A stream of furious French issued from his lips and he scrambled out, shaking his fist. But the car responsible for the crash had quickly backed up, then roared off down the street before anyone could get the license number.

By this time Mr. Drew had gently helped Nancy to her feet and the taximan assisted Bess and George from the car. Although badly shaken, the cousins' first concern was for Nancy.

"Are you hurt?" they asked.

At first she did not answer. The breath had been knocked from her and she had fallen heavily on one shoulder. Nancy admitted it hurt.

"Nothing's broken, though. I'll be all right. How about you girls?"

"Okay," George said gamely, rubbing the back of her neck. "We're lucky."

Mr. Drew was greatly concerned for his daughter and her friends. "We'd better give up the party and go back to our hotel."

"Oh, no!" Nancy insisted. "I just wish we'd seen the person who crashed into us. It was certainly deliberate!"

Grim-faced, her father agreed. No one had caught even a glimpse of the culprit. Mr. Drew paid their fare and the banged-up taxi rattled off.

The door of the mansion had opened and the doorman, who evidently had heard the crash, came hurrying down the steps. Upon learning that Mr. Drew and the girls had an invitation to the soirée, he said quickly:

"I will take you to bedrooms so that you can refresh yourselves." When he saw Nancy rubbing one shoulder, he told her there was a doctor at the party. "I will send him upstairs."

Nancy protested, but the doorman was insistent. "I know Monsieur Tremaine—your host—would want me to do that."

He escorted the American guests to elegantly furnished bedrooms on the second floor. Heavily carved furniture was set off by velvet flower-patterned rugs and large tapestries which hung on the walls. The one in the girls' room showed a hunting scene with women seated sidesaddle on their horses. The costumes made the girls smile.

The women wore bodiced dresses with long skirts and large hats with plumes.

"I wonder if those women ever really did any riding or whether they just sat on the horses and posed," Bess remarked.

A few moments later the doorman brought in the physician and introduced him. He was very gracious and seemed glad that Nancy and the others spoke French, since he said he spoke little English. He examined her shoulder thoroughly and reported that it was neither broken nor strained.

"But you have a bad bruise. I suggest that an ice pack be put on it at once and that you get some rest."

Then the doctor examined Bess and George. He seemed pleased that their injuries were minor and prescribed ice packs for the bruises.

Mr. Drew summoned a maid, who quickly brought some ice. The girls lost no time in applying it.

Presently Nancy declared, "I feel all right now. Let's go down to the party."

Bess helped her put on fresh make-up and combed her hair. George brushed the dirt off Nancy's dress and used some water to remove a couple of spots.

"Thanks a million, girls," she said. "All set?"

With a smile Mr. Drew gave Nancy his arm and they led the way downstairs. News of the accident had spread among the guests and many had gathered in the reception room to meet the newcomers. Beyond, the girls could see a ballroom gleaming with crystal chandeliers.

Monsieur and Madame Tremaine were very solicitous, but Nancy and the cousins assured them they felt fine. "We are grateful to you for inviting us to the soirée," Nancy added, not revealing she knew why the party was being given.

"I should like to introduce you to some of our other guests," Madame Tremaine said.

After she had presented them to various friends, she escorted the four Americans into the ballroom where Monsieur Leblanc was standing, and introduced them. A tall slender man with iron-gray hair and mustache, he spoke English fluently.

Nancy thought, "He is handsome and has a charming smile."

"Mr. Drew," said the financier, "you are fortunate to have such a lovely daughter." His eyes beamed with admiration as he looked at Nancy. Then, turning, he smiled at Bess and George.

"Ah! We Frenchmen pride ourselves on the good-looking women in this country, Mr. Drew, but if Mesdemoiselles Drew, Fayne, and Marvin are examples of the young women in America, perhaps our women have to take second place, *non?*"

Nancy, Bess, and George as well as Mr. Drew

carried on the banter. Then Nancy adroitly brought the conversation around to another subject with the question, "You are alone this evening, Monsieur Leblanc?"

"Unfortunately, yes," he replied. "Madame Leblanc is at our house in the country. She did not feel well enough to attend."

"I'm so sorry," said Nancy. "I would have liked to meet her."

She had the feeling he might have invited the group to do so, but at that moment they were interrupted by an announcement from the leader of a small string orchestra. He introduced a young woman soprano who had just joined the Paris Opera Company. The listeners were spellbound by her clear silvery voice, and after she had finished two solos, the applause was thunderous.

Directly afterward, Monsieur Leblanc murmured *"Pardon"* to the girls and Mr. Drew, and went off. The young opera singer graciously gave an encore, then said she must leave.

As the orchestra resumed playing, Nancy, Bess, and George began to talk in subdued tones to Mr. Drew about Monsieur Leblanc. "He seemed attentive to the music," Nancy remarked, "but I did notice that once in a while during the singing he had a faraway look in his eyes."

Bess said dramatically, "Maybe he's been hypnotized and is being coerced into selling his securities!"

"At any rate," George declared emphatically, "I have a hunch it won't be easy to get information out of him!"

Mr. Drew nodded. "I've already learned that. But I really think you girls may have better luck."

Some of the guests they had already met began introducing the River Heights group to others. Two debonair young men asked Bess and George to dance. Another young man was just making his way toward Nancy when Monsieur Leblanc returned.

Bowing low, he said, "May I have the pleasure?"

Nancy did not want to dance—her shoulder was aching—but she felt she should not miss this opportunity to talk with the financier. As they circled the floor of the ballroom, he began to query her about her trip to France. Instantly she wondered if he suspected something, but if he did, Leblanc gave no evidence of it.

She said, "Whenever Dad's away from home he misses me very much. My mother died when I was a child and he and I have always been close pals. He asked me to join him here. Bess and George often go on trips with me."

"I wish," Leblanc said, "that I might have the honor of showing you and your friends around. But I am very busy and unfortunately have little time to myself."

When the music stopped, the Frenchman escorted Nancy to a chair, then excused himself. A few minutes later George made her way to Nancy's side, saying:

"I have something terribly important to tell you. I told my partner I'd be back in a few minutes. See that man in Arabian dress standing in the doorway?"

When Nancy nodded, George went on, "Well, what do you think of this? After Monsieur Leblanc left you, I heard him say to the Arab—in the doorway to the palm garden, where I was—'I told you not to come here, or anywhere else, unless we were alone!' "

Nancy sat straight. "Go on!" she urged.

"The Arab replied, 'But 9 is coming up. You must meet me.' "

"This is exciting!" Nancy remarked. "What else happened?"

"Monsieur Leblanc answered, 'Tomorrow—99.' Then the men separated."

"Ninety-nine!" Nancy echoed softly, her eyes lighting up. "I'd like to follow the Arab!"

At that moment Mr. Drew walked over and Nancy repeated what George had told her. He too was extremely interested, but said he would not permit Nancy to do any more sleuthing that evening.

"Don't forget you were banged up a while ago.

You must get back to the hotel and go to bed. I'll make a bargain with you, though. Tomorrow we'll follow Monsieur Leblanc."

"All right, Dad. Now, may I make a bargain with you?"

He smiled. "What is it?"

"I'd like to shadow the Arab here just for a few minutes and see what I can find out. Please!"

Mr. Drew agreed to give his daughter twenty minutes. "Be very careful," he warned her. "We don't want anyone becoming suspicious."

Just then a young man, Henri Durant, came up and asked Nancy to dance. She accepted and as the music started he led her onto the floor. The young sleuth glanced about as casually as possible. Suddenly her gaze fixed on the far end of the ballroom which opened onto the indoor garden with palm trees and exotic plants. She spotted the Arab in the garden!

An idea quickly came to Nancy. "I hope it works!" she thought.

As they moved along to a lively tune, Henri complimented Nancy not only on her dancing but also on her ability to speak French so well.

Nancy laughed. "You dance very well yourself." Then, seconds later, she said, "Would you mind going into the garden and sitting out the rest of this dance? My shoulder is aching."

Henri was most solicitous and at once led her to a bench in the heavy foliaged garden. At first she could not see the Arab. Then suddenly she spotted him among the palms. He was staring intently at her!

Did he know who Nancy was? Had he guessed that she was trying to solve the mystery of the 99 steps? Was this man a new enemy of hers?

Turning to her companion, Nancy asked, "Do you know who that Arab is?"

"No, but I'll be glad to find out," Henri answered.

He arose and started toward the man. But instantly the stranger turned and hurried off to the far end of the garden where there was another entrance into the ballroom.

Nancy caught up to Henri, thinking, "That Arab certainly acts suspiciously. I mustn't let him get away without finding out who he is!" Smiling, Nancy said to Henri, "I want to speak to that Arabian man and I thought he might be leaving."

This seemed to satisfy Henri and he accompanied her to the edge of the dance floor. Nancy caught sight of the Arab's turban as he disappeared out the doorway which led to the hall. She and Henri made their way through the crowd of dancers as fast as they could.

By the time they reached the hall, however, the Arab was going out the front door. Apparently he had not bothered to say good night to the Tremaines. Hurrying to the doorman, Nancy asked him who the stranger was.

"I do not know the gentleman," he replied. "He had a proper invitation, so of course I admitted him."

"I must speak to Monsieur!" said Nancy, and the servant opened the door.

She ran outside and from the top of the long flight of steps gazed up and down. The Arab was striding quickly toward a small, dark car parked up the street. There was a driver at the wheel and the motor was running.

"Come on, Henri!" Nancy urged.

CHAPTER IX

Startling Headlines

TOGETHER, Nancy and Henri dashed down the steps of the Tremaine mansion. By this time the mysterious Arab had jumped into the automobile. The driver pulled away and the car shot forward.

Suddenly, in the glare of two street lamps in front of the Tremaine home, the Arab took off his turban. With it came a wig and false whiskers.

"Oh!" Nancy gasped.

The man was Louis Aubert!

"Is something the matter?" Henri asked.

"That man was in disguise. I have an idea he had no right to be at the party. We should tell the Tremaines."

"Do you think he is a thief?" Henri looked perplexed. "Is that why you wished to stop him?"

Nancy hesitated, then answered truthfully, "I'm not sure. But I do have reason to suspect that the man is dishonest."

Henri accepted her reply as if sensing Nancy did not wish to divulge anything else. The couple re-entered the house.

Monsieur and Madame Tremaine were at the back of the hall saying good night to several guests. Nancy waited until they had departed, then asked her host who the Arab was. He and his wife

exchanged glances, then Monsieur Tremaine responded:

"We did not catch his name. He suddenly appeared and told us he was a friend of Monsieur Leblanc's. Do you wish me to ask him?"

"He has already left," Nancy told them. "He seemed to be in a great hurry."

The Tremaines frowned. Obviously the man had displayed very bad manners! Nancy was saved from explaining the reason for her query because Bess, George, and Mr. Drew joined them. The lawyer said he thought they should leave now.

Henri smiled at Nancy and said good night. Monsieur Leblanc then came up to the group. His manner seemed perfectly natural as he expressed the hope of seeing them all again some time in the near future.

Nancy's brain was in a whirl. She wondered if the financier might be staying in town and planning to meet Louis Aubert early in the morning. Smiling, Nancy asked Leblanc, "Will you go way out to the country tonight?"

"Yes, indeed. I love it there. I sleep much better."

George had caught on to Nancy's line of questioning. She spoke up. "Do you commute to your office every day, Monsieur Leblanc?"

"Yes. I will be at my desk by nine o'clock tomorrow morning, as usual," he replied.

Nancy had come to a conclusion. He would meet Louis Aubert either in Paris during the daytime or out in the country the next evening. "I can't wait to follow him," she thought.

The girls went for their wraps, and after thanking the Tremaines for a delightful evening, left with Mr. Drew. Nancy, although bursting with her news, decided not to tell it until they were alone at the hotel. Once there, she asked her father to come to the girls' room.

Nancy told about the Arab being Louis Aubert and added her suspicion that the invitation might have been obtained fraudulently.

"It could even have been forged," she said. "Remember, his brother Claude is a wanted forger. Louis could be one, too."

George in turn repeated the conversation she had overheard between Louis and Leblanc.

"These are excellent clues!" the lawyer exclaimed. "They may tie in with something I heard this evening from Monsieur Tremaine. He is one of the people who is greatly alarmed about Monsieur Leblanc's irresponsibility in business affairs."

Nancy asked eagerly, "Can you tell us why?"

"Oh, yes. Today Leblanc received a very large sum of money—thousands of dollars in francs—for the sale of certain securities. He had insisted upon having it in cash. I assume that he had the sum with him tonight."

Bess's eyes grew wide with excitement. "You mean that perhaps the poor man is being blackmailed by Louis Aubert?"

The lawyer smiled wryly. "I'm not making any definite statement yet, but what we've heard and seen tonight seems to add up to some kind of secret dealing."

He and the girls continued to discuss every angle of the mystery for nearly an hour. In the end, all agreed that the whole thing remained very puzzling.

"I still can't fit Mrs. Blair's strange dream into the picture," Nancy remarked, "yet I'm sure there's a connection."

One by one the foursome began to yawn. Mr. Drew stood up and said he was going to bed. "I'll see you all at breakfast," he added, then kissed each girl good night.

As Nancy undressed she looked woefully at her bruised shoulder. There was a large black-and-blue area. Bess asked if she wanted more ice, but Nancy shook her head.

"The doctor said I was all right and I think a good night's sleep will help a lot."

In the morning her shoulder did feel better, although it was very sensitive to the touch. Nancy smiled. "Just a little souvenir of Paris."

When the girls joined Mr. Drew in the hotel dining room, they found him reading the morning paper. As he laid it down, a headline caught Nancy's eye and she gasped.

"Monsieur Leblanc robbed on the way home!" she repeated. "And of thousands of dollars! It must have been the money he received from the securities!"

Her father nodded. "I'm afraid so."

"Have you read the whole article?" George asked Mr. Drew.

"Yes. Leblanc's car was waylaid by two men on a lonely stretch of road not far from his home. The bandits did not harm Leblanc or his chauffeur, but they did take every penny which both carried."

"How dreadful!" Bess exclaimed. "Have the thieves been caught yet?"

Mr. Drew said No, and there was probably little chance the police could do so. After the holdup, there had been rain and any footprints had been washed away.

"Mr. Drew," Bess asked, "could one of the holdup men have been Louis Aubert?"

"I confess I'm baffled," Nancy's father replied. "If that make-believe Arab is blackmailing Leblanc and was going to meet him today, why would he rob him last night? On the other hand, he may have feared Leblanc would change his mind so he decided to get the money right away."

Nancy spoke up. "One thing we haven't followed up about Louis is his being a scientist. My hunch is he's a chemist."

Bess sighed. "It's going to be hard to find out about his work if nobody knows or will tell where Aubert lives. I'll bet if Monsieur Leblanc has the address he isn't going to reveal it."

The others agreed and felt that pursuing this lead would have to wait. Nancy said, "I'd like to find out if Monsieur Leblanc plans to stay home because of the robbery."

"Why don't you call up and find out?" Bess suggested. "You can act terribly upset and sympathetic over what happened."

"I'll do that," Nancy said. "I'll phone his office."

Shortly after nine, Nancy put in the call. She learned from the operator that Monsieur Leblanc was there, and appeared to show no ill effects of the incident. "He is busy in a conference," the girl told her. "Would you like to leave a message?"

"No, thank you. I just wanted to make sure that Monsieur Leblanc is all right." Nancy rang off before the operator might ask who was calling.

When Mr. Drew heard his daughter's report, he decided to get in touch with Monsieur Tremaine and suggest that a private detective be retained to watch Leblanc's office building that day and follow the financier wherever he might go.

Mr. Tremaine readily agreed and asked if the detective should continue his assignment that evening also.

"Thank you, no. The girls and I will take over then."

Nancy was eager to pursue her sleuthing, but she went sightseeing with her friends and had lunch aboard a pleasure boat on the River Seine. Later, while buying some souvenirs, Nancy said, "Look! A musical coffeepot! I'll buy it for Hannah Gruen!"

Late in the afternoon Mr. Drew and the girls picked up a car he had rented earlier. They drove to Monsieur Leblanc's office building and parked nearby.

Immediately a man in street clothes walked up to them. Smiling and tipping his hat to the girls, he inquired, "Monsieur Drew? Monsieur Carson Drew?"

When Mr. Drew nodded, the man presented a card identifying him as the detective assigned to watch Leblanc.

"Monsieur Leblanc has not come out all day," the detective reported. "Do you want me to stay longer?"

"No, that won't be necessary," Mr. Drew replied. "We'll relieve you now."

Not long after the detective had left, the financier emerged from the building. He walked briskly to an automobile with a chauffeur at the wheel and got in.

A few seconds after Leblanc's car started off, Mr. Drew pulled out and followed him easily, but for only half a block. Then the dense rush-hour traffic closed in, making it impossible for Mr. Drew to keep close to their quarry. In a few moments he had lost sight of the financier's car completely.

Nancy sighed. She was very disappointed. "What if Monsieur Leblanc stops for a rendezvous at the 99 steps!" she thought. "We'll miss a perfect chance to find out where they are."

As the Drews were debating what to do next, Bess spoke up. "I'm absolutely famished. Couldn't we stop somewhere for just a quick bite—and then look for Monsieur Leblanc?"

Nancy started to agree when a sudden idea struck her. "First let's go back to Claude Aubert's old apartment!" she exclaimed.

"Why?" Bess asked.

"Monsieur Leblanc might be heading there right now—to meet Louis!"

CHAPTER X

A Sinister Figure

Mr. Drew threaded his way through the Paris traffic to the Left Bank. When they reached the apartment house, the travelers scanned both sides of the street. Leblanc's car was not in sight.

"I guess he didn't come here after all," the lawyer said.

Before leaving the area, however, Mr. Drew drove around the two adjoining blocks. Still no sign of Monsieur Leblanc.

"He probably went straight home," Bess remarked. "Do we eat now?" she asked hopefully.

Mr. Drew chuckled. "Right away."

Soon he pulled up at a small cheerful restaurant which was willing to serve dinner earlier than was customary in Paris. Bess regarded the menu suspiciously.

"Snails!" she exclaimed. "And fish served whole—I just can't stand to look at the eyes of a fish on a platter!"

Mischievously Nancy pointed to another item. "Why not try this, Bess? It's very popular here—raw beef mixed with chopped onions and an uncooked egg."

Bess was horrified. "That's even worse!"

The others laughed and George said, "Why, Bess Marvin, I thought you were a gourmet!"

"Sorry," said Bess. "I'll stick to good old cream of tomato soup, medium-well-done roast beef, potatoes, asparagus, salad, some cheese, and then fruit."

George looked at her cousin disapprovingly. "You'll be bursting out of your clothes within three days if you eat like that!" As a compromise, Bess said she would not have the soup.

The food was delicious, and everyone enjoyed the meal immensely. It was seven o'clock before they left the restaurant.

"How far away does Monsieur Leblanc live?" Nancy asked her father.

"About twenty miles outside of Paris."

On the way, Nancy did not talk much. She was mulling over the various angles to the mystery. There was no doubt now but that both her case and her father's revolved around the 99 steps. Her one clue to them so far had faded out.

"If I could only unearth another clue to the right steps!" Nancy said to herself.

Mr. Drew had come to an area of handsome

homes, most of them with extensive grounds. The girls exclaimed over their attractiveness. In a little while they reached an estate which Mr. Drew said belonged to Monsieur Leblanc. It was surrounded by a high stone wall, and the entranceway was almost hidden by a grove of sycamore trees. Nancy's father pulled in among them and stopped.

"I'll hide the car here," he said. "It will be easy to take out and follow Leblanc if necessary."

"What if he doesn't come outside?" Nancy asked. "Shall we go up to the house when it's darker?"

"We'll have no choice."

They waited in the car for over fifteen minutes, then George burst out, "I need exercise! Let's do some walking!"

The others agreed and Nancy added, "We can try a little sleuthing too."

Mr. Drew locked the ignition and took the key. As the four passed through the driveway entrance, they noticed a great stone pillar on either side. Tall iron gates were attached to them, but they stood open.

"Just put here for decoration," Mr. Drew observed. "I imagine they're never closed."

Nancy suggested that the group separate. "Bess and George, suppose you take the right side of the driveway up to the house. See if you can pick up any clues as to what Monsieur Leblanc is frightened about. Dad and I will take the other side and meet you there."

Mr. Drew added, "If you two girls see Leblanc leaving, give our birdcall warning and run as fast as you can back to the car so we can follow him."

Bess and George set off among the trees that grew along the driveway. It was dark under the heavy foliage and they kept stumbling over roots.

"I wish we'd brought flashlights," Bess complained.

"We couldn't have used them, anyhow," George retorted. "Someone would spot us right away."

They went on silently for a few minutes, then Bess whispered fearfully, "I don't like this. There may be watchdogs prowling around."

"Oh, don't be silly!" said George and hurried ahead.

Suddenly Bess let out a scream. George dashed back. "What is it?"

Bess, ashen-faced, stammered out, "There! Hanging from that tree! A—a body!"

George turned a little squeamish herself, but decided to investigate. She went over, felt the object, and then laughed softly.

"It's only a stuffed dummy," she declared.

"Why is it hanging there?" asked Bess, still trembling. "It must be some kind of a sinister warning. I'm not going another step. Let's go back to the car."

"And run out on Nancy? Nothing doing," George replied firmly. "Do you know what I think this figure might be? A punching bag!"

"You mean, like football players use in practice?" Bess asked.

George nodded.

Finally Bess summoned up enough courage to go on, and presently the cousins found themselves at the head of the driveway. On the far side stood a large and imposing chateau. The girls would have to cross in the open to reach it. They discussed whether or not it was wise to do this.

The front of the mansion was well lighted. Several windows stood open, but not a sound came from inside.

"I wonder if Monsieur Leblanc is at home," George murmured.

Before she and Bess could make up their minds what to do, the front door opened. A tall, slender woman, holding a mastiff on a leash, walked down the short flight of steps. Hastily the cousins ducked back among the trees as the woman turned in their direction. Had she heard Bess's scream and was coming to investigate?

"I told you they'd have a watchdog!" Bess groaned. "We'd better go before she lets that beast loose!"

George did not argue, and the two girls began to retrace their steps hurriedly.

Meanwhile, Nancy and her father had made their way cautiously toward the rear of the big house. A little way behind it was a five-car garage, filled with automobiles. The Drews recognized the car in which Leblanc had ridden earlier.

"Dad, this must mean he's at home," Nancy said.

Directly behind the house was a large flower garden. The Drews entered it and walked along a path. Fortunately it was dark enough so that their figures could not be seen in silhouette. They passed what Mr. Drew said were the kitchen and dining room. Just beyond was a brightly lighted room with a large window, partly open, that overlooked the garden.

The room was lined with bookshelves, and comfortably furnished. In the center stood a mahogany desk. The Drews could see no one.

A moment later a telephone on the desk began to ring. The door to the room opened and a tall man strode in.

"Monsieur Leblanc!" Nancy whispered excitedly. "He *is* home! Now we can follow him if he leaves!"

Her father said, "Remember, he may already have met the man we think is Louis Aubert. Let's wait and see what happens."

Monsieur Leblanc did not lower his voice and

through an open window his part in the phone conversation came clearly to the Drews.

"I told you the money was stolen!" the financier said. "If I did not have the money, what was the use of my coming?"

Another long pause. Then Leblanc said firmly, "Now listen. People are beginning to show some suspicion. I will have to be more careful."

There followed a long silence. At last he spoke again. "It is against my better judgment. Let us not do anything more for a few days."

Nancy was hardly breathing. She did not want to lose one word that this enigmatic financier was saying.

Leblanc's voice grew angry. "Why can't you wait? I know you said 9 was coming up, but even the thought of it brought me bad luck. Every cent I had with me was taken."

The next pause was so long that Mr. Drew and Nancy began to wonder if the caller had hung up. But finally they heard Monsieur Leblanc say in a resigned tone, "Very well, then. I will go to the orange garden." He put down the telephone.

CHAPTER XI

Clue From Home

NANCY squeezed her father's arm and whispered, "The orange garden! Do you think it's here?"

Mr. Drew shook his head. "I know every inch of these grounds."

The two became silent again as they wondered where the orange garden might be and if the telephone caller had been Louis Aubert. "I'm sure he was," Nancy thought, and hoped Monsieur Leblanc would start out immediately.

The Drews watched him intently. Leblanc did not leave the study, however. Instead, he took off his jacket and slipped on a lounging robe. Then he sat down at the desk and wrote for several minutes.

"It doesn't look as if he's going out tonight," Nancy remarked.

At that moment the Frenchman picked up a book from his desk and went to a large leather easy chair. He sank into it and began to read.

"I guess this settles the matter," said Mr. Drew in a low voice. "We had better go."

His daughter lingered. "Maybe Monsieur Leblanc is going out later."

Mr. Drew smiled. "I think it's more likely he'll stop at this mysterious orange garden on his way to the office. But we can't stay here all night. Remember, you girls leave for the Bardots' chateau tomorrow."

Reluctantly Nancy started back with her father. Just then they heard a series of deep-throated barks. "That's the Leblancs' guard dog," Mr. Drew said.

"Oh!" Nancy cried out. "It may be after Bess and George! We'd better find out!"

The Drews hurried from the garden and raced quickly down the driveway. The barking continued. When Nancy and her father reached the entrance, the gates were locked.

There was no escape!

"This is bad!" Mr. Drew exclaimed. "Nancy, I'll boost you to the top of the wall. The dog won't harm you there."

"But how about you?" Nancy argued. "And where are Bess and George?"

At that moment the cousins appeared, running like mad. The mastiff's barks were closer now.

"Quick! Over the wall!" Nancy said. "The gates are locked!"

Bess and George did not say a word. Quickly

Mr. Drew helped them to the top of the stonework, then he boosted Nancy upward. She and George lay flat on the wall and grasped the lawyer's hands. The dog, his leash trailing, had reached the scene and managed to tear one cuff of Mr. Drew's trousers before the girls yanked him to safety.

Out of breath the group dropped to the ground and went to their car. As they headed for Paris, Mr. Drew remarked, "I guess we got what we deserved. We *were* trespassing."

Bess said, "Thank goodness we escaped. Two scares in one night are two too many for me."

She and George told the story of the figure hanging from a tree. When Mr. Drew heard George's idea that the dummy was a punching bag for Monsieur Leblanc, he laughed heartily. "I've been calling him the frightened financier, but maybe I'll have to change it to the fighting financier!"

The girls giggled, then George eagerly asked what Nancy and her father had found out. When they were told about the orange garden, the cousins agreed it was an excellent clue.

"How are you going to follow it up, Nancy?" Bess queried.

"Right now I don't know. But I intend to find out where the orange garden is."

Nancy went on to say that one thing was very puzzling: Why did Louis Aubert have such a hold over Monsieur Leblanc, when his name had once been forged by Aubert's twin, Claude?

Her father said this mystified him too. "I'm afraid we'll have to wait for the answer to that question, Nancy, until you turn up more evidence about the exact relationship between Louis and Monsieur Leblanc."

Next morning, when the girls came downstairs to breakfast, Mr. Drew said, "I've rented a car for your trip to the Loire valley, girls."

"Wonderful! Thank you, Dad," said Nancy. "You think of everything."

The lawyer smiled. "I have another surprise for you." He pulled a letter from his pocket. "Some news from Hannah Gruen."

Nancy excused herself and read the letter. Marie and Monique were having a good time in River Heights. The sisters were popular and they had made some warm friends. There were two special messages for Nancy. One was from Chief McGinnis. The River Heights police had caught the stilt walker! He had been paid, he said, by a James Chase to do the job.

"Claude Aubert again!" Nancy murmured, then quickly told the others about the stilt walker's arrest. She read on. Suddenly she said excitedly, "Oh, listen to this, everyone!

" 'Here's the other special message for you, Nancy. Right after you left, Mrs. Blair phoned to say she'd had the dream about the 99 steps, as usual. But this time she was a child, playing with her governess. Presently the woman tied a dark handkerchief over the child's eyes for a game of blindman's buff. Later, Mrs. Blair came across another clue in her mother's diary—the name of the governess. It was Mlle. Lucille Manon.' "

Nancy looked up from the letter and burst out, "How's that for a marvelous clue?" Mr. Drew, Bess, and George were elated by the information.

The girls had packed before leaving their room, so soon after breakfast they checked out of the hotel and were on their way to the Bardots. Nancy, at the wheel of the small French car, found it took some time to make progress. The morning rush hour was in full swing, with its hurrying crowds and hundreds of taxis scooting recklessly in and out of traffic.

The route to the Bardots led past the famous palace of Versailles. Nancy paused briefly so that the girls could view the huge building and gardens.

"Let's see," Bess mused, "wasn't it Louis XIV who built Versailles?"

Nancy nodded. "It has a fascinating history. Imagine a German emperor being crowned here! You remember that Germany once controlled all of France."

"But the French finally got their country back," George remarked.

Suddenly Bess chuckled. "The thing I remember is that Louis XIV was supposed to have had over a hundred wigs. He never permitted anybody to see him without one, except his hairdresser."

Presently the girls came to the Bardots' home. Set far back from the street, it was approached by a curving driveway. The stone dwelling was in the style of an old French period when buildings were square and three stories high. It had a flat roof with a cupola for a lookout.

"Isn't it lovely here?" Bess remarked as she looked around at the green lawns, the well-trimmed shrubs, and the flowering bushes.

As Nancy stopped the car at the front entrance, the door opened and Monsieur and Madame Bardot came out to greet them. At once the girls could see that Marie resembled her mother and Monique her father. The couple were most gracious in their welcome and led the visitors inside.

The furnishings were charming but not elaborate. They gave the chateau an atmosphere of warm hospitality, which was enhanced by vases of beautiful flowers.

The Bardots spoke perfect English, but upon learning that the girls could converse in French, Monsieur Bardot advised them to speak only in French during their visit. "I believe it will help you in your sleuthing," he added.

No further reference was made to the mystery at the moment, for suddenly excited barking came from the rear of the house. The next moment a miniature black poodle raced into the living room. She jumped up on the girls, wagging her tail briskly.

"Fifi! Get down!" Madame Bardot commanded.

"Oh, we don't mind," said Nancy. "She's very cute."

The girls took turns patting Fifi. When she finally became calm, Nancy said, "Monique told me that the dog sleeps in an antique kennel."

Madame Bardot smiled. "Actually, we should call it a bed, since we keep it in the house. Would you like to see it?"

She led the guests across the center hall into a combination library and game room. In one corner stood the most unusual dog bed the Americans had ever seen. The square frame, surrounding a blue satin cushion, was of gilded wood with an arched canopy of blue velvet. The headboard was covered in blue-and-white-striped satin.

"This was built in the early eighteenth century," Madame Bardot explained.

"How darling!" Bess commented. "Does Fifi really sleep in the bed? It looks so neat."

Monsieur Bardot laughed. "Every time Fifi comes into the house she is brushed off and her feet washed!" His eyes twinkled as if he were teasing his wife, who pursed her lips in pretended hurt.

The visitors' baggage was brought in, and the girls were shown to Marie's and Monique's bedrooms. They loved the wide canopied beds and dainty gold-and-white furniture. Bess and George said they would share the same room.

Conversation during luncheon was confined to Marie and Monique and their trip to the United States. Nancy told about the madrigal singing and how the people of River Heights loved it. The Bardots beamed with pride.

When the meal was over, their hostess arose. "Shall we go out to our patio?" she suggested.

The Bardots led the girls to the rear of the chateau and through a garden filled with roses, mignonettes, and summer lilies.

As soon as the group was seated in comfortable lawn chairs, Madame Bardot leaned forward. "Now please tell us, Nancy, have you had any success with my sister Josette's mystery?"

Nancy had decided it would be wise not to mention her father's case and had instructed Bess and George not to. She and the cousins described the various warnings received by Nancy, the helicopter incident, and the Aubert twins.

"I think," Nancy went on, "that Claude, the one in the United States, left the warnings at the request of his brother Louis."

"And," said Bess, "Louis calls himself Monsieur Neuf."

George put in, "We thought we had found the 99 steps but we were wrong."

"We may have a new clue to them," Nancy added. "Do you know of an orange garden in this area?"

After some thought, Monsieur Bardot replied, "At Versailles a double flight of steps leads down from a terrace to L'Orangerie, the orange orchard."

"You mean," Nancy said eagerly, "that there are 99 steps in them?"

The Frenchman smiled. "Actually there are 103 in each flight, but they are called the *Cent-Marches*."

"The hundred steps!" Nancy exclaimed.

"That's close enough to 99," George declared.

"It's worth investigating," Nancy agreed.

Her host suggested the girls drive to Versailles that very afternoon. "I'm sorry that my wife and I cannot accompany you, but we have an engagement."

Within an hour the trio set off. When they reached the palace of Versailles, Nancy parked the car and the girls walked up to the huge, sprawling edifice. They went to the beautiful gardens at the south side, exclaiming over the pool, palms, orange trees, and velvety grass.

Nancy spotted the imposing double staircase

leading down from a broad terrace of the palace. Excitedly the girls mounted the steps, counting them.

Presently Bess gasped and called out, "Look!"

On the 99th tread was a black chalk mark—M9!

"M9—Monsieur Neuf!" George exclaimed. "Then what you overheard at Leblanc's last night, Nancy, was true! Louis Aubert must have come here. But when and why?"

"Maybe," Bess spoke up, "it has nothing to do with Louis Aubert after all."

Nancy shook her head in disagreement. "I believe Aubert chalked this M9 here as the spot where Monsieur Leblanc was to leave something—probably money. Let's do a little sightseeing in the palace and then come back in case Leblanc stops here on his way home."

The girls went down the steps again and walked to the main entrance. Inside, they stared in wonder at the grandeur of the palace. Walls, ceilings, and floors were ornate, but what amazed the girls most was the lavish decor of Louis XIV's bedroom.

"It's absolutely magnificent but it sure doesn't look like a man's room," George said.

"At least not a modern man." Nancy grinned. "Don't forget, back in the seventeenth and eighteenth centuries this was the way people in power liked to live, men as well as women."

When the girls came to the famous Hall of

Mirrors, a guide told them it was here that the peace treaty between the United States, England, and France on one side and Germany on the other had been signed after the First World War.

"They couldn't have picked a more beautiful spot," Bess murmured.

When the girls left the palace, Nancy glanced at her wrist watch. Very soon Monsieur Leblanc might be stopping at L'Orangerie. The three friends went back to the steps and waited. Minutes dragged by.

Finally George said, "I can't stand this inactivity another second. Nancy, I'm going to climb these steps again."

The next instant George was running up the flight of steps. When she reached the 99th, George stared in amazement, then turned around and called down to the others:

"The M9 mark is gone!"

The words were barely out of her mouth when she noticed a door in the palace being opened. No one came out, and she wondered if the girls were being spied upon.

"I must find out!" George said determinedly as she sped across the terrace.

Just as she reached the door a man's arm shot out. In his hand was a cane with a large curved handle. Suddenly the crook of the cane reached around George's neck and she was yanked inside the building!

CHAPTER XII

The Red King Warning

As the door of the palace closed, Bess shrieked and Nancy gasped. George was a prisoner! Whose? And why?

"M9 has kidnapped her!" cried Bess. "What'll we do?"

Nancy was already dashing up the steps. She crossed the terrace and tried the door. It was locked!

"Oh, I must get in!" Nancy thought desperately. She turned to Bess, who had followed her. "You stay here and watch. I'll run to the main entrance and see what I can find out."

She sped off and tried that door. It, too, was locked!

Desperate, Nancy banged on the door panels as hard as she could. In a few minutes a guard came out.

"The palace is closed for the day, mademoiselle," he said, annoyed.

"But listen!" Nancy pleaded. "A friend of mine was forced inside by somebody near the top of the L'Orangerie steps."

The guard looked at Nancy skeptically. She knew he was wondering if she had suddenly gone mad.

"This is serious," she said. "I'm not fooling. Please! My friend is in danger!"

Suddenly the guard seemed to sense that perhaps Nancy was telling the truth. He admitted her, and together the two raced up a staircase and to the door in question. No one was in sight.

The guard gave Nancy a look of disgust. "I do not like people who play jokes," he said brusquely. "Now you had better leave. And quickly!"

Nancy was at her wit's end. How could she convince this man? Then her eyes lighted on a pale-blue button from George's blouse. She picked it up from the floor.

"Here's proof," she said to the guard, and explained where the button had come from.

"Then where is she?" he asked, now worried himself.

"We'll have to find out," Nancy replied.

She led the way, practically running from room to room. There was no sign of either George or her abductor.

"Maybe the fellow sneaked down one of the stairways and went out," the guard suggested.

As the two stood debating where to search

next, they suddenly saw a man in uniform dash from one of the rooms and head for the main stairway.

The guard with Nancy muttered, "Very odd. I am supposed to be the only one left on duty."

Nancy cried out, "That man may be a fake! Come on!"

They dashed after the uniformed figure, but by the time they reached the top of the staircase he was out of sight. A door below slammed.

Out of breath, the guard said worriedly, "The fellow has probably escaped. I hope he did not steal anything."

Nancy had a different idea—that the fugitive had grabbed George with the crook end of the cane. "He must have left my friend behind. We'll have to keep searching!"

Nancy and the guard pressed on. Presently they reached Louis XIV's bedroom and stood still in amazement.

George Fayne lay on the ornate bed asleep!

At least Nancy hoped that George was *asleep*. Fearfully she went toward her friend. Just as she reached the bed, George opened her eyes. She looked around wildly, murmuring, "Where am I?"

"Oh, thank goodness you're all right!" Nancy cried out.

The guard's expression was one of utter disbelief. For a moment he could only stare at George as if she were an apparition.

"George, how do you feel?" Nancy asked solicitously.

"I—I guess I'm all right," George answered shakily. "When something hooked around my neck I blacked out." She started to sit up.

By now the guard was thoroughly alarmed. "No, no!" he insisted. "Do not move. I shall call a doctor. And I must also inform the police at once." He hurried off.

George protested, but Nancy agreed with the guard and insisted that George lie still. It seemed an endless time before the man returned with a physician and two police officers. After examining her, the doctor said that George was all right but should rest. Then he left.

Suddenly George burst out laughing. "This is so ridiculous! I can't believe it really happened!" Between gales of mirth, she said, "Imagine me sleeping in Louis XIV's bed!" Finally Nancy, the guard, and the policemen were also laughing.

George's eyes became so filled with tears of merriment that she had to wipe them away. As she pulled a handkerchief from the pocket of her blouse, a folded sheet of paper fluttered to the floor. Nancy picked it up and handed the paper back to George. When she opened it, a strange expression came over her face.

"What's the matter?" Nancy asked.

"Somebody put this note in my pocket! It's another warning!"

The two officers instantly became alert. "What do you mean?" one asked.

"First I'll read the note," she said. "Then my friend Nancy can tell you the rest." George read aloud the typed message:

" '*You girls mind your own business or grave consequences will come to you!*
The Red King' "

"The Red King?" the second officer repeated. "*Mais*—but who is he—this Red King?"

"That's a new name to us," Nancy answered the question. "Other warning notes have been signed Monsieur Neuf and the Green Lion."

She explained sketchily about Mrs. Blair's mystery which had brought Nancy to France. The officers said that they had never heard any of the names.

"Earlier today we noticed that on the 99th step of the stairway from L'Orangerie someone put M9 in black chalk," Nancy went on, and told the whole story of what had happened.

The officers and guard were impressed. All said that these pretty American girl detectives were brave indeed to undertake such risks.

Nancy inquired, "You are sure that none of you knows a man named Louis Aubert?"

The three shook their heads. One of the policemen asked, "Does he live around here?"

Nancy said she did not know his address. "We saw him in Paris twice—once he was dressed as an Arab. I suspect he's involved in this mystery, and that he's the man in a guard's uniform we saw running away from here a while ago."

"We will make an investigation," the officers assured the girls. One of them reached for the note. "And examine this for fingerprints. You will come to headquarters if necessary?"

Nancy smiled. "Of course." She told where they were staying.

"*Très bien*. Very good!"

George insisted that she felt much better. "Let's get back to Bess. She's probably frantic."

The two girls hurried to rejoin their friend. Bess was relieved and delighted to see her cousin safe, but horrified to hear what had happened.

When the girls reached home, the Bardots were very much worried by the girls' adventure. "It is quite evident this Monsieur Neuf knows you three are on his trail. He is getting desperate," said Monsieur Bardot. "From now on you girls must take every precaution." They promised they would.

That night after dinner Nancy asked the Bardots where Josette Blair had lived as a child.

"Only a few miles from here," Madame Bardot replied. "Would you like to see the place? I'll take you there tomorrow morning after church."

"Oh, wonderful!" Nancy exclaimed.

The journey took them through rolling, verdant country. There was acre upon acre of green pasture and farmland filled with a profusion of growing vegetables and flowers in bloom. It was late morning when they reached another attractive, old-time chateau surrounded by gardens.

In the front a man and a woman were busy snipping off full-grown roses. Madame Bardot turned into the drive and asked the couple if they were the present owners.

The woman replied pleasantly, "Yes, our name is Dupont. May we help you?"

The visitors alighted. After making introductions, Nancy explained that Mrs. Blair, a very good friend of hers, had lived there as a little girl. At mention of the strange dream, the Duponts were greatly interested.

"Ah, *oui,*" said Madame Dupont. "I do recall that Mrs. Blair lived here when she was little, but we cannot explain the dream."

Nancy asked, "By any chance do you know her governess, who was Mademoiselle Manon?"

"We do not exactly know her," Monsieur Dupont answered, "but a woman did stop here about five years ago. She told us she had once lived here as governess to a little girl but had lost track of her."

"This is very exciting!" Bess spoke up. "Can you tell us where Mademoiselle Manon lives? Mrs. Blair would like to know."

"I'm sorry, but we cannot help you," said Madame Dupont. "At the time of her call she wanted to get in touch with Mrs. Blair but had no idea where she was. We could tell her only that Mrs. Blair had gone to the United States."

Nancy wondered if the couple could give any kind of clue leading to Mademoiselle Manon's present address.

"Did she happen to mention where she was going?" Nancy inquired. "Or where she might have come from?"

"No," Monsieur Dupont replied. "But she did say she had married. Her name is Mrs. Louis Aubert."

CHAPTER XIII

Schoolmaster Suspect

WHILE Nancy and the other girls were mulling over the startling bit of information about the governess, the Duponts' maid came from the house.

"*Pardon,* madame. I could not help but overhear your conversation about a man named Aubert," she said. "Perhaps I can be of some help to the young ladies."

Everyone looked eagerly at her, and Mrs. Dupont said, "Yes, Estelle?"

The maid, who was a little older than the girls, turned to Nancy. "I come from Orléans. I went to school there two years ago, and one of my masters was Monsieur Louis Aubert."

This statement excited Nancy still more. Was she on the verge of a really big discovery?

"Tell me about the man. Was he in his fifties?" she asked.

"Yes." Estelle described her schoolmaster in

detail. He certainly could be the Louis Aubert for whom Nancy was looking!

"Can you give me his address?" she asked the maid.

"I am afraid not, except I am sure his home is in Orléans."

"Did you ever meet his wife?" Nancy inquired.

Estelle shook her head. "I do not even know her name."

Nancy thanked the girl, saying, "What you've told us might be of great help." She also expressed her appreciation to the Duponts, who said they were very happy to have met the Americans and wished them luck in their search.

During the drive home, the entire conversation revolved about Louis Aubert. Bess remarked, "Do you suppose he's leading a double life—one as a respectable schoolteacher, and the other as a crook?"

"It certainly looks that way," George said.

Nancy suggested, "How about going to Orléans and checking?"

Everyone thought this a good idea. After an early breakfast the next morning the three girls set off, prepared to stay overnight if necessary.

Madame Bardot kissed them good-by, saying, "If your sleuthing in Orléans should take much time and you girls plan to stay, please phone me."

"I certainly will," said Nancy, "and let you know how we're getting along."

A short time later the girls' conversation turned to the city of Orléans and its place in history.

"From the time I was a child," said Bess, "Joan of Arc, the Maid of Orléans, was one of my favorite heroines."

George added, "The idea of a girl soldier appeals to me. What terrific courage she had! That much of her story I do remember well."

Nancy smiled. "I wish we had Joan on this trip with us. She was a pretty good detective, too."

"Imagine a young peasant girl saving her country!" Bess remarked.

"Yes," said Nancy. "Joan was only seventeen when she requested a horse, armor, and an escort of men from a French commander to help fight the English invaders."

"I'll bet he laughed at her," George remarked.

"He did at first," Nancy continued, "but finally consented. Joan also wanted to help put Charles VII, the Dauphin, on the throne at Reims, which was held by the English. Charles was a weak man and had little money."

"And still he wanted to be crowned king?" George asked.

"Yes. He didn't want the English to take over France," Nancy went on. "When Joan arrived at

Charles' castle and offered to help, the Dauphin decided to test the peasant girl's ability."

"How did he do that?" George interrupted.

"By slipping in among his courtiers and asking one of the nobles to sit on the throne. But he couldn't fool her—she showed up the hoax at once."

Nancy smiled, brushing a strand of hair from her forehead. "Joan glanced at the man on the throne, then walked directly to Charles and curtsied. Everyone was amazed, since she had never seen the Dauphin in person."

Bess put in excitedly, "Yes, and Joan claimed she had seen a vision of the Dauphin. That's how she knew him."

George wrinkled her brow. "Joan finally did succeed in getting the king to Reims, didn't she?"

"Oh, yes," said Nancy. "Charles gave her a sword and banner and troops. In 1429 she rode into Orléans and freed the city from the English. Then the king was crowned."

"Unfortunately," Bess added, "she was captured a short time later and burned at the stake for heresy!"

"And you know," Nancy concluded, "twenty-four years after Joan's death at Rouen she was declared innocent. Now she's a saint!"

The girls became silent, thinking about the brave peasant girl and viewing the lovely countryside of the Loire valley. The soil was rich and the air sweet with mingled scents of fruit and flowers.

Later, as Nancy pulled into the city of Orléans, Bess requested that they go directly to the famous old square called La Place Ville Martroi, where a statue of Jeanne d'Arc on horseback graced the center. Nancy parked on a side street, and the girls went to gaze at the figure in armor high on a large pedestal.

At that moment the girls heard music. "That's a marching tune," said George. "Wonder what's up."

A crowd had begun to gather in the square. Speaking in French, Nancy asked the man standing beside her the reason for the music. He said a small parade was on its way. Soon the square was filled with onlookers.

Again Nancy spoke to the man. "*Pardon,* monsieur, but do you happen to know a schoolmaster in town named Louis Aubert? I should like to find him."

He nodded. "*Mais oui,* Monsieur Aubert is the bandleader in the parade."

Nancy and her friends could have jumped in excitement. In a few moments the schoolmaster suspect would appear!

As the music came closer, the girls strained their eyes to see the beginning of the parade. Suddenly a small boy standing near Nancy found he was too short to see the parade. He jumped over the flowers and onto a section of bench that surrounded the base of St. Joan's statue. Like a monkey he clambered up the pedestal.

"Oh, that's dangerous!" Bess cried out. "He'll fall!"

The boy was just pulling himself to the top of the pedestal when Nancy saw one of his hands slip. Instantly she jumped onto the bench. "Hold on!" she called to the boy.

The lad clawed wildly at the pedestal, but lost his grip. With a cry he dropped into Nancy's outstretched arms. The shock knocked the two into the flower bed. Neither was hurt.

"*Merci,* mademoiselle," the boy murmured, as they got to their feet.

By this time the crowd had begun to cheer. Nancy was embarrassed, particularly when the boy's mother rushed up and threw her arms around Nancy. In voluble French she expressed her thanks over and over again.

Nancy smiled, freed herself gently, and made her way back to Bess and George.

"Great rescue, Nancy," said George. "But in all the excitement we missed seeing the beginning of the parade. The band has gone down another street."

Dismayed, Nancy's instinct was to run after the band and try to spot the leader. But that was impossible. Several policemen had appeared and re-

The shock knocked them into the flower bed

fused to let the bystanders move about until the entire parade had passed.

"It's a shame!" George declared. "Maybe we can catch up with Louis Aubert somewhere else."

Nancy sighed. "I hope so."

The man to whom Nancy had talked earlier turned to her and said, *"Pardon,* mademoiselle, I see you have missed your friend. Would it help for you to speak to Madame Aubert?"

"Oh, yes!" Nancy replied.

"She is standing in that doorway across the square."

Nancy caught a glimpse of the woman as the marchers went by. But by the time the square was clear and the girls could cross, Madame Aubert had vanished.

"We've had so many disappointments today," Bess said wistfully, "something good is bound to happen soon."

Nancy urged that they try to catch up with the band. The trio ran after the parade, but by the time they reached the line of marchers, the band was breaking up. Nancy asked one of the drummers where she could find Monsieur Aubert.

"He has left, mademoiselle," was the answer.

"Can you tell me where he lives?"

The man readily gave the Auberts' address, but he added, "I know they will not be home until this evening, if you wish to see them."

Nancy thanked him, then turned to Bess and George. "Would you like to stay here overnight?"

"Oh, yes!" Bess's eyes danced. "Orléans is such an intriguing place. Let's have a long lunch hour, then do some more sightseeing."

"The place I'd like to see next," said Nancy, "is La Cathedral St. Croix, where there's another wonderful statue of Jeanne d'Arc. Shall we go there after lunch?"

The others agreed, and the three girls walked to a delightful little restaurant, where they ate a fish stew called *macelote*. It was served with a frothy white butter sauce to which had been added a dash of vinegar and shallots. For dessert they had plum tarts, which, on the menu, were listed as *tartes aux prunes*.

The stout friendly owner came to chat with the visitors. "Today people do not eat much," he said. "Banquets in medieval times—ah, they were different. Once at the country wedding of a nobleman near here this is what was served." He pointed to a list on the back of the menu.

9 *oxen*
8 *sheep*
18 *calves*
80 *suckling pigs*
100 *kids*
150 *capons*
200 *chickens*
120 *other fowl*
80 *geese*
60 *partridges*
70 *woodcock*
200 *other game*
3000 *eggs*

"Wow!" George exclaimed. Even food-loving Bess said the idea made her feel squeamish.

The restaurant owner was called away, and the girls left a few minutes later. They went back to the square to visit the cathedral. Though not considered so grand as Notre Dame, it was a beautiful edifice with spires and domes. What interested the girls most about it was the statue they had come to see.

The sculptor had pictured Joan of Arc more as a saint than soldier. She was not wearing a suit of armor as usual, but was dressed in a long simple white robe. Her hair was short—cut in a bob—and in her clasped hands was her sword.

"Isn't the expression on Jeanne's face marvelous?" Bess said.

Nancy nodded. "Serene and spiritual. The sculptor certainly caught the spirit of her life."

As the girls finished speaking, a voice behind them said, "*Bonjour,* Nancy. I thought I might find you here."

Nancy turned. "Henri!" she exclaimed. "*Bonjour!* Where did you come from?"

Henri Durant, grinning broadly, greeted Bess and George warmly. He said, "I phoned the Bardots and they said you three were coming here. I offered to do an errand in Orléans for my dad," the French boy added, "so he lent me his car. Nancy, I hope you and your friends aren't too busy to take a ride with me."

Bess and George graciously declined, but urged Nancy to go ahead.

"Are you sure you wouldn't like to come along?" she asked. The cousins said No, they would go at once to the hotel where they had decided to stay. Nancy handed her car keys to George and said she would meet them at the hotel later.

The group left the cathedral and Henri led Nancy to his car. "Have you found that Arab yet?" he asked. When she shook her head, Henri added, "I was in the post office here this morning and saw a man who looked like the one in the taxi."

"In disguise?" Nancy asked.

"No, in regular clothes. He was just leaving the stamp window."

"That's very interesting, Henri!" Nancy exclaimed, wondering if the man could be Louis Aubert, the schoolmaster. It certainly seemed plausible. "I'll find out tonight," she thought, then determined to enjoy the afternoon's outing.

Henri drove to an attractive area of the river and rented a canoe at Collet's boat dock. They paddled in and out of various small coves. Nancy was enchanted by the landscape, some pastoral, some wooded.

Her companion proved to be humorous and told of his life as a student at the famous Sorbonne in Paris. "Someday I hope to be a lawyer." He grinned. "Then I shall give you some mysteries to solve." Henri said Madame Tremaine had told him confidentially that Nancy was an amateur sleuth.

"I can't wait for your first assignment," she said, her eyes twinkling.

Time passed quickly and only the lowering sun reminded Nancy they should get back. As Henri pulled up to the dock, the owner said a telephone message had come for him. "You're Monsieur Henri Durant?" When the young man nodded, Collet told him he was to call his father the instant the couple landed. The man walked off.

Henri laughed. "My dad certainly guessed where I would be! Please wait here, Nancy. I will be right back."

Almost as soon as he had left, a rowboat slid out from under the dock and bumped the canoe. Startled, Nancy turned to look squarely into the face of a heavily bearded man. Instinct told her to flee and she started to scramble to the dock.

"Oh no you don't!" the man said gruffly. "You are trying to solve a dream. Well, I will give you something to dream about!"

Nancy started to scream, but the stranger reached up and covered her mouth with one hand. With the other he slapped her face so hard she fell, dazed, into the water!

CHAPTER XIV

Amazing Number 9

THE cold water shocked Nancy back to semiconsciousness, so she automatically held her breath while plunging below the surface. Rising again, she tried to swim but had no strength to do so.

"I—I must turn over and float," Nancy thought hazily, and barely managed to flip over. A drowsiness was coming over her. "I mustn't let myself go to sleep," she thought desperately.

By this time Henri was on his way back. Seeing Nancy floating motionless in the water, he sprinted to the end of the dock and made a long shallow dive toward her.

"Nancy!" he cried.

"I'm all—right. Just weak," she replied.

Henri cupped a hand under Nancy's chin and gently drew her to the shore. Here he put an arm under her shoulders and helped the wobbly-kneed girl to the boat owner's office. Monsieur Collet's eyes blinked unbelievingly, but he asked no questions. Instead, he poured a cup of strong coffee from a pot simmering on a gas plate.

Nancy drank the coffee and soon felt her strength returning. Finally, able to talk, she told her story. Monsieur Collet was shocked and called the police at once to report the bearded stranger.

Henri frowned. The incident, he told Nancy, seemed to tie in with his telephone message. His father had not called him. "Evidently this villain planned the whole thing to harm you, Nancy. I shouldn't have left you alone."

"Don't blame yourself," Nancy begged him. "And now, if you don't mind, I'd like to go to the hotel and get dried out. Henri, will you bring my handbag from the canoe—if it's still there."

Fortunately it was, and not long afterward Henri dropped the bedraggled girl at her hotel. "I will telephone you tomorrow to see how you are," he said.

"Thanks a million for everything," Nancy said, "and I'll let you know if I find that Arab!"

When she reached the girls' room, George and Bess began to tease her about Henri having dunked her in the river. But they soon sobered as Nancy unfolded her story.

"How terrible!" said Bess.

"It does seem," George remarked, "as if you

aren't safe anywhere, Nancy, and what did he mean about the dream?"

"I guess he found out somehow about Mrs. Blair's dream," Nancy replied. "Who can he be? Everything happened so fast I didn't notice anything but his whiskers."

"I'll bet they were false!" George declared.

Nancy's spirits revived after she showered and changed into fresh clothes. She insisted that they call on the Auberts directly after a light supper. The girls had a little trouble finding the couple's house, but at last they pulled up in front of a small bungalow. As they alighted, the trio wondered if they were finally to face their enemy Monsieur Louis Aubert!

Nancy's ring was answered by a man who was definitely not the suspect. She politely asked if he were Monsieur Aubert.

"*Oui,* mademoiselle. You wish to see me?"

"Yes, if you can spare the time. And I would also like to talk with your wife."

"Please come in. I will call her."

He led the girls from a hallway to a neat, simply furnished living room. Then he returned to the hall and went upstairs.

A few minutes later the girls heard descending footsteps of two people. They tensed. Were they going to meet Mrs. Blair's governess? Would she solve the mystery of the disturbing dream?

The schoolmaster and his wife entered the living room and he introduced her to the girls. Madame Aubert, slender and dark-eyed, wore a puzzled expression. "You wish to see me?"

"Yes," Nancy replied. "We were directed here by a former pupil of Monsieur Aubert's. Please forgive our unannounced call."

The woman smiled. "As a matter of fact I am flattered that you have come to see me. Usually our callers ask for my husband."

Nancy explained how the Duponts' maid had overheard the girls say they were looking for Monsieur and Madame Louis Aubert. "Estelle directed us here. Mrs. Aubert, by any chance, was your maiden name Manon?"

To the disappointment of Nancy and the cousins the woman shook her head. "No. May I inquire why you wish to know?"

Nancy explained about the Lucille Manon who had been Josette Blair's governess. "We are eager to find her so she can give us some information about Mrs. Blair's childhood."

The schoolmaster and his wife were sympathetic and promised if they came across any lead to the other Madame Aubert they would let Nancy know.

George spoke up. "Monsieur Aubert, did you ever happen to run across another man with your name?"

"Yes. I have never met him personally, but mail for him has come here by mistake."

Nancy at once recalled Henri's statement about the man at the post office. "You mean his mail came to your home?"

The teacher smiled. "I am well known at the post office. When any letters for Monsieur Louis Aubert arrive in Orléans without a street address, they are naturally delivered to me."

Nancy asked eagerly, "Was there a return address?"

Aubert shook his head. "No. That is why I opened the envelopes. Of course, when I found out they were not intended for me, I returned the letters to the post office."

"How were they signed?"

"There was no signature—just the initial C."

The girls exchanged glances. "C" might stand for Claude—Louis's brother!

Excitedly Nancy asked, "Could you tell me what the contents of some of the letters were?"

Aubert replied, "Ordinarily I would not remember, but these letters were unusual. They were written almost entirely in symbols and numbers. The number 9 was especially prominent."

The three visitors were elated. Surely they had stumbled upon a valuable clue!

Bess spoke up. "Have you received any of these letters recently, Monsieur Aubert?"

"No. None have come in the past two weeks."

During the conversation that followed, it developed that as a hobby the schoolmaster had studied a great deal about alchemy. At once Nancy told him that only recently she had learned a little on the subject and mentioned the Green Lion symbol in particular.

Her remark set Monsieur Aubert on a lengthy but very interesting discussion of the medieval science. He brought a portable blackboard from another room and with a piece of chalk drew a circle with a dot inside it.

"That was the symbol for the sun," he said.

Next, he drew a half moon on the left and on the right of the blackboard drew what he said was the alchemist's sign for it. The symbol looked like a quotation mark, only a little larger.

"In olden times alchemists and astrologers worked hand in hand. The positions of planets on certain days were very important. Metals and chemicals were named after heavenly bodies. For instance, mercury—which we use in the laboratory today—was named after the planet Mercury."

He sketched the symbol and Bess began to giggle. "That's a sassy-looking sign. It reminds me of a scarecrow with only a smashed-in hat on!"

Everyone laughed, then the teacher continued, "I translated one of Aubert's letters to mean, 'Turn all gold to silver quickly with mercury.' Very odd to correspond in this manner. The writer must also be interested in alchemy."

Nancy herself had exactly the same idea. Not

only was Monsieur Neuf the mysterious chemist, but his brother might be one also! But how did this connect either brother—or both of them—with Monsieur Leblanc's secret? Was the financier buying up the rights to some important formula concocted by the Aubert twins?

As Nancy was speculating on this, the schoolmaster took up his chalk again. "The story regarding numbers is really quite fascinating," he said. "Take the 9, which appears so frequently in that other Louis Aubert's letters. The number was considered a sign of immortality."

On the board he wrote 9 = 9, and then the number 18. As if he were addressing students, the teacher went on, "The sum of digits in successive multiples of 9 are constant. For instance, if we take 18, which is twice 9, and add 1 plus 8, we get 9." He grinned. "Who can figure out the next multiple of 9?"

Jokingly George raised her hand. "I feel as though I were back in school," she said with a laugh. "The third multiple of 9 is 27. The 2 plus the 7 equals 9."

"Trés bien," the schoolmaster said. "And, Mademoiselle Marvin, how about you answering next?"

"I never was very good at arithmetic," Bess admitted, giggling. "But I do remember that 4 × 9 is 36. Add the 3 and the 6 and you get 9!"

"Exactly," said Monsieur Aubert. "This is

true all the way to 90. After that, the sums become multiples of 9."

The girls were fascinated and would have loved to hear more, but Nancy said they had taken up enough of the Auberts' time.

"We've had a wonderful evening," she added, rising.

Twenty minutes later the girls were back in their hotel. While getting ready for bed, Bess remarked, "I still think Louis Aubert, alias Mr. Nine, has cast some kind of a spell over Monsieur Leblanc. All this alchemy business sounds like black magic."

George scoffed at the idea. "I think Monsieur Neuf is just a plain crook who's robbing Monsieur Leblanc unmercifully. All we have to do is prove it."

"A big order." Nancy knit her brow. "I feel what we must do now is find Lucille Manon Aubert. I have a hunch she is the key that will unlock at least one mystery."

The following morning the girls set out early for the Bardot chateau and two hours later pulled into the driveway. Madame Bardot herself opened the door. At once the girls detected a worried expression on her face and sensed that she had bad news for them.

"What is wrong, Madame Bardot?" Nancy asked quickly.

The Frenchwoman's voice quivered. "My darling poodle Fifi has disappeared!"

"Oh dear!" Bess exclaimed. "You mean she ran away?"

Madame Bardot shook her head. "Fifi was locked in our house and could not possibly have left it of her own accord. But somehow she has just vanished!"

CHAPTER XV

Missing Gold

"POOR Fifi!" cried Bess. "She must have been stolen!"

"But that seems impossible," said Madame Bardot. "Every window and door on the first floor was locked. If some thief did get in, he must have had a key. But where did he obtain it?"

"Do you mind if we make a thorough search of the house?" Nancy requested.

"Oh, please do. We must find Fifi!" Madame Bardot's eyes filled with tears.

The group divided up to hunt, but with no success. As time went on, Nancy became more and more convinced that some intruder had been able to enter the house. On a hunch that the dog might have been hidden, she began a systematic search of all closets but did not find Fifi. Finally the only place left was the attic tower of the house. There was a door at the foot of a stairway leading up to it. Nancy opened the door and ascended. At the top she looked about at the small square room lighted by a tiny window on each side.

"Oh!" she cried.

In the center of the floor on a faded rug lay Fifi!

Since the dog did not move at Nancy's approach, she was fearful the pet might not be alive. In a moment she realized Fifi was breathing, but unconscious. There was a strong medicinal smell about the animal, and she guessed the dog had been drugged to keep it from barking the alarm.

Nancy was angry. Who would do such a mean thing? But there was no time to think about this at the moment.

Taking the steps two at a time, Nancy hurried to the second floor and called out loudly, "Come quickly! I've found Fifi in the tower!"

Madame Bardot rushed from a bedroom. "Is she all right?" the woman asked worriedly.

"I think so," said Nancy, "but a veterinarian should see her as soon as possible. She's unconscious."

By this time Monsieur Bardot had appeared in the hallway. He offered to phone the doctor and the police while the others hurried to the attic. Bess and George were indignant also at the mistreatment of the poodle.

In a short while the veterinarian arrived. He

examined Fifi and declared that the intruder had injected a drug that produced sleep for a long time. "She will be all right, however," he assured Madame Bardot. "And I do not think she needs medication. Just let her sleep off the effects."

As the veterinarian was leaving, two police officers drove up. They talked briefly with the doctor, then began to quiz the Bardots.

"We have little to tell," Monsieur Bardot replied. "My wife and I heard no unusual noises last night." He introduced the American girls, singling out Nancy. "Mademoiselle Drew is here trying to solve a mystery. Perhaps she can be of some help to you."

Both policemen frowned, and Nancy felt sure that the suggestion was not a welcome one! Quickly she said to the officers, "I'm sure you won't miss any clues the intruder may have left. But if you don't mind, I'd like to do a little looking myself."

The policemen nodded stiffly, then said they wanted to see where the dog had been found. The Bardots led them to the tower.

After they had gone, George whispered, "Nancy, I dare you to solve the mystery before those policemen do! Bess and I will help you find some clues before they get back downstairs!"

Nancy grinned. "All right. Let's start!"

While the girls were searching the first floor,

Bess remarked, "Nancy, do you realize that several houses—or buildings—you've been in lately have been entered by an intruder?"

"That's right," said Nancy. "But in this case, I hardly think the person was out to find me or take anything valuable of mine."

"If he was," said George, "he certainly got fooled, because we were away and had our passports and money and jewelry with us!"

Nancy examined the outside kitchen door. It had a Yale lock, but when she tried the key, she discovered that it was hard to turn.

"This must be how the prowler got in," she concluded. "He tried various keys before he found the right one, and almost jammed the tumblers."

"He's just a common burglar then," George declared. "He probably stole things from the house."

By this time the police and the Bardots had reached the first floor.

George blurted out, "Nancy discovered how the intruder got in!" She explained about the lock, then added, "The intruder put Fifi to sleep so she wouldn't bark and awaken anyone. Then, to keep the Bardots from notifying the police right away if they found the dog unconscious, he carried her to the tower."

The two officers stared at the girls unbelievingly. Finally both grinned at Nancy and one said, "I must admit you do have a good detective instinct, Mademoiselle Drew, and your friend here too. Perhaps you three girls can give us some more help."

This time Bess spoke up. "Yes, we can. I believe Monsieur and Madame Bardot will probably find some things missing."

At once Monsieur Bardot went to the desk in his den. He yanked open the top drawer, then said, "Well, at least the burglar wasn't after money. The bills I had here in an envelope are intact."

Meanwhile, Madame Bardot had hurried upstairs to her room. In a moment the others heard her cry out, "They're gone!"

The policemen rushed up the stairway, followed by the girls and Monsieur Bardot. They crowded into the bedroom.

"All my gold jewelry!" Madame Bardot gasped. "Some of it was very old and valuable—family heirlooms!"

This second shock was too much for Madame Bardot. She dropped into an armchair and began to weep. Her husband went to comfort her.

"There, there, dear, do not let this upset you," he said. "Fifi is going to be all right, and you rarely wear the old jewelry, anyway."

His wife dried her eyes. By the time the police asked for a description of the missing pieces, she had regained her composure enough to give them a list.

Nancy asked if any other jewelry had been taken, and Madame Bardot shook her head. This set Nancy to thinking. The intruder must have been after gold only! She inquired if there was anything else in the house made of the precious metal.

"Some demitasse spoons in the buffet," Madame Bardot replied, "and a lovely collection of baby cups."

She rushed downstairs to the buffet and opened the top drawer. "The spoons are gone!" Pulling the drawer out farther, the Frenchwoman cried out, "The baby cups too—all of them! I had one that once belonged to a queen. It is priceless!"

The Bardots opened every drawer and closet in the house to examine the contents. Nothing else had been taken. The police made no comment, but took notes.

Nancy herself was wondering if the intruder had a mania for gold. Suddenly she thought of the Green Lion, and Monsieur Neuf—Louis Aubert!

"Is he the housebreaker?" she asked herself.

Nancy was tempted to tell the police her suspicions about the man but decided that without any evidence she had better not. Instead, Nancy decided to consult her father about her theory.

After the police had left, she put in a call to Mr. Drew and fortunately reached him at once. He listened closely to Nancy's account of her adventures and agreed with her that Louis Aubert was indeed a likely suspect for the chateau thefts. "He must have known Madame Bardot owned objects of pure gold. I hope they can be recovered," the lawyer said.

Nancy mentioned the strange letters which Monsieur Aubert the teacher had received in error. She asked her father if he thought the elusive Louis Aubert, assuming he was a chemist, wanted the gold to use in an experiment.

"Very probable," Mr. Drew answered.

Nancy's father said he had news of his own. He had learned that Monsieur Leblanc had recently purchased a lot of uncut diamonds. "The reason is not clear," Mr. Drew added. "It would not be feasible for him to have such a large quantity of stones cut for jewelry, and diamonds are certainly of no commercial value to him—they're not used in his factory work as sharp drilling tools."

Mr. Drew went on to say that Leblanc had served notice his factory was closing down in a month. "Of course his employees are in a dither."

"That's dreadful!" said Nancy. "Dad, what are you going to do?"

Mr. Drew sighed. "I don't seem to be making much headway, but I have invited Monsieur Leblanc to luncheon today. I hope to find out something without his becoming suspicious."

"Please let me know what happens," Nancy

requested, "and I'll keep you posted. I wish you luck, Dad. Good-by."

A short time later the Bardots and their guests sat down to luncheon. Suddenly Madame Bardot said, "In all the excitement I completely forgot! A letter came from Marie and Monique. They have some news of special interest to you, Nancy. Incidentally, everyone at your home is fine, and our daughters are having a wonderful time. I'll get the letter."

Madame Bardot arose and went to the living room. Presently she returned and handed the envelope to Nancy.

"Shall I read it aloud?" Nancy asked.

"Please do," Monsieur Bardot said.

The message for Nancy was near the end of the long letter. It said that the night police guard presently in charge of Claude Aubert understood French. The day before the sisters' letter was written he had heard the prisoner mumble in his sleep, "Hillside–woods–ruins–go Chamb–"

"Whatever does that mean?" George spoke up.

"It is only a guess on my part," said Monsieur Bardot, "but I think the "Chamb" could be Chambord. That is one of the loveliest chateaux in the Loire valley."

"I certainly will investigate," Nancy said eagerly. She recalled the reference in Mrs. Blair's diary to the haunted ruins of a Chateau Loire. Perhaps the girls would have a chance to go there, also. Nancy now asked if there were any special stairs at Chambord.

Monsieur Bardot smiled. "If you are asking me about 99 steps, I cannot tell you. There is a double spiral staircase which is architecturally famous, and for that type, unusually wide and ornate."

As soon as the meal was over, Nancy suggested she and the cousins visit Chambord. Bess and George were enthusiastic and eager to go. In case of an unexpected overnight stay, the three took along suitcases.

They climbed into the rented automobile and Nancy headed down the driveway. As she neared the street, Nancy noticed a car approaching and pressed the foot brake. To her dismay, it did not work. Her car moved on!

Quickly Nancy leaned over and pulled on the hand brake. This would not hold either! With a sinking heart she realized there was no way to stop her car. It rolled onto the road directly into the path of the oncoming vehicle!

CHAPTER XVI

Followed!

THE three girls sat petrified. There was nothing Nancy could do to avoid a collision. The other car was too close!

But with a loud screech of brakes its driver swerved sharply and managed to avoid a collision by barely an inch. Nancy's car coasted across the road and stopped against an embankment. The shaken girls murmured a prayer of thanksgiving.

The man at the wheel of the other vehicle had stopped and now backed up. "Are you *crazy?*" he yelled at Nancy, his face red with anger. Then he went into a tirade in such rapid French that the girls could catch only part of what he was saying. They understood enough to learn he had had a dreadful scare also. "I ought to have you arrested!" he shouted.

Nancy started to apologize but did not get a chance to finish. The irate driver put his car into gear and sped off down the road.

Nancy turned shakily to the cousins. "Do you realize how lucky we were?" she said.

"Sure do," George replied fervently. "What went wrong anyhow?"

Nancy told her that neither of the brakes would work. "I'd better move and not block the road." She steered slowly back into the driveway and stopped by rolling against the sloping edge.

The Bardots had seen the narrow escape from a window and now came rushing out. "Thank goodness you are all right!" cried Madame Bardot. "What happened?"

Nancy told them quickly and at once Monsieur Bardot said, "Did you have any trouble with the car this morning?"

"None at all. It worked wonderfully." She frowned. "I'm sure someone tampered with the brakes."

"But when?" Bess asked.

"Probably during our search in the house," Nancy replied. "I also think the person who did it was trying to keep me from investigating some ruin near Chambord, perhaps even the Chateau Loire."

"Whom do you suspect? Louis Aubert?" George put in.

"Yes," Nancy answered. "He probably came back here after the police left and eavesdropped on our conversation. When he heard what his brother had mumbled in his sleep and learned our plans, Louis decided he had better do something quick to stop us."

"He must be a good mechanic to know how to damage brakes," Bess commented.

Nancy reminded her that the man was supposed to be a scientist. If so, he probably had a technical knowledge of machinery. "A simple thing like letting air out of our car's tires wouldn't have delayed us long enough, so he chose something more important."

Monsieur Bardot hurried indoors to telephone a service station. He returned with disappointing news. "They can send a man to pick up the car, but they cannot have it ready until tomorrow. If they tell me there was sabotage, I will report it to the police."

Nancy smiled wanly. She did not say how bad she felt at having to give up the trip. Apparently the Bardots sensed this.

"You must take our automobile," their host offered.

"Oh, thanks, but I couldn't," Nancy said. "You might need it."

Madame Bardot smiled, saying they had many friends close by who would help them out in an emergency. "I think you girls are on the verge of making an important discovery," she added. "We want you to go to Chambord. Perhaps you will solve the mystery of my sister's strange dream."

Nancy finally agreed. The baggage was transferred to the Bardots' car, and once more the girls set off. Their recent harrowing experience was almost forgotten as the three gazed enchanted at the countryside on the way to Chateau Chambord. Due to a late spring, poppies still grew in profusion along the roadway and fields were dotted with marguerites and buttercups.

When they reached the town of Chambord, the girls soon realized why the main sightseeing attraction was the chateau. Nancy parked near it and the trio alighted, exclaiming in admiration and awe.

The castle-like building stood in the center of a park and was approached by a long walk. The main part of the building was three stories high and there were many towers. A pinnacle in the middle, shaped like a gigantic lantern, stood as high again as the chateau itself.

On either side of its main entrance, and at each corner of the vast front of the chateau, was a huge rounded tower that rose well above the roof.

"I can't wait to see the interior!" Bess exclaimed.

But at the entrance, a guard told them, "Sorry, mesdemoiselles. The last tour of the day is just ending."

Nancy glanced at her wrist watch. It was later than she had realized. Nevertheless, smiling beguilingly, she said, "Please, until the tour group gets back here, couldn't we look around just a little?"

The guard softened. "I cannot let you go by yourselves," he said, "but I will show you a few things."

He let them in, locked the door, and led them straight ahead. When the girls saw the double spiral staircase of stone they gasped in wonder. The guard said with pride that the design was a unique one.

"You have to see it to believe it," said Bess. "What period does it belong to?"

"The Renaissance. This staircase, and in fact the entire chateau, is one of the finest examples of Renaissance architecture. It was built by King Frances I. He was fond of hunting, and the woods here at that time were full of deer and wild boar. The monarch also loved art and brought it to a high degree of perfection in France."

The group climbed to the second floor and he showed them several rooms. The girls agreed with their guide—the decor, although ornate, was in excellent taste.

The man grinned. "You might be glad not to see everything here—this chateau has 440 rooms, 13 large staircases, and stall for 1200 horses."

Bess exclaimed, "Think of all the servants and gardeners and grooms King Frances I must have had to take care of his home!"

The guide laughed. "You are right, mademoiselle. But in those days, a king was a king, and he had to have an extensive retinue!"

Regretfully the girls followed him back to the first floor. At the entrance Nancy thanked the man for the "special" tour, then asked if there were any ruins on the property.

"No," he answered. "You can see this place is very well kept. There are, however, a couple of ruins in the town—and, of course, some are scattered around the countryside."

The girls decided to walk through the streets of Chambord. They had not gone far before Bess complained, "I have the strangest feeling we're being watched. It makes me nervous."

Nancy had paid little attention. She was too busy absorbing the atmosphere of the chateau town. But presently she became aware that two young boys had come from one of the houses across the street and seemed to be trailing the girls. Whispering to her friends, Nancy suddenly did an about-face. Bess and George did the same, and the three girls started in the opposite direction. The two boys stopped, and after a momentary conference, they also turned and once more kept pace with the girls.

"I'll bet they're purse snatchers," Bess said fearfully. "Hold on to your bags."

Nancy did so, but her mind was suddenly running in another direction. Hunting for the ruins to which Claude Aubert had referred was like looking for a needle in a haystack. The young detective decided to concentrate first on learning if there were a chemist in the neighborhood. If so, he might be Louis Aubert!

Excusing herself, Nancy hurried into a pharmacy. To her annoyance, the two boys followed her inside! In a low voice she put her question to a white-coated man who came forward.

But his answer could be heard by everyone in the place. "I do not know any chemist who lives around here. Why do you ask?"

Nancy thought quickly. She must think up an excuse!

"I am interested in chemistry," she said. "And I believe a brilliant chemist lives somewhere in this vicinity."

Out of the corner of her eye, Nancy could perceive that the two boys seemed to lose interest in the conversation.

"I am sorry. I cannot help you," the druggist said.

Nancy bought some hard candy, then left the shop. When she reached the sidewalk, the boys were standing halfway up the block, apparently debating between themselves whether or not to continue following the girls.

Apparently they decided not to and turned in the opposite direction. For an instant Nancy was tempted to ask them what they were trying to find out. But she refrained. The boys might have been engaged as spies by some enemy of hers. "It would be better to leave well enough alone," she thought.

As the three walked back toward the main street, Nancy asked a passer-by if there were any interesting ruins outside town.

"*Oui,* mademoiselle," the friendly man replied. "Chateau Loire. I would advise you young ladies not to go there alone now. You had better take a strong male escort with you. The ruins are some distance from the road and the access is difficult. Besides, it is rumored that tramps are living among them."

Bess spoke up promptly. "Definitely we're not going there. Nancy, I can't let you take such awful chances. Your father would never forgive me and George."

The man to whom they were talking smiled. "Ah! *Oui!* A most sensible decision."

Nancy thanked him for the information and words of caution. She and her friends walked on to their car. Just as Nancy started the motor, a white sports sedan roared down the main street. The girls were close enough to catch a good glimpse of the driver.

"Monsieur Leblanc!" George cried out.

"It certainly is!" said Nancy, swinging the car into the road. "Let's follow him!"

CHAPTER XVII

Knight in Armor

IN moments Nancy and the cousins were heading after Monsieur Leblanc. But he was driving at such terrific speed Nancy felt wary of trying to overtake him.

George did not seem worried. "Step on it!" she urged.

But Bess had other ideas. "If we have a blow-out, good-by to us," she warned.

Fortunately the road ahead was straight and Nancy thought she could keep the financier's white car in sight for a while. George remarked that Monsieur Leblanc might suspect he was being followed.

"Yes," said Nancy. "And if he does, he certainly won't go where he plans to unless it's on legitimate business."

The sports car sped on for several miles. Then, a short distance ahead, Nancy noticed a sharp curve. Monsieur Leblanc did not slacken speed and roared around it.

"I mustn't risk that," Nancy told herself, and slowed down enough to take the curve safely.

As they reached the far side of the turn, George said in dismay, "He's gone!"

"But where?" said George. "To meet Louis Aubert perhaps?"

Nancy stepped on the gas and drove for another few miles. Their quarry had vanished. "I guess it's no use," she remarked. "We've lost him!"

She concluded that Monsieur Leblanc must have left the main road not long after passing the curve. "Let's go back and watch for any side roads." She drove slowly and presently the girls spotted a narrow dirt lane through the woods. There were tire tracks on it.

"Better not go in there," Bess advised. "What would you do if you met somebody driving out?"

Nancy smiled grimly. "How right you are!"

She parked the car along the roadside, and the girls proceeded on foot down the rutted, stony path. The tire tracks went on and on.

Presently Bess complained that her feet were hurting. "This must be a lumberman's trail that nobody ever bothered to smooth out," she said. "Where do you suppose it leads?"

"I hope to a ruin," Nancy answered. "The one Claude Aubert talked about in his sleep. It could be the Chateau Loire."

A little farther on the girls stopped and stared. Before them was a tumbled-down mass of stone and mortar. It had evidently once been a small, handsome chateau. Little of the building was intact, but as Nancy and her friends approached, they saw one section which had not yet suffered the ravages of time and weather. The tire tracks ended abruptly, yet there was no car in sight.

"I guess Monsieur Leblanc didn't come here," Bess surmised. She looked around nervously, recalling the guard's mention of tramps.

Nancy did not reply. Her eyes were fixed ahead on a series of stone steps leading below ground level. She assumed they had once led to a cellar or perhaps even a dungeon!

"Let's do some counting," she urged, and took out her pocket-size flashlight. Bess and George followed her to the steps. Would there be 99?

Nancy descended, counting, with the cousins close behind. When they reached thirty-five, Nancy stopped with a gasp. About ten steps below, at the foot of the stairs, stood a knight in full medieval armor! He was brandishing a sword!

George exclaimed sharply and Bess cried out in fright. But Nancy boldly took another step down. As she did, the armored figure called in French in a high ghostly voice, "Halt! Or I will run you through!"

Bess turned and fled up the steps. Nancy and George stood their ground, waiting to see if the figure would come toward them. He did not, but again warned them not to advance. This time his voice seemed a bit unsteady.

At once Nancy became suspicious. To the surprise of the other girls, she spoke up calmly, "Come now, Sir Knight! Stop playing games!"

The figure dropped the arm which held the sword. He fidgeted first on one foot, then the other.

"Take off the helmet!" Nancy ordered, but her voice was kind.

The knight lifted the visor to reveal a boy of about twelve! Bess and George marveled at Nancy's intuition.

Smiling, Nancy asked the boy, "What is your name?"

"Pierre, mam'selle. I was only pretending. Do not punish me. I did not mean seriously to threaten you."

"We're not going to punish you," Nancy assured him. "Where in the world did you get that suit of armor?"

The boy said it belonged to his father, who let him play with it. "I knew about this old ruined chateau and I thought it would be fun to come here and make believe I was a real knight."

Bess, looking somewhat sheepish, came back down the steps. "You had me fooled, young man!"

Nancy added with a chuckle, "I guess you didn't expect visitors to see your performance."

"Halt! Or I'll run you through!" the knight cried out

Pierre grinned and admitted he certainly had not. Now the girls asked him about the ruin and he told a little of its history. The place dated back to the fifteenth century and was not the Chateau Loire.

"Are there any other ruins near here?" Nancy queried.

The boy said there was one across the road, deep in the woods. "I guess it's Loire. But do not go there," he advised. "Funny things happen."

"Like what?" George questioned.

"Oh, explosions and smoke coming out of the ruin and sometimes you can hear singing."

"Singing?" Bess repeated.

Pierre nodded. "It is a lady's voice. Everybody believes she is a ghost."

"Who's everybody?" Nancy asked.

"Oh, people who wander around there to explore. Some of my friends and I have gone as close as we dare to the ruin, but something strange always happens. We have not been near it in a long while because our parents forbid it."

Nancy was intrigued by this latest information. She asked for directions to the mysterious ruin.

"You go about a mile up the road toward Chambord. If you look real hard, you will see a narrow lane which leads to the place."

"Thank you, Pierre. Have fun." Nancy winked at the boy. "Don't let Sir Lancelot come and overpower you in a duel!"

The girls left Pierre laughing, and set off once more in the car. Nancy drove slowly and finally they spotted the entrance to the lane, well camouflaged by low-hanging branches.

Nancy pulled over and parked. Then the searchers trudged through the woods. Again the way was rugged and bumpy. Projecting underbrush kept catching the girls' clothes.

"If Monsieur Leblanc came this way," said George, "he sure scratched up his car."

"I doubt that he stopped here," Nancy replied. "No tracks." Suddenly she asked, "What's the date?"

George told her it was the 17th. "Why?"

"I'll bet," replied Nancy, "that tomorrow will be an important day here. It will be the 18th. One plus 8 makes 9, the magic number!"

Bess's eyes opened wide with fear. "Please! Let's get out of here fast! We can come back tomorrow and bring the police."

But Nancy and George wanted to proceed. Nancy said, "We'll need proof, Bess, if we expect police help. We don't know yet that this is Monsieur Neuf's hideout. Are you willing to go?"

Bess gulped hard and nodded. The three girls walked on.

A few minutes later Nancy stopped short. "Listen!"

The cousins obeyed. Somewhere ahead a woman was singing softly! Nancy whispered,

"That's one of the madrigals Marie and Monique sang." An electrifying idea struck her. "Girls! The singer could be Lucille Manon Aubert, the governess we're trying to find! Her husband Louis might be here too!"

Excitedly Nancy started to run toward the singing sounds which seemed to be coming from the woods to her right. George and Bess hurriedly followed her.

"We're getting closer!" Nancy said, breathless with suspense.

CHAPTER XVIII

Dungeon Laboratory

THE singing ceased abruptly. Had the footsteps of Nancy and the cousins alerted the woman? A moment later the girls heard someone scrambling among the bushes ahead, but the underbrush was too dense for them to see anyone.

"Do you really think that was Lucille Aubert?" Bess whispered.

George answered, "If she had nothing to hide, why would she run away?"

"What puzzles me is," said Nancy, "if she is Mrs. Blair's former governess, how did she get mixed up with a crook like Louis Aubert?"

The words were hardly out of her mouth when George caught her friend's arm. "Look over there!"

Some distance ahead in a clearing on a hillside the girls glimpsed the corner of a tumble-down chateau. A woman had darted from the woods toward the ruin. She was a tall, slender, graying blonde of about fifty-five.

"Do you think that's the governess?" Bess asked.

"She's about the right age," Nancy replied. "Come on!"

The three girls dashed forward up the hill, but when they reached the ruined chateau, there was no sign of the woman. Was she concealed nearby or had she gone on through another part of the woods?

Suddenly Nancy said, "Perhaps we shouldn't have given ourselves away. The woman may have gone to warn somebody else that we're here. We'd better hide!"

"Oh yes, let's!" Bess begged. "I don't want to be caught off guard by that awful Louis Aubert."

The girls ducked behind a cluster of trees and waited for over ten minutes. There was not a sound except the chirping of birds. No one appeared. Finally Nancy said, "I guess it'll be all right to investigate now. Shall we see if we can track down a few ghosts?"

"I'm game," George answered, and Bess reluctantly agreed.

Nancy led the way in the direction the woman had taken. They did not see her, but Nancy was fascinated to discover a very steep flight of stone steps leading down into the basement of the chateau. Suddenly the girls became aware of a faint roaring sound coming from below.

Nancy was very excited. Intuition told her she had found the right 99 steps! "I must go down there!" she exclaimed.

George grabbed her friend's arm. "Not alone!" she said with determination.

Bess did not want to participate in the venture. "I think you're taking a terrible chance, Nancy. You know what you promised your father. And frankly I'm scared."

George snorted. "Oh, Bess, don't be such a spoilsport. This could be Nancy's big chance to crack the mystery."

"Tell you what, Bess," said Nancy. "We really should leave somebody on guard here at the top of the steps. Bess, suppose you stay. If anybody comes, give our secret bird whistle."

"All right, but don't go so far underground you can't hear me if I have to warn you."

Nancy descended the steps, counting as she went. George was at her heels. Farther down, the daylight grew dim. To the girls' amazement two lighted lanterns hung from the crumbling walls. Somebody *was* below!

When Nancy reached the bottom, she could hardly keep from shouting for joy! She had counted exactly 99 steps!

Ahead was a narrow corridor leading to a huge

old-fashioned wooden door. In the upper part was a small square opening containing parallel iron bars.

"This must have been a dungeon!" the young sleuth thought. Cautiously she and George peered through the barred opening. Nancy gasped. A medieval lab! Maybe it once had been an alchemist's prison!

The laboratory was fully equipped with an open furnace in which a fire roared, and there were numerous shelves of heavy glass beakers, pottery vessels, assay balances, crucibles, flasks, pestles, and mortars. At the rear were several long benches, one of which held bottles of assorted liquids.

What amazed the girls most, however, was a man in Arab garb standing sideways at one of the benches! Nancy and George glanced at each other. Was this Louis Aubert again in disguise? The light was too dim for them to be sure.

The girls watched the man intently. In his left hand he held a black chunk which the girls guessed might be charcoal. In his other hand he had a knife and was busy gouging a hole in the chunk.

Evidently deciding it was large enough, the Arab picked up a large nugget of gold from the bench and dropped it into the hole. Next, he opened a jar and with one forefinger took out gobs of a pasty black substance and filled the opening.

Immediately Nancy recalled the old alchemists' experiments with metals and wondered if the nugget were real gold. Watching closely, she detected a look of satisfaction on what little she could see of the man's face. Now he set the charcoal on the bench, walked to the rear end of the laboratory, and went out a door. Before it closed, Nancy and George caught a glimpse of a corridor beyond.

The girls were wondering what their next move should be, when they heard Bess give the secret birdcall. The sound came loud and clear and was instantly repeated. The double call meant:

Someone is coming. Hide!

"Hide where?" George asked in a whisper.

Without hesitation, Nancy opened the laboratory door and motioned George to follow her. She tiptoed across the room to several large bins holding logs and charcoal. The girls ducked behind them.

They heard footsteps descending the stairway and a moment later Monsieur Leblanc strode in! Immediately he reached up above the barred door and pulled on a cord which rang a little bell. Within seconds the Arab walked in through the rear entrance. He bowed and said in a deep voice:

"Monsieur, you are welcome, but are you not a day early? Tomorrow is the magic number day. But it is well that you came." Suddenly his manner changed. He added gruffly, "I cannot wait longer."

Monsieur Leblanc's face took on a frightened expression. "What do you mean?"

The robed chemist replied, "I have finished my last experiment! Now I can turn anything into gold!"

"Anything?" The financier grew pale.

"Yes. Surely you do not doubt my power. You have seen me change silver into gold before your very eyes."

Monsieur Leblanc stepped forward and grabbed the Arab's arm. "I beg you to wait before announcing your great discovery. I will be ruined. The gold standard of the world will tumble!"

"What does that matter?" the Arab's eyes glittered. "Gold! Gold! All is to be gold!" he cried out, rubbing his hands gleefully. "The Red King shall reign! And when everything is gold, the metal will no longer be rare and precious! The value of money will collapse." He laughed aloud.

Monsieur Leblanc seemed beside himself. "Give me a little time. I must sell everything and buy precious stones—they will never lose their intrinsic value."

The chemist walked up and down for several

moments. Then he turned and said, "Monsieur Leblanc, your faith in me will be profitable. Watch while I show you my latest experiment."

He picked up a bottle filled with silvery liquid which Nancy guessed was mercury. He poured a quantity into a large crucible.

"Now I will heat this," the Arab said, and walked over to the open furnace on which lay a grate. He set the crucible on it.

The chemist waited. When the liquid was the right temperature, he took the piece of charcoal from the bench and started it burning. Presently the man dropped the mass into the crucible.

Nancy and George never took their eyes from the experiment. Once George leaned too far out beyond the bin, and Nancy pulled her back.

Blue flame began to rise from the crucible. The Arab placed a pan on a bench near the furnace, then picked up the crucible with the tongs and dumped its contents into the container. The charcoal had disappeared, and out of the mercury rolled the lump of gold!

Monsieur Leblanc cried out, "Gold!"

George looked disgusted, and Nancy said to herself, "That faker! He has Monsieur Leblanc completely bamboozled. Why doesn't he see through the trick?"

Both girls had a strong desire to jump up and expose the whole procedure. But Nancy was afraid the swindler would break away from them, and decided that it would be better for the police to arrest him.

Monsieur Leblanc seemed to be in a daze, but presently he pulled a large roll of franc notes from his pocket and handed them to the Arab. "Take these, but I beg of you, do not make your announcement yet. I will come at this same time tomorrow with more money."

"I will give you twenty-four hours," the Arab said loftily. "This time the price of my silence will be five thousand dollars."

The demand did not seem to faze the financier. As a matter of fact, he looked relieved. He said good-by and left the same way he had come in. The Arab went out the rear door.

The two girls arose from their cramped position, hurried outside, and up the 99 steps. Bess was waiting anxiously at the top.

"We must run," Nancy exclaimed, "and notify my father immediately that Monsieur Leblanc is being swindled!"

CHAPTER XIX

Nancy's Strategy

IT was bedtime when Nancy, Bess, and George burst in upon the Bardots. Twice en route Nancy had tried unsuccessfully to get her father on the telephone.

The couple could see from the girls' excited faces that something unusual had happened. Nancy quickly poured out the whole story, feeling that the time was past when she had to keep her father's case a secret.

Monsieur and Madame Bardot were shocked. "You think this Arab you saw in that laboratory is really Louis Aubert?" Madame Bardot asked.

Nancy nodded. "Something should be done as soon as possible. I don't want to call the police until I talk to my father and ask his advice."

She telephoned Mr. Drew, but found he was not in. The switchboard clerk at the hotel, however, did have a message for Nancy.

"Your father said to tell you if you should call that he tried to reach you at Monsieur Bardot's but received no answer. Mr. Drew is an overnight guest of Monsieur Leblanc."

"Thank you," said Nancy.

After she put down the receiver, the young sleuth sat staring into space. She was perplexed by this turn of events. Nancy had so hoped to alert her father that Monsieur Leblanc was being hoodwinked by an alchemist's trick! Had Mr. Drew also learned this? Or had he come upon another lead in the mystery of the frightened financier?

"I'd better try contacting Dad at once," she told herself.

She called Leblanc's number. A servant answered and said that both men had gone out and would not be back until very late.

"Will you please ask Mr. Drew to call his daughter at the Bardots' number," Nancy said.

"Yes, mademoiselle."

When Nancy reported this latest bit of news to her friends, the others looked puzzled. She herself was fearful that her father might be in danger —perhaps from attack by Louis Aubert! Resolutely she shook off her worry. Surely Carson Drew would not easily be caught off guard!

The three girls, after a late, light supper, tumbled wearily into bed. In the morning Mr. Drew telephoned Nancy. She thought that his voice did not have its usual cheerful ring to it.

"I'm leaving here at once," he told his daughter glumly. "I will come directly to see you."

A sudden idea flashed into Nancy's mind. "Why don't you bring Monsieur Leblanc along? I have some exciting things to tell you which I am sure will interest him too."

Nancy did not dare say any more for fear some servant might be an accomplice of Aubert's and be listening in on the conversation.

"I'll ask Leblanc. Hold the wire." The lawyer was gone for a minute, then returned to say that his host would be happy to see Nancy again. "He'll postpone going to his office until this afternoon."

When the two men arrived, Nancy greeted Monsieur Leblanc graciously. Then, excusing herself, she took her father aside. "Dad, tell me your story first."

The lawyer said he had tried diplomatically to impress Leblanc with rumors he had heard of the financier's transactions. "I told him that reports of his selling so many securities was having a bad effect on the market and that his employees were panicking at the prospect of his factory closing down."

Mr. Drew said Monsieur Leblanc had been polite and listened attentively, but had been totally uncommunicative.

"I can understand why!" Nancy then gave a

vivid account of the girls' experiences of the previous day.

When she finished, Mr. Drew said he could hardly believe what he had just heard. "This Arab alchemist must be captured and his racket exposed, of course. The question is what would be the best way to do it without tipping him off? I certainly don't want Monsieur Leblanc to be harmed."

Nancy suggested that they tell the financier the whole story from beginning to end. "Then I think he should keep his date with the Arab this afternoon and turn the money over to him as planned.

"In the meantime, Bess, George, you, and I could go with a couple of police officers and hide near the 99 steps. Then, at the proper moment, we can pounce on Louis Aubert, or whoever this faker is."

Mr. Drew smiled affectionately at his daughter and put an arm around her. "I like your idea very much, Nancy. I promised you a lovely gift from Paris. Now I think I ought to give you half my fee!"

Nancy's eyes twinkled. "Only half?" she teased.

She and Mr. Drew returned to the others and Nancy whispered to Madame Bardot, "Would it be possible for you to find errands for the servants outside the house so that nobody will overhear our plans?"

"Yes, indeed. I'll send them to town."

As soon as the servants had left, Mr. Drew said, "Monsieur Leblanc, my daughter has an amazing story to tell you. It vitally affects your financial holdings and perhaps even your life."

The man's eyebrows raised. "This sounds ominous. Miss Drew is such a charming young lady I cannot think of her as having anything so sinister to tell me."

Bess burst out, "Nancy's wonderful and she's one of the best detectives in the world!"

Monsieur Leblanc clapped a hand to his head. "A detective!" he exclaimed. "Do you mean to say you have discovered why I am selling my securities?"

Nancy smiled sympathetically. "I believe I have."

Then, as Monsieur Leblanc listened in amazement, she related the story of Claude and Louis Aubert. She told about the many ways they had tried to keep the Drews from helping Monsieur Leblanc, and finally how she and George had seen the financier come into the secret laboratory at the foot of the 99 steps.

"You saw me!" he cried out. "But where were you girls?"

When Nancy told him they had hidden behind the bins, he knew she was not inventing the story. Leblanc sat silent for fully a minute, his head buried in his hands.

Finally he spoke up. "To think I, of all persons, have been duped! Well, it is only fair I give you my story. In the first place, if this chemist is actually someone named Louis Aubert, I do not know it. To me, the man is Abdul Ramos. I never saw him in any other clothes than Arabian."

Monsieur Leblanc said that Abdul had come to his office one day a couple of months before and showed him several very fine letters from Frenchmen, as well as from Arabs, attesting to his marvelous experiments.

Nancy at once thought of Claude Aubert. He could very well have forged the letters!

The financier continued, "Abdul wanted financial backing for a great laboratory he planned to build. Because of the letters, and some experiments he later showed me, I was convinced he knew how to turn certain things into gold. Yesterday when I saw the solid gold emerge from the heated charcoal—" Monsieur Leblanc's voice trailed off and he shook his head gloomily. "How could I have been so foolish!"

After a pause the financier admitted what Nancy had already overheard—he had intended to sell all his holdings and put the money into precious stones. "Since gold is the standard for all currency in international trade, I really feared the economy of the world would be disastrously harmed when Abdul's ability to transform substances into gold became known."

Mr. Drew remarked, "That explains the large quantity of uncut diamonds you bought recently."

The Frenchman looked surprised but did not comment.

Nancy spoke up. "Also, you figured that diamonds would replace gold as the world standard."

"Precisely. I realize now that my self-interest is unforgivable. It was neither patriotic nor humanitarian. Instead I've been unforgivably greedy. Thank you for showing me up. This has been a great lesson to me and I shall certainly make amends for it."

George asked, "Monsieur Leblanc, what about the number 9?"

He explained that Abdul Ramos knew a great deal about astrology and the magic of numbers. "He convinced me that on the 9th, 18th, and 27th days of each month new secrets were revealed to him and he threatened to announce his discoveries to the world."

George next inquired if he had left money on the 99th step at Versailles where M9 had been chalked.

Monsieur Leblanc nodded. "I did not see Abdul that day, but left the money there at exactly the time he had told me—directly after lunch."

When Leblanc was told of George's experience, the Frenchman was shocked. "All I can say is I am very sorry. I was foolish to let that man control me and cause so much worry." He shook his head sadly.

Bess, too, had a question for him. "Is Abdul married?"

The financier shook his head. "I have never heard him speak about a wife."

Nancy had been mulling over Leblanc's remark that he had allowed himself to be controlled by Louis Aubert and would like to make amends. She described her plan for exposing the fake alchemist.

"I will be glad to cooperate in any way," said the Frenchman, and Mr. Drew nodded approval. Soon afterward, Monsieur Leblanc left for his office.

Late that day three cars converged on the chateau ruin in the woods near Chambord. One vehicle carried Mr. Drew and the three girls, another two police officers, Beaumont and Careau. In the third was Monsieur Leblanc. The first two cars were well concealed among the trees and the passengers proceeded cautiously on foot through the woods.

At the small clearing near the ruin, they paused until they were certain no one was around. Then they darted to the 99 steps. Again the lanterns were lighted. The group tiptoed down.

Nancy peered through the barred opening of the door. Everything inside the laboratory looked the same as the day before, even to the glowing fire in the open furnace. The grating lay over it and she wondered if Abdul planned to show Leblanc another experiment.

Softly Nancy opened the door and one by one the watchers went inside and hid themselves behind the bins. Ten minutes went by, then Monsieur Leblanc strode in. He tinkled the bell and in a few seconds the Arab came through the rear door.

"Ah, I see you are on time, monsieur," he said smugly, with a little bow.

The financier reached into a pocket and brought out a roll of bills. He did not hand them over at once, however, saying, "Do you agree to a waiting period in return for this?"

"Have I not always kept my word?" Abdul said haughtily.

Leblanc laid the bills on a bench and immediately the Arab snatched up the money and tucked it into a pocket.

"How much more time do you wish before I reveal my great work to the world?" he asked.

"At least a week," Monsieur Leblanc replied. "I have several big transactions I must complete first."

"A week?" Abdul repeated, and began to walk around the room.

Presently he paused at the door which led to the 99 steps. The hidden group could see him reach toward it and heard something click. Nancy wondered if he had used a secret latch to lock the door and why. Were they all in danger?

Suddenly apprehensive, she watched the Arab intently as he returned to the furnace. He gazed at the fire, then with a brisk movement picked up a small sack from a bench. He hastened to the rear door, opened it, and whirled about. His eyes held a menacing gleam.

"Leblanc," he cried out, "you have double-crossed me! I know you have spies hiding in this room because I followed you to the Bardots! But I shall not be caught. Everyone of you shall perish!"

Without warning, the Arab threw the sack onto the furnace grate, then backed out, slammed the door and bolted it from the other side!

CHAPTER XX

Surprising Confession

IT took but the fraction of a second for Nancy and the others trapped in the laboratory to realize the danger they faced. The sack hurled onto the furnace might explode at any moment!

Instantly Officer Beaumont jumped from his hiding place and made a grab for the bag. Fortunately, it had not yet ignited. As a precaution, he dropped it into a pail of water which stood nearby.

By this time everyone else had jumped up. Nancy exclaimed, "We mustn't let that awful man Abdul get away!"

She started for the doorway through which the Arab had fled, but then remembered he had bolted it from the outside. Those in the room were prisoners!

Nancy collected her wits. First she thanked Beaumont for saving them all. He shrugged this off and said, "We will have to break down the door and go after that crazy fool!"

Suddenly Nancy stared across the room in horror. Monsieur Leblanc had collapsed and was lying on his back, apparently unable to get up. Bess had already noticed this and was searching in vain for fresh water to revive him. Frantically she dug into her dress pocket and pulled out a small vial of perfume. Bess held it under Leblanc's nostrils. He took a deep whiff and almost instantly sat up.

In the meantime, the two policemen and Mr. Drew were heaving their bodies against the rear door. There was a loud splintering sound and finally the door began to give way.

The second it crashed down, the officers scrambled out and dashed up the corridor. Nancy started to follow, but her father held her back. "Let those lawmen handle the job," he said. "Beaumont was right when he called the faker crazy. No telling what he'll do."

The young sleuth became agitated at the delay. But only ten minutes had elapsed when they heard footsteps and voices in the corridor. Everyone gazed out and in the dimly lighted area they could see the police officers returning.

With them were Louis Aubert and the grayish-blond woman!

"She was the one who was singing the madrigals!" Nancy exclaimed.

Those in the laboratory could hear the woman saying, "My husband is a great scientist! He could not do anything wrong!"

"We'll see about that," said Officer Beaumont. "Anybody who wears a disguise and cheats people out of money by pretending he can turn almost anything into gold has a lot to answer for!"

Careau added, "To say nothing of threatening lives!" Madame Aubert said no more.

As the four entered the laboratory, Louis glared malevolently at Leblanc, Mr. Drew, and the girls. At first he would answer no questions, but when confronted with accusations from the financier, Nancy, Bess, and George, the would-be scientist broke down and admitted to engineering the holdup of Monsieur Leblanc as well as practically all of the other charges against him.

Bess, proud of Nancy's sleuthing, said, "He has confessed to just about everything you suspected him of—even the canoe incident and to hiring two boys to follow us and get information."

Nancy, too, was elated—not only at the capture, but also because her father's mystery had been solved. There were still a few questions in her mind which she now put to the prisoner.

"Your brother Claude forged the letters of recommendation which you showed to Monsieur Leblanc, didn't he?"

"Yes."

Aubert also revealed that it was Claude who

had written the letters about a helipad being built on the Drews' roof.

The young detective suggested that the various other happenings in River Heights had been Claude's work, while those in France were Louis's schemes.

"That's right. I suppose you'll get it out of me sooner or later how I knew about you Drews, so I might as well tell you. A servant at the Tremaines is a friend of mine. It was he who stole an invitation for me to the soirée. He used to eavesdrop on conversations and found out that Mr. Drew had been retained secretly to investigate why Leblanc was selling his holdings.

"I did not want my scheme ruined, so I sent Claude to the United States. With his ability to forge all kinds of documents it wasn't hard for him to enter your country under another name. Unfortunately your father had left. But he did learn that you were coming and he did his best to frighten you into staying home."

"You used lots of names besides Abdul," George said to him. "Monsieur Neuf, the Green Lion, the Red King."

Aubert admitted this, adding that Claude, too, had used Neuf and the "Lion" on the warnings to the Drews. The prisoner bragged, "I know a lot about astrology and the practices of ancient alchemists. That's what gave me the idea about the gold and using alchemists' symbols." The M9 chalk mark had been left by Aubert at L'Orangerie as the place for Leblanc to leave money, but he had rubbed it out upon spotting the girls there.

During the interrogation, his wife had been sitting on a bench, pale with shock. She kept daubing her eyes with a handkerchief and murmuring, "I knew nothing about this."

Nancy went over and sat down beside the distraught woman. The young sleuth had not forgotten she had a mystery of her own to solve!

In a kind voice Nancy asked, "Were you Mlle. Lucille Manon?"

"W-why, yes!"

"I'm a friend of Mrs. Josette Blair. You were her governess many years ago. She has a recurring dream that frightens her. We thought perhaps you could explain the meaning of it."

The woman looked puzzled. "I do not understand," she said. "I took care of Josette when she was only three years old."

"Her dream dates back to that time," Nancy explained, and told about the nightmare.

As Nancy finished speaking, the woman began to weep aloud. "Yes, yes, I can explain. In a way Louis was responsible for this. I suppose he has always mesmerized me—as he has Monsieur Leblanc. During the time I was taking care of Josette, he was a guest at a chateau where the little girl and I had been left for a short time while her parents were away."

"Louis and I fell in love, and as it was not considered proper for a guest and an employee to date, we had to meet secretly."

Madame Aubert went on to say that Louis had already come upon the ruin with the underground alchemist's laboratory.

"It became our meeting place. One day I had to bring Josette along. He did not want her to recognize him or to see the laboratory for fear she would tell others about it. Louis wanted to keep the place a secret until he was ready to reveal a great scientific fact to the world."

The ex-governess went on, "I thought up the idea of playing blindman's buff. I took Josette to the woods and then blindfolded her. After we had played the game a while, I led her here. When I told her she was going down steep steps, Josette became afraid. I said I would hold her hand and she should count. Of course she could not count very far, so I did the rest."

"And the total, of course, turned out to be 99," Nancy put in.

"That is right," Lucille Aubert answered. "Louis thinks the alchemist who built this place chose that number of steps because it's a multiple of 9, a magic number for alchemists. The chateau dates back to the fourteenth century."

The ex-governess continued, "After Louis and I had looked at his laboratory, we three went back up the steps. Josette was still blindfolded. Just as she reached the top, she lost her balance and started to fall. Louis caught her, but for a long time after that, poor little Josette used to cry out in her sleep."

"No wonder the 99 steps made such a deep impression on her," Bess remarked.

Madame Aubert hung her head. "Not long after the incident, Josette's mother discharged me. I guess she suspected I was responsible for scaring her daughter. A short time later Louis and I were married."

Her husband spoke up. "When I found out the Bardot sisters were going to the Drews' home, I eavesdropped at the Bardots a good deal. One day I heard Madame Bardot read a letter from Mrs. Blair about the dream and I decided to send the warning note to her. Claude carried on from there. My wife didn't know anything about it."

Nancy said she was sure that when Mrs. Blair heard the story, her nightmares would cease. Nancy expressed her sympathy to Madame Aubert for her present predicament.

At that moment Officer Beaumont walked over to them. "I'm sorry, madame," he said. "You must come with us for further questioning."

Tears rolling down her cheeks, the woman arose. But suddenly she turned and said to Nancy, "Remember me to Mrs. Blair and tell her I loved her dearly."

Nancy felt her own eyes becoming a little dewy. "I'll be happy to," she replied.

Louis Aubert was made to release the secret lock on the door leading to the 99 steps. Before mounting them, Nancy suddenly remembered one part of the mystery was still unsolved. She asked Beaumont, "Did you search the Arab costume?"

The officer admitted they had not. "Wait here!" he directed, then hurried back into the rear corridor. He returned holding the robe, turban, and false hair. Beaumont searched the various pockets the costume contained. As Nancy had suspected, Madame Bardot's missing gold pieces were hidden in several of them! After a search, the rest were found hidden about the laboratory.

Everyone looked at Nancy admiringly. The officers shook their heads and Beaumont commented, "Mademoiselle Drew, *vous êtes merveilleuse!*"

George grinned. "In other words, Nancy, you're the greatest!" Her words were to prove true again when Nancy met her next challenge in *The Clue in the Crossword Cipher*.

The Auberts were led away. Then Nancy beckoned the others to precede her from the laboratory. Smiling, they all exchanged knowing glances. The young sleuth wanted to be the one to close the door to the mystery of the 99 steps!